Frederick Wentworth, Captain

A Novel in Two Parts

Book 2

FOR YOU ALONE

by

Susan Kaye

Wytherngate Press
2008

2008 Wytherngate Press

Cover photograph
iStockphoto, Inc.

Cover art direction: Margaret Coleman
Cover design: Galina Vishnevski

ISBN 0-9728529-5-6   ISBN 13 978-0-9728529-5-1
LCCN 2008936528

Wytherngate Press website: wytherngatepress.com

The principal text of this book was set in a digitized version of 10 point
Baskerville. Title appears in Edwardian Script.

Printed in the United States of America on acid-free paper.

Kaye, Susan.
   For You Alone/ Susan Kaye.
   228p.; 21 cm. Revised ed.
   Series: Frederick Wentworth, Captain; 2.
   ISBN 13 978-0-9728529-5-1
   1. Regency–England–Fiction. 2. Regency fiction. I.
Austen, Jane, 1775-1817. Persuasion. II. Series:
Frederick Wentworth, Captain; Book 2.

   813.54   2008936528

—&—

To my family who continue to smile and shake their heads.
To my online readers and the Austen communities of
Pemberley.com
DerbyshireWritersGuild.com
and Firthness.com

—&—

Chapter One

L ouisa insisted on standing and even took the few steps to the window. She has pronounced the day to be beautiful, Captain." Mrs. Harville smiled at Wentworth as he stood at his usual post near the only window with a view of the sea. There was nothing beautiful in the alternating rain and fog that had been Lyme's weather for the past week. She said quietly and only to him, "She is still weak as a kitten, but I think it a good sign that she wants to be up." In a normal voice she said, "I shall send word to the Musgroves at their lodgings. They will be beside themselves with joy. Now, to get her something more substantial than beef tea." She patted his arm as she passed to the kitchen. Clearly, she presumed he, too, would be beside himself with joy at the news.

"*Thank God*," he thought. If Miss Musgrove were up and around, she would soon be out and on her way home. The sooner she was fully recovered, the sooner he could disentangle himself from his close connections to Uppercross. While the elder Musgroves had endlessly assured him that his position as a close intimate of the family was not affected in the least by the accident on the Cobb, he was feeling the need to separate himself and move on. This meant going to his brother in Shropshire as soon as possible. He would miss Sophia and the Admiral's company, but he would not miss living in Anne's family home or miss the portrait of her mother which evoked in him no end of difficult memories.

The note was sent to the Musgrove's lodgings, and Mrs. Harville bustled about with offerings of solid food to tempt the palate of the rapidly recovering Miss Louisa. With the good news came again the accounts of worry and fright of the first few hours after the girl's injury, the impressive actions of Miss Anne Elliot, Miss Louisa's first days of slow progress, and now her sudden gains in health. Wentworth could measure the recovery of his own spirits by those of the girl. All this talk of the past week was threatening to undo all the gains a great deal of solitary riding and walking had accomplished. Finally, Miss Louisa was back abed and resting, and the activity of the day seemed to be over. He could excuse himself for the rest of the afternoon and evening.

"If she's awake and up to it, I can't see a thing in the world wrong with allowing Frederick to see his fiancé. A quiet, somewhat private visit will do Miss Louisa a powerful lot of good if you ask me," Captain Harville said to his wife, who had finally taken a seat and was sharing a pot of tea. "Surely, the Musgroves cannot have any objection if you act as chaperone, Elsa."

Fiancé! From the moment of the young woman's fall, a knot had constantly been present in Wentworth's stomach. It had worsened when he was required to escort Anne Elliot home to Uppercross instead of her sister, Mary Musgrove. The agony of emotions and awkwardness of the seating—he had had to sit between Anne and Louisa Musgrove's elder sister, Miss Henrietta, in order to drive the carriage—had caused great strain on his body and his mind. He'd not thought it possible, but things had been aggravated still more by the arrival of the Musgroves on the second day. It was only in the last few days, with the improvement of the patient, that the knot had loosened. Harville's statement firmly-cinched it again. It was abundantly clear that his friend was under a horrible misconception concerning his affection towards Louisa Musgrove.

Before Mrs. Harville could make a reply, Wentworth turned to face the couple. It was vital that he put a stop to this new and ridiculous speculation, but to his annoyance, James Benwick had joined them at the table. The smallness of the house required a closeness that was allowing for more attention than was comfortable.

"There is no engagement." The declaration interrupted their conversation. It was graceless and sounded more rough-edged than he had intended. All three faces reflected shock and puzzlement. Though he was not sure how to explain himself, a clarification was obviously in order.

"I have made no promises...and I have seen no indication on Miss Louisa's part that she is partial to me...that she expects anything of me..." Except for the first little blast about there being no promises, all the rest were lies; and he knew it. Miss Louisa was very partial to his undivided attention and had demonstrated her willingness to manipulate whomever she must in order to insure it. Moreover, she had proven she was willing to jeopardise her own safety and reputation both in public and private, a clear indication she very much expected him to reciprocate her blatant affections. In lying to his friends, he was, for the first time, admitting the unadorned truth to himself.

Harville rose and joined Wentworth at the window. "You needn't worry, old man; I am sure that in spite of there being no formal declarations, Miss Musgrove knows how you feel about her. A visit will go a long way to proving that."

"But there is nothing to prove, and I do not think it would be prudent to—"

"I know, I know, you do not wish to excite her beyond what her condition will bear. That is admirable, Frederick. But really, Elsa will keep a close watch on her and see that she is not overtired." Quietly, for Wentworth's hearing alone, he said, "I understand you regret the accident and that it has caught you up short. As soon as you knew how you felt, you should have asked, but this is your chance to mend that. Visit her, and when she is well enough, do the right thing." It was shocking to see that his friend had not gleaned an ounce of understanding from what he had said.

"There is nothing to mend—"

"That's the spirit! Go straight at the task. No one will think any less of you for waiting so long. Even if there are some hurt feeling on the matter, once a proposal is made, those will disappear forever."

This tack is useless, he thought. He put his faith in another direction. "Really, Timothy, I do not think it wise to see her without the approval of her parents—"

"A courtly gesture to the in-laws is wise but unnecessary; I am sure. Come on man, a glimpse of you will be just the tonic the girl needs! The encouragement of the man she loves will do wonders."

The man she loves. That is the central issue, he thought. He had come to know his own feelings plainly enough. Nevertheless, it was her feelings that mattered the most at this juncture. Timothy's insistence that he should risk a visit with Miss Louisa made him wonder if the girl was saying things to Mrs. Harville, which then Elsa was communicating to her husband. The two women spent a lot of time together now that Miss Louisa was conscious, and he imagined that they managed to converse about all manner of subjects. Mathematical odds, not his own vanity, dictated that at some point he would be one of those subjects.

"—besides, they shall be here soon. You can enquire of Mr. Musgrove then. He will surely bless a visit, and Mrs. Musgrove can oversee it." Timothy made a face. "If my stairs can withstand the strain." Mrs. Musgrove's considerable size made climbing the steep, narrow stairs of the Harville house an awkward and time-consuming process. The man had even gone beneath and braced the frame to protect against any future embarrassment or injury. "I haven't room enough for another invalid," was all he had said as he had put away his tools.

A commotion at the door diverted their attention from Wentworth's objections. "My dear, dear sister is up and about, and I must be the first to see her. I simply must." A bonnet and cloak flew at the maid, revealing not Miss Henrietta Musgrove, but Mrs. Charles Musgrove. One of the little boys was unlucky enough to be in her path as she made for the stairs. Fortunately, children have an amazing sense of self-preservation, and he just missed being trampled. The rest of the Musgroves entered, talking loudly. *Certainly joy is understandable,* he thought, *but the hilarity of it seemed more appropriate to a circus tent rather than a sick room.* The mass arrival required that Harville should quit Wentworth's company and play host. This gave Wentworth an opportunity to slip out the door and away from the aggravation of the misunderstanding to contemplate his options. There would be no need to make himself available at Harville's until the next day. With all the fresh excitement, he would not be missed if he stayed away.

His customary haunt being off limits, he considered a ride along the scenic cliffs extending east of town. This prospect raised no real interest, and he thought of a walk by the shipbuilder's along the waterfront. This was always a pleasant diversion, but today, because of its close associations with the worries of career, his mood was not inclined towards it. Instead, he bought a fortnight-old copy of the *Plymouth and Cornish Advertiser* and headed back to the inn for a drink. As he exited the shop, he saw Miss Henrietta Musgrove and Charles Hayter walking down the street, undoubtedly heading to Harville's. They were deep in conversation and not a happy one by her sad eyes and his knitted brow. Wentworth hesitated injecting himself into the couple's conversation, but on the off chance they had already seen him, he stepped forward.

"Miss Musgrove, Mr. Hayter, good day. I am surprised you are not at Harville's celebrating Miss Louisa's progress."

"The same might be said of you," Hayter said. Miss Musgrove looked at each man and then cleared her throat.

"Good day to you, Captain. We are just on our way there." She tightened her grip on Hayter's arm, looked up at him and said, "But it will be a precious short visit on account of my sister." Wentworth said nothing, and his judicious silence was rewarded. "My dear Mr. Hayter has just arrived from Winthrop, and now my sister-in-law is insisting that he should ride back this very night with a letter for Miss Anne telling her of the good news concerning Louisa's recovery."

"You have heard from Anne ... Elliot?"

"She is with Lady Russell now and, I am sure, must have lots of time for writing letters." The young woman sighed and then looked into her young man's eyes. "Considering Miss Anne's good sense, I am sure she would not think this a good reason for Mr. Hayter to forgo rest and be parted from me so soon."

This explained the grave look on Miss Musgrove's normally cheery face. A plan began to take shape, and he, too, agreed it would be a shame for the young couple to be so soon parted. If *he* were to offer to take the letter, a side trip to Kellynch Hall would not be out of order. He had only written a hasty note the day of the accident, leaving his own family with little but the village gossips for news. Having a definite commission to deliver the letter to the Lodge would also afford him the opportunity to enquire after Miss Anne's health and deduce her state of mind. No matter how any other inhabitants of the place might feel, such politeness on his part would be expected. It would be rude if he did not ask to see her. When he made the offer formally, even prickly Mr. Hayter's face shone with delight. For once this past week, rather than bearing ill tidings, his words brought happiness.

He began to regret his largesse later that evening when he had a drink with Musgrove at their lodgings while waiting for the letter to be finished. In the beginning, Mrs. Charles scratched away quietly while the gentlemen traded predictions concerning the next day's weather, rejoiced upon the felicitous news concerning Miss Louisa's first few steps, debated whether Wentworth should take a horse from the inn or use Musgrove's gig—he opted for the horse when Mrs. Musgrove opined she longed for a ride to Charmouth so she and her husband might explore the lovely little place—and they were well into concluding that the port they drank was some of the foulest stuff on earth when Mrs. Musgrove clumsily hinted that the Captain's presence and conversation was an impediment to her thoughts.

"My sister expects such perfection when it comes to correspondence, and simply knowing someone is waiting for it is causing me no end of troubles," he overheard her saying to her husband when he returned from a breath of fresh air. "I am quite rattled now and may not even be able to finish it." Wentworth's only comfort in the lady's complaint lay in being equally blamed along with Anne. After making it clear that he would be around in the morning for the letter, he quickly took his leave. His suspicion that the letter would never be finished was put to rest when Charles brought the four-page monster around to the inn at nearly midnight. They shared another drink, and then Wentworth saw him off, feeling a bit guilty for the effusive thanks heaped on him by the thrifty, younger Mr. Musgrove.

The next morning's weather was precisely what one could expect so early on a late November morning: cold clean air, sporadic rain, and gusty breezes chilling the bones of anyone who must be out and about. The weather mattered nothing to him, for he was away from Harville's ill-conceived notions about Miss Louisa and him. No less was he also pleased to be away from the celebratory clamour of the Musgrove clan. He did not begrudge them their happiness, but it was a constant reminder of his part in the evil. He did not appreciate them, quite unconsciously, stirring his conscience. The quiet of the road was a pleasant change from the stifling surroundings to which he had become accustomed.

He progressed at a good pace, his horse more than up to a run now and then. The scenic landmarks that had become so familiar over five daylight trips were slipping by in quick succession. No memories of any of the trips save the one with Anne came to mind. A bad patch of rutted road forced him to slow to a trot. As he allowed the horse to pick her way through the channels, he convinced himself that this was the very spot where the carriage had slipped from the road and he had rescued her from a certain fall from the carriage. He felt ashamed that he could look back upon it with a certain pleasure, for the incident had not only put her in danger, but into his arms. There had been no pleasure in it for her. He recollected the disappointed looks they exchanged over the remainder of the trip. Such reminiscences nudged out any sort of satisfaction and brought on a renewed sense of guilt. His only hope was that Mrs. Charles's letter would relieve Anne's mind concerning Miss Louisa and begin building a new foundation for an improved opinion of him.

This journey passed as quickly as the others, and soon he found himself in the environs of Uppercross. As he passed through the village, he was greeted here and there by the bustling residents. The closer he drew to the Mansion, he could not help noticing hard stares and was certain if he looked back, he would see more harsh opinions in evidence. Before Mrs. Charles had become agitated by his presence, she had emphasised that her sister would be now installed with her godmother at Kellynch Lodge. "I shall render you a map, so that you will have no trouble in finding the place," she proudly told him. "Everyone rates my artistic skills as superb." He had glanced over at Musgrove for a confirmation of such a declaration but the man's expression was unreadable. Later, when the letter was delivered and he had a chance to look at the map in his chambers, he thanked God that no lives depended up the cartography skills of Mary Musgrove. It was so badly drawn that, were he foolish enough to be guided by it, he would miss the Lodge by a mile or so. The map was burnt that very night. Nothing would stand in the way of the promised delivery or in the way of an opportunity to see Anne.

A young man was quick to meet him and hold his horse as he dismounted. When questioned, the groom said that the ladies were home and that not a soul had been in or out of the house so far this morning. Standing before the door of the Lodge, he harried his cuffs and neck cloth as he buffed his boots on the backs of his trouser legs. It was not the first time he had stood on the steps of Kellynch Lodge, but for the first time, he felt more than equal to the place and all it stood for. He touched the letter in his breast pocket one more time and smiled, taking a wicked sort of pleasure in bearing a document guaranteeing him admittance into Lady Russell's home. "You care little for doing good, and are enjoying the idea of the poor woman's suffering far too much," his brother, the Reverend Edward Wentworth, would have lectured. *Poor woman*, he scoffed.

"Captain Wentworth." The butler stood aside to allow him entrance.

The use of his name caught him off guard. The man at the door was the very same butler of years before, but he was at a loss for the fellow's name, putting him at a disadvantage that he did not care for. He removed his hat, though no offer was made to take it.

"May I ask your business?" The question was simple enough. However, it reeked of disapproval and the condescension so easily assumed by servants of the middling gentry.

"I am on an errand for Mrs. Charles Musgrove. I have come to deliver a letter to Miss Anne Elliot...Longwell," he added, the name popping into his head.

Longwell offered a silver salver. "I shall see it is delivered promptly."

The letter was his charm to get past this dragon and through the gates to the citadel. *In fact*, he thought, *it shall see me safely by both dragons. To surrender it now would insure failure.*

"I cannot. I gave my word that I would deliver it to her personally." No such promise had been asked for, and no such promise had been given. He prepared to tell the man he knew Miss Anne was at home were he to offer her absence as an excuse. Longwell said nothing further but turned and went through one of several closed doors facing onto the entryway.

Every move he made in the marble entry echoed and accused him of smallness compared to the mistress of the house. He decided against taking a seat, choosing instead to examine a landscape hanging near one of the closed doors. As he studied the scene of haying in the golden midsummer of some unknown county, a piano began to play somewhere nearby.

Unless Lady Russell had taken up the instrument in the intervening nine years, it could only be Anne. The tune was gay and one he had heard before. He did not know its name or composer but would ask

11

Anne in the course of their conversation. She knew he was fond of music and this, he hoped, would not seem to be merely a polite bit of banter. The music stopped. He quickly peered into a glass and did some moderate preening in preparation of his summons to her.

The door opened, and Longwell motioned for him to enter. Wentworth followed, but before he could catch a glimpse of Anne, the butler asked for his hat. A stay of some length was anticipated. The door's quiet click was his cue that they were alone.

His eyes were drawn immediately to the pianoforte that stood prominently in the room. Anne was nowhere near, and all that moved was two thin tails of smoke from the recently extinguished candles. Although alone, he tried not to gawk as he widened his study of the room. Nothing had changed; the Lodge's sitting room was still severely formal and elegant without a hint of comfort. He remembered his first visit years ago. He had stupidly commented that the room was as pretentious and straight-backed as its owner. Unfortunately for him, he had said this to Anne Elliot before he understood fully the relationship of the younger woman to the older. That evening, she had made him appreciate how intimate with and dependent upon Lady Russell she was. His profuse and, at the time, sincere apology had brought Anne's full forgiveness for his biting wit. Though he had repented of distressing Anne, his opinion of the woman had only grown firmer over time. He was not ashamed of holding such an opinion, but he did regret not having the wisdom to keep it to himself on several other occasions. He was certain it was this loose talk that had sunk him in the eyes of Lady Russell and caused her to take a position against him concerning Anne and their engagement. This incident had forced him to see that there was almost no difference between his own little wooden world and the small society of the country. He was not surprised that the room had worn well. This was to be expected since Lady Russell spent a good portion of the year away from the area. *Harassing her few friends and family, to be sure,* he thought.

It was then to his dismay, that he noticed that a lone, older woman sat at a small table tucked into a corner of the room facing onto a sodden autumn garden. The dragon nodded towards a chair to indicate he should sit. Still, Anne was nowhere to be seen.

"Captain, you must join me." The command was polite in tone and her expression composed. Perhaps it was not only the furniture of the Lodge that had worn well. Perhaps, the lady had softened over time and was now willing to acknowledge him properly.

He bowed and joined her at the table. The formalities of how he took his tea and whether he cared for cake or a biscuit were observed although he could not help wondering what sort of plan the woman was working as she did so. Never, in all their short association, had she treated him with such courtesy. He took a sip of his tea and was disturbed to find it prepared just how he liked it. She was up to something, but he salved his uneasiness with the reminder that Lady Russell was not an overly clever woman. No, not clever...but persuasive enough when she wanted to be.

"Longwell said you have a letter to be delivered. I must say I am astonished to see you lowering yourself to playing messenger, Captain."

He had not expected that she would goad him in such an obvious fashion. "Mr. Charles Hayter has been gracious enough to bring word of Miss Louisa's condition on practically a daily basis. I was presented with an opportunity to spell him in these messenger duties and so offered to bring the letter from Mrs. Mary Musgrove to Miss Anne. I thought to visit my own family as well."

"How kind," she conceded. "I have been told all the particulars of the sad accident that has befallen Miss Louisa Musgrove."

Steady on, Captain, this is her angle of attack, he thought.

"Yes, it was most distressing." He put down his cup and looked directly into her eyes. "It was a horrible thing to witness, but I must say, even in the height of such panic, it was Miss Anne who showed the greatest strength and was most in control of her senses. We all looked to her for direction, and despite her own feelings, she kept the rest of us from falling into utter disarray. I, in particular, owe her a great debt of thanks."

The pride in Lady Russell's eyes was unmistakeable, and for a brief moment the two were in agreement about something concerning Anne.

"My goddaughter is a most intelligent and resourceful woman. I am sure it was anguishing for you to see the woman so dear to you the victim of such a dire accident."

He was about to agree and confide that to see Anne so discomfited by his own carelessness was a hurt from which he would not soon recover. Something made him hesitate, and in the short lull, he realised Lady Russell was speaking of Louisa Musgrove as the victim. He was about to assure her that no person with a heart could see such a thing and not be moved, but she gave him no time to respond and continued.

"I would not think, with her sister-in-law in such precarious health, Mrs. Musgrove would have time to write casual correspondence." The lady's mild expression was unchanged as she looked at him over the rim of her cup. In the company of a more sympathetic listener, Wentworth would have elaborated that there was nothing to keep Mrs. Musgrove from writing reams and reams of casual correspondence, as she had nothing else to do. Between Mrs. Harville, the Harvilles' nurse, and the nurse brought from Uppercross, Miss Louisa had a small army of women caring for her every possible need. All that Mary Musgrove had

13

to occupy her during the course of the day was deciding how deeply she was personally affected by each new improvement in Louisa Musgrove's health.

"It is not a casual letter, Ma'am. Miss Louisa's condition is greatly improved, and Mrs. Musgrove wanted immediately to tell her sister the good news."

"Ah, improved you say. That *is* good news. I am sure *you* are particularly relieved."

"No more so than her family, I assure you."

"Of course. As I said earlier, my goddaughter gave me all the details of the regrettable affair. She was particularly disturbed by the recklessness and lack of judgment that brought the incident to pass." Perhaps the woman was more clever than he gave her credit for. She could neither have used words more damaging to his already bruised conscience nor chosen ones which could more readily pierce through his confidence as a man. The question was: were these truly Anne's thoughts on the matter or were they Lady Russell's alone?

"You may leave the letter. I shall see that that it is given to her."

"Thank you, Ma'am. But, I would prefer to see it delivered myself. I am well able to answer any questions she might have. Or, should she wish to send a reply, I am returning to Lyme this afternoon and could carry it directly to Mrs. Musgrove."

It was a simple enough explanation, so when Lady Russell's cup clattered in the saucer and she stammered something about such fuss not being necessary, Wentworth was puzzled for a moment. Her face coloured quickly, and she hastened to fill his nearly full cup. She kept glancing out the window behind him. He turned to look. It was clear that whatever was out there she desired he not see it.

He scanned the view and saw Anne making her way from the Lodge. She pulled her cloak close against the light wind. Carrying a covered basket, she walked through an arch that led her out of his sight. He assumed that her godmother had hurriedly arranged whatever errand dispatched Anne into the cold and rain. For a moment, he nursed the hope that she might be on her way to Kellynch Hall. *Even Lady Russell is not so foolish as to send her there to avoid me*, he thought.

"As you see, my goddaughter is unavailable."

He looked into her cool expression, and said, "Unavailable to me, you mean."

"Captain, must I remind you that my goddaughter is a very thoughtful young woman? Sometimes too thoughtful; she takes on the cares of far too many people. Since she has been with me, she has endeavoured to hide the fact that the events in Lyme and how they will affect the Musgrove girl's future wear very heavy on her. You cannot expect that I would allow her to be subjected to your presence and the suffering that would surely accompany it." The woman's words did not describe the Anne Elliot of a week ago who so adeptly directed matters concerning Louisa's immediate care, consoled the dispirited, and was willing to stay to nurse the girl at his particular request.

Anne Elliot was indeed caring and thoughtful, and this was certainly proven by the fact she had taken matters into her own hands and seen that provision was made for him when he rode back to Lyme that horrible night. If her godmother was telling the truth, in the intervening days, her opinions and thoughts now flowed against him.

"So, you can see that your only option is to leave the letter with me and get on with the rest of your errands."

It nearly strangled him to admit she was right. Short of refusing to leave—which would give her an excuse to summon the young groom from earlier and see him ejected—he must leave the letter and exit with some of his threadbare dignity intact. He reached into his coat.

She was not so rude as to extend her hand, but she watched with an avid eye as he took the letter from his pocket and placed it before her.

Rising, he folded the napkin. "I will be at Kellynch Hall visiting my sister until noon should Miss Anne need me."

Lady Russell's eyes brightened. She took the letter and studied it for a moment. Meeting his gaze full on, she said, "I assure you, Captain Wentworth, my goddaughter has no need of you."

Chapter Two

The half-mile ride to Kellynch Hall was not remarkable, except that the Captain was able to relive the entirety of the disastrous meeting with Lady Russell exactly four times. Each re-enactment gave him an opportunity to triumph in the verbal joust with only the slightest variations of cunning wit and brilliant wordsmanship. He thought it a pity that none of the imagined victories could change the results of the actual clash. Passing through the Hall's gates, he nodded to the gardener, who sent a boy to announce the visitor. "Don' worry, sir. I'll see that she's brushed good and gets me special blend of oats," the groom assured Wentworth as he dismounted. In the mind of the Kellynch groom, the animal's care was quite obviously lacking.

He's no doubt right. I've ridden the poor beast too hard, too often, the Captain thought, stripping off his gloves. *And yet never able to outride my difficulties.* The footman greeted him with no indication that he had any opinions on the matter and directed him to the dining room where the Crofts were finishing breakfast.

"Frederick, dear, you look terrible," was the first thing his sister said, taking him gently by the arm as though he were suddenly feeble.

"Thank *you*, sister, dear. I have been riding all morning just hoping to hear your melodic voice."

The Admiral chuckled from behind his newspaper, and Sophia dipped in a mock curtsey. "I'm sure you did not come all this way just to tease me."

Bussing her cheek, he saw her to her seat and then took the empty one to her right. "And who else would I ride all this way to see?"

She paused as she poured him tea. "There is no one, I suppose. All the Musgroves are with you in Lyme, and that leaves just the Admiral and me. Oh, and the Pooles." She looked to the Admiral, lifted a brow and returned to appraise her brother. "Have some breakfast; you look as though you're perishing." So, his horse was not the only one suffering from lack of decent care.

He took the platters offered and allowed the comforting smells to entice his appetite. Of late, when he occasionally dined alone, he chose simple meals and drank more than was good for him. It was difficult not to spend those solitary times toasting to the foolish nature of men and the ache of lost love. When dining at the Harvilles' and the various configurations of Musgroves that daily presented themselves, he had strained to listen to the noisy, circular conversations between the members, expecting any day that his part in Louisa's accident would be mentioned. It would also not have been a surprise if the family spoke of an engagement. Surely, the idea would come to them just as it had come to the Harvilles. He never allowed himself to go any further in his conjecturing.

"So, what is the news of Miss Louisa today? Does she continue to improve?" Sophia asked.

"Yes, she does. She is beginning to stand, in fact. Her progress is excellent."

"Just see that she doesn't over tax herself. But, I suppose Elsa Harville would know not to allow her to do too much."

"Mrs. Harville has done an excellent job. She can not be thanked enough."

"I should think not," the Admiral said, finally adding to the conversation. He folded the paper and continued. "This is a strange new ritual you've added to courting, Frederick. I have my doubts though as to it catching on with the common folk...especially the ladies." He took a drink, the cup not quite covering his wide smile.

One part of him welcomed the Admiral's attempt to lighten the mood, the other knew his brother-in-law would never let loose of this particular bone. Wentworth knew that even if a miracle freed him from obligation to Louisa Musgrove, he would forever have to endure this sort of harassing. He would be explaining to his children why their uncle was always taking about ladies falling—

"Have you plans to visit Miss Anne?"

The sound of her name so casually spoken was a surprise. Frederick paused. He then took his time drinking his coffee. When he'd composed himself sufficiently, he said, "I had no plans to do so. Has she made mention of my visiting?" He was disappointed that his voice did not, to his own ear, sound more indifferent, more detached.

"No, we've not seen her since her return. She is still settling in with Lady Russell, I imagine. No doubt, she will make us a visit soon. I just thought, being connected to the Musgroves and the accident after a fashion, she might like to know the latest good news."

A footman took his empty plate. Perhaps it was the comfort of being with his family, or, perhaps, it was the fortification of a good meal, but

Frederick thought Sophia and the Admiral should know as much about that day as possible.

"I brought a note from the Musgroves and left it at the Lodge. She'll learn the latest from that. Although I know her modesty will never allow her to admit it, it was only she amongst us who kept her head. Only she prevented a chaotic disaster from becoming a tragedy." He paused, thinking of the events in quick succession. "If I had had my way, it would have been her to stay rather than her sister. She was very gracious and more than willing to remain and care for Louisa, but others thought better." He could see that Sophia desired to say something but kept it to herself.

"My only hope is that she did not suffer exceedingly from the shock. I should hate to think … there are more ways than the physical to be damaged."

Sophia rose and patted his shoulder. "Frederick, please, I assure you again, we are not all fine china. Women see shocking things all the time and survive quite well. In fact, we are strengthened by them. Do you think you came into this world by a tidy and gentle passage? Our mother—"

"Well, now," the Admiral said, rising as well, "I think we've talked enough of the shocking events of the past weeks." He took Sophia's arm. "Frederick, let's go out. You can give me advice on a pointer I'm thinking of buying."

He stayed a while longer and talked about the pointer, though he possessed no specific knowledge that might help the Admiral decide, then left the Crofts to discuss their genteel country life. Returning to the house, he made arrangements for his possessions to be sent to his inn at Lyme.

"…so please see it sent immediately. I have no intentions of returning here."

"Very good, sir. And these books, sir," Harkness said, indicating two sitting on the table by the bed.

"Yes, the red one is mine to be packed. Return the other to the library."

Harkness picked up the one, glanced at the title, then at the Captain. Wentworth had found the novel in the library and tried to read it on one of the nights when sleep was impossible. It was a dreadfully affected tale of desperation, separation, and eventual madness. Further, steeped as it was in such overwhelmingly depressive elements, it had also managed to be sloppy and maudlin. He wondered if Anne had ever read it. If she had, surely she had despised it as much as he? He slipped his own volume into his pocket and looked around the room.

"Will that be everything, sir?"

"Yes, Harkness, I believe so. You have the name of the inn and her keep. Please send it on as soon as possible." Harkness bowed and followed Wentworth to the door. He took a moment to look about the room. "I cannot say I am going to miss the country."

Harkness opened the door and stood aside. "Well, sir, for some it takes more than a mere visit or two to come to embrace the charms of the country."

Wentworth nodded to the man as he passed. *Blast the man.* He was sorely tempted to stop and force him to disclose what he was hinting about. It seemed more reasonable than ever that the man—and, perhaps, all the servants—knew about his past relationship with Anne Elliot. While he was sorely tempted to have the truth, he was equally afraid of what he might hear.

The Captain rode out of the yard at the stroke of noon. As he passed the Lodge, he was unreasonably disappointed that Anne made no appearance. She was either not interested in gaining further intelligence about Louisa's condition or the source of the information put her off. Either way, he was obliged to return to Lyme by evening. Mrs. Harville had promised that Louisa would be well enough to receive a short visit from him. He was thankful for the seventeen-mile ride in which to work up the proper enthusiasm for such a duty.

~ ~ ~ ~ ~ ~ ~ & ~ ~ ~ ~ ~ ~ ~

To his relief, he was freed from that particular obligation when it was revealed that Louisa had overdone and was now suffering from a monstrous headache, restricted from having visitors. "She worked too hard in anticipation of your visit no doubt," Mrs. Musgrove said. Had Wentworth been able to detect the tiniest nut of ill feelings on her part, he might have suffered less, but there was none. Her expression and tone were completely genuine. When she walked away, she patted his arm in commiseration with his assumed disappointment.

After his luckless mission to Kellynch, the days began to move by quickly. Louisa's recovery was full of stops and starts. This was in his favour. When she was doing well, he stepped aside and graciously allowed her mother, sister, and brother to take their time with her. When she was genuinely ill or just out of sorts, he stayed back, not wishing to force himself upon her. If anyone noticed the ploy, they said nothing.

While he was not masquerading as a moral paragon, he was riding and walking through the countryside about Lyme, Charmouth, and Up Lyme. Many adventurers came to Lyme Regis for the views of the sea from the dramatic cliffs west of town. The more studious came to dig for newly discovered remains of what were thought to be ancient sea creatures trapped in the soft earth along the shore. The locals shook their heads at some of the proclivities of the visitors as they went about their daily business. Those who belonged and those who were visiting gave Wentworth plenty to study as he made his rounds of the area.

As long as he was able to keep himself physically occupied with things to do his thoughts bothered him but little. It was in the middle of the second week after the accident that the wind and the rain conspired to keep everyone prisoner. Twice a day, in the short walk from his inn to the Harvilles' house, Wentworth endured a soaking. The arrival of the Musgroves would soon exhaust the tiny house of places to hang sodden hats, coats, shawls and even stockings after the puddles filled and over-flowed. When the storm passed the three-day mark, he understood why caged animals sometimes did themselves harm trying to escape their confinement.

"As soon as this squall lets up, we are going back to Uppercross," Charles Musgrove said one evening to Wentworth, Harville and Ben-wick.

"You would go before Miss Louisa is well enough to travel?" Ben-wick asked. His tone betrayed shock at the proposition.

"No, not all of us. Father is concerned that things will go awry if there's no one to watch over the labourers. He and mother will stay for sure, Henrietta most likely as well. Just Mary and I will be heading off."

Wentworth looked to Harville to see if he could detect his opinion. His friend seemed satisfied with the situation.

"Besides, Mary's not heard from Anne and is anxious to know how things go with her father in Bath."

"Were I to give you something for Miss Anne, could you see it de-livered to her?" Benwick asked.

"Certainly! As long as it's not a love letter or such," Charles laughed to himself, not noticing that the others grew quiet and avoided looking at one another.

Benwick coloured at the implications of the jest and hurriedly ex-plained. "It is a book. Miss Anne highly recommended the author as a very insightful man who is himself intimately acquainted with grief. She mentioned this title in particular and said she was very anxious to read it for herself." He went to a shelf and brought down a black volume. "I found it at the local shop and wish to make her a gift of it." Wentworth noticed his friend stroking the book's spine. He wondered if Benwick was loath to part with it, or, perhaps, he was imagining Anne's delight upon receiving the token of his friendship. The former was definitely a possibility, but it was the possibility of the latter that drove him to make

20

an excuse and abandon the close quarters of the house for some fresh air.

When word circulated that the younger Musgrove couple was leaving for home, Wentworth determined this to be a prime opportunity for him to withdraw as well. The close family setting and any stray, underlying expectations concerning Louisa and him might be weakened by his departure. Should questions be asked, he would enlist the claims of his brother's recent marriage, his duty to welcome his new sister to the family, and the unpredictable weather of the northern climes as reasons for his departure. It all sounded well, and he hoped everyone would accept his explanations.

With his decision made, Wentworth went directly to the elder Mr. Musgrove with his plans. Were he given to self-flattery, the Captain might have credited the possession of an extraordinarily honourable nature and its demand for forthrightness. The truth was much simpler: he was tired of skulking about, endeavouring to avoid the gentleman whenever possible. And when he couldn't, he had grown weary of his own feigned geniality. Every meeting with Musgrove, he felt, was an opportunity given by Providence to lay the blame for Louisa's misfortunes squarely on the shoulders of Frederick Wentworth. The interview, though, exceeded all his expectations. Mr. Musgrove listened carefully to his explanations, responding only that he wished the Reverend Wentworth and his new bride happy. Wentworth was astonished.

No one else pursued the matter. He was assured several times that his absence would be deeply felt. Curiously, no one save Harville asked the length of his intended stay. He supposed no one was interested in the affairs of anyone outside their own circle, or they assumed he was absolutely obliged and would return promptly, not wishing to be too long away from Louisa.

On Tuesday morning, when he had made his last visit, he was surprised to find James Benwick making plans to travel with the younger Musgrove couple. The normally melancholic face was bright with anticipation of the journey. "I have found and read several of the books she recommended. And I am anxious to discuss with her some of the finer points of the various authors' thinking." Wentworth was persuaded Benwick hid his true intentions behind talk of books and conversation.

"And there is also the book you wish to give her," Wentworth said. Benwick brightened to incandescence, thanked him for reminding him of the gift, and hurried off to retrieve it from Musgrove so that he might deliver it himself.

Wentworth thought, for all the aid he was rendering Benwick, he might just as well offer to stand up with the couple when they exchanged their vows. He was leaving at the best of times. With his friend neatly installed at Uppercross, he knew he would drive himself mad imagining all sorts of interesting and romantic scenarios involving the like-minded pair.

Benwick returned with the volume. "Thank you for reminding me. I hope she likes it." After a brief and subtle questioning, it was clear Benwick believed Miss Anne would be on the doorstep of Uppercross Cottage, cheerfully awaiting the arrival of her family and being pleased no end upon welcoming a visitor. Benwick's expression changed markedly when Wentworth informed him that Anne Elliot was ensconced three miles away at the residence of Lady Russell, the godmother and chief protector of the young lady in question.

"The woman is a gorgon to be sure, but she'll not eat you all in one bite," was Wentworth's parting jibe. He was both angered and amused that quiet, studious, remarkably unconnected Benwick was liable to please Lady Russell no end and that, if Anne was in the least hesitant, her godmother's power of persuasion could be again called upon to point out Benwick's qualities in abundance. Approval on the one front, coupled with a fortnight of James's increasingly irritating talk of "Miss Anne's elegance, sweetness, and beauty," forced Wentworth to acknowledge that if he was to hear news of their impending nuptials within the quarter year, he would not be shocked in the least.

~ ~ ~ ~ ~ ~ ~ & ~ ~ ~ ~ ~ ~ ~

The clamour and confusion of the streets of Plymouth were, paradoxically, a tonic to Wentworth's exhausted mind. He felt completely at home as he and his horse waded through the fray. Plodding country wagons laden with goods, wives, children, and sometimes angry drivers made their way alongside fine carriages with nervous, high-stepping teams controlled by drivers indifferent to the other traffic. To add to the disorder, Wentworth was one of many solitary riders dashing around the slower moving vehicles. Most made pretence of avoiding those on foot, but it was really a show. Those trying to cross the street were at the mercy of wheels, hooves, and the good will of others. Battling his way up the street was an ordinary, though all too brief, distraction from the dunning thoughts concerning the place he had left earlier in morning.

Wentworth settled himself in a modest, clean room at the *Main and Mizzen*. He ordered dinner be brought to him, along with two bottles of a decent Spanish wine. Once he was renewed by the second-rate meal, he spent the rest of the night silencing his inner turmoil by losing himself in the noisy and oddly musical clatter of life in Plymouth.

The next day, he walked out just as a pitcher of hot water was brought to his room. "But you asked for it last night, sir," the boy said.

He looked at the dour, skinny lad and wished for the likes of the affable Mr. George Tuggins from Portsmouth. "Take it to someone else with my compliments," he said, heading down the stairs. At the stables, he summoned his horse and rode out of town to admire the views of the ocean in quiet solitude.

~ ~ ~ ~ ~ ~ ~ & ~ ~ ~ ~ ~ ~ ~

Pulling a short glass from his pocket, he looked out to the lighthouse. He envied it its place in the middle of the channel. It stood alone and was responsible for nothing more than shining its light. It was the responsibility of those piloting the incoming ships to be warned and show some skill as they headed inland. It was the light's good fortune to be insensible; it cared nothing when a captain or master was dashed on the rocks and his ship destroyed.

He sat for some time watching jealously as the rough sea pounded and tossed the ships struggling to make their way into port. With even more envy, he watched those pushing out to open sea. When he was afloat, life was very simple: he did whatever he must to keep his crew happy and occupied. When enemies came within range, he did whatever he must to subdue them and take them as prizes. When disturbing thoughts would begin to trouble him, he subdued them by turning his mind back to the first two.

Urging his horse to a walk, he let her pick her own way down the hill. This left his mind to wander, as it would, into dangerous paths. For instance, his reunion with Anne had reawakened those latent desires of the heart and flesh with a vengeance. It was lamentable, he reflected, that even if he were able to put to sea this very minute, those needs would not quiet easily. Short of being sent into the heat of raging war, he would most likely find only a cold sort of comfort in the simplicity of his former existence.

His second meal at the *Main and Mizzen* made him regret leaving Elsa Harville's excellent cooking. Still, he would not exchange the peace he found being left to his own thoughts for a decent bit of beef and a tender, generously fruited pudding. As he contemplated alternate uses for a runny plum duff, he heard a familiar laugh. Through the haze of the snug, he caught sight of his old friend, Gilmore Craig, sitting with a table full of older men. Most of the fellows were outfitted in dated frock coats and cheap scratch wigs while Gil was his usual jaunty self. He looked to have a fashionable trim to his hair and a new coat, cut in what was most certainly the latest style and colour. Wentworth rubbed his unshaven cheeks and considered whether he should even draw Craig's attention. His shabby and tired appearance would get him no sympathy, a great deal of ribbing, and a whole host of questions. But, he was coming out of his brown mood and the thought of some cheerful company was surprisingly attractive.

When the serving woman came to collect his tableware, he asked that she take a drink to his friend. She cast an eye to the table. "The youngest one. In the grey coat?" A seductive smile came over her face.

"A good brandy, nothing more," Wentworth added.

Barely a shadow passed over her expression. She nodded at him with the same look and took care to leave him with a fair prospect of the showy sway of her hips as she disappeared into the back room. In due course, she returned with Gil's drink and put it before him, pointing towards Wentworth's table. Craig smiled wide upon seeing him and signalled that he would join the Captain soon. After three-quarters of an hour, Wentworth was finishing a brandy of his own and Craig was still signalling his soon arrival. Finally, he rose, shook the hand of each of the gentlemen and approached Wentworth.

"What are you doing here?" Craig asked, taking a seat. "I thought you were rusticating in the wilds of Somersetshire." The serving woman came back around, and Gil ordered a good bottle. Settling in for the evening, he said, "I'm sorry I couldn't join you sooner, but those are the business fellows I was telling you about this summer. We were lamenting our losses to rats...both the two and four-legged varieties."

Wentworth hesitated. There was nothing to say that would not be open to comment and question. He deemed it best to push the conversation along in another direction.

"So nothing has changed in the wilds of Plymouth then." Aside from the keep and the girl earlier, he'd spoken to no one for nearly two days. His own voice sounded foreign.

"Of course nothing changes. Men have ever been liars, both in business and in love."

"My brother would chalk it up to original sin."

"What? Business or love?" Craig laughed and took a drink.

"Both, I imagine." Wentworth tipped his glass in a little toast. His own behaviour in the business of war was, he believed, exemplary. Recently, in love, it was stained and littered with the marks of a repentant sinner. The drink was a sort of baptism into this disquieting realisation.

Craig topped each of their glasses, raised his and said, "Here is to me, chief of sinners, but redeemed, and out of the business of love."

Wentworth raised his glass but was a bit hazy as to what they toasted. "You have taken a monk's vow then?" he asked.

Craig laughed again and touched his glass to Wentworth's. "Hardly! I am married."

24

The news was a shock. The last time they met Gilmore Craig was still grinding his teeth over the lovely, but unobtainable, Miss Hammond. She was a beauty, smitten with Craig, but also the niece of an India-bound admiral with no good opinion of any man not in service to the King. Either his friend had won over the girl or his affections had migrated to another with the speed of summer lightening. He chose the first of the propositions.

"So, Miss Hammond is now Mrs. Craig?"

The man's smile widened. "You are correct! See, you *are* a romantic. You *do* hope for tender happiness even in the most dreadful circumstance."

There again was that blasted accusation! He stood firm in his mind. He was *not* a romantic. Neither Sophia nor the Admiral had accused him of being a starry-eyed, poetry-spouting simpleton. Even Benwick had not done so.

"I believe there was a trusted auntie left to stand watch over Miss Hammond. Did I not say you had the power to sway the old girl in your favour?"

Craig studied him for a moment, took a drink, and studied him some more.

"I know I look a bit rugged. I've not shaved for a day or so, but your examination makes me nervous, Gil." In the past, his slightly sodden friend had shown an annoying propensity for speaking the precise truth concerning Wentworth's feelings, and the Captain was not eager for it to manifest itself again this evening. "When did the happy event occur?" he asked, hoping to steer clear of any conversation relating to him.

Gil roused himself and took a drink. "Not many days after you left Plymouth. I think Anne is very happy with her choice." He continued to study Wentworth and then leaned forward. "You look dreadful, old man. Things not going well?"

Wentworth was shaken by his words. He'd forgotten that Miss Hammond's Christian name was Anne, so Gil's familiar use of it had startled him. Then there was the sympathetic question, which was so broad and inviting that he feared he might take his friend up on the offer to share his woes. "Everything is well enough. I am just allowing myself to be reenergized by the sea." It was true he hoped for a revival of sorts, but he was already certain there was none to be had. These bits of truth and lies, along with Craig's silent study, made him suddenly drain his glass, set it precisely on the table, and stand to leave. Craig stood as well.

"It has been a pleasure, Gil. I hope to see you again before I leave." This was pure palaver as Wentworth intended to leave Plymouth without so much as a nod to anyone if he could help it.

"Come to dinner tomorrow night." Gil's expression was of old and not the intense scrutiny of minutes earlier. There was genuine desire for his company in the invitation.

"I am not certain—"

"Please, Wentworth. Come break bread with us and see what a happy home looks like." He extended his hand; Wentworth accepted. "I shall send the carriage for you. You are staying here?" Craig pushed in the chair and stepped aside as the serving girl came round.

"Yes, I'm here, but no need to trouble with a carriage. I shall walk."

"Good. Anne will look forward to seeing you again, I am sure." He nodded and left Wentworth standing in the middle of the snug feeling tired and put out that he had accepted the invitation.

~ ~ ~ ~ ~ ~ & ~ ~ ~ ~ ~ ~ ~

The following day began slowly and continued at a snail's pace through the morning. It occurred to Wentworth that he had no proper attire for even a casual dinner with his friend. It could not be helped. When he had packed his things at Kellynch Hall, he had made no contingency for any sort of society besides that of the Harvilles' and the Musgroves. His trunks had not even arrived when he had decided to flee. His only thought to his belongings had been to request Harville send them on to Plymouth. It would take several days for his trunks to catch up to him, but he did not feel like putting off the invitation until he could make a better show.

As he again brushed his undress uniform coat, he hoped that Mrs. Craig was not the sort of woman who would take offence when he showed up looking more like a common swab than a gentleman. Noticing a button missing from the faded waistcoat, he called for a needle and thread and moved a button from the bottom to the empty place. Carefully, he worked his neck cloth into an acceptable knot that would hide a hurried darn, muttering, "Vanity, vanity, thy rank is captain."

He made his way through the busy streets, again taking comfort in the bustle and hubbub. So much activity all around kept the ghosts at bay very nicely. Immediately before he was to turn off the high street to the Craig residence, the doors of a respectable-looking establishment flew open and out poured a large group of ordinary sailors. The keep was obviously tired of their shenanigans. He waved a white cloth, loudly and crudely informing them of his annoyance. Passing slowly through the crowd, he recognised a great many of the men. Nearly all had sailed with him on *Laconia's* last voyage.

"To Captain Tanner!" one shouted, and the others haloo'd.

Captain Tanner, Wentworth surmised from the exuberant pack, had no doubt just been made into a new command. *Lucky bugger*, he thought.

"Captain Wentworth, sir!" Turning in the direction of the voice, he saw a small man with a wide grin, an unruly beard, and a filthy jersey coming towards him. Wentworth stopped. "Captain Wentworth," the man repeated, making his obedience.

"And you—Greer!' he said, suddenly remembering the man. "You look to be celebrating."

"Aye, sir, we is. I know this sail won't be the same without ya, but I hope ya don't begrudge us poor swabs our chance at a bit of fortune." The man's eyes were a brilliant sparkling green. Wentworth wondered if it was wine or anticipation of a windfall fuelling such a look.

"No, Greer, I would never begrudge a man a bit of fortune. I wish you and the other lads well." He made to continue on, but Greer was not finished.

"That's very good, sir, cuz I don't mind tellin' you, I think your ill-will could bring us greater misfortune above any man's."

What Greer said made no sense until his attention was drawn to the door of the pub again. Obviously Captain Tanner was leaving the establishment, and his new crew was anxious to draw as much attention to themselves and their new master as their recent refreshment could muster.

Tanner looked Wentworth's way. Though he did not recognise him, Wentworth nodded and it was returned.

"All *Laconias* this way," Tanner roared with a huge sweep of his arm.

At the call, Greer hared off to join him. What seemed to be hordes of men separated from the gathered throng of spectators and followed the man heading towards the docks. Wentworth could do nothing but stare at the single straight blue-clad back leading the way. Another man was now at the helm of his beloved *Laconia*.

Dinner with Gilmore Craig and his new wife was even less appealing than when he'd accepted the invitation. But, it would only last a few hours and then he could return to his room and continue punishing himself for all his ignorant misjudgements. He'd been told once the imposing house had always been in the possession of the Craig family. The story went that it was built to its present magnificence from a lean-to where the first occupants kept sheep. Over the years, the Craig men and, when necessary, the odd woman had learnt the ways of trading which led to the family's present prosperous state. Gilmore Craig was an only child who now commanded the family holdings. Wentworth

27

surmised that the newly minted couple would begin producing heirs as soon as possible so the house could finally be filled with little Craigs, ensuring that the family line would not quietly die out. As he stepped up to the door, he thought how common it was becoming these days to allow things to die away without much notice

The door opened and a fine, liveried footman ushered him inside and then took his hat and coat. When his less-than-elegant undress uniform was noticed, the fellow reminded Wentworth of sour old Longwell of The Lodge.

He was in no mood to endure the sneering disapproval of a man who, if they were onboard a ship, would be subject to his absolute authority. The thought reminded him of the sight on the street. While he was greatly relieved that his dear *Laconia*—for dear to him she would always be—was not broken up into scrap, she was still under another man's hand. As with Anne, another man would now enjoy the place he once occupied.

Wentworth's mood improved as he was shown into a small drawing room where Mrs. Craig welcomed him. "Captain, it is good to see you again and that you are free to dine with us." She dropped a proper curtsey, evidently not minding his casual attire. A glass of a very fine brandy was soon warming in his hand as Mrs. Craig explained that Gilmore would be a little late. "There has been some sort of crisis at the warehouse. It seems that some hoaxing jobber is trying to pass off a few casks of bad cod." Their laughter was thin and forced. "That is what his note said," she added hesitantly. There was nothing else to laugh about, so both made a study of their refreshments.

"Congratulations on your marriage." He wished to acknowledge the couple's quickness once Admiral Hammond left the area but doing so seemed in poor taste. "It was accomplished not long after I left the area, I think." This seemed tasteful enough.

"No, no, not long. A fortnight is all. It happened so quickly after you left." Her look was odd, as was the repetition. He wondered if Craig had taken his advice too much to heart and had pressured the lady with too much vigour. Remembering the mutual state of their feelings, he thought that to be impossible.

"You have returned to Plymouth on business?" Again she was hesitant, her voice insipid, having only enough vitality to carry it to his hearing and no further.

"No, not business." Unless dodging responsibility could be considered a business.

"H-has your time in the country been enjoyable?" She finished her sherry.

"Uh, no. Others seem to find a great deal of enjoyment in the country, but I found little." Surely he should have stretched a little and told a convenient lie for the sake of sociability.

"I am sorry to hear that–" Mrs. Craig placed her glass on the small table beside her chair, knocking it off as she withdrew her hand. It did not break–the delicate crystal remained unharmed thanks to the thick rugs–and the footman cleared it way immediately. As the man moved off, she touched a handkerchief to her lips. Wentworth wondered if she was ill. Before he could inquire, she said, "So, you returned to Plymouth hoping to find…"

He found the question extremely intimate, and it angered him for a moment. His normal confident temperament was taking a remarkable beating lately. Perhaps the anger was because the question of why he had come to Plymouth was one for which he had no credible answer. While he had all the reason in the world to put as much distance as possible between himself and Louisa Musgrove, he could have gone directly to his brother's to accomplish that. Why had he chosen to sequester himself in the place where all that was seemingly successful in his life had begun that summer to go sour?

"I suppose, I hoped to find things here unchanged." Now he hesitated. "I wanted things to be just as they were the night of the Farewell Ball." That night he was still, though just barely, *Laconia's* captain, he was still in active service and he was not a man facing his most regrettable past mistakes or an uncertain future.

Mrs. Craig rose and went to the window, wringing the kerchief as she went. She stood at the window for a few moments, saying nothing but managing to mangle a perfectly nice arrangement of red flowers. The silence was beginning to be awkward. He was casting about for something intelligent to say when she jammed a bloom back into the vase, nearly knocking it over. Turning, she gaped at him, pink and panicked. "Gilmore is coming up the walk. Things are not as they seemed the night of the Farewell Ball. Anything you may have thought about me … about us…is not how I genuinely feel or ever felt." She swept by him, and out the door.

"God, he murmured, why did you make women completely inscrutable?" He downed the last of his brandy and stood to greet Craig.

Chapter Three

Voices echoed in the entryway as she greeted her husband. They came into the room arm-in-arm. If possible, she looked more ill and he wore an inscrutable expression.

For a moment they all stood looking from one to the other. Finally, Craig bowed and said, "Captain, good to see you don't stand on ceremony, though I must play host and present a good front. You will excuse me while I go up and change." He looked again at Mrs. Craig. "I am sure the two of you will continue amusing yourselves." He nodded to his wife and left them quickly.

Mrs. Craig was still pale as ever, but now wore a dash of scarlet on her cheeks. She went back to her chair and sat down. The handkerchief she had mangled earlier was getting another round of punishment. She was closer to tears than Wentworth cared to see.

He chose to stand near the window, well out of her sight. Were the floodgates to burst, taking all her dignity in the torrent, she would have an illusion of privacy if nothing else. But even after a few minutes, there were no sniffles or sobs. He glanced back at her. She sat straight and still as a statue. Before Craig rejoined them, though it was none of his affair and inquiring was impertinent, he wished to know how things stood. Would she tell him?

"Craig looks as if the jobbers may have gotten the better of him." A small group of people passed by the house, and he was made acutely aware that he was completely adrift and alone with his particular friend's wife.

"I know not; he said nothing about them." She moved in the chair. "Captain, I must be honest with you." She had left her chair, her voice was much closer to him now. "My behaviour the evening of the Farewell Ball was inexcusable...and all an act"

He turned to see her earnestly addressing him. The pause was to orchestrate her next statement. "I stood close to you and pretended to be so...amiable to make Mr. Craig jealous. If you thought—"

"I thought nothing, Miss Ham–Mrs. Craig." So this was it. He had thought her a bit intoxicated, but she had merely been baiting Craig into making his move. He should resent being used as a pawn in her silly game, but he could not fail to see the humour in it. "I assure you I have always held you in the highest regard, but…" Tact dictated that he go cautiously. To say he was not in the least interested in her as a woman might open a Pandora's Box which would never be closed on top of the ridiculousness already afoot. "…I have known Craig's feelings concerning you from the beginning. I would never in good conscience have done anything to betray him."

Mrs. Craig relaxed visibly. She even managed a feeble smile. "I must say I am glad. I played a part, and while it worked–Gilmore came around almost immediately to speak with my aunt–I never thought it would have such repercussions. I assured him of my feelings before we wed, but when he came home last night his jealousy was palpable." Perhaps this explained Gil's quizzical looks and close examination of the previous evening. Wentworth's brown mood had at long last worked for him. No sane person could look on his dishevelled person and melancholic demeanour and mistake it for interest of any kind, much less interest in a married woman.

"Would it help you if I left?"

Her smile was wide but brief. "If you leave there will be no chance to set things aright with him. I hate to think I have ruined such a deep and abiding friendship."

The smile on his face was genuine and the relief he felt, liberating. He moved towards the doorway with her alongside. "Mrs. Craig, blacken me as dark as you must. Make him know what a reprobate dog I am in accepting an invitation I never intended to keep." He stopped and faced her. "Play another part–a woman completely disgusted with my poor sense of style, lack of social acumen, and utter disregard for people's feelings. Make him understand you never want me in your house again." He headed to the door, hoping she could pull off this new role.

She called to him. "I regret that you must sacrifice your friendship with my husband because of my silly gamesmanship." Her expression was utterly guilty.

"You needn't worry, Mrs. Craig. I shall return to Plymouth one day– after your affection is thoroughly established in his mind. We shall have a few drinks, I will do the polite and apologise profusely for upsetting you, and all will be well."

Now there were tears. "I am so sorry for this."

"Don't be. You've helped to remind me how dangerous it is to play a part. Especially one you don't particularly feel." He took his hat and coat as he thought about the near calamity to which he'd been party. Leaving the house, he determined it was time to move on.

~ ~ ~ ~ ~ ~ ~ & ~ ~ ~ ~ ~ ~ ~

The stable attached to the *Main and Mizzen* was crowded. The warm, stinking air surrounded him closely and reverberated with the voice of the hostler bawling orders. One poor soul seemed to be the particular object of his wrath to the exclusion of all others. While Wentworth was in a restored frame of mind, it was not so much repaired that he would tolerate being ignored and forced to witness the brutal display.

"Sir," he called out. All eyes turned towards him, including those of the hostler. "No doubt the boy needs a good thrashing, but I have a horse that must be tended." The hostler continued to leer at Wentworth, and tossed aside the boy.

He approached the Captain, pushing up his filthy sleeves. "You mean to be tellin' me my business?" His face was inches from Wentworth's. The man's foul breath reeked of his last meal and burned the Captain's eyes.

"No, merely pointing out that I am in need of your service. Surely you realise that while beating that squeaker may be amusing for a short time, it will put nothing in your pocket. Tending my horse will." Ignorant bluster met with natural authority and took a beating of its own.

The man thought for a moment, took the few steps necessary to grab the boy and dragged him along as he came to the Captain. Shoving the child at Wentworth, he said, "Here. I know enough to say that brat ain't worth my time and trouble. Since you's so concerned, you take him."

The vicious shove caused the boy to slam into Wentworth's legs and fall with a grunt at his feet.

The boy wisely stayed on the ground but looked up into the Captain's face. A nod of recognition passed between the man and the boy.

"Well, as I live and breathe, we meet again, Mr. Tuggins."

~ ~ ~ ~ ~ ~ ~ & ~ ~ ~ ~ ~ ~ ~

George Tuggins wolfed down his second bowl of stew, pausing between bites only long enough to sop gravy with hunks of bread. Wentworth motioned for another glass of small beer for the boy and a pint of ale for himself. For such a small thing, Tuggins could certainly put away the victuals. As soon as he was finished with his meal, Wentworth would take him to his room and see to the cut over his right eye. It hadn't bled much, but it needed cleaning...along with the rest of Mr. Tuggins.

"So how do you come to be in Plymouth, Tuggins?"

"Well, sir, you said if I was ever in Plymouth, I should look you up. I weren't going to make a fortune at the *Crown*, so I come here."

"And found I was gone."

"Aye, sir. I asked around before leavin' Portsmouth, found your ship's name was *Laconia*. When I got here, I asked around again and found she was in ordinary and that you was gone." He looked down to his bowl and with great precision wiped every bit of gravy from the bottom.

Wentworth marvelled how there was no complaint in the lad's voice. When they had spoken earlier in the year, he meant only to leave the boy with an understanding he was inclined to help him were they to find themselves meeting again. It was obvious George had taken his words as an explicit invitation. To find Wentworth departed would have stopped other boys cold, but not so Mr. Tuggins.

"I knew I would have to start over, so I went lookin'. There's always a job shovelling sh—" He hesitated as there was a young serving girl passing the table. George looked over his shoulder as she walked away. "There's always something somewhere that needs shovelling, sir."

Wentworth liked the boy's polite consideration and powers of observation. His feeling that Tuggins was a rarity was strengthened. "When you finish that glass, I shall order water sent up to my room, and we'll see you cleaned up."

Like most young boys, Tuggins took on an air of reluctance at the mention of hygiene.

~ ~ ~ ~ ~ ~ ~ & ~ ~ ~ ~ ~ ~ ~

The cut was deeper than he had thought, and for a moment, he wondered if a doctor should be called for stitches. Examining it more closely, he saw that it was now only weeping a bit and already beginning to close of its own accord. "Hold this on it," he said and handed the boy a clean cloth.

Pouring the bloody water into a slops pail, Wentworth said, "You'll have a scar, but it shouldn't be too bad. It'll come in handy when you're older."

"Sir?" Tuggins looked at him from under the cloth.

Wentworth turned, wiped out the bowl, gathered the rags, and placed them all on the dresser. "The ladies, boy. The ladies like scars...so long as they are few and well placed."

George got up and looked at the cut in the mirror. "I didn't know that ladies like such things, sir."

"Oh yes. Above the eye is good, as well as along the cheek. Just here." He moved his finger along his own cheekbone. "I was mates with

33

a fellow who had a nasty scar across both lips. Got bashed in the mouth with a belaying pin, somehow. Anywise, poor devil couldn't pucker up his lips properly. To hear him tell it, the ladies were inconsolable." He smiled, wondering what wisdom Mr. Tuggins would have to impart upon hearing of the loss of such a vital skill.

"Poor fella. That is a real shame." Placing the cloth back on the wound, he turned to Wentworth. "But I didn't know that ladies particularly liked men who could whistle. Whenever I whistle 'round a lady, they turn all red, and I'm sure to get thumped."

It was all he could do to keep from shouting in laughter. The revelations of Lyme had cast a shadow on his entire life, but it would seem that the Almighty had his cure in the form of one George Tuggins.

~ ~ ~ ~ ~ ~ ~&~ ~ ~ ~ ~ ~ ~

Wentworth sat for a moment and let the dark, dreary night press in upon him. An overcast sky,and the accompanying freezing rain had stayed with them since setting out that morning. Despite the fact that he'd had no sun with which to gauge time or direction, he was confident that the clock in his head was true. He'd heard no sound save the rain and George's teeth chattering for some time. "Walk on," he urged the horse. It was fast approaching midnight.

Determined that they would make Crown Hill without spending another night on the road, he had been disappointed by their lack of progress and had only begrudgingly stopped once to dry out, take a meal, and rest a bit early that afternoon. The Captain was glad they were closing in on their destination. The boy was not eating or sleeping well. But how could he? The child would only pick at his food and would not sleep in a proper bed electing to curl up with Anne's blanket near the fire instead. He regretted taking the fellow from whatever sort of life he had cobbled together for himself in Plymouth.

The Captain was heartened when the landscape began to change and the number of houses increased. In short order, they were riding onto the high street. As could be expected for the time of night, the only lights were from the inn. The only movement on the street was a small but loud group of men moving away from the village centre. For a moment, Wentworth considered foregoing the inn and riding over to ask them for directions to the rectory. He decided against it. Though the town was small and, no doubt, peaceful, he would trust the directions of a sober innkeeper over those of men whose state of sobriety was questionable.

He dismounted and said, "Come inside and warm yourself while I ask about my brother."

34

The rain was heavy enough that he could see nothing, but George's voice rang out plainly, "I shall stay with the horse, sir." There were neither eaves nor overhang under which to shelter the pair. The enquiry would have to be quick. These were the most words the boy had strung together all day. Wentworth put his growing quiet down to extreme discomfort and, perhaps, George was nursing a little regret of his own.

"Suit yourself," Wentworth said, heading to the door. As he sloshed his way through the mud, the Captain shoved aside snatches of the alarmed conversation they had exchanged when the boy found out Edward Wentworth's occupation.

"*You never said he was a preacher, sir.*" George's tone was approximately that of a trapped animal.

"I did not think it was significant. Besides, what did you imagine a brother of mine do for a living?" They were just settling in for the first night's rest.

"Well, as we're going into the country, sir, I thought perhaps he was a farmer or a blacksmith or something useful. But not preacher, sir."

Wentworth generally agreed with the boy. He, too, believed most clergy were at best of little use, but he could not feel this way about Edward. Naturally, his brother was the exception that prevented all his brilliantly conceived ideas about religion and its practitioners from settling themselves neatly away in his mind. To his shock, the Captain found that the boy's incensed tone caused something of a defensive sensation rise up within him.

"My brother may be a man of the cloth, but he is useful. When my parents died, he raised me until I went to sea. I owe him a great deal." He never thought of his relationship with his siblings in terms of debt, but he did owe much to Edward. "He is a good man."

Tuggins eyed him for a moment. "You were reared by a preacher?"

"No, he went into that after I left home."

"So, you don't know nothin' of him since?"

"I've stayed with him a few times I've been on shore."

"You don't know what he does to people though."

He hesitated. "Other than behaving like a dyspeptic spinster at times, I think my brother is quite harmless. His preaching goes long occasionally. I think that is a hazard of having your audience captive and unable to escape." He chose not to enlighten Mr. Tuggins to the fact that it was very nearly the obligation of all those in authority to bore their inferiors on occasion. "If he looks to be heading down that dangerous road, I'll challenge and you can be my second."

"Aye, sir. At least you're safe when they's in the pulpit." And that was the last that George would say on the matter.

Few of the tables in the public room were occupied and then only by one or two stragglers, most likely single men with no proper homes. The keep returned from his rounds of the tables and asked how he might help him.

"I am looking for the parish rectory."

The keep eyed him up and down. "You look to be better than keeping body and soul together, if you ask me. You don't look to be needin' help from the poor box."

Wentworth was always surprised at the lack of modesty of country people when it came to stating things that were none of their direct concern.

"You are right, I do not. I am looking for my brother. He is the rector of this parish."

The man frowned a moment then brightened. "Ah, you'd be the Captain! Oh, well, why'd you not say as much? The Rector is always speakin' very highly of you, sir."

He wondered that his brother spoke of him at all, but it was good to know that any ill opinions of him were kept quiet and not bandied about with the rustics.

"And with him bein' just married and all, he's happier than I've ever seen him. Not that he weren't a cheerful enough fellow to begin, mind," the keep added.

Frederick had given little thought to the new Mrs. Wentworth during his travels. He did begin to wonder what the woman would have to say about his sudden appearance—along with that of his young protégé. It was not a subject he would consider discussing with his new acquaintance and asked again about the location of the rectory.

"Well, I would send you the shorter way, due to the rain and all; but the path is pret' near invisible in the dark, and I'd hate to be the one to send you off into the river." He leant closer. "It's the rector's business to forgive, but I think he'd have a devil of a time, seein' as how you're his favourite brother and all."

The keep straightened and wiped the water from the counter that had dripped from Wentworth's coat. "I do appreciate that. So, can you tell me the long way to his house?"

"Oh, yeah. Now which way did you come in?" The Captain told him. "Well, then, you'll want to turn around and go back until you come to the last house. The fella keeps pigs so you can tell by the smell..." The man went on to tell of a tortuous route he was sure promised to drop him and George in the river by the morning. "And once you see the cemetery, you'll know you're about in his yard. Just be careful of his garden. Not that there's much there this time of year, but he's particular that people stay out of it."

"Thank you for your time, sir," he said. Walking to the door, he tried to make some order of pigs, a high stone fence, and an overgrown hedge. Then there were a few other landmarks that the man assured him he would not see by night and the worry of trampling his brother's garden. He exited the inn, looking to see if the loitering men from earlier were still about. They were gone. *Obviously more rational than I gave them credit for. Gone home and snug in bed by now,* he thought.

He joined George at the horse and prepared to turn back up the street.

"Sir, I think I spotted the church. Wouldn't your brother live in that?"

Wentworth smiled. "Somewhere near it, I would imagine. Where away?"

"Over there. There are a few lights between those trees. Let your eyes get used to it, and you can see the spire."

"Well done, Tuggins. Your sighting is all we have to go by. Stay on-board and I shall walk her." With the noise of the rain nearly deafening, he wanted to have his feet firmly on the ground if they were indeed close to a river. In short order, without pigs or fences or hedges, they came to a house all alight. If nothing else, he would ask directions to the rectory. Not sure how the house was situated, he walked around until he found the back entry. Wentworth hesitated, not wishing to alarm those inside. Years earlier, he had learnt in one of Edward's other parishes that some country folk answered the door, no matter the time, with weapons in hand. Even a frail, old woman can be a frightening sight with a blunderbuss primed and ready to fire.

The horse stamped its foot, and George made a small noise as he shivered. The house would give them either shelter or hope of it soon. Before Frederick could get to the stairs, the door opened and his brother stepped out, holding a small lamp aloft.

"It's about time, my boy!" He joined him. "Give me your bags, and you can take the horse to that shed over there." He indicated with the lamp a small building a short distance from the house that looked to be little more than a lean-to. Just then, a sneeze drew the attention of both men. Edward raised the lamp higher and went to the horse. "What's this?" George sat up taller and pulled the oilcloth coat from over his head. Edward looked back at his brother. "Frederick? Who is this?"

"This is George Tuggins, Edward." In all the time he'd had to think while journeying to Shropshire, Wentworth had never formed a precise explanation of his relationship to the boy. "He is a—"

"I am Captain Wentworth's second, sir." Wentworth had forgotten that they had discussed such a thing. It suited for the time being.

37

Edward laughed and looked at the boy. He leaned close to Frederick. "Have the two of you had much cause to be duelling along the way? It is illegal, you know." He continued to smile as he awaited his brother's answer.

In the past, Edward had never welcomed him in such a full and energetic manner. Frederick had always come to the door and been greeted like the proper visitor that he was. Edward even being awake at this time showed he anticipated Frederick's arrival. Everything about his brother was upside down from what he knew. Even his appearance was extraordinary.

Edward had always fought his deep black beard with all the precision of a military campaign. Some days, when he was required to appear at an important social function, it had been necessary from him to shave twice in order to look the part of the proper religious gentleman. It seemed that he had tendered his surrender. He'd also rarely seen his brother without his black suit coat. On the occasions they had shared a home, Edward had always been scrupulous about his appearance even in private. More than once, his brother had explained that a religious man never knew when his clerical services would be needed and that it would not do to be caught undressed. Frederick had often wondered if there was the religious equivalent of the Articles of War setting down requirements for the particular uniform to be worn when performing one's required duties. It was either that or his brother was merely fussy.

Not that Wentworth was careless regarding his own appearance. When he'd appeared in Monkford, fresh from a well-publicised battle and sporting a handsome new uniform, Edward had muttered something about no man in the area standing a chance against such gilded glory. He could admit still to a bit of pleasure in wringing such an admission from his brother. That time in their lives was long gone, and this brother might be quite interesting, if for no other reason than he possessed a new look. Perhaps it was a portent of a deep, substantial change.

"No, there has not been any reason to. The trip was uneventful. But cold—"

"And wet," piped a small voice.

"Mr. Tuggins!" There had been a few discussions about the need to learn the proper comportment if he wished to sail with Wentworth. This included holding his tongue and not interrupting his betters.

Edward looked from one to the other. "Well, you are come at last. I had begun to think you shanghaied!" he said, with a smile. He offered his hand.

Now the formalities would begin. He'd barely taken Edward's hand when the rector pulled him close to embrace him. This startled Wentworth.

The last such show of affection between the brothers had been when Frederick had gone to sea at fourteen. On the busy, smelly Liverpool docks, Edward had stood with tears in his eyes, doing everything humanly possible to keep them from falling. Frederick had wanted to cry as well, but even then he was acutely aware others aboard the ship would be watching him and making judgements. This being so, any unmanly behaviour was to be avoided at all costs. At Edward's last touch, he'd stood ramrod straight and made no move to reciprocate the tender gesture. His fears had been baseless; not even in jest had anyone commented on the act.

Edward pulled away, looking embarrassed by his unreserved actions. Frederick realised he had just reacted with the same lack of affection as he had on that scandalous Liverpool dock. The rain was beginning again and Edward raised a hand over his face, blinking away the drops. "I am glad to welcome you, Frederick. I shall take all the bags in, and you can take your horse around back and put him in with my poor old cob. There's a good fire and plenty of food when you're finished." He took the bag and urged George into the house before him.

He meant to hurry as his brother had suggested, but as he stripped off the horse's saddle and hefted it over the stall's wall, he couldn't help pondering his brother. *Apart from the beard, the man looks and sounds like Edward.* He unbuckled the bridle and carefully removed the bit, hanging the gear on a nearby peg. *But he looks nearly naked without his full black uniform.* He gathered up some hay and dropped it into the manger. The horse's velvety lips greedily sought it out. She raised her head and chewed with an unperturbed regularity. "I always knew he could pry it off if he cared to," he confided to the mare. "I'll observe him closely and let you know what I find."

He gave her a pat on the forehead and stood quietly for a moment, preparing himself to enter the house. As he did so, he couldn't help noticing the slovenly construction of the tiny stable. Had the builders felt it their duty to keep the occupant of the rectory from thinking more of himself than he ought? For Wentworth's part, they had succeeded. No one being forced to use such a building would ever mistake himself grand or even respected. A small bay horse of indeterminate age stood quietly watching him. The beast seemed to be further proof of his theory.

He found a brush and took a few swipes over his own horse's back. The mare nickered her approval. No matter how the evening went, their arrival was a relief. He admitted to himself that both man and horse were showing signs of wear from being so much on the road and in the foul weather.

He ducked through the door and latched it for the night. The darkness was thick and seemed to wrap itself more tightly around him as he felt the strengthening wind. He stood in the yard for a moment, enjoying the silence. The rain had stopped and the clouds were moving on. A crystalline sky and pinpricks of starlight were already promising hard beauty on this freezing December night.

As he approached the house, he especially appreciated the homey warmth it gave off. Frederick hesitated at the door and watched Edward through the kitchen window. George was nowhere to be seen. While a man in the kitchen seemed odd–which was a silly notion considering in his world men did all the cooking, sewing, and nearly every manner of womanly work–it seemed to fit exactly the apparent changes in his brother's life.

The warmth of the kitchen embraced him as he entered. The good smells of the promised meal teased his empty belly. "You look frozen to the bone," Edward said, as he stirred a pot on the fire. "Hang up your things and remove your boots–stockings as well. The bootjack is outside; bring it in if you must. Then come and warm yourself." Glancing at him, Frederick noticed the smile was missing. His brother's voice lacked the enthusiasm of earlier and had taken on all the charm of a surly bull. He wondered if the boy had said anything untoward.

"What have you done with Mr. Tuggins?" He hanged his coat and hat on pegs near the door then set about removing his boots. The ancient jack had a loose upright, useable only if wedged against the sole plate. As he held the contraption together and worked his foot from the boot, he studied the garments already there. The great coat he'd bought his brother nearly eleven years ago occupied one of the pegs. Edward's fussiness paid off, for it looked practically new. Alongside the coat there hung an apron and a straw bonnet with grey ribbons. This was the first evidence of the new Mrs. Wentworth he'd seen so far. It suddenly struck him that it was odd that she was nowhere to be seen.

"He's eaten and is in bed." He was pulling crockery from a shelf and paused. "Is he yours?" The bowls clattered when he set them on the table.

Wentworth was at a loss. It had not occurred to him how it looked that he had the boy. Of course people would assume they were father and son. Edward did not wait for an answer. "You should get out of those wet clothes. Are your things in the bag wet? Most likely! Shuck it all off, and I shall fetch something dry," Edward ordered, leaving the pot and the fire for the door.

40

Abandoning the jack, he stood with one boot still on, the other falling to the floor. "Excuse me?"

"What? I don't need you getting sick from a cold. Get undressed, and I shall be right back." He seemed put out by Frederick's reluctance to strip down in the kitchen.

"And what of your wife?" When it was strictly the two of them—with no fear of a female appearing suddenly—certain proprieties could be set at naught, but a woman changed all that.

Edward stopped and smiled. "Ah yes, my lovely wife." He laughed. "Catherine is well away from here. She's with her parents in Kidderminster. Her father is buying a horse, and her mother needed company while he makes the rounds of the sales. Anywise, you'll not be compromised." He laughed, shook his head, and left the room.

"Compromised, indeed," he muttered, working off the second boot. He wondered where his brother had put the boy as he moved closer to the comfort of the fire. Another chair held the boy's clothes. He'd never examined Tuggins very closely and now realised how worn were his coat and pants. It was impossible not to notice how small the boy was as well. The remains of Mr. Tuggins's meal were evident on the table. He took a small piece of bread, dragged it through the stew's gravy, and ate it. Pulling a chair onto the hearthstones, he peeled off his stockings and warmed his feet. The sound of the stew bubbling in the pot was as soothing as it smelled rich and inviting. His stomach growled in anticipation of more, and the warm stones around the grate felt wonderful on his cold feet. He made a silent concession to his brother: he would remove his soaked outer garments but keep his shirt and trousers firmly in place until he examined what Edward brought him.

He'd never worn his brother's clothes before. When Edward returned from the West Indies to care for Sophia and him, Frederick had been a short, wiry 12-year-old barely able to fill out his own clothes. Now, as adults, Edward was half-a-head shorter than he and more solidly built. And, if he was not mistaken, marriage had added not only to Edward's happiness but to his girth as well.

The rector's clothes were examined and deemed acceptable when compared to the Captain's sodden ones. The resulting outfit was rather comical. "I'm sorry the pants are too short. They fit me very well," his brother said, spreading the wet articles over the backs of two chairs.

"Well, they would, wouldn't they?" Frederick said, pulling on heavy woollen stockings.

"It is not my fault that you're the taller of us."

"I didn't say it was."

Again, there was nothing of Edward's previous warmth, or perhaps, it was his own grim mood putting them at odds. "Where is George

sleeping?" He was beginning to realise the boy would serve as a convenient diversion when feelings ran a bit high.

Edward was filling bowls with stew. He motioned to the fireplace
with a large spoon. "There is a small room behind this wall—quite warm
and snug—with a bed. He ate and was practically asleep when I returned
from getting him something to wear." He paused in his serving and
studied Frederick. He began to say something, thought better of it, and
resumed his task. Finally, he said, "The boy seems like a good sort." He
finished with the food and picked up the tray.

~ ~ ~ ~ ~ ~ ~ & ~ ~ ~ ~ ~ ~ ~

"Were Catherine here, we would certainly be in the dining room,
but with her away I have become like a hermit in my own house. I
spend most of my mornings out visiting, and the local ladies have taken
pity and pass me around as a dinner guest. That leaves my evenings
spent mostly in here. I only venture into the kitchen or the bedroom out
of necessity."

They were seated before a roaring fire in Edward's study. Frederick
was amused by his brother's enthusiastic hospitality. Edward insisted
that he take the better of the two battered red leather chairs and a
mismatched upholstered footstool. Above the change of clothes, he was
offered a blanket, which he refused, and now he ate a bowl of stew that
could feed three men along with a chunk of bread able to sustain four. It
was a far cry from former days—days not all that long ago—when Edward
had to be careful of every mouthful he consumed or provided.

"Would you like more?"

Frederick's bowl still held a fair amount. He held up his hand in re-
fusal and placed it on a small side table from which Edward served them
both. "You are a better cook than I remember."

"Better circumstances. I still receive gifts of food— they are occasionally suspect in quality, mind you—but for the most part, people are doing
well here and are quite generous. What's more, Catherine's family is
very adept at seeing we never return from our weekly visit empty-
handed."

This was another change. In the past, Edward gladly accepted the
spotted and blighted offerings of whatever poor parish he served. When
he was given anything in good repair and useable, he bristled. In those
bygone days he seemed to feel he deserved only that which was fit for
the trash heap, anything of decent quality was above him and should be
humbly refused. Frederick was glad to see things changed. He'd eaten
enough meals concocted from those dubious offerings to last him a

lifetime. Possibly Mrs. Wentworth's family had something to do with the change.

"Would you like to see a picture of Catherine?" Edward asked. He'd been quiet for a while, perhaps thinking of her. Frederick said he would, and Edward brought a framed picture from his desk.

Mrs. Wentworth was not a beauty in any sense. She, in fact, gave the impression of being rather severe, if the drawing was in any way true to the subject. Her grey eyes lacked any brilliance and her complexion was nothing at which to marvel. Her hair was a nondescript brown and her shoulders were somewhat narrow. It was not a formal portrait but an amateur composition with an ill-organised flower arrangement in the background. Even with nature at her back, it did her no real favours.

Edward took the picture. "I hope to have something better done in future. This was rendered by a young cousin of hers a few years ago." He touched the frame and replaced it. "She will be the first to tell you she is not pretty." He sat down. "When she takes the time, she says she is tolerable. It angers her that I insist on telling her she is beautiful. 'I know better than that, Edward Wentworth,' she'll scold."

Frederick glanced over to his brother. Edward stared blindly into the fire. "So, why do you tease her if it upsets her so?" Edward had never shown a propensity to mock anyone.

He looked at Frederick with a countenance that warred between frown and smile. "You know better! No matter how loud the protest, ladies like a compliment. Besides, I am not teasing her." He sat back and put a foot on the unused stool. Frederick pushed it towards him. "I do find her beautiful. Love does that I suppose. It has been my duty to baptise some of the most awkward-looking children ever born, but their mothers, particularly, see them as perfect little babies." He was quiet for a time. "I know that Catherine does not fit the accepted mould of what passes as a beautiful woman these days, but I like to think that because I love her, I am able to see her more clearly than other men."

Frederick had no response for this theory. "I am pleased to see you happy, Brother." And he was. At least one of them should be lucky in love.

"Thank you. I am happy. One of the older parishioners told me she thought me one of the most cheerful men she'd ever known. But, after I married, she said I surpassed even that. I had always thought myself quiet and introspective. I guess I badly misjudged myself all the way around."

You and I, both, it would seem, Frederick thought. From the cheerful greeting outside, his brother's mood had shifted between a light airiness and his customary earnestness. At some point, it had begun an inextricable move towards this more genial side. There was none of the distance and condemnation Frederick had felt in the past. Could a marriage make this much difference in such a short time? Perhaps. But the innkeeper had said Edward was a happy man even before that. Where had that brother been all these years?

"Anywise, we are happy, and that accounts for it, I think."

"How did you meet Mrs. Wentworth? Is it a longstanding acquaintance? Or did you see one another and just know it was love?"

"I have known Catherine since I moved to Glencoe—a market village just up the road—three years ago. I had it in my mind to pursue a trade of some sort."

"But God is your trade."

Edward raised a brow and looked at Frederick for a moment. He was clearly deciding something. "God is neither a trade nor a commodity to be bought and sold. Anywise, I was worn to the bone and thought a complete change would be just the thing."

He did not ask why his brother was worn and had contemplated a change in occupation, but it was odd and something to keep in mind.

"I was doing some teaching and met Catherine through her brother. I was tutoring his son in mathematics. Her family resides there. We saw one another at social gatherings, and she would take pity on a poor, hapless man who dances poorly. I noticed one evening that she had the habit of rescuing me by starting unusual theological discussions. We'd be left to ourselves in short order once anyone got wind of the topic. After a time, it was known that I was only good for deep philosophical conversations, and then, none of the ladies expected any dancing from me." Edward smiled as he gazed into the fire.

"That's rather inappropriate, isn't it? Two single people conversing so intimately?"

Edward chuckled. "Yes, it was. I did once mention that she opened herself to great and unwelcome speculation on the condition of her soul by doing this. Her answer was that in the country everyone is so closely tied and that practically anyone at any time could know what she was about. There was no opportunity for her to be up to mischief. Besides, the conversations were not always about theology. She is keen on practically all matters, and we merely took advantage of the circumstances."

"So, did the two of you fall immediately in love, or did it take time?"

"You probe rather deeply, my boy."

The rebuke made him realise he was being amazingly meddlesome. "Sorry. I am just interested in the change of affairs. Ignore me."

"No, I'm glad to tell someone. We were merely acquaintances. She had almost decided it was not her lot in life to marry. One day, we met outside the shops, and she showed me a cap. She said she might buy it.

44

'It is not too gruesome, but it will send a clear message to those who think themselves eligible,' she said."

"I must say that even as a single woman, she was quite frank."

"Very much so. After that meeting, I began to contemplate our separate situations and found that a solution would be for us to marry." Edward shifted in his chair but did not look at Frederick.

This struck Frederick as absurd. "I can scarcely believe the happiness you describe is the result of convenience alone."

Edward glanced Frederick's way, but quickly looked back at the fire. "It is not. God has an amazing sense of humour. I proposed, and she accepted. There were smiles all 'round, handshakes of congratulation. I suspect her family knew what I was about. They saw me as Catherine's gallant knight come to save her from spinsterhood. Though, the truth be known, she has saved me." He turned away and kicked off his shoes, setting them precisely by the leg of the chair. After he sat up, he continued. "Just a few days before the wedding, I began to think myself very unfair. I would be quite comfortable in the arrangement, but what if Catherine harboured secret ideas about romance and such?"

"You said she is intelligent; didn't you think she also understood this to be a practical matter?" Frederick knew he should scold himself for going more deeply into a subject that was clearly none of his concern, but he was fascinated.

Edward leaned over the arm of the chair. "And what if she did not? I have seen perfectly rational people turned into idiots by weddings and ideas of love. I began to think very carefully about what I might have started." He sat back. "And that was when I decided that I had to make everything clear to her. That very night I was dining with the Keyes. My stomach was so tied in knots I thought I must be ill."

"Is Mrs. Keye such a bad cook?" Frederick asked, not able to resist the jest.

"Please, Frederick. Put that brilliant wit aside for a moment. So, I dined with them. I was perfectly senseless the entire meal. My hands were shaking, I dropped so much cutlery I spent more time under the table than upright. I mutilated a perfectly good chop to look as if I had eaten. Thankfully, we adjourned to the sitting room. Catherine's brother was to read us something of his own composition...as he always must."

Frederick could not help noticing the sarcasm-laced reference to Edward's brother-in-law. It was not his usual way. He was beginning to enjoy this man he had thought he already knew.

"Catherine took a seat next to me, as she usually did. I would normally have endured the recitation with a modicum of grace but not this time. He began, and I noticed immediately that her presence was quite unnerving. We had always been perfectly at ease, but that night ..."

The Captain knew what confession was to follow. He took a drink rather than laugh.

"I began to feel ill again, and I quit the room with as much aplomb as my haste would allow." Edward rose and faced the mantle, denying his brother a look at his expression. "I stood in the vestibule for a moment, considering what I should do. The heat in the sitting room was excessive; it was cooler there. Dusk was falling and the candles had not yet been lit," he paused to poke at the fire. He took a deep breath. "Catherine came to me. She asked if I was ill." He paused for a long time.

Curiosity was getting the better of Frederick. "And you told her–"

He turned to face Frederick. "I told her nothing. I stuttered and stammered and finally, I kissed her."

That was the outcome Frederick had suspected. He could not help but laugh.

"What is so funny?"

"You intend to tell her it's all for convenience sake, and that, perhaps, she needs to think again; and to prove it, you kiss her. That makes no sense, Brother." He continued to laugh quietly.

Edward laughed in agreement and settled back into his chair. "No, my actions do not. But love doesn't really make any sense, does it?" He took a drink and raised a toast to love and the confusion it brings to mankind.

"I was astonished at it all. I had not been in love with her when I proposed, but then there I was. The greater surprise came when I realized that she fully returned my...affection. We, um, parted, and all I could see was the most beautiful woman ever created. As I looked at her, I realized we were becoming part of one other. It was like–"

"–seeing your own reflection looking back at you in a mirror. It is not your face, not even your sex. But, it is you."

The sentimentality passed over his lips before he could stop it. The shimmering coals of the fire were his only refuge, but after a moment or two, he looked over to see Edward nodding in agreement. Sentimental the thought may be, but it obviously had a ring of truth to it.

"I now understand more fully how crushed you were when Miss Anne Elliot broke your engagement." The unexpected mention of Anne's name made Frederick catch his breath. "That night, had Catherine said she thought better of marrying me, I would still be shattered, I think." His tone was hushed, and Frederick assumed he was counting his blessings that such a thing had not happened.

Frederick wanted distraction, so he rose and went to the window. There was nothing to see in the dark but a few lights scattered in the distance.

"How is Miss Anne? Sophia is very taken with her. Though, of course, I cannot tell from her writing if she is much changed."

This second mention of Anne was more than unsettling. "I see no change in her at all." He could not bring himself to add more.

They were quiet a few more moments. Edward broke the silence. "I know you have always thought my advice about your engagement to her was meant to wear it down, wither it on the vine, or kill it outright. It was never meant in that way. I had a sort of understanding about how you felt and what you wanted. I know she loved you deeply, but she was so young, and so vulnerable to those who could only see you as a—" He stopped to find a word.

"Go on."

"As a proud young man with little more to offer the daughter of a gentleman than a handsome face and a sharp wit."

"Fortunately, I have learnt to use the sharp wit in ways that are to my advantage and not to harm myself as in former days." Lady Russell's disapproving face when she was the object of that unleashed wit came to his memory.

"Miss Anne's godmother was only doing what she thought was best for her. The Elliot family's position in the area was quite attractive and probably brought out all sorts of undesirable fellows. A young woman in Miss Elliot's circumstances—her mother deceased and father so—needs good advice in life. I imagine she still takes it from time-to-time."

Frederick could hear Louisa's voice that day on the walk to Winthrop. "...she persuaded Anne to refuse him." "I have been told she, indeed, still does." He noticed that his brother looked at him, puzzled. "What?"

"I said, I think you still have feelings for her."

He looked back into the fire. "And what have I said that makes you think this?" He would make short work of whatever his brother said, and then excuse himself for bed.

"It is not what you say, but what you keep to yourself." Edward sat back.

That is not fair, he thought. He was about to ask where he was to sleep when Edward spoke.

"I am glad you are come Frederick. I should not be surprised if this visit we find we are more alike than you know."

"I would not be opposed to that." He was relieved that the conversation had turned.

Edward roused and stood. "Your room is ready, and I must tell you, you look as though you need it desperately." He headed towards the door. "Come."

The rector lit a candle by the bed's side, and Frederick could see the room was indeed prepared for his occupation. The fire was low but had been given enough time to warm every corner of the room and make it more than comfortable. The bedclothes were pulled back, beckoning. Several blankets were at the ready at the foot of the bed. He wondered for a moment if he should check on George Tuggins but decided against it.

"This will have to do for the night. I laid out the contents of your bag and that shabby blanket, as well. Are you sure it shouldn't be in the barn with the horse?"

"No, it belongs here with me. Go to bed, Brother," Frederick said, taking the candle. "You need some sleep. I can handle this."

Edward smiled. "Yes, I suppose you can." He made for the door, and then turned. "Forgive me, but I must ask. When I address Mr. Tuggins at breakfast, should it be as a guest or as a nephew?"

Chapter Four

N ephew or guest," Frederick muttered. The question had taken him by surprise, though he could understand how it could be asked with complete sincerity. Explaining why and how he came in possession of Mr. Tuggins would be one of the first things he did the following morning.

He turned on his side yet again, hoping that the unyielding mattress would relent just this once. It did not, and he soon turned onto his back. He did not wish to dwell on his troubles, but he could not help thinking about Edward's question about Anne.

'She is so altered, I would not have known her.'

There was a physical sting to the remembrance. When he had said it to Miss Henrietta, he'd tried to phrase it in such a way as to seem innocent. But now that Edward had smoked out the truth about his feelings, he had to wonder how much had been said knowing the cutting remark would make its way back to her.

Yes, how different life would be if stupidity were valued, as it ought. He wished he could be happy with a pretty face and body that could satisfy his baser urges and leave the idea of an equal partner in love by the wayside. In his travels, he had seen many beautiful women, but most of them were not overly concerned with the inward self. Rather, their concern lay with the outward, and that only as deep as a comparison of their appearance with that of other ladies. A few of the more beautiful ones were callous to the very centre of their hearts. Women of beauty and quality were difficult to come by.

'I suppose you know he wanted to marry Anne?' The words from that long-ago walk caused his pulse to quicken and the room to warm noticeably. While he would never say anything against Charles Musgrove as a man or an acquaintance, he, also, would never mistake him for a scholar. Had Anne, too, found that intelligent partners were rare? There was no reason, other than the opinion of the Musgrove's, to believe that

it was Lady Russell who had found the man lacking. Still, as Anne's judgment on the matter was unknown, his questions remained unanswerable.

He rose and stirred the fire. The room was finally cooling to a comfortable degree, but his mind would not allow the rest he craved. To his way of thinking, it was infinitely better to be active and doing something than to lie helplessly by, allowing a parade of harassing thoughts to tramp through his mind.

~ ~ ~ ~ ~ ~ ~ & ~ ~ ~ ~ ~ ~ ~

Surprisingly, Frederick was not stiff when he woke. He had no desire to sit for any length of time, but for the most part, he was in fine shape for having ridden so far in so few days.

"George!" He must get to the boy before Edward.

All his clothing was completely dry; although, he would look as though he had spent the night in them. It could not be helped. As he attempted to tie his neck cloth, he rushed through the rabbit warren of halls on the ground floor, following the scent of coffee and ham to the kitchen. Thankfully, he found the boy sitting at the table, peacefully eating his breakfast while Edward sat by the fire, chatting and toasting bread on a long fork. Wentworth felt slightly foolish as he realised George had nothing to tell regardless of any questions Edward might ask.

The Rector glanced to the doorway. "It's about time, Brother." He examined the slice of bread, deemed it sufficiently brown, and tossed it onto a plate on the table. "In that little oven is a platter with your breakfast on it. You'll serve yourself." He took another slice of bread and went back to toasting. "So, George, you think I am likely to be unexciting and a bit tedious, eh?"

The boy's fork hung between the plate and his mouth. He looked to the Captain with wide, pleading eyes.

Edward hitched himself around to look at Frederick. "I take it you feel the same." He turned back to the hearth.

Mr. Tuggins quickly filled his mouth and began scraping around on his plate under Wentworth's withering glare. It was clear their unflattering conversation about the clergy had been referenced in some way, and Edward was offended.

Frederick took a plate and went to the warming oven, hoping to think of something at the best, clever, and at the least, soothing. A blackened piece of bread appeared before him. He took it and went to the table. "I fear that you have misunderstood, Edward. We were speaking of clergymen in general, not you in particular. And you must own that Mr. Tuggins, being rather young, may have mischaracterized, inadvertently, of course, some things I said." He took a good piece of toast from the plate and began to eat.

Edward did not turn around this time. "I don't know about that. But I am told that the word 'spinsterish' was used." He hung the long fork on a peg, turned the chair back to the table. It placed him directly next to Frederick. "Have I indeed misunderstood?" His brown eyes gave the Captain no clue as to his thoughts.

Frederick looked over to Mr. Tuggins, catching his eye just before he took a drink from his mug. The boy was afraid to his very bones. Wentworth softened his expression and noted that in future there would need to be an in-depth discussion of confidences between gentlemen and how keeping them was especially important at sea. He turned to Edward and met his gaze full on. "I indeed said something to that effect,but it was not meant maliciously—"

Edward didn't change his expression and waited patiently for Frederick to finish. He might as well have done with it and tell the whole truth. "It's just that you can be bloody peevish and silent as a grave to the point where people..." It was the whole truth he should speak. "*I* think you are like an old gouty man just waiting for the grave." There it was. He was certain he had now goaded his brother too far. He gave a fleeting thought to his trunk that was making its way to Plymouth and wondered if, when he and the boy were shown the door, he might intercept it somehow.

His brother's expression was unchanged for a few seconds. Then, like a flash of lightening, he smiled and began to laugh. Edward stood, clapped Frederick on the back and told George he needed to eat some more. It took a little time for his laughter to fade as he went upstairs.

George turned back from staring at the door, puzzled. "Is he angered or mad?" He took a bite of ham and chewed, awaiting the answer.

The Captain turned back to his own plate. "No, no he is obviously not angry." He looked back at the door for an instant then to the boy. "As to the state of his mind, I cannot say, Mr. Tuggins."

~ ~ ~ ~ ~ ~ ~ & ~ ~ ~ ~ ~ ~ ~

The next day was spent visiting members of the rector's parish. When it had been proposed the evening before, Frederick had agreed without much thought. The Captain could not help but wonder if he had made a mistake in assenting to the project as Edward readied the cart, telling him all about his parishioners.

"...and so the mother-in-law is always interfering with her daughter-in-law. I have tried to point out that her son is a man and under no obligation to please his mother but to no avail." Was the second or third domestic drama to which he had been made privy? He foresaw a boring morning.

The morning was indeed boring, but during it, he saw aspects of his brother that had left him mystified. First, Edward's attention to the boy was significant. He asked him all sorts of questions to which Wentworth had given no thought. Such as, where were his parents? Frederick had assumed the boy had no desire to speak of them, wherever they might be, and so, had left the subject alone. He asked about siblings. Again, Frederick had given no thought to them. George had one sister who had died a while ago. When asked about his favourite food, he said figgy pudding, which put him in good stead with the Rector, as he was partial to the sweetmeat himself.

Another aspect of his brother that set Wentworth thinking was the hearty and genuine greeting he had for each of the families they visited. By the second household, Frederick's notions of Edward being spinster-ish were completely demolished.. Edwardwas treated much like a well-loved family member and not a superior in anything but benevolence. To Frederick's embarrassment, when it was learned that he was *the* Captain Wentworth, hero of numerous battles at sea and piles of prizes, he was the one treated with deference boarding on worship.

~ ~ ~ ~ ~ ~ ~ & ~ ~ ~ ~ ~ ~ ~

"I hope you appreciate how they all admire you," Edward said after the final visit ended. He sat crooked in the seat with his legs crossed, giving George as much room as was possible on the seat made for two.

Frederick would be unjust if he did not admit that the parishioners of Crown Hill were extraordinary. In four visits, he had been shown the brownest of cows, the woolliest of sheep, and laying hens of infinite colours, sizes, and abilities to produce. He also could not help but notice that each household seemed to have an unmarried daughter, sister, or aunt who just happened to be in the vicinity. This was all done respect-fully, but the hopefulness in the eyes of the family members was unmis-takeable. "I'm sure they are as courteous a people as one could find anywhere. Tell me Brother, if I was the object of such affection, why is it that I feel like a prize pig at the fair?"

"Think how those poor women feel." Edward's laugh nettled him. "You forget, Frederick, this is the country. You are a long way from the civilities of life by the bell and the strict disciplines of the sea. These are simple people who offered up their best. Now, you didn't fail to notice that most took you to inspect their prize farm animals well before they introduced their female relations." He laughed again, more quietly this time. "Oh, and sorry about your boots. I'll clean them myself."

"I can do it," Frederick said. "You never told me that I would be tapped for duty as a mule."

"The cart was stuck; there was nothing else to be done. The man overworks himself dreadfully. You did no more than he did himself."

An old parishioner had gotten his pony cart stuck in a muddy field and begged the help of the rector. When they had it up and out of the mud, there had been thanks all around and an offer of something to restore them. It would be no trouble to the lady of the house, as the refreshments were kept in the barn. The rector politely refused, and they hastily said their goodbyes.

"The stuff he offered is homemade. It is rumoured just having a jug of it in the place keeps the rats out of the hayloft," Edward said, explaining why they had passed on the man's offer. "We must also be an example to this young man." He winked at George.

"Home at last." He manoeuvred the cart around the house then jerked them suddenly to a stop. "Take the reins," he mumbled, shoving them towards George, as he dismounted.

"What the…" Frederick said, watching his brother walk quickly away. Looking in the direction Edward headed, he could see a woman. The Captain could only guess that the inestimable Mrs. Wentworth was home. Wentworth took the reins from the boy. "That would be the rector's wife."

Edward's behaviour was odd but fascinating. The man was dazed and stumbled around the wooden shack that housed the horses onto a path leading to the garden farther past the house.

The boy watched as well. He scratched his nose and said, "I wonder what she will think of me being here." He'd not moved when Edward left them. Wentworth felt him move a little closer as he spoke.

Mrs. Wentworth was facing towards the garden, away from him so it was impossible to know what she looked like in the flesh. Just then, it occurred to Frederick that he and George were intruders on this intimate scene and they should take themselves elsewhere. Before he could act, Edward reached out and touched his wife's arm. He could hear the low strains of Edward's voice but no distinguishable words.

The woman turned to her husband. From this position, Wentworth still could not see her face clearly but did discern a wide, welcoming smile. The couple stood face-to-face. Edward reached up and swept off her bonnet. Neither of them showed the least bit of concern when it went straight to the ground. The woman continued to smile as her husband spoke. They were quite oblivious to the fact that anyone other than themselves might be present. Edward laughed loudly and, reaching out, took her in his arms. The passion with which Edward kissed his wife shocked Frederick. He was also a bit shocked at her eager response as well.

He quickly dismounted the small carriage, took George from the seat, and put the horse between them and the romantic scene playing out in the garden. He tapped George on the head when he noticed the boy straining to look past the horse. When they had nearly reached the shed, he heard his name.

"Frederick! Come here, Brother, and meet Catherine," Edward called. Frederick breathed deep. To George, he said, "We must put on a front that we've not seen a thing. She would be quite embarrassed."

"What have we seen, sir?" George's face was open and quite innocent of any notions of impropriety.

The boy was such a curious mix of innocence and wisdom that Wentworth was not willing to go further. "We've seen nothing. Make a first-rate leg when you are introduced and stand quietly." With orders given, he himself fought to prepare a severe countenance, one that would not give away his amusement, puzzlement, and intense interest.

The couple's heads were close together and they were talking intimately. Frederick trod with a heavy foot to warn them of their approach. Edward, instead of turning to greet him, laughed, took his wife's face in his hands and kissed her again and again.

Between kisses, Frederick heard her voice for the first time.

"Edward, please," she said. Her voice was low, but the tone was filled with laughter and held no hint of embarrassment or shame at her husband's last antic.

Neither was Edward ashamed as he made the introductions. "Mrs. Wentworth, please meet Captain Frederick Wentworth. And this is George." They all watched as the boy made a very proper bow to the lady.

Mrs. Wentworth acknowledged the Captain and then knelt down to the boy. "Well, George, the Rector neglected to tell me I am an aunt on his side of the family. You are a fine looking young man." She touched his shabby coat and straightened his neck cloth.

Realising his mistake, Edward whispered, "This is not Frederick's son." He helped her stand. "I should have said this is George Tuggins. He is Frederick's travelling companion at the moment." He looked at Frederick. His expression meant a further conversation about the boy was in order.

Catherine's countenance never faltered. Her finger briefly caressed George's still-bruised forehead. "In any case, you look to be a fine young man. I am happy to see that you have come through the terrible weather unharmed, Captain. Your brother has been beside himself to get you here." She took her bonnet from Edward but did not put it on.

The picture in the study had captured her features in the strictest sense, but the subject was certainly not dull as the drawing had led him to believe. The artist simply had not the talent necessary to capture the essence of the woman.

Catherine Wentworth's medium-brown hair was tucked under a modest cap. She possessed plain features, but the shine in her grey eyes was irresistible, and the set of her mouth was positively mischievous. Her want of strikingly beautiful features would put everyone at their ease and certainly be a comfort to the insecure. Someone of an unconfident disposition might, in fact, be drawn to her because of her lack of beauty. He speculated that, initially, beautiful women felt honestly superior to Mrs. Wentworth. He suspected this pleased her a great deal. Such a circumstance would allow her careful and close scrutiny of many a character. He used such a tactic when in the presence of superior officers who actually believed superiority was measured by yards of gold braid. His first instinct was to like her. Mrs. Wentworth was, without doubt, worth knowing and staying within her good graces.

"Yes, our dear Sophia has told us of some of your business," she said, smiling and taking Frederick's arm. She touched George lightly on the shoulder to draw him along as well. "We will go into the house, and I shall make us something refreshing. Then you shall tell us of your other bits of 'business.'" Catherine Wentworth was, it appeared, like a force of nature that could be resisted only with a great deal of strength.

He took a look at his brother. There was no getting his attention. Edward was smiling like a fool as he fell in step behind them. The Captain had the distinct impression he was now a prisoner of war. One that would be gently treated, to be sure, but a man captured nonetheless.

~ ~ ~ ~ ~ ~ ~ & ~ ~ ~ ~ ~ ~ ~

A housekeeper, Mrs. Bell, had been added to the household now that Mrs. Wentworth was returned. The plump, middle-aged woman moved around the sitting room, dispensing tea and sweets. "Please take George out to the kitchen, Bell, and make him something hot. He needs a meal more substantial than tea." He was sitting close to her, and when he rose to leave, she patted his arm.

Frederick wondered if he should begin to assert some authority and start treating Mr. Tuggins as though he was being trained for the sea and not as though he was a pet.

For You Alone

"She was a very young woman, a maid in my family's house, when I was born. I have no idea what life would be like without Bell as part of it. You shall grow accustomed to her, Edward, I assure you."

"I doubt it. How do we come to have her?"

Catherine paused for a moment. "It is at Mother's insistence. She feels that with your position and at this juncture in our marriage, it is necessary to have Bell take care of the household. You know how Mother can be." She cocked her head with an air of general understanding.

He replaced his cup on its saucer. "No, I don't know how your mother can be. She has always struck me as a good and sensible woman and not given to insisting other people live by her edicts." Edward raised a brow and waited for an explanation.

Frederick was completely out of his depth in this. The two already had looks and gestures that telegraphed emotions and understanding that he could not begin to fathom. Perhaps the best course of action was to make an excuse and leave them to discuss their household without the impediment of his presence.

Catherine glanced at Frederick. "We are putting your brother in an awkward position, dear."

"Are you feeling awkward, Frederick?"

Before he could answer, Catherine's brow rose. "My dear, I would like her to come and help me. I find the duties of this house, while there are only two of us, to be more than I can manage. This is Christian charity extended to your own wife, Edward." She again cocked her head and, if Wentworth was not mistaken, batted her eyes.

Edward knew he was caught. "More people in the household, even those installed due to Christian charity, make for a chaotic situation. Servants particularly! They are so quiet they inevitably startle me while I am working. All our privacy is gone."

She looked at Frederick. "For one dedicated to serving his fellow man, your brother is more like a hermit than anyone I know."

Edward's lament in relation to their privacy being disturbed hit home. Frederick was the first to intrude, bringing with him the burden of an extra mouth, and now there was to be a servant. Unlike Frederick, his brother was not used to having people surrounding him and imposing on his peace all day and night. In the past, he and his brother would pass hour upon hour without saying a word. Frederick doubted much had changed now that his brother was older. It was impossible to not feel guilty for upsetting the household.

"I do have a question, Catherine. Where will we put her?"

She lowered her cup. "In the room behind the kitchen, where all the housekeepers have slept, I imagine."

56

"Mr. Tuggins is occupying that space at the moment."

Catherine frowned. "I suppose I could ask Father if the groom could bring her back and forth, but that would be an awful imposition on her."

"The boy could sleep in my room." Frederick looked from Edward to Catherine.

It was Edward's turn to frown. "No, there is no need. Catherine, it would be an imposition for the boy to be in Frederick's tiny room."

"Perhaps it would be an imposition on Mr. Tuggins as well." Catherine smiled at Frederick. "But, if he is willing, dear, might we not try it for a while?"

"Are you sure, Frederick?"

"I would not have offered if I weren't sure." To Catherine he said, "I am sorry, madam, that I have thrown your house into chaos."

"It is a very welcome chaos, Captain, very welcome, indeed."

The conversation turned to the visits, and Edward began to bring Catherine current on all the neighbourhood news. Vowing to make his presence as unobtrusive as possible, he studied Edward and was actually hard pressed to see a trace of any sort of pique at this upset in their routine. Frederick could not help noticing that while the rector stood well away from Catherine, there was no real distance between them.

When he passed by on the way to the tea table, the rector grasped the Captain's shoulder. Then, as Mrs. Wentworth poured his tea, he leaned down and spoke something in her ear. Her expression blossomed into a smile accompanied by an appealing pink flush. She whispered back, and he laughed all the way back to his place by the fire. As he had been earlier in the day, Edward was cheerful, laughing, and affectionate. Nevertheless, the old spinsterish brother, he suspected, was still lurking nearby. Frederick wanted an explanation but was baffled as to how he might obtain one.

~ ~ ~ ~ ~ ~ ~ & ~ ~ ~ ~ ~ ~ ~

A note was dispatched to Catherine's family stating that a new battle plan was being formulated and the Rectory was in need of another bed. Particulars of the situation were given, and in hours, a child's bed once used in the nursery of the Keye family was being set up in the far corner of the Captain's room.

Frederick, on the whole, was not ordinarily grudging with his privacy, but he could have wished the room the size of the one he occupied at Kellynch. It did not really matter; he would become accustomed to Mr. Tuggins's company over the past few days and sharing the room would present no real difficulties.

Along with the bed, Mrs. Wentworth had requested that if there were any of her brothers' clothes left from their youth, they should be sent along as well. It appeared that Mrs. Keye—Catherine's good and sensible mother—was scrupulous to keep everything that might in the future be deemed useful.

"I am sorry, George, there is not much here that will fit you."

"That's a'right, Ma'am. I ain't had any new shirts for a long time. Two is a lot to have. And these trousers." He held up a pair of particularly ugly brown wool trousers that would have to be shortened for him. From the expression on his face, the trousers might as well have been custom tailored and spun from the finest silk in the Orient.

"Oh, Ma'am, what is this? It's like the one the Captain has." George reached into the bundle, snagged a corner of something blue, and began to pull. It was a deep blue, brocade waistcoat, several sizes too large. The delight on his face faded quickly.

Catherine glanced at her brother-in-law. "Well then, I shall enlist Bell's help in cutting it down to fit." She held it up against him. "The colour suits you wonderfully, George." She gave him a few other things to sort through and then went to the Captain. "He is quite smitten."

"How so?"

"He admires you a great deal, sir." She turned back to look at the boy. "You have done a wonderful thing in taking responsibility for him."

"I never meant that he should think of me so ... warmly. I only meant to help him when I have another command."

Catherine thought for a moment. "He can't help it. All the people in the world who are supposed to care for him are gone. You have shown him that care. Don't be afraid, Brother, such feelings will only make him a better man—and sailor." She smiled and touched his arm. "You are a great deal more like Edward than I imagined."

She gathered the clothing with George's help and left the room. Frederick closed the door, went to the window and opened it. The room was suddenly stifling; he welcomed the fresh air.

A cold breeze carried the smell of wood smoke, the scent of food cooking, and various reminders of the damp vegetation surrounding the rectory. Standing at the top of the house, looking over the small northern village gave the illusion of his having a simple life. When this comforting notion was challenged by Catherine's observations that he was now responsible for George and about the boy's growing affection, he winced to think he could be so generous to a stranger, but to the woman he loved, he had had nothing to offer but coldness.

~ ~ ~ ~ ~ ~ ~ & ~ ~ ~ ~ ~ ~ ~

The news of Frederick's arrival blew through the farthest reaches of the parish like a warm summer wind. Those less fortunate families who missed out on the first visitation now took it upon themselves to invite the esteemed gentleman into their midst. The Rectory was awash in invitations, and its calendar was filling for weeks into the future.

"You always liven things up when you stay with me," Edward said one morning as he was accepting the invitation for "the gentlemen of the Rectory" to dine at the table of a very prominent parishioner the following afternoon. "If these people have their way, you will almost never be home. This fellow has two marriageable daughters, barely out of school, and I suppose he hopes you will see them and be instantly taken with one or the other."

Frederick was discomfited by the situation and its eerie resemblance to that of Henrietta and Louisa Musgrove. Thankfully, he had learnt his lesson. In the maelstrom of social activities, he did not allow himself to be charmed into the ranks of any one family. He took extreme care not to cast a shadow of undue interest in the direction of any of the ladies presented, and the only enthusiastic conversations in which he engaged were about the Navy, sailing in general, or horses. Now, even talk of hunting left a disagreeable taste in his mouth.

This increase of social obligations quickly became a part of the household's daily routine. Another routine he noticed was that Mrs. Wentworth was almost never seen any time before early afternoon. On days when the gentlemen were not engaged, Edward either kept her company in their bedchamber or made visits about the parish. Frederick would ride or read or walk the grounds around the church and nearby fields. George, surprisingly, seemed quite satisfied to be traded back and forth between the brothers.

After spending a significant portion of the day with only himself or the boy, it was fortunate for him that, when Mrs. Wentworth did appear, she was more than ready to entertain him. Her natural curiosity proved her open to a vast number of subjects. Nor was she shy in asking questions of him about sailing, the various parts of the world to which he had travelled, and even the intrigues of Whitehall. He had yet to find an appropriate topic in which she was not interested.

Thanks to his sister-in-law's seemingly endless curiosity, he forgot most of his troubles for days on end. Intermittently, he was acutely aware that they might be mounting with each passing hour. At those times, he took hard and punishing rides in the cold countryside. Only when his body was exhausted could his mind fall quiet.

On the whole, the visit to his brother was going very well. The only disconcerting aspect of his presence was that the couple were still newlyweds. Frederick was as likely as not to catch the rector and his wife in a pose of full-blown affection. The Captain assumed he and poor Bell to be sailing the same seas in this, and he pitied her. It soon became a habit to walk heavily, clear his throat, whistle, and generally make a fuss before entering a room. He quickly understood they were fond of the rector's study as a place to exchange their connubial demonstrations.

After a fortnight of grey skies, there dawned an uncommonly brilliant morning and, as was usual, he found himself with only Mr. Tuggins for company at the breakfast table. When asked about the master and mistress, all Bell had to say was, "They're bein' quiet by themselves."

George watched the woman leave and then volunteered his observations. "I saw a man come earlier. He went with the Rector upstairs." Wentworth reminded the boy not to speak with his mouth full. "Sorry, sir. He called the man Abernathy." He wiped his mouth on his sleeve.

Wentworth handed George his napkin. "Did he say anything else to the man?" George was proving to be as useful a source of information as a distraction.

He shook his head vigorously. "No, sir. He took him upstairs to Mrs. Wentworth and never came back down."

Wentworth stirred his coffee slowly and contemplated a male visitor to the wife of the house. "Did the man have a bag with him? A satchel like mine only black and smaller?"

The boy was in the habit of swinging his feet, and his head bobbed as he thought. "Yes, sir. I think so. He told the Rector there was no need to worry." He made a point to let Wentworth see him wipe his mouth on the napkin.

Bell re-entered the room, cleared away George's dishes, and asked if the boy might help with some odd jobs out of doors. The Captain consented. After coming to no conclusions about a doctor visiting, Frederick decided that he should write to Harville and ask for news from Lyme. If Miss Louisa was well on her way to good health, the sooner he could bid farewell to his role of villain in this convoluted melodrama.

As he approached the study, he tapped absently on the wall in case he'd missed the doctor's departure. He coughed several times for good measure. After knocking on the door, he stepped in and was somewhat surprised to find his brother. He'd thought he was still upstairs.

With the rector was a young man whose bag at his feet obviously marked him as the doctor. The young fellow was a pleasant-looking and well-dressed man for a country healer, but that did not explain the reason that they should be raising wine glasses in a toast in the morning.

Edward interrupted his drink when he caught sight of Frederick. "Brother, come in, please. Captain Frederick Wentworth, please meet Doctor Michael Abernathy. Doctor, Captain Wentworth."

The doctor bowed and extended a hand. "I am happy to finally meet you Captain Wentworth. Your brother has been good enough to share with me some of your more brazen exploits at sea." He grasped Frederick's hand firmly, shook it enthusiastically, and was quite anxious that the Captain should take the better of the leather chairs, which he had vacated.

Frederick thanked the doctor, took the seat and a glass of wine that Edward offered. He was surprised that Edward knew of anything of his life at sea, much less exploits. Frederick never wrote to tell of any particular actions or captures. The Captain assumed his brother would not be at all interested.

"So, we toast to the future, Rector." Abernathy's smile was open and generous. Whatever they toasted was a happy event. He turned to Wentworth. "The way your brother speaks, I should not be surprised if he names a boy after you." Abernathy turned back to Edward.

Frederick's realisation of what the doctor meant took an instant or two, but it dawned quickly enough. He studied this happy, slightly dazed Edward. Edward glanced Frederick's way and signalled what Frederick took as an apology for the news being delivered so abruptly.

To see his brother happy in his new life should have filled the Captain with joy, but, in the way that humans are at times, it only reminded him of his own faults and sadness at his own missed opportunities. The confidence in his own abilities that had carried him so remarkably through the earlier years seemed to be deserting him. All he had wanted for himself—had wanted for Anne and him—were now playing out before his eyes in the life of another man, and it galled him to the core, even if it was his own dear brother.

To add jealousy to his *repertoire* of jumbled emotions was ridiculous, childish in fact. He was beginning to appreciate the attitude of those others who seemed to resent his success. He was now eating the crow that he enjoyed feeding to others. Forcing a smile, Frederick raised his glass to the future of the Wentworth Clan. "May its chief find joy in his family and in his life." He raised the glass high and endeavoured to genuinely take pleasure in Edward's look of contentment.

Chapter Five

E dward looked embarrassed at the overly flattering toast. The doctor joined in with a call for a speech. "Thank you, gentlemen. I am happier than I can convey and am glad to have such good friends to mark the occasion. Gentlemen." He lifted his glass again and then drank the glass dry.

While the others chatted, Frederick took the opportunity to fill his glass. It was then he spied a copy of the *Naval Chronicles* on his brother's desk. There had never been any mention of such a thing the past, and he had never seen a copy in his brother's possession.

"You read more widely than I knew." Edward looked and saw to what Frederick referred. He hesitated for just an instant. Just as quickly the moment vanished. He laughed. "Yes, I have subscribed for years. How else would I keep up with your activities? Your adventures are kept pretty much to yourself." To prove himself, he opened a drawer and tossed several well-worn magazines in his brother's direction.

The banner of the topmost announced the *Naval Chronicles* latest issue and several of the stories found within its pages. When it came out twice yearly many readers read every copy, and most officers were buried in its pages for days. Wentworth had missed this particular issue, but he calculated it would tell of three small captures to the credit of *Laconia*, Captain Frederick Wentworth commanding. There would be Benwick's name on the list of Lieutenants stepping up to the rank of Master and Commander. There would be no announcement of Fanny Harville's death. She was not the wife of Captain Benwick, and Captain Harville was not important enough to have family tragedies listed. Only truly important events in the life of the Navy's privileged ever graced the pages of the *Chronicles*.

His mind jumped to the next issue that would appear early in the following year. The only announcement he cared about was that *Laconia* had been put in Ordinary. Without an accompanying notice of his being awarded another ship, all would know he was now ashore on half-pay. If things were timed just right, there would be an announcement that *Laconia* was placed back in active service and that Captain Tanner was now at the helm. Went-worth's private business would be there for all to read and to speculate upon. His thoughts only glanced at the idea that a future issue would announce his marriage to one Miss Louisa Musgrove of Uppercross, Somersetshire.

"Frederick?"

He looked away from the magazine. Both Abernathy and Edward were expecting an answer. "I'm sorry, I don't follow." He scolded himself for allowing idle speculation to overtake him.

Edward was about to enlighten him on what he had missed when the door opened and a woman entered. Edward and Frederick rose. The rector gave the woman a very stiff, very proper bow and then introduced his brother to Mrs. Michael Abernathy.

Frederick wondered how George had missed seeing the woman enter with her husband. He bowed and looked up in time to see that the woman's curtsey was as shallow as could be made and still be considered movement.

He noticed first the intricately arranged mass of chestnut hair. Her eyes were a pleasing brown and her features were regular, though nothing out of the ordinary. Other men of a more generous character would call her complexion alabaster but pale was a much more apt description. Overall, he would say she was not unattractive, and he fully understood how a man might be drawn to her.. Nonetheless, he had certainly learnt his lesson with Mrs. Wentworth about making judgements concerning a woman's character by her features, and he could not help being put off by the frigid air of this one.

She stepped forward with a lifted chin and confident expression. "Captain Wentworth. My cousin, Rear Admiral of the Blue Daniel Fuller assists the First Lord at Whitehall." She folded her hands, making it clear that her credentials were now stated and it was his turn to do the same.

As luck would have it, he did know Admiral Daniel Fuller. They had met in Portsmouth early in the year when Fuller was the guest of the Port Admiral. Mrs. Abernathy's careful enunciation of his full title did not negate the fact that, while the man did, indeed, assist the First Lord, he was merely one of an over-stuffed retinue of toadies chosen solely for their ability to trumpet the importance of the powers that be and, in doing so, ensure that all observers understood how important they were as well. General opinions of Fuller's talents as a sailor and an officer were mixed. From what Wentworth had heard, Admiral Fuller's most impressive talent was his memory for gossip. The man was a treasure trove of embarrassing peccadilloes that ensured the least of captains, sailing the least of ships, in the least important stations, would remain so. He was just the sort of man who would land himself at Whitehall, snugged up against the most powerful of officers. He was just the sort of man Wentworth endeavoured to avoid.

Frederick nodded in acknowledgement. "Ma'am, I believe I have had the pleasure of dining with your cousin once or twice. He is an officer we all do well to watch." The obfuscation was quite clever in his opinion and would give the lady the impression he thought highly of her cousin. But, when he looked into her face, the tiniest narrowing of the woman's eyes informed him she was not fooled by his shrewdness and that she fully understood Went-worth had no good opinion of her family member.

If possible, she straightened her shoulders even more. "As you should, Captain. He is quite an example to the entire family." Just then, Abernathy cleared his throat. His glass rang out when he put it down on the table. Mrs. Abernathy took her eyes from Wentworth's and glared at her husband. She turned to Edward. "I would think it too early for wine, Rector."

The doctor moved away from the desk and picked up the battered black satchel sitting on the floor next to his chair. His movements were stiff and precise. "It was my doing, Julia. We were toasting the Wentworth's good fortune of a child." He took out a small bottle and handed it to Edward. "Have your wife take—"

Mrs. Abernathy interrupted. "I helped Mrs. Wentworth to dress." She looked directly at the rector. "She is resting now. You may go up when we are finished." Nothing could be done until she had stated the instructions. The woman's tone made it clear she had no expectation of anything but utter obedience on the part of the rector.

In nearly the same thought, Frederick put aside his distaste of Mrs. Abernathy's manner and awaited the doctor's instructions for Mrs. Wentworth. Other than how they came into being, Frederick knew next to nothing about babies and was uncertain that medicines were a part of the usual procedure. His stomach knotted at the possibility of something seriously amiss for his little family.

Abernathy continued as if there was no interruption. "Have her take this every evening. It may help with the sickness in the mornings. If not, it'll only last another month or so." He shut the bag with a snap. He bowed to Went-worth with his back to his wife. He smiled as broadly as before his wife joined them. "It was an honour to meet you, Captain. I hope I have another chance to speak with you during your visit." The smile vanished; he turned and joined his wife at the door. "Well done, Edward," he whispered back to the rector before he followed her out.

Edward took a deep breath and relaxed. He absently parted the tails of his coat and took his seat. With Mrs. Abernathy's departure, air and life seemed to flow quickly back into the room. Frederick was about to say as much when he looked at his brother. Edward was remarkably placid. It was clear that his mood was not in the least dampened by the doctor's wife. He pulled one of the chairs from in front of the hearth and placed it next to the desk. "So, I am to be an uncle." It was ridiculously to even speak it, but he was at a loss to say anything else.

Edward still smiled and now nodded. "Yes. She's going to have a child. My child."

Frederick thought they each were stupefied in their own respective ways. His emotions seemed to gravitate to petulance and jealousy. The rector's was shock manifesting in a slightly daft grin. As he thought about it, his brother's faraway look had been in place since Mrs. Wentworth's arrival home. They had known about the child for some time and, for some reason, had chosen not to share the news with him. Again, he felt a touch of something unpleasant and wrong.

Edward knocked on the desktop and stood. "I didn't think that woman would have the audacity to come right in." He put away the wine and put the glasses to the side to take away later.

It seemed odd that Edward preferred to speak of the doctor's wife rather than the joyous news of a child. "Audacious seems to be a most apt description for Mrs. Abernathy. They are a very contradictory couple."

Edward nodded vigorously. "Yes. Their marriage is the product of haste and gross misjudgement." He took his seat.

The statement was ripe with possibility having not only to do with the departed couple, but with him as well. Frederick took a seat in preparation. "How so?"

"He comes from a London family of great wealth. There are no titles, but there is immense influence. She wished to rise above her upbringing of moderate means and saw him as a wealthy man with an interest in medicine. He turned out to be a man of compassion who happened to possess a great fortune and a great zeal for treating the sick.. Abernathy says she assumed that if he did practice it would be in London, not in the wilds of Shropshire. She pictured her life as one of grand society and ease. The truth of it has proved to be extremely disappointing."

Did Louisa Musgrove also assume life as the wife of a Naval officer more interesting and exciting that it was in actuality? "You said there was an element of haste involved." The Abernathys seemed to be an example tailor made for his study.

"Yes, he saw her at a ball, gained an introduction, and they were married in a matter of months." The rector picked up a quill and began to sharpen it. "She hates living here. She acts as his nurse, though she despises dealing with us provincials." Each stroke of the knife punctuated every few words of the statement. "He thought he could love her enough that she would change her mind. But that has proven impossible. So—" He held up the quill for study and then looked at Frederick. "So, Mrs. Abernathy makes life difficult for the doctor most of all, but for the rest of us to varying degrees, as well."

The couple's hasty marriage sounded extraordinarily like Anne and him. It was a sad tale but it proved the situation was not so unusual. If the worst happened and he was expected to marry, Frederick thought his observations months ago of going to sea and leaving a wife to reside close to her family at Uppercross an excellent solution to any of the stated difficulties. There would be no inconvenience to anyone, and no one would have to deal with anyone's disappointments...except of course, Louisa and him.

Edward pulled a pot of ink to him. He put aside the quill and began fiddling with the lid. "I know for ages previous to ours and for ages to come man and women will marry for things other than love. Even I was bent upon it. For the most part, people find a genuine sort of happiness. But a marriage like Abernathy's gives one reason to think very hard." The lid was fixed, and he dipped the quill and began to scribble on a paper.

Frederick wished to leave the uncomfortable topic of the doctor's marriage as soon as possible. He rose and poured them each another glass of wine. "Difficult marriages are a subject for another time. I wish to toast to the joyous announcement of a brand new Wentworth on the horizon." He raised his glass and took a sip. He wished his heart were lifted high as well.

Edward thanked him and leant back in the chair.

"You don't seem happy." His brother's face mirrored his own emotions. Edward's expression when Frederick entered the room was completely different than this one.

He looked out the window for a moment and then to Frederick. "I am happy. It's just that Catherine and I never spoke of children. Of having them together I mean. She is not too old for it—obviously—but I am 48-years-old, Frederick. I am just surprised by it all."

"You may be shocked, but you are certainly not out of the game. Obviously." His brother's lack of consideration on the matter amused him.

Edward looked up. "No, not at all. In fact, I have told Catherine many times that I have always thought of you more as my boy than my brother." He returned to the desk and fixed his attentions on the trimmings from the quill.

Frederick was now taken aback. He knew Edward had always had mixed feelings about him. There had been times of great closeness when Edward returned to England to care for him and Sophia. As Frederick grew a little older, the feelings grew stronger on both sides. After Edward had seen him off on that Liverpool dock, things had grown strained. He was still, "my boy" on most occasions, but the warmth of the words had disappeared over time, replaced with a perfunctory sort of tone. Only since his arrival in Crown Hill had they regained some of their previous tenderness. Edward's admission touched him, and in the Captain's ragged emotional state, it was a soothing thing to hear. Although, he now realised, since Catherine's arrival home, Edward had not used the endearment at all. "And now you may have a true son of your own." Frederick knew he was loosing a little something with this declaration, but it was the right thing to say.

"Yes, but in a way he'll be my second son. When you heard it, you looked torn. Are you disappointed that you may not inherit my vast fortune?" He laughed. Frederick enjoyed the jest as well.

"How could I begrudge the child a heaping pile of theology books and your mended surplice? Oh, and that horse."

"The horse isn't mine. A fellow in Ludlow just lets me have use of it."

They sat for a moment, amused with their banter. Soon, Frederick realised that most lives were the sum of all that, even his, with all his money and all the possessions he might ever obtain. At this moment, his brother, with the love of a woman he admired and a child on the way, was far richer than he might ever be.

"There is something that has worried me since Catherine told me of her suspicions."

"What is that?"

"What if I am like him?"

There was no having to guess who his brother meant. Edward had suffered at the hands of their father in ways Frederick only knew from Sophia. Rarely did anyone ever mention the man who gave them life, and when one of them did, it was only in passing. All the Captain knew was Edward left just after turning sixteen. A savage beating had been the impetus. Frederick had been only two at the time. When he was older, it was not unusual to find his mother crying and his father raging. More often than not, Edward's name was connected to those violent scenes.

"You are nothing like Phillip Wentworth." He could think of no two men related by blood more dissimilar.

For You Alone

"I did not think so, either. Then I wondered if it was having children that made him so … hateful. I could not help but wonder if it was not my birth which touched off something inside his mind."

"You are nothing like him. Nothing at all."

"How do you know? How can anyone know what sort of parent they will turn out to be?"

"You came to Sophie and me when we needed you. You were good and kind to us. You hardly even raised your voice to us. You are not that sort of man."

Edward stared at him intently. "You cannot say that for certain. You do not know everything about me." He finally looked away.

Frederick had to admit that Edward was a puzzle to him and that he did not know all there was to know about his brother and his life away. But he knew enough that he was sure there was not a trace of their father's violence in him.

Frederick rose and walked to the door. His only hope was that his comments would bring comfort and reassurance to his brother. For good measure he turned and said, "If either of us is in danger of turning out like Father, I think you can rest easy and know it is me."

"What makes you say such a thing, Frederick?" Edward scowled.

Frederick paused, uncertain he wished to reveal so much of himself on such a happy day. "I have, at times, taken pleasure in the punishments to which I have sentenced certain men." He gestured. "Just a kernel of pleasure for men who I felt deserved to be punished. So you see, Brother, we all have pitiable things to regret." He left before Edward could respond.

Edward's supposition, at first, was ridiculous, but the more he allowed it to get into his mind, the more Frederick saw some merit in it. He had said what he did to Edward to ease his mind and put him off that disturbing path. He had not really thought himself any more like their father than Edward. Now, as he made his way through the house to take a walk, he pondered the idea that an event could be so harmful to a person that it would fundamentally change them from sensible and rational to violent and ugly. Thoughts of his mother's harassment by Phillip Wentworth made it clear that some thing at some time had released a beast that had no trouble inflicting such agony.

~ ~ ~ ~ ~ ~ & ~ ~ ~ ~ ~ ~ ~

The customary afternoon walk led nowhere. The Captain's need to be alone made walking for pleasure impossible. Plump drops of occasional drizzle made it downright unpleasant at times. For some time now, Frederick had rested on a stile and watched a man rebuilding a section of stone fence that was broken down. In the distance was a small farm surrounded by an unremarkable stand of woods. The farm itself seemed to be of no real distinction either. All the buildings were constructed of the same stone as the fence and, though the rain intensified the few shades of colour offered by the brownish grey winter landscape, they seemed to fade away into the surrounding forest.

The man had not acknowledged his nod when he'd taken his seat on the stile, and he did nothing to indicate he cared that Wentworth watched him work or that he would prefer him to continue on his way. The man did, though, occasionally glance the Captain's way as he lifted or placed one of the stones. Frederick glanced away occasionally as he surveyed the area and tried to decide whether to continue walking or return to the warmth of the Rectory.

The man eventually placed the last stone in the wall. To check his handiwork, the farmer laid hands on various stones and seemed to give them a shake. Frederick wondered if this was to check his craft or prove to his observer that he was a capable builder. The man gathered a few things lying out of Frederick's view and placed them in a pouch he slung over his shoulder. Frederick nodded when the man glanced his way, but the fellow merely turned and walked off in the direction of the farm.

~ ~ ~ ~ ~ ~ ~ & ~ ~ ~ ~ ~ ~ ~

After he returned home, Wentworth was still in the mood for solitude. His trunks had arrived from Lyme the previous morning, and he retired to his room to shift a few things from them to his travelling case. As he looked through his possessions, it was clear that a man's life could easily be winnowed down to a very few square feet of space. "Not counting the coffin," he muttered. He chose a few new articles of clothing to wear, took out a book, and then put it back. When he thought he'd taken out all he needed, he spied the blanket Anne had sent with him on his journey back that dreadful night. He was tempted to shut it away in the trunk and get it out of his sight. Such an action was useless. He would know it was locked up in there, its presence teasing and begging him to view it. At least with it in the open he could pretend it was proof of her sympathy towards him. It, along with the food and drink she had sent him, let him know she had thought of him, even if it was only in the most perfunctory of ways.

He placed it at the end of the bed and wondered if she had touched it herself. More than likely, she had merely pointed to it and directed the serving woman to include it in the bundle to be taken to him. A picture of her picking it up and deciding to include it played out in his mind. It was ridiculous and overly sentimental to think she'd made any such effort on his behalf. He kicked off his boots and lay back on the bed, slipping his feet beneath the blanket.

Anne would be in Bath at the beginning of the year. For now, she was with her godmother. There would, of course, be no mention of his doing the favour of delivering the note from Lyme. Without any knowledge of his actions and an uncertain opinion of the events, Anne might even take it upon herself to give her version of Louisa Musgrove's accident to his sister.

During his visit at Kellynch Hall, there had been little discussion of the matter. There were no probing questions. Disinterest—he suspected something more like discretion—rendered the barest facts as satisfactory to both Sophia and the Admiral. There had been talk of Lady Russell's return to the neighbourhood and how they expected a visit from her. Because of the close association, they could look forward to a visit from Miss Anne, as well. Anne's reaction to some trivial changes around the house would provoke more interest than knowing anything about him or his state of mind.

He was just beginning to sink into a daydream of her when someone sat on the end of the bed. He opened his eyes and there was George. Wentworth hitched himself up a bit and put his arm behind his head. "What can I do for you, Tuggins?" By the look on his face, the boy was in trouble or thought so.

"I went into the study, and they were in there."

"You forgot to knock."

"No, sir. The door was open. A little bit." He looked down and twisted a button on his prized blue waistcoat. This would be the moment to address how to announce one's entrance, but Wentworth was in no mood to launch into a lecture. His own manners were suspect enough. The boy picked at a snag on the blanket covering the Captain's feet. "Why do you keep this horse blanket in here?" Mr. Tuggins had a knack for redirecting Wentworth's thoughts.

"It's not for a horse. And it is ..." He had just been over it all in his mind, but what to call this token? "It is a gift from someone I care for very much."

George frowned, and Wentworth could read his thoughts. How much could a person care if they gave only a scruffy coverlet? "I treated this person very poorly—rudely, in fact—but she gave it when I needed it." He hoped the questions would end. The more he talked about it, the more foolish it seemed to endow the covering with remarkable, touching qualities.

The informal nature of the conversation allowed Mr. Tuggins to forget himself and settle more comfortably on the end of the bed. "It was a girl? Girls do nice things for people they care about." He looked at Wentworth expectantly.

"Yes, it was a girl. A lady." He was surprised he answered with such frankness, but he saw no harm in telling someone who hadn't any interest in the matter at all. "I was very unkind to her. Giving me this was a kindness I did not deserve."

"Like the ladies on the streets who buy me sweets. One gave me an umbrella once. It got ruined in the wind though." The boy's innocence was touching. Unfortunately, it would not be long before he discovered more about those ladies that might taint his naive opinion. "My sister was like that." This last was said very quietly.

"Was she?" As Wentworth remembered, his sister was dead.

"She was nice. She kept the butler from hitting me so much."

"You two worked in a big house?"

"Yeah. It was Reverend Thornton's father's house. He yelled a lot."

"The reverend?"

"No, his father. Jane told me to run away; so I did."

It would seem the boy had figured out that the fewer ties to his past, the simpler it was to create a future and so had lied about having a living relation. He wondered if his parents, too, were the victims of an urchin's expediency. "Do you know if she is still there?"

"I think so." He shifted to face the Captain straight on. "That is why I followed you. I know a boy on a ship does not make much, but if there is prize...and if I become an officer, I could give her a home." His face showed perfect faith in his simple plan.

Frederick sat up. "A very worthy ambition, sir. I only wish I could see the future so clearly and with such hope." A knock at the door interrupted the gentlemen's philosophising.

Both turned to see Edward. Frederick immediately wondered how long his brother had been at the door. He invited Edward to enter. His stomach clinched when he noticed the rector bore letters. "These are for you." Edward looked at the address. "This is from Harville in Lyme. And the other is from ... a ... C. Musgrove, Uppercross, Somersetshire." He handed them over. "Is Harville well? I always liked him."

"He does well enough." Frederick made no effort to inform Edward of Harville's health, shattered career, or anything that might entice his brother to remain. Edward grasped the situation and turned to leave. He then turned back. "Come to me later, Frederick. We need to talk." To George he said, "And we shall talk now." The boy swallowed hard and went with the rector.

Frederick stared at the letters, dreading the contents of each. Bad news could be put off. Good news would free him of all his anxieties, and he could celebrate his continued good fortune. His skills of divination were quite poor. There was no hint of news of one kind or the other. He reached into his pocket, pulled out his clasp knife, and cut through the wafer sealing the first letter.

Captain,
We were happy to hear from you and hope all is well with your brother and new sister. You will be glad to know that Miss Louisa is making great strides daily. She is up for several hours a day and walks with Benwick both morning and evening. He is impressed that she is regaining her strength so quickly. Elsa is vigilant that the girl does not overtax herself. Life in the house has calmed a bit now that Charles and Mrs. Musgrove have decamped back to Uppercross. It looks as though the balance of the family will be leaving in time to meet the rest of their children for Christmas. Mr. Musgrove, in particular, is anxious to get back to his own home and hearth permanently. We older gentlemen like our homely comforts. I hesitate to mention your returning to Lyme, but I think as soon as you have had your fill of Mr. Wentworth's piety, you may wish to return and re-establish yourself. There are pressing matters that require your attendance.

Frederick rose, dropped the letter on the bed, and went to the fireplace. '*Matters that require my attendance.*' Rather than think precisely about those matters, he busied himself with the fire. The hearth was warm but the rest of the uncarpeted floor was too cool for him to remain barefooted. After he pulled on his boots, he picked up Musgrove's letter.

Captain Wentworth,
I hope this letter finds you in good health. All of us, save Louisa, of course, are the same. By the time you receive this letter, my wife and I will have returned to Uppercross. Before leaving Lyme, Father is anxious that I write and bring you current about my dear sister's condition. She was just beginning to sit up and is somewhat more clear-headed but is still exceedingly weak. She has no capacity for noise or confusion. Few are allowed in to see her, except Mother, Mrs. Harville and the nurse, although Benwick and his poetry are pressed into service with some frequency when she's agitated. The surgeon fears that her slow recovery indicates more damage than was first thought. Mrs. Harville has declared there is no telling when we might bring her home, but she has assured us that she will not mind if it takes up to half a year. Their hospi-

tality will remain constant. They have truly been the saving of us.

Every line offered its own evil interpretation. It was clear by the dates that each letter had travelled its own tortured path, and that explained the deviation in reports. Louisa had progressed considerably since Musgrove's letter. Mr. Musgrove's anxiety that Wentworth know of Louisa's condition was growing as well. Undoubtedly, this was the matter about which Harville spoke. All involved understood the Captain's duties to the girl and were determined that he should not forget them either. The blame now grew heavier with the knowledge that the surgeon's initial diagnosis was overly optimistic and each of the letters strengthened the understanding that the girl's health and the responsibility for her care were Frederick's. To shirk those duties was to damage his already battered sense of honour.

The Musgroves might present themselves as simple country folk, but he was sure the old man cagey enough to know when he had the advantage. Wentworth was trapped by the expectations of the Musgrove family and by his own sense of responsibility. He must and would do what was necessary to make things right for Louisa Musgrove. He folded the letters and put them in his breast pocket. Before he left the room, he folded Anne's blanket and put it out of sight.

Chapter Six

The evening was quiet and convivial. Everyone gathered in the sitting room as usual. There was not much conversation except about church matters which left Frederick free to read Edward's copy of the *Naval Chronicles*. There was no information volunteered about George and what had transpired between him and the rector, and Wentworth didn't care to ask just yet.

Mrs. Wentworth had been sewing. Out-of-the-blue she rose, said, "I nearly forgot," and left them.

"A letter from Sophia." Edward told Frederick.

There seemed no respite from the reminders of things he'd rather forget. "I put it on Edward's desk thinking it would remind him to give it to you." She handed it to him and went back to her sewing.

Wentworth read it anxiously, searching for any indication that the intricate web of country gossip was marrying him off to Miss Louisa. He read it through and was relieved that Sophia's main reason for the letter seemed to be to make comment upon the return to Uppercross of the younger Musgrove couple.

...for an excursion that ended so badly, I must say that Mrs. Charles Musgrove was a good soldier and made the best of it. We were treated to a lengthy recounting of all the sights she managed to see, the entertainments she partook to refresh her mind, and the large number of books she read while attending so faithfully to her sister's every need. I was surprised that a small coastal town, practically deserted for the winter, had so much to offer the visitor. Perhaps, she came home to rest herself, but I suppose you would know better than I whether she was help or hindrance, Frederick.

The rest assured him that Miss Anne had little to say about the unfortunate events directly but seemed pleased that he had taken such trouble to bring the note to her from Lyme. "And she seemed especially pleased that you made us aware of her great exertions, even to volunteering to remain with Miss Musgrove." The rest was to mention that Miss Anne was also glad to see the changes they had made about the Hall. He folded the letter and returned the letter to his brother. One thing stood out; there was no mention of Benwick in the neighbourhood, and Harville had mentioned twice daily walks with the man. So, the much anticipated trip to Uppercross had not come off. The reasons were not important.

Edward tucked it in his pocket. "You were in Lyme, then." No doubt, he was remembering the other letters. Thankfully, he seemed not to notice the reference to Anne.

Frederick knew he must now take particular care. His brother might be a happy man, but his curiosity was not so dulled by marital bliss that he would not begin to make out Frederick was not being completely open. Perhaps, he already was aware. "Yes, the fellow who sent the letter—Charles Musgrove—his wife and his sisters accompanied me there to visit Harville and his family."

Edward considered a moment but was interrupted by Catherine. "It is unfortunate her sister fell ill." Her tone was casual, and she did not look up from her sewing.

Frederick took no comfort in this. "She had an accident. She took a bad fall." Catherine now looked up, her curiosity roused. "But, she is recovering well from what Harville has told me." His sister-in-law murmured thanks for that. Unfortunately, Edward was giving it all some intense thought.

After Mrs. Wentworth retired—Edward going up with her for evening prayers and the like—Frederick went to his brother's study as he had been ordered.

Edward joined him and took a seat before the fire. He gazed into it and then turned to Frederick directly. "I heard your conversation with Mr. Tuggins."

"I wondered." The house was small, and it was only a matter of time before his private affairs became known.

Edward shook his head and sat back in the chair. "I am more disgusted than I can say. Catherine and I discussed it, and she thinks I must do all I can to make this up to the boy and his sister." His fingers tapped the arm of the chair in a rhythmic tattoo. "It is no wonder the clergy are mistrusted and bring such shame on the Church." He stared into the fire and chewed thoughtfully on his thumbnail.

Frederick was relieved. It seemed his confession to George had occurred before Edward's arrival. "Yes, it is a disgrace that anyone would treat vulnerable children so badly."

"When I spoke with him, he was able to tell me the name of the father, though I shall write to this Reverend Thornton straightaway. It can't possibly be that he is ignorant of what goes on in his father's house. He obviously oversees it and is therefore responsible. But then again…"

"And what of George's interruption earlier?" He might as well get all troubles pertaining to the boy out of the way.

Edward smiled a little. "He did nothing wrong. We were merely having tea in here. The boy came in, saw us, and flew out of the room. I think he's become oversensitive." Edward rose and fetched glasses and the decanter. "I told him there was nothing wrong in entering the study, but that all of us must be courteous and knock from now on." He handed him a glass.

The wine was murky in the firelight. Frederick held up a hand. "I think I should retire—"

Edward offered the glass again. "We're not finished here." He held the glass. "I also heard you speak to George about Anne."

The Captain took it, tasted it, and swallowed though it was very nearly the dregs. He watched Edward return to his seat and waited for the next salvo.

Edward took a drink. "Catherine says all of us have secrets. Allowing things into the light are freeing. What is the burden she sees in you?"

The Captain was startled that the conversation shifted so suddenly.

"You know some of it. You said you think I still care for Anne Elliot. You are right. I still love her very much." As Edward had said, it felt good to allow some things into the light. If only he would have acknowledged such feelings earlier, so much anxiety and pain could have been spared.

"As you've said nothing about this until now, I have to assume the lady is in the dark."

"You are right. Unfortunately, I have only come to understand myself in the last few weeks."

"And why are you not making arrangements to see her and let her know your mind?" It was clear Edward had been observing him and thinking about what little there was to observe. "Does this have anything to do with your trip to Lyme?"

"That is part of it. Though, I think most of the damage was done well before Lyme." Frederick leant back and rested his head against the chair.

"Damage?"

He frowned without looking at his brother. Frederick felt suddenly like a child again, having to admit to mischief. He continued to hide himself. "When I first heard from our sister, I misunderstood something she said and thought Anne was married. I believed myself safe until I was in the midst of her family. I immediately realised my mistake." He paused, now perfectly understanding what tack he'd taken with her. "An officer I knew told me that the way to punish another officer, someone you felt was inferior and needed a lesson, was not to degrade them or harass them in any way. The best way to make them know your displeasure is to hold them at a distance. This works particularly well if you have been close." He looked at his brother. "If you truly wish to wound someone, ignore them. Act as if the past intimacy is nothing, that it is forgotten completely. So, I did that."

The first salvo of shame was launched. It would not be long before Edward insisted on the second.

Edward frowned and bit his lip as he meditated on the words. "That is brilliant." He sighed. "It is the most despicable, soul crushing scheme I've ever heard, but it is brilliant."

He bristled at Edward's sketch of his behaviour, but it was accurate and very well deserved. "There is more." The fire popped and a bit of it crumbled through the grate.

Edward's chair creaked as he moved. "More?" He rose and went to the tray.

The tone was enough that Frederick did not dare to look. "I may have obligated myself to someone else. The young woman in Lyme."

"Miss Musgrove."

"Yes, I behaved badly—"

"Just *how* badly?"

"I am not quite a reprobate—I have not spent my time meddling with young girls. I paid her too much attention, was too much with the family. My behaviour could easily invite romantic speculations." He could not rise to defend himself more. Even as he spoke of Louisa Musgrove, Anne's face reminded him of all the opportunities he missed.

"I see." There was silence while Edward thought. "You said you *may* have obliged yourself. What makes you uncertain? Surely, the family has made their view known."

Suddenly, Frederick realised how ridiculous it all sounded that he was completely dependent upon the mistaken opinion of Harville and his wife. Musgrove had seemed to say the family had expectations, but nothing had been expressed outright. His plan of separation may have done all he hoped, but he had no sure way of knowing. Edward was going to have much to say about this.

And he did.

After Frederick outlined what had occurred in Lyme and how he had left things, Edward asked for more details. He now knew as much about the fiasco as anyone. "So, you are hoping to hear from Harville, and then you will do whatever you must."

"Honour demands it."

"Honour is a harsh taskmaster."

"What are we without it?"

"Happier sometimes."

"Are you advising me to shirk my duty if I am expected to marry her?"

"No, certainly not! I will say that if it comes to that, you can be happy with her."

"Does that really matter?"

"I think it would matter to your wife...and eventually to your children."

Children. The word made his stomach twist. He had hoped bringing his troubles to light would make them easier to bear. It would seem, the more his brother spoke, the heavier the burden became. "How could I be happy with a woman I do not love?"

"By putting away all thoughts of the one you do love."

Edward was being sympathetic, and Frederick knew this advice was a hard thing to say. It was clear the rector in no wise wished for his brother to give up concerning Anne unless it was absolutely necessary. Frederick looked away, back to the fire.

Edward cleared his throat. "You need to have some faith, Brother."

It seemed a preposterous statement. "Religion will save me?"

"No, I mean that when we are caught up in our pride and so certain we know what Providence has for us, we can change. The circumstances can change as well."

"Yes, yes...as with you and Catherine." He did not bear to hear of their triumphant tale of love over expediency again.

"I hadn't thought of that, but what you say is true." There was a pause. "I was thinking more along the lines of my return to England."

Frederick studied his brother. During this visit there had been more genuine exchanges than the Captain could ever remember. It was all so strange, and at another time, when his own affairs were more certain, it would have been refreshing. But now he knew too much about too many people and knew that the truth always tainted even the most carefully weighed opinion. Besides that, there were things about him and his career that he wished no one knew: judgements he had made in the past that he would change if such a possibility presented itself, words he had spoken in haste that he wanted back, actions towards people he cared deeply for that proved quite the opposite. "What have you done?

What makes you think you understand my situation?" This was the crux of it; Edward's behaviour intimated that he was guilty of something.

Edward was still silent and staring into the fire when Frederick rose to pour them each a glass of wine. He handed it to Edward. "Now, tell me what this is about. I am tired of all our secrets and manoeuvres." He took his seat and waited.

"When I ran away from home, the first ship I found leaving Liverpool was bound for New Holland. They were short a steward for the First Officer, and I was taken in that capacity."

Frederick took a drink of the frightful wine. It did nothing to sooth his impatience. It was clear Edward was going to go about revealing himself in his own way.

"So, aside for the few months I was stuck in Ireland, that voyage began nearly seven years of seasickness and learning the hard way to keep body and soul together." He looked at Frederick and then relaxed.

Frederick wasn't certain why Edward's countenance suddenly eased and his frame seemed to have a great weight lifted from it, but that was how it was. Edward took a drink and then stood. "I left after Father beat me viciously. I had to leave, else he'd kill me—or I would kill him. Either way, nothing good would come of my staying, so I figured that leaving both of us alive was the best for all concerned." He brushed at the mantel. "After nearly seven years, I was never rated more than a landsman. So, after many years of hating life aboard ship, one night I failed to return when the gun sounded."

Frederick now understood one aspect Edward's reluctance to speak about his life at sea. The revelation that he had walked away from his ship required further investigation. "You said you were rated as a landsman. You were in the Navy then?"

Edward seemed happy to relieve him. "No, you needn't slap me in irons and find the nearest admiral to hand me over as a deserter. I had managed to avoid impressment. Only God knows how, but I never abandoned my country in that sense."

"Even if you had, desertion is not punished with much more than a fine these days. With the war ending, they would not likely care what happened ages ago...but this is good to know." He should feel more comforted, but he did not. "Where did you ... in what port did you leave your ship?"

"I jumped ship in Bridgetown. Barbadoes."

It was all clear now. In any given port city, there were scores of filthy things his brother might have been about, but the port was Bridgetown. The possibilities narrowed. The only question was: was it sugar or slaves?

"I had taken none of my things so I was a bit desperate for the first day or so, but the third day I was sitting on a wall, looking over the docks, when a fellow came and asked me if I could read and write and do sums. When I proved that I could, he asked if I wanted a job. I said I did, and he took me to the house of a Dutch fellow who had ships coming in and out from Africa to America."

They quietly looked at one another. Edward had efficiently answered the question. There was no reason to enquire further. The docks of Liverpool had provided all the education Frederick would ever need having to do with the slave trade. The smells alone were enough to make a decent human instinctively know the evil of the practice.

Upon his return, it took little time for Edward to know Frederick had a deep desire to go to sea. He began to form connections with captains who would be willing to take the boy out for short runs up the Mersey and the occasional trip to Blackpool. He had been careful to keep his young brother from certain sorts of captains and certain sorts of goods.

It was on one of these sallies that Frederick had made a good impression on a naval captain making his way home after several years in Gibraltar. "You're a bit old, but I see you have some skills. I would not mind having at least one midshipman on my next posting with a brain in his skull." Edward had not been convinced that the man meant anything by the compliment, but on Frederick's insistence, he did write to this Captain Croft. To his great surprise, the officer remembered Frederick, and he was further surprised to find the offer of a place on his ship was genuine.

Croft would be returning to Liverpool in a few weeks, and a meeting was arranged. Within two month's time, Frederick was to report as a midshipman aboard the fifth rate, *Bainbridge*. It was aboard the *Bainbridge* he first came into contact with a packed slave ship at sea. There were no words for the experience, and only occasionally did he allow the sights, sounds, and smells to attack his senses. Frederick was not certain whether it was his brother's reputation he wished to protect by remaining ignorant of the past or if it was to save himself from his own memories.

"My main duty was to oversee the docks, making sure that the manifests and the actual cargo matched. It was mostly a matter of counting the living and the dead." Edward looked at his brother and did not flinch with the bloodless, matter-of-fact revelation. He continued. "I was also responsible for seeing that all the money added up after the auctions." Edward finished his wine and stood before the fire, studying the glass. "I don't think we need go into all my other duties. You understand the life well enough." He poured another bumper of wine and took his seat.

80

Frederick looked around the room and wondered how many others had poured out their closely guarded secrets to his brother. The irony of life now made it his brother's confessional. That made the captain a sort of priest, not that it was new to him. He'd listened many times to his men when they acknowledged their wrongdoing and been obliged to mete out their punishment. He played no such role this time. Or did he?

"It was a desolate and shameful life. To be honest, I can't even say it was a life. Maybe a sort of existence, but not anything more." He put the nearly full glass of wine on the table and leaned forward, rested his elbows on his knees, and bowed his head.

Frederick needed to know nothing more about Barbadoes. He knew men who had done much the same, worse in fact. There was no loathing or condemnation on his part. This was his brother, and his repentance for his filthy past was unmistakeable. Any stone that Frederick might have been tempted to cast slipped through his own guilty fingers.

"I know what I did was more vile—the loss of life alone..." He still did not turn to look at Frederick. "But you need to know that there is forgiveness. You can make amends, and you can have some peace... no matter how despicable your actions."

"The scale of our respective deeds is not even comparable. I tell you this, not so much for your benefit, Brother, but for my own." He sat up and turned fully to Frederick. "I tell you this because for years I have done what you did to Anne Elliot. I held you at arm's length and made our former close relationship of little value. Not to hurt you, for it cost me more than I can tell you, but I did it out of fear. I was afraid that if you knew this about me, you would rightly reject me. It was better that you and I would have a scrap of our former closeness than nothing." He heaved himself from the chair and went to his desk. Out of the bottom drawer, he took a wooden box decorated with marquetry flowers. He returned to the chair, opened the box, and offered it to Frederick. "Don't tell my wife."

Evidently, some secrets were to be kept no matter what. He looked in the box. He laughed and took out some candied walnuts.

Edward took some for himself. "She thinks I eat too many sweets. She's right, of course, but I need something just now." Never looking away from the fire, he began to eat the clandestine pleasure.

After a few minutes of no sound but the crunch of the hard sugar coating, Frederick dared to open the conversation again. "Did you grow tired of Barbadoes, as you had your life on ship? Is why you returned to England?"

Edward's gaze was gentle, and Frederick could tell he was again bringing his thoughts together, trying to measure his words. He likely never intended to tell any of what was to come, or he would have been more prepared.

Edward looked away. "After father died, I was urged by father's man of business to return. Mother was not well and there were things that needed my attention. I ignored the letter." He reached over without looking to take his glass. Wine sloshed a bit and ran down the side of it.

Before Edward could do anything, Frederick had his handkerchief out and tossed it on the deep red puddle. The fire was in need of stoking, but the Captain was too tired to attend it.

"When the second letter came in a few week's time, I was informed that my mother was now dead and that my siblings needed a guardian." He did not answer the half-hearted accusation and was careful to choose words stripped of all affection. Frederick wondered why.

"During that interminable voyage, all I thought about was putting you in any school that would have you and finding Sophia a place as a governess or companion. I never gave a single thought to caring for the two of you myself." He took a deep breath. "All I had when I landed that hellish August night was the address of a Mrs. Greene. She had taken you and Sophia when Mother died. Do you remember her?"

"I do, and I well remember her small army of boys. They all hated me. I was daily pelted with rocks, and they chased me down like a pack of rabid dogs." The memory of them was stronger than he imagined it could be after so much time.

Edward burst out laughing.

"You find it funny that I was terrorised?" Frederick was shocked that his brother did not sympathise with his younger self.

Edward stopped laughing but still smiled. He touched his lips with the back of his hand. "After she could trust that I was going to stay, Mrs. Greene came to talk to me about you." They exchanged looks. "She said that she could see you were a very smart boy but that if I did not take you in hand soon, you would be wayward for sure."

Frederick sat straight and leant over the arm of the chair. "Me! She called *me* wayward! With her tribe of heathens, she would dare to say that?" He could not believe such a thing. He flopped back against the chair.

"You must be fair; she said you *might* become wayward. It seems that you had found a book of knots, traps and snares. Do you remember digging a pit in order to trap Peter Greene?"

He had not thought of the Greenes in ages and had never once thought about hunting them down one-by-one until tonight. He could not help but laugh as well. "I do remember. His brother Paul followed him right in. But in my own defence, it was only as deep as their knees."

"Only because you were rather short for being just twelve-years-old. You do remember that you filled it with water?"

"Ah, yes."

"She said you always managed to get them dirty or wet or both. I think the terrorising was divided equally."

"I got in a great deal of trouble not only for the hole but for stripping the branches off a bush in order to cover it. I think I killed the bush."

Edward laughed quietly. "You have always been an ambitious young man with a knack for the original. And that is why I have always admired you."

He could not look at Edward just now.

"Anyway, when I got to Mrs. Greene's, she said I could sleep in the attic where the two of you were staying. The stairway narrowed as you went up, and it grew hotter and hotter with each step. The room was like an oven, but all that went out of my head when I opened the door and first laid eyes on Sophia." He paused. "The last time I had seen her she was only eight-years-old. There she was, a beautiful young woman... so much like our mother." His voice was shaking. "And then you." He paused again. "You were lying on the floor in a patch of moonlight. You'd tossed off your nightshirt, and I could see that you were thin—blond, all elbows and knees—but I just knew you were strong and healthy." He turned and the chair creaked. Frederick looked over. "And to confirm the bad behaviour of the Greene boys, you had a gash on your cheek." He smiled and unconsciously touched his own. "I couldn't stand the heat any longer and went to the window, intending to open it. I could see our house from that vantage. It would not be markedly cooler there, but there was no reason to remain in that oven—"

"And you told Sophia to get my things and that we were going home." Frederick felt the heat and heard the words as though it was no longer winter in Shropshire, but a hot Liverpool night.

"You remember?"

"Every night I had prayed to God that He would rescue me from the Greene's and that He would rescue me from that attic room."

"Why the room?"

"It was packed with casks and boxes and shadows. The house made strange noises at night, and I was frightened out of my mind most of the time." It was his turn to pause. "That night I awoke to strong arms lifting me from my bed and a deep voice saying we were going home. It was the first prayer of mine that was ever answered."

Edward's hand came to rest on the arm of the chair. "I can never do enough to get out from under the guilt I feel about Barbadoes. I am resigned to that. But I sometimes feel that I was at my worst when I wanted nothing more than to cast adrift my own flesh and blood."

This was harder to hear than anything earlier had been. "But you did not do that; you came and stayed."

Frederick rose and stood behind Edward's chair. Both men were done in. Neither of them had the energy for any more emotions or revelations.

"Good night, Brother." Frederick rested his hand on Edward's shoulder for a moment.

"Good night, my boy."

They were finished for the night.

~ ~ ~ ~ ~ ~ ~ & ~ ~ ~ ~ ~ ~ ~

The day following, the brothers went out of their way to be polite, but not in any way affectionate. It would take some time before the gentlemen were comfortable with knowing so much about one another. The Captain noticed Catherine watching them, but she said nothing. He wondered if she knew about Edward and about their talk.

Several days passed. Then, as Frederick was tending his horse, he happened to glance out the stable window to see Edward and Catherine walking around the garden. They held hands as they stopped and looked over the bare canes of berries, broken hills where potatoes had been dug, and frost-wizened tops of beets still in the ground. As they were coming out, passing under a little pergola covered with withered grapevines, they paused and stood very close together.

Frederick stopped brushing and watched. Edward took his wife's hands, slowly removing her gloves as he spoke. She listened attentively. When he had finished, he kissed each hand and slipped them into his own pockets. This action drew her closer still. She smiled at first and then laughed when he said something in her ear. They stood looking at one another, silent. Very slowly, Catherine closed the tiny gap between them and kissed him. His brother's hands came out of his pockets, and he took her in his arms. They stayed together, locked in the embrace for a very long time. Frederick continued to stare but no longer saw them.

Had he treated Anne with some friendliness when he arrived at Uppercross, they might have found a way to heal his angry wounds. They might be on their way toward marriage had he exercised something resembling intelligence.

As he came out of his reverie, he noticed, to his horror, that Catherine now rested her head on Edward's shoulder; and her gaze had him in her line of sight. She smiled at Frederick and waved a little with her fingertips.

There was nothing to do but return her gesture. He turned quickly. *I shall never be able to look the woman in the eye*, he thought, brushing his horse with a violent sort of vigour.

~ ~ ~ ~ ~ ~ ~ & ~ ~ ~ ~ ~ ~ ~

It was over two months since Louisa Musgrove's fall, and Frederick suddenly felt a renewed sting of the event. He excused himself from the usual after dinner conversation and went out intending to take another walk. He did not wish to risk meeting strangers or slight acquaintances, and so sought his refuge in Edward's winter-hardened garden. The plot perfectly reflected the landscape of his heart. Overall, the ground was uneven, making walking difficult. The greens and browns that made up the garden's colour palette were dull and muddy. What had once been vibrant with life was now brittle with frost and gave little indication that anything good could ever appear again.

There had been no other letters from any of the Musgroves. This was a relief in the short-term. Without letters piling up, it was simple to imagine that there was nothing of importance outside the world of the rectory. In reality, the lack of communication could also mean the Musgroves were taking their time in marshalling their arguments for marriage between Louisa and him . He must do something soon or be at the mercy of a situation for which he had no defence.

At times like this, he thanked God for a fair amount of control over himself. His passions of late had taken wild swings from being reconciled to the situation to a deep desire to mount his horse and ride away from the obligations. Intellectually, he knew that his course lay somewhere between the two. The pain in his heart came from knowing that Anne was not to be found in any of the solutions.

"If you continue to excuse yourself when the pudding is served, I shall be forced to think it is not to your liking, Captain. In fact, none of my cooking has managed to entice your appetite today." Catherine's voice startled him. She was looking over the stone wall that surrounded part of the garden.

He approached her. "Not at all, madam. I merely wanted fresh air. Your puddings are a triumph, and I shall have two pieces when next we dine."

She paused under the pergola to pluck a dead grape vine. He waited for her at the garden's end. "No need to flatter me, sir. My husband is enthusiastic enough about my cooking to keep your bad opinions from stinging too much." She took his arm. "He is a very enthusiastic man in general. By the way, Captain, please never mention what you have seen between him and me. Edward would be mortified to know."

He wondered if his brother's mortification could possibly surpass his own at that moment. *It could,* he decided. "I shall take my knowledge of his excesses to the grave."

Catherine laughed and thanked him. "I did come looking for you. You were very tense during dinner, and I think I know why."

They continued apace as he wondered if he might have , given her a clue to the truth of his circumstances. Edward surely would keep his confidence, but what exactly was the priority of keeping a brother's secret from a wife? Was there any at all? Regrettably, wives had more powerful weapons at their disposal than brothers would ever possess. The only solution was to walk and listen.

Catherine crushed the leaf and watched the brown bits flutter to the ground. "I think you are still concerned about Edward and his...secret."

The relief he felt was instant. There was no doubting he was still coming to terms with his brother's past, but his particular bit of spleen today had nothing to do with anyone's past but his own. "So, you know."

"Yes, he told me before we married. It was almost our undoing."

"But you forgave him."

"Yes. It was the most despicable thing I'd ever heard of, but he is a changed man. And I love him. A woman who truly loves a man will forgive him a great deal."

She knew about Anne. Her expression and tone said as much. "What if you are an exception?"

"I am not. Most women will choose to love a man when his heart is in it."

The statement was inscrutable and applied to many things all at once. Frederick had no idea how to open the subject further or if he even cared to. He said nothing more.

They came to a bench, nothing more than a low shelf built into the stone wall. He brushed windblown debris from the seat for her. Thanking him, she sat and looked over the desolate garden. He imagined it had been lovely in summer and how the two of them would have spent evenings here. Edward would titivate, pruning and weeding while Catherine talked or, perhaps, read aloud to him. The warmth of summer would make it a sweet place for a couple to be alone and enjoy one another's company. It was appropriate that growing things were so friendly to lovers.

"Well, here you are." Edward had come upon them without a sound.

Catherine patted the bench, and he joined her. "I came to see that the Captain was feeling well."

"And is he?"

"I am."

He held out a letter. "Good. Here is that item from Harville for which you've been waiting." The small packet of paper shook a little in his hand.

Frederick took it and began to put it in his pocket. Edward would have none of that. "Be off with you, Brother. I feel sure it is good news." Edward took Catherine's hand and patted it.

He took his brother's permission as an omen. "Excuse me, please." He could hear Catherine's voice fade as he walked away.

He chose to stand at the mouth of the pergola and read.

—so it falls to me to tell you that Miss Louisa and James are to be married. No one but Elsa saw it coming. She tried to warn me, but I told her she was misreading the situation com-pletely. Always listen to a woman in matters of love. Now that I will listen, she has told me she suspects the girl was exagger-ating her condition at times so that she might spend time with him. Don't blame James. Moreover, I suppose, you cannot blame her either. I counted on his broken heart to be a shield against any sort of affection. They were thrown together in such anxious and intimate circumstances that this is a natural result. Had you only returned—

So, that had been it! The matters Harville had mentioned were Louisa and James, not concern that he do his duty by the girl. He was never so happy to be wrong.

By the time he reached the end of the letter, his heart was pounding and his hands shook. He made a mess of refolding it and, instead, jammed it into his coat pocket. Stepping ever more quickly over the small hummocks of dirt, he began to order his departure. There was packing to do and the horse to ready. He must pen a letter to inform Sophia of the felicitous news about Benwick and Louisa's engagement. In the letter, he would mention that he was tired of the country and had decided to make a visit to Bath. With a little luck, she would offer her dear little brother a place to stay.

"Frederick! Where are you going?" Edward shouted.

He realised he was nearly to the door of the house, leaving the two of them staring at him from the garden. "It is time for me to be off! I shall be in Bath on Wednesday," he shouted, jumping the steps and opening the door in one graceful motion.

The warmth of the kitchen welcomed him as he entered the house. Its present, cosy atmosphere was the antipodes in comparison to the night he arrived. Such a change could only be attributed to the letter and the wonderful news it bore. He stopped and pulled off his coat by the fireplace. Bell was nowhere to be seen. Suddenly, he was starving and ate one or two small jam tarts that beckoned to him from the table. He paced as he ate the first of them. After gulping a slosh of wine, he pulled out the letter and read it again. The words might just as well have been set to music for the joy they brought to his heart. After the second tart, he folded the letter properly and slipped it into his breast pocket.

He grasped at the hope that Anne retained some feelings towards him; her occasional looks and willingness to help with Louisa were the most obvious clues to that. The blanket he took from Uppercross had been her doing and was a tangible expression of some sort of concern for him. Everything came down to whether or not his boorish behaviour at Uppercross had been enough to kill any regard she might have nursed over their years apart. Were the attentions of James Benwick and the pointed notice of her cousin enough to make her cast off any remaining feelings towards him? He earnestly prayed that if this was the case, his newfound willingness to make amends would renew her feelings for him and sweep away any interest in fresh associations that were part of her new life.

If all went according to his plans, he would be in Bath soon and would, perhaps, be in Anne's company in less than a week. He lifted the nearly empty glass.

"To us, my girl." He thought of her and downed the wine.

~ ~ ~ ~ ~ ~ ~ & ~ ~ ~ ~ ~ ~ ~

As he made his way up the stairs, Edward caught up with him. "So, the news is good."

"The best possible. Miss Musgrove is engaged."

"But I thought–"

"As did I, but evidently I am not the man that my friend James Benwick is. So, I leave in the morning for Bath."

Edward leaned against the wall. "That is wonderful news, but what will you do with George? You can't really take a small boy with you when trying to curry favour with a woman." A cough sounded above them. They looked at one another. George stood in the doorway of the bedchamber he and the Captain shared.

Frederick started up the last few steps. "Come, Mr. Tuggins, we have business to discuss." Wentworth took his travelling bag from the closet. "I am leaving in the morning."

The boy smiled and looked about. "What can I put my new clothes in, sir?' He turned to the rector. "Can I have a sack, sir? Anything to take my things."

Frederick looked at the little boy's face. There was such trust and faith that he would keep his promise,and now, his one chance to make things right with Anne would dash all the little fellow's hopes for the future. Was every good thing tainted with some sort of evil?

Before he could speak, Edward took the boy's hand and led him to his bed. He sat and looked George in the eye. "The Captain must leave in the morning for Bath. Just now there is no place for you."

Frederick could not see George's face, but the boy's shoulders sagged.

"Now, now, Mr. Tuggins, there is much to do here." Edward looked up and winked at Frederick. "I don't suppose the Captain has told you what a blockhead he was about mathematics before I taught him algebra and geometry and all he needed to know." The boy perked up. "It is only thanks to me that my brother can navigate across a pond, much less an ocean. And we will use this opportunity to teach you."

George turned and looked at the Captain and then back at the rector.

While Edward spoke to George, Frederick packed his satchel. "I have two books with very fine maps that I have used to keep track of my brother's travels, and you can study them so that, when he has a ship, you will have a very good working knowledge of the world's geography. No ignorant blockhead will you be!"

George turned again. His expression was still grave. "Why are you going to Bath?"

The question was impertinent and Frederick bristled, but he was practically abandoning the boy and maybe that deserved a decent explanation. "Remember me telling you about the lady who gave me that blanket?" George nodded. "I have just gotten word that there is a very small chance for me to make things right with her. If I can, there is another small chance that she will marry me." The boy was bright; perhaps he would understand the urgency and understand his being left for now.

George went to the Captain's bed and picked up the blanket. He brought it to him. "Make sure to pack this. It will bring you luck...and I think you will need all the luck you can muster on this mission. sir."

Edward laughed and said, "Out of the mouth of babes, Frederick."

He took the blanket from the boy. "You are quite right, Mr. Tuggins. You are quite right, indeed."

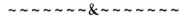

Frederick walked around his horse, pulling at various straps and buckles. Everything was ready for his departure, and he was anxious to be away. He would miss the rectory and its occupants, but he knew they both understood. Nothing had been said, but he was certain Catherine had been told at least some of the details and understood the reason for the Captain's hasty removal. He suspected that any disappointment would soon be replaced with their good wishes. He looked towards the house and saw them approach to see him off.

Edward extended his hand. "I wish you great success in your endeavour. Considering that Bath is well past its prime, you will have few things to distract you from planning your strategy."

"You *will* remember to have my trunk sent after me. My uniforms are in it, and—"

"And your sword and instruments and other dunnage; I know. For the third time, I'll send it on to Gay Street as soon as possible."

"Right. Oh, here is something to keep the boy…and a bit to keep my niece or nephew." He pulled several coins from his purse and offered them to his brother.

"That is not necessary."

"Yes, it is. Take it. If the child is a boy, buy him a book on knots and traps and snares along with a little shovel."

"Suppose the child is a girl?"

Taking Edward's hand, Frederick put the coins in it. Keeping hold, he said, "Considering how stupid I've been the last few weeks, it might not be a bad thing for a young lady to know about traps and snares." The Captain stared into the rector's face. "I want to make sure that my family is well-cared for." When he felt Edward's fingers take hold of the coins, he released him.

"Thank you, Frederick. I shall miss you as well. I've grown quite used to having you underfoot again."

"I'm sure I will return sometime. Perhaps sooner than later." He paused. "Besides, I have a promise to keep to someone." He nodded to George.

"Aye, we'll take good care of him. You will be more than welcome no matter what the outcome." Edward sighed and put the coins in his pocket. They stood, silent and awkward.

"If I am able to put things right, I shall bring Anne to meet Catherine. If I fail—" He'd admitted as much as he could stand. He would not begin a campaign with talk of failure.

Edward scowled. "You cannot fail. You will succeed."

He turned to Catherine. Her eyes were red and her handkerchief at the ready. She kissed him and said, "We expect to hear good things when you write."

To Mr. Tuggins, he saluted, then knelt. "Listen to the Rector. He's right. I was a blockhead, and he taught me quite a lot. When I return, I will teach you more."

George stood straight and tall. "Aye, sir," was all he said.

Frederick rose and began to mount. His foot was in the stirrup and he was just beginning to hoist himself up when he paused. He headed back to his little farewell committee, removed his gloves, and then pulled out his purse. Without looking at the coins he fished out, he took Catherine's hand and placed them in it. "Don't let him have this or he'll give it away. For the love of God, get some *good* wine in this house!"

He didn't look at them until he was at the edge of the road. He then turned and waved. It would go on forever if he let it, so he tuned and spurred his horse on to Bath.

Chapter Seven

I am sure I speak for both of us when I say we are delighted to have you quite unexpectedly appear at our door, Frederick," Sophia remarked as she took a sip of her tea.

"And for that, I apologise. I would have sworn any number of oaths that, when I wrote, I had told you I was coming to Bath." Had his sister not shown him the letter, in his own hand, he might still think that she had misread his intentions. But, after the commotion of his arrival and several rounds of playful accusations of forgetfulness on one or the other's part, the letter was fetched and Sophia proven correct. He had written and conveyed the news of Benwick and Louisa Musgrove's engagement, ending with his hopes of happiness for the pair. He had, to his credit, taken a scant line to wish the Crofts good health and enjoyment of the delights of Bath. Not a word of his own travels to Bath were written or implied. It was now with embarrassment that he remembered rushing to post the letter so that he might get on with packing for the journey.

"You will, of course, stay with us, Frederick. It is no trouble, but I wonder that you left Edward so suddenly to come here. Bath is not quite the sort of place I imagined you would like to visit." She refreshed his tea. "I do not imagine you are here to take the waters."

The idea of wading into the pools with the ancient or infirm was repulsive. Not wishing to insult his brother-in-law, he made noises that it was not for his health that he came but to see old friends and to take in a little culture in the form of plays and concerts.. In truth, he did have one particular friend residing in Bath, and if his luck held, the man would be at home for the winter. "I hear that fireworks are quite the thing here. You know how I like a good rousing display of fireworks," he said.

"They are pleasant enough, but fireworks are never so stirring as when they are lighting the taking of an enemy frigate, eh Captain?" The Admiral had been absent upon his arrival but now joined them with a pleased expression as he pumped Frederick's hand vigorously.

"It is true, Admiral. In many cases, fireworks can mean a handsome profit is to be made."

They all settled in while Sophia explained to the Admiral how surprised she was at her brother's sudden appearance and, further, that he would stay with them and that he was hoping for some good entertainment while in town.

"Well, I must tell you that the most entertaining thing I have found to date is watching the crowds at any of these gatherings. It's quite a sight to watch the swells puff and prance and try to outdo one another."

The Admiral's expression indicated that he had much more to say on the matter. Wentworth looked forward to their after dinner chat, which was certain to give him an opportunity to take a survey of the territory. When he asked about mutual acquaintances that were in residence, the pair began a running recitation of who was about, speculations on their fortunes, and hints towards various romances and intrigues. He was about to ask after Patrick McGillvary when Croft mentioned meeting Anne Elliot.

"...it was on Milsom Street. You know, dear, by that shop with the paintings. More often than not, they display paintings with sails and pennants blowing in opposite directions. I have no idea how you can watch a ship sailing and..."

"And how is Miss Anne?" Sophia asked her husband. Frederick blessed his sister's timely curiosity. Turning to him, she said, "Before leaving Kellynch, we offered to take anything that Mrs. Charles Musgrove might wish to send her family. She sent a gigantic letter, and that allowed us to easily re-establish the acquaintance. This is the first time either of us has met with any of the Elliots while we've been out and about. Thankfully, from the gossip we've gleaned, we will not be moving in the same circles."

"And what do we need with the Elliots when we have Sir Archibald Drew and those shabby Brand brothers? Oh, by the bye, while I was walking with Miss Elliot, I saw Captain Brigden. Don't be surprised if the rumours begin to circulate." He laughed and winked at his wife.

"Be nice," she said.

"And how is Miss Anne, sir?" Wentworth repeated his sister's question, hoping to sound somewhat disinterested.

At once Admiral Croft's expression sobered. He asked for another cup of tea and then said, "To begin, she seemed very well. I told her about your letter and the engagement of James Benwick to that Musgrove girl. She didn't seem surprised in the least."

"I dare say her sister gave her the news in the letter we brought. You did say that Captain Harville wrote to you from Uppercross, did you

93

not?" Frederick nodded and waited to drive the conversation back to his object of interest.

"Well, that explains it then. Anywise, she listened nicely as she always does. She is terribly polite; is she not, Sophie? Much different than her father."

The couple began discussing their various prejudices concerning the Elliots. Wentworth was about to come out of his chair, dash his cup against the mantel, and demand the Admiral tell of the meeting without benefit of the small talk and personal asides. Instead, he took a piece of cake and battered it into a plateful of crumbs.

"I am curious to hear Miss Anne's opinion of the match," Sophia said, rather loudly. Evidently, she had noticed Frederick's preoccupation. To him, she said, "I find that I usually agree with Miss Anne, when she will venture an opinion, that is. I would like to know her better. I am sure she has some very astute things to say when she feels free to speak her mind."

His sister on intimate terms with Anne was a fascinating, though horrible, thing to contemplate. He could only hope, if Fate were kind and such a thing came about, that Anne's loyalties would lie with him over the enjoyment of entertaining his sister with tales of his past stupidities.

"That is true, dear. The girl has a good head on her shoulders. Anywise, on the matter of the letter, she seemed to be most concerned about your feelings, Frederick." He took a drink of his tea and began speaking to his wife about some other fellow he'd seen prior to meeting Anne.

Concerned for me. This was good. This was a felicitous bit of information he might try, ever so slightly, to exploit when they must eventually meet. While he would take no advantage by pressing hard the role of the jilted lover, he would take his time correcting her if she wished to feel a bit sorry for any perceived disappointment on his part. But this would be only long enough to secure a friendly, open footing between them.

He put his cup down and was about to excuse himself when the Admiral said, "When you see Miss Anne next, you might tread lightly on this subject, my dear. And you as well, Frederick."

This enigmatic statement roused his curiosity, so, settling back into his chair, he asked, "And why should I take care in this matter, sir?"

The Admiral looked over to Sophia, who also looked puzzled. "As I said, in the beginning of the conversation she seemed exceedingly concerned about your feelings on the matter. Now that I look back, I wonder if perhaps she had harboured some tender feelings for Benwick."

"What on earth makes you think this, dear?" Sophia asked.

Wentworth shifted in his seat. The idea was not new, of course, but he had hoped that the engagement had laid this ridiculous notion to rest forever.

"Just a guess. She was quite adamant that Benwick is a fine fellow and hoped that if Frederick was feeling ill-used, it would not affect their friendship."

"That is a very kind thought," Sophia said.

So, her concern extended not only towards himself, but also to dear, dear James as well. As Sophia and the Admiral discussed other particulars of his trip, Frederick tormented himself with various possible meanings of Anne's remarks.

~ ~ ~ ~ ~ ~ ~ & ~ ~ ~ ~ ~ ~ ~

Sophia's revenge for his careless intrusion was exacted when she showed him his rooms after supper. "Were we staying here permanently, I might be inclined to change it," she said. They stood in the doorway of a room so feminine that the sight of it was an affront to his masculine senses. The floor was covered with a fine rug of green, scattered with intertwining stems of white and yellow roses. The window draperies were dark green, to mimic foliage no doubt, with under curtains of tiny multicoloured rosebuds. The wallpaper nodded with hedges of fat pink and red roses. The painted surfaces were a trompe l'oeil garden. The various plants, trees, expanses of lawn, and fountain, complete with angels spitting water out their mouths, surrounded the occupant in a grip that was startling to say the least. The room might as well be filled with discordant bells that rang all the time. It all clashed and screamed against any sort of order.

Frederick took it in, knowing his sister was enjoying herself more than he should allow. Finally, he said, "Not to hurt your feelings, Sister dear, but it is a monstrosity."

Sophia stepped around him and went to open the curtains. "You don't hurt my pride. The woman who did this is in London just now, perhaps doing the same to some other unsuspecting room." She turned. "The only other accommodation I can offer is a sofa in the sitting room."

He finally stepped fully into the room, allowing the effect to surround him. His chest tightened.

She came close and grasped his arm. "Be of good cheer, Brother, the only time you will be in here, it will be dark." She patted him and snickered as she walked to the door.

He was just able to make out his empty case on the counterpane's riot of flowers. "Yes, but it is just the knowledge that this madness is going on all the time, asleep or awake." She had turned at the door, and he motioned to the case.

"I had a blanket in there. Where has it gone?" He could not lose Anne's blanket now.

"Harkness is with us. I told him to unpack. I'm sure he's seen to it."

Frederick willed himself to be calm about it. There was no sense rousing Harkness's curiosity. He glanced over the room again and thought it might all be worthwhile just to hear Harkness's opinion on the decorations.

Just as he was about to thank her, Croft entered, laughing. "So, you've found the garden. When it's raining too much to be out, we take a turn in here."

And so the little jokes went. If the room were a symphony, every instrument was out of tune, but the place was dry and warm. He was in Bath, and so was Anne.

~ ~ ~ ~ ~ ~ ~ & ~ ~ ~ ~ ~ ~ ~

The next day he was amazingly tired from the breakneck pace he'd set coming from Shropshire. He idly wondered if his horse fared any better. The large bracket clock on the mantle struck the quarter hour, and he moved away, hoping to remember to be out of the room when it repeated itself on the next quarter. Instead of exiting the room, he moved towards the window overlooking the street.

"Frederick, my sitting room is not your Quarter Deck. Your pacing is going to wear a trail in my carpets, not to mention what it is doing to my nerves," Sophia said, pulling a thread taut and tying it off. "There are many interesting shops to visit in Bath and quite a lot of interesting architecture to study."

In his mind, Frederick could hear her adding, "Find some of it and be out of my hair ."

The Admiral lowered his newspaper and leant forward. "I'm sure you will find some pretty girls who are also in need of a bit of exercise." He winked and went back to his reading.

This suggestion to walk took on a new shade of interest when he realised that, perhaps, Anne Elliot might be out shopping or studying the local architecture as well.

"I think you're right, both of you. I need to get out and see the sights of Bath." Just then a blast of rain hit the large window overlooking Gay Street. The Admiral didn't stir, and Sophia looked up only long enough to take it into account. "There is a brand new umbrella in the stand by the door. Feel free to make it your own, for if you wait for the rain to quit in Bath, you will never stir out of your house."

"Right," he said, and headed to the door.

~ ~ ~ ~ ~ ~ ~ & ~ ~ ~ ~ ~ ~ ~

Several hours later, after walking what felt to be every street in Bath, looking in every shop window and avoiding every crowd of fine and not-so-fine ladies, sailors, tradesmen and even children, he headed down Milsom Street for home. The shops on Milsom were some of the finest he'd encountered and surveying the merchant's offerings was not a terrible trial. He was amazed that there was so much in the way of trifling rubbish on which people could spend their money. "Loads of trash for the buying," he said to himself. It was not until he came to a watchmakers' shop that presented a select grouping of telescopes, compasses, and quadrants that was he persuaded that there might be something genuinely useful to be had.

In a short time, a man in the store came to the window and indicated he would be pleased to show the Captain any of the fine, gleaming brass items. As he was about to be lured in, a voice behind him said, "Enter at your own peril, they are some of the finest craftsmen in the whole of England, Captain Wentworth."

The use of his name and rank by the strong voice from behind startled him. Turning he was shocked to be face-to-face with his oldest and dearest friend, Admiral Patrick McGillvary.

"I know how you hate to part with any of your significant fortune, so I thought I'd give you fair warning." They greeted one another as only old sailing friends are able. "So, have you come to this glorified watering hole to buy navigation equipment or expand your mind with the cultural wonders available?"

"Neither and both, I suppose. I am visiting my sister. You remember Croft? They are living here for the winter."

"And they allowed you a place to lay your weary head."

"Yes. You are living here still?"

"I'm afraid I must. The old man's usury business is here, and the family pile is comfortable. I'm too lazy to go off and make a home of my own; so I just took it all over when father passed."

"Did you ever retire?"

"God, no! But Whitehall is happy to have me out of their hair on a daily basis and sopping up merely half-pay. I live a quiet life now." The look in McGillvary's eye said that his definition of a quiet life and what that generally meant were very different, indeed.

Before any more was said, a group of three ladies and a gentleman joined them. Introductions were made. Wentworth was glad to note that one of the ladies was married to the other gentleman and, in a short time, their rapid-fire conversation established that the other two were also attached to men not present.

The rain had picked up again, and the group packed themselves under the modest awning of the watchmaker's. To Wentworth's amusement, the six of them blocked nearly the entire sidewalk. He had noticed during his ramble that if there were a walkway, someone would eventually encamp, thinking it the perfect place to hold court. When the genial gentleman from the shop rapped on the window, it was suggested that they should move on to Molland's, a nearby teashop, and leave the crowd on the sidewalk to sort itself out.

McGillvary and the rest of the party made their way across the street and like barbarians at the gate entered the shop. He observed they moved through the shop with the coolness of very frequent, very favoured customers. As he brought up the rear, Wentworth caught the tip of his umbrella on the cloak of a woman exiting. A sharp look was all he received for his apology. Inside, the warm, damp air, fragrant with the smells of spices, sugar, and coffee enveloped him. The babble of the local, genteel society burst on him like that of a jungle he'd once trekked across, a place that assaulted the senses and teemed with life, some parts of which lay ready to attack.

Suddenly, all was silent. There stood Anne Elliot.

As he moved toward her, he noticed the room growing inordinately warm and that everyone standing between them seemed to clear away to open a path. Soon, he was bowing with all the elegance of an oaken plank and imposing upon her with an insipid salutation of, "Good morning, Miss Anne." As if that were not enough, he immediately turned away from her look of surprise before she could even respond. *No, no, you bloody idiot, don't walk off!* He rebuked himself with every step. *You've searched Bath for hours looking for her! Here she is, and you retreat like a raw coward. No! Not a coward, but like the bumbling ass you've become.*

"There you are, Wentworth. Thought I'd lost you in the throng," the Admiral said. "We are over here." He pointed to the happy group gathered around a small table, giving their orders to a waiting woman.

"I shall join you presently, sir. I have seen a friend I wish to speak with."

McGillvary's eyebrow arched. "A friend, eh?" he said. "Take your time."

Anne still stood in the midst of the maelstrom. Again, the noise, movement and bodies of those between them seemed to fade away. He stood before her, silent. A faint smile came to him but he could think of nothing to say.

"You look well, Captain," she finally said. It was not much of an opening, but he could not expect that things should be made simple for him.

"Thank you, Miss Anne. I am well. And you? And your family?"

She answered in the affirmative. "The Admiral and Mrs. Croft, they are well today?" she asked. Her interest seemed genuine, but he wondered if he was merely a channel for information about them.

Answering in the affirmative, he added, "Though Bath is a very crowded place, I think even this mob is barely equal to the parties at Uppercross. Not that they were this large, but that there were so many with the Hayters and the rest." *Did that make a bit of sense,* he wondered. *And, by all means, dolt, do bring up the wretched past.* Her open smile at the comparison eased his mind a bit.

"Yes, Bath is very busy. It would seem that everyone has chosen to stop into Molland's today." She glanced around briefly and then put her full attention on him again. He, too, looked around and saw her elder sister seated at a table with another young woman, both of them making preparations to leave. He would have to be quick and try to separate Anne from the rest of her party with an offer of his arm.

"The Musgroves, I think, would like all the commotion of Bath. I heard last autumn that they were planning to come and spend some time here this winter," she said.

"Ah, well, I am sure they will enjoy themselves." Not satisfied to leave well enough alone, he continued. "And, if she comes, perhaps Louisa could take the waters. Though she is much better, I am assured."

Just then, Miss Elliot and her companion left their seats and began smoothing coats and poking at their hats in preparation for an imminent departure. Miss Elliot looked at him directly. As he prepared to bow, she looked away and then turned her back to him. *Still not good enough,* he thought. *So be it.* When he turned again to Anne, he found her red. She had obviously witnessed the snub and was sensitive enough to be embarrassed for the discourtesy. He had determined to prove her sister's cold shoulder meant nothing to him when a finely liveried servant approached and announced a carriage for the "Miss Elliots." The elder sister made such a stir it was impossible for the crowd not to know that she was the object of the declaration. The two women joined the servant and left the shop.

Turning back, he tilted his head towards the door. Surely, she was not staying just to converse with him. To be allowed to take her home was a delightful prospect, but one he could not hope for so soon upon his arrival.

"I am much obliged to you, but I am not going with them. The carriage would not accommodate so many. I walk. I prefer walking." This was no surprise. Anne's nature would seek any means to be excluded from her sister's social spectacle. He was happy to see that being amongst the fashionable of Bath had not changed her.

He glanced out the window. "But it rains."

"Oh, very little. Nothing that I regard." She smiled and then seemed awkward and looked away.

He would take the opportunity to escort her home if she would allow it. Then again, she may genuinely wish to be alone. Or, perhaps, solitude was not her real object, and she just wished to be away from him. The spinning thoughts and incessant second-guessing were becoming tiresome. He determined that it was best to build the foundation of their re-acquaintance slowly but firmly. "I came only yesterday but have equipped myself properly for Bath already, you see." He held out the new umbrella to her. "I wish you would make use of it. Though, I think it would be more prudent to let me get you a chair."

"Thank you very much, Captain, but the rain is so light and not really worth the expense of any sort of covered conveyance. Besides, I am only waiting for Mr. Elliot. He will be here in a moment, I am sure."

The mention of Elliot was an unexpected blow. The morning in Lyme came painfully back to him. The look they exchanged on the Cobb and the time she spoke to him on the stairs before going down to breakfast he recalled with bright clarity. Now, his suspicions that the fact that they were cousins would make a meeting inevitable had come to pass. The only question was whether her statement betrayed any anticipation of the cousin's arrival. or, better yet, could he hope she was disappointed at being previously engaged? The answer was not long in coming as Elliot entered the shop.

"I am sorry to have left you alone, Miss Anne. You must be bored stiff," he said as he claimed a place at his cousin's side. "I was detained at the chemist's shop. The cold preparation for Mrs. Clay took longer than expected." He glanced at Wentworth but did nothing to acknowledge his presence. "Shall we set off? The rain is unpredictable today." He offered her his arm and smiled with sunny anticipation.

Anne glanced at Wentworth and blushed, sighing as she took her cousin's arm. "Good morning to you, Captain," was all she had time to say as the man whisked her towards the door. Wentworth refused to stand like a love-struck mooncalf in the midst of the busy shop and watch her leave him behind. He turned and walked away.

The meeting of the Elliot cousins had not gone unnoticed by his group. As he joined them, his ears burned with their blithe conversation: "Mr. Elliot does not dislike his cousin, I fancy?" one of the ladies said to the other two.

"Oh, no, that is clear enough. One can guess what will happen there. He is always with them, half lives with the family, I believe. What a very good-looking man!" She glanced towards the door with an avid eye. Wentworth resisted the temptation to do the same.

"Yes, and Miss Atkinson, who dined with him once at the Wallis's, says he is the most agreeable man with whom she was ever in company."

"She is pretty, I think. Anne Elliot is very pretty when one comes to look at her. It is not the fashion to say so, but I confess I admire her more than her sister." He wondered how closely Anne's cousin looked at her. Did he notice what was so obvious to casual onlookers?

"Oh, so do I."

"And so do I," said the third. "No comparison. But the men are all wild after Miss Elliot. Anne is too delicate for them." The lady's tone was mocking and drew laughter from all the others. For a moment, Wentworth was angry that they would ridicule Anne, but considering their previous claims and listening as the conversation resumed, it was clear their derision was aimed at the arrogant Elizabeth Elliot.

~ ~ ~ ~ ~ ~ & ~ ~ ~ ~ ~ ~

"The tea is like wash water, but the coffee is good." The Admiral handed Wentworth a cup. "The ladies like the chocolate. So do I, but not in public. It gives a man an air of being a bit frail and insipid." He took a drink then stepped closer. "So, you are acquainted with the Elliot clan." Taking another drink, he looked over the rim of his cup, inviting Wentworth to confirm the statement.

"I am acquainted with both the Miss Elliots, Miss Anne more so than the other."

McGillvary nodded, a smile playing on his lips. Wentworth was not certain he liked the thoughts he assumed lay behind Patrick's cheeky expression.

"And what about the fellow? You know he's a cousin?"

"Yes, I became aware of him on a short trip to Lyme late last year."

"What do you think of him?"

"Nothing. We did not meet face-to-face then, and I have never spoken with him." McGillvary was either trying to find out about the man for his own reasons, or he was merely taking a survey of Wentworth's personal information. He added, "I did come to understand that Sir Walter, the father of Miss Elliot, and this fellow were not on good terms. That seems to have changed."

Casting a look over the ladies embroiled in more intense gossip, he said, "Ah, Frederick, my friend, you will learn that not only in the waters of Bath are miracles to be found. I have seen the social fortunes of many marvellously resurrected after submersing themselves in the company of the right hostess or wading through the proper rout. As you heard, William Walter Elliot is now a favourite at the Baronet's residence on Camden Place."

Patrick also knew something of Sir Walter, using his title without hesitation. The feelings of being put upon when first meeting McGillvary were quickly dissipating. His good friend would no doubt be a fount of information concerning anyone and everything of great or little importance in Bath. True to her prophesy, he would have to thank his sister for having insisted he take a stroll in the rain.

~ ~ ~ ~ ~ ~ ~ & ~ ~ ~ ~ ~ ~ ~

After an hour of gossip and coffee, he left McGillvary's company and returned home to Gay Street, taking the time to carefully go over the latter parts of the afternoon. Even as he shed his coat, hat, and umbrella, he was still unsure how to comprehend his meeting with Anne. He could detect no particular pleasure or unhappiness in her manner, although she seemed much more at ease than during their former, indifferent meetings together at Uppercross.

Thankfully, the Croft home kept traditional naval time and dinner was just ready when he arrived home at three. The food was generous in amount, and as he had noticed the day before, the gossip was also served in generous portions. He decided to work this to his favour and see if there was any more to know about Anne, or her cousin.

"I met Miss Anne Elliot today. A place called Molland's. Do you know it?"

"Yes, Frederick. It is one of those places one goes to watch and listen. From what I have been told, some of the choicest morsels that come out of the place are not any delicacies which Mrs. Molland creates."

Eureka! He thought. "The surroundings are certainly fine, but one could not help noticing it shares many of the same features of the common scuttlebutt." Croft particularly liked this. He then told about meeting McGillvary and how the group's main source of entertainment was commenting and speculating upon those entering or leaving the shop.

"Don't misunderstand me, I like the place," Sophia said. She did not elaborate on whether it was the cooking or the gossip she most admired. "You said you met Miss Anne. Was she looking well?"

"Very. She and her sister were there, waiting for the rain to ease."

Sophia's expression shifted quickly from friendly interest to a smiling mask of disdain. Obviously, Miss Elizabeth Elliot was not a favourite. If the Admiral was even listening, his opinion of the elder Elliot daughter was not important enough to take his mind off finishing a piece of treacle tart. Frederick smiled. Being ignored by the likes of Admiral Croft would probably aggravate the woman to the highest degree.

"And she was no doubt all smiles and polite chatter."

Not wishing the conversation to turn heated in regards to Miss Elliot's social expertise, he decided to keep her rudeness to himself. "No, we exchanged no words. Someone was waiting for her and she had to leave immediately."

The Admiral was just finishing his sweet but thought it important to add, "Luck was on your side then."

"So, once Miss Elliot left, did you and Miss Anne have a good chat?"

It amused him that his sister was, no doubt, rubbing her hands together, entertaining visions of him and Anne tucked away in a quiet corner. "Good enough. We talked about the rain and how she doesn't mind walking in it. I offered to hail her a chair, which she refused, and then her cousin arrived to take her home."

"And that is all?" Sophia asked.

"No, I then had a great time with Admiral McGillvary and his friends." He went on to tell some of the more interesting bits of gossip, enjoying the fact that he was thwarting his sister's sudden interest in his connections with Anne Elliot.

~ ~ ~ ~ ~ ~ ~ & ~ ~ ~ ~ ~ ~ ~

The sidewalks were crowded the next morning. A heavy shower in the predawn hours had left the air damp and cool, making heavy wool feel just right on the body. Men and women were walking quickly here and there in case the rain returned. Wentworth questioned if, in their hurry, any of them noticed the fresh, sweet scent that overcame even the smell of the horses pulling the numerous carriages up and down Pulteney Street.

There was no reason he should feel so positive. He could not call their meeting bad. Yet, he had no idea when they might again meet, though his sister had spoken about some social events she assured him were the sort Sir Walter and his daughters were wont to attend.

"To be sure, most of their socialising takes place in private salons, but I have seen them on rare occasions enduring the masses."

"I must say, Sophia, you are much more down on the Baronet than I remember when we were at Kellynch," he said, at the breakfast table that morning.

"You are right. There is really no reason for me to be so cross. It is just that the first thing from anyone's mouth is that we lease Kellynch

103

Hall, the family seat of the Elliots. It's like a little crier is going before us everywhere and announcing it. I can't imagine how the news has gotten around so quickly. Or why!"

"Never underestimate the swiftness of gossip on the lips of sailors with no commission to occupy them," he said.

And while that was the truth, any gossip not involving Anne Elliot was of no interest to him. He stopped for a moment to get his bearings and then headed in the direction he thought would take him to Molland's. Lost as he was in persuading himself that he had made a good impression on Anne the day before, he hoped that they might meet at Molland's again. It was a silly notion, and one that left him as soon as he saw Lady Russell in a carriage, staring directly at him.

He was not surprised that she did not acknowledge him. It would be deemed ill-mannered to be seen waving and hallooing from a carriage. Even so, a nod would not have been out of line. He was now further convinced that the more gently-bred a woman, the more likely she was to be rude to any man she did not deem suitable.

Lady Russell looked away. She appeared to be talking with someone in the carriage with her. Anne then emerged from behind her godmother and looked at him as well. The carriage passed, and all he could see were two bonnets withdrawing down the street. Suddenly, the cool sweet air was gone and the wool coat oppressive. Looking around him, there was nothing of interest to keep him on this street. He could think of nowhere else to go at the moment and continued on to Molland's.

~ ~ ~ ~ ~ ~ ~ & ~ ~ ~ ~ ~ ~ ~

The clink of china cups being placed on their matching saucers was both maddening and seductive: maddening in the randomness of the clatter and seductive in that careful listening exposed a rhythmic undercurrent that made a perfect background to the voices of the other customers.

Gad, he thought, *I'm going barmy. Benwick's philosophising has infected me.* He turned his attention to the people walking just outside the window. At times, someone looking into the shop would meet his gaze; it was then he thought he knew how fish in bowls must feel. He turned a bit away from the window and thought again of Benwick, which led to thoughts of Anne and the conversation she had with the Admiral concerning their mutual friend.

Anne's' protective comments were laudable but troublesome. There was no way around the possibility that she might have been disappointed with the news of Louisa and Benwick's engagement. *Another love affair blighted,* he thought. Were he a better man, he might feel sorry. As he did not, it was obvious he was rather small, indeed.

A tap on the window drew him back into the present, and he looked up just in time to recognise Lady Russell's man, Longwell, turning away and then crossing the street. Wentworth could not help but think the man had drawn his attention on purpose. It made no sense, unless he merely wished to ascertain his identity. If that were the case, the fellow would be scuttling back to the lady's lair to report on Wentworth's whereabouts. Was this bit of reconnoitring the first salvo in keeping him from Anne?

He left the shop and headed to Gay Street. Even the name was annoying to him just then. What was there for him to be gay about?

Chapter Eight

Thankfully, there was no one about the family rooms when he returned, and he was able to make a quiet retreat to his room. He pulled off his coat and tossed it on the bed, suddenly resenting the imposition of such a feminine setting. The flowers, the lavish drapes, the delicate, slim-limbed furniture, and crushing garden motif immediately wore on his patience. Pulling out a chair from the little tea table, he hesitated. He was not a giant of a man, but taking a seat on the slight chair would be practically the same as sitting on furniture for a child's nursery. The only place to relax was the bed.

He stretched out and enjoyed the luxury of a broad, immobile bed. Being landlocked did offer certain amenities, such as the absence of worry about falling out of a hammock in a rolling sea. But then there were the pillows. He'd never given them much thought until now. He held up a frothy confection of lace and colourful, finely woven fabric for scrutiny. A small square of cloth stuffed with feathers was what he was accustomed to, but in this den of excess, the bed was overloaded with them. He launched a small one, drenched with frills at a huge, gaudy tassel that hung from the bed's canopy. The tassel swung crazily, and he caught it, satisfied that he'd hit the mark for the third time since taking to the bed. He tossed the little missile again and returned to the idea of presenting himself at Camden Place. To what end? He would be forced to interact with the Baronet with no guarantee that Anne would be present. If she was, there would be no privacy; she might not even see any reason for privacy. A picture of them sitting together, silent and awkward, being watched by her family was highly disturbing.

That idea scrapped, he took heart that his reconnoitring had paid off. She took tea at Molland's. He could frequent the shop at regular intervals in hopes of meeting her "accidentally" again. It was a chancy proposition, and there was always the possibility she had only gone to Molland's on that particular day to please her sister or the nefarious cousin. Perhaps her usual place for refreshments was elsewhere, closer to home. He would keep Molland's in mind but would not rely on it to figure heavily in his plans.

After more thought, he also put aside any advantage her driving out with Lady Russell on Fridays might mean to him. An open, crowded street would do him no good at all. He needed to meet her in a place where she could openly acknowledge him and where they would have the opportunity to talk. The Pump Room came to mind—Sophia had said she and the Admiral often met friends there—but the results of it would be as haphazard as haunting Molland's would be.

He rose and waded through the pillows that he'd one-by-one tossed, launched, slapped, or flipped off the bed. Later he would find a place to store them out of his way. Just now, he had to find Sophia and question her about the social habits of the Elliots and their set.

~ ~ ~ ~ ~ ~ ~ & ~ ~ ~ ~ ~ ~ ~

Saturday was again spent wandering Bath. Again, the mission met with failure on almost all fronts. The only exception was that he now knew where all the major and minor attractions lay. He also knew where the better hotels, restaurants, and music venues were gathered. He'd gotten a bead on McGillvary's massive Belsom Park mansion and grounds. He had also noticed and followed the nefarious male cousin for a time. When the man met with a lobster colonel, he had gone his own way back to Gay Street. Perhaps Saturday had not been as much of a loss as he had first thought.

~ ~ ~ ~ ~ ~ ~ & ~ ~ ~ ~ ~ ~ ~

Sunday proved to be diverting. Church was dull, but several gentlemen joined the Crofts for dinner. It proved to be as entertaining a meal as he'd had in some time, although his sister was not pleased with the great wine stain that came from reworking several minor battles that had led up to the Trafalgar action. It was not the small spots that came from quickly shifting glasses out of the way of the battle lines, but the one that took up a quarter of the table when a bread plate, representing a French hulk, tried to cut down a significant part of the English fleet, represented by a nearly full bottle of a lovely dark red burgundy.

After the older gentlemen directed the conversations towards events long before his time, Frederick excused himself, collected his umbrella, and went walking again.

The previous evening Wentworth had resisted the urge to haunt Milsom Street and Molland's. The walk to Camden Place was too distant considering the setting sun and the cool evening breezes. He had taken a new street, Westgate, and had found a grimy and sad but quiet part of Bath.

It was a neighbourhood that would have been considered fine at one time. Most of the buildings would offer rooms of generous size judging from the placement of the windows. The street was not cramped and narrow as in neighbourhoods where planning depended completely upon the caprice of the builders. Unfortunately, as new areas of the city were built and those with money moved up and out, areas such as Westgate Street, notwithstanding their amenities, lost more and more of their value until they could offer little more than physical protection from the elements. That could disappear as well if the charitable feelings of the owner changed. As Wentworth admired the mature trees lining the walk, he was surprised to find Patrick McGillvary, along with a surveyor, studying one of the many run-down buildings lining the avenue.

"I may buy it, though I am not fond of being a landlord," McGillvary said after Wentworth greeted him. "The bank is forced occasionally to take one in a foreclosure, but we try to rid ourselves of it as quickly as possible. The aggravation of trying to collect the paltry rents is never equal to the expense of keeping the place from tumbling in on itself." He spoke as one who had never scrambled to make even a paltry payment. The surveyor consulted with him as the equipment was carefully packed. The two agreed to meet the next day, and then Patrick was at his leisure. The conversation was unremarkable, but it had ended with an invitation to Belsom Park for dinner the following day.

After refusing his friend's offer of a ride to Gay Street, Wentworth made to turn off Westgate Street completely when a fashionable barouche came around the corner. The gleaming, warm polish of the box and flash of the spanking new brass made the vehicle stand out remarkably from the dreary regimentation of the buildings. It was something interesting in an otherwise uninteresting walk.

McGillvary had spoken about the properties in the area and made it clear that one of the reasons he would be reluctant to buy was that most of the poorest residents made their living from various illegal and immoral means. "Between the destruction that is inevitable with fights and drunkenness, the number of fires around here is alarming. One good blaze can wipe out an entire block of these shambles in no time. Not that I begrudge a man, or particularly a woman, making a living by whatever methods they are willing to undertake, but those sorts are not precisely careful about their surroundings." This being the case, Wentworth wondered if the proud owner of an expensive carriage like this one might not be up to some mischief.

Any ill behaviour on the part of the smarter set was really none of his affair, and he was about to move on when curiosity got the better of him. He chose to blend in rather than cower and took a seat on a set of stairs a safe distance away. Even with the wide avenue, the driver's turn was too wide and the wheels on one side of the carriage jerked over the low kerb, and dropped heavily back to the street level. Something was said from inside the carriage and was answered with strong feelings by the driver. Frederick entertained visions of the fine occupants being jostled about like cats in a sack. To his further delight, the door opened and out of the carriage stepped none other than the shining likes of Mr. Elliot. Following him was Miss Elizabeth Elliot's companion from Molland's. She was obviously not wanted wherever Elliot was headed as he bid her to remain. She re-entered the carriage. It shook when she slammed the door.

"He won't like that," Frederick muttered. On cue, Elliot cried out an epithet and tapped the window sharply with his walking stick. Evidently satisfied with his set down, he went immediately to a particularly decrepit looking building.

It was only one room wide and four floors high, crammed between two larger buildings. It might have been a single house at one time, or perhaps still was, elbowing for its place amongst the shabby lugs surrounding it.

There was no hesitation as Elliot stepped up to a door with most of its black paint peeled away. He used the stick to knock. There was only a little wait. He was recognised quickly and entered.

Wentworth doubted Elliot was visiting the poor or tending the sick. After his exchange with his female friend, he doubted that Elliot knew very much about charity. An uneasy feeling kept him spying on Elliot, but good sense made him give up any notions of doing more than watching in spite of what might unfold.

~ ~ ~ ~ ~ ~ ~ & ~ ~ ~ ~ ~ ~ ~

The next day over dinner, McGillvary found Wentworth's intelligence work interesting and highly amusing. "So, the conniving little pettifogger was in there for an hour. Certainly long enough to do all sorts of despicable things." McGillvary considered the possibilities for a moment and then began to slice his beef with energy. "Though, I think him too pale and slight to have the sort of stamina required for an hour-long rendezvous."

"I doubt that was his business. There was a woman outside in the carriage."

"Oh please, Wentworth, you know some men are thrilled by the prospect of getting up to no good just outside the view of a woman. He's just the sort; believe me." He paused a moment. "But, in this case, if he was down on Westgate, he was doing business."

"What sort of business?"

"Don't know," McGillvary said. He quietly chewed and considered. "He may have heard I've been nosing around down there and decided to take a look for himself."

"He deals in real estate then?"

"Not generally. But of things legal, there's not much going on down there otherwise. No, come to think on it, Elliot enjoys dealing in smaller, more manageable items than plots of land and buildings." With a smile, Patrick twitched his brow and took a generous bite of beef.

"Is he above the law?"

"Somewhat. He's a lawyer. You know them. They can write themselves all sort of writs and statements and briefs that bind up the courts and decent people for ages. I do know there are rumours he is not the most loyal subject of the Crown. In any sort of confrontation between powers, he is not averse to profiting from both."

"You seem to know a lot about Mr. Elliot. How is that?"

"I do a little business with him, as little as possible. Enough so that in his eyes I am considered a "friend," and it keeps me safe from any chicanery he might care to pull."

"He has that sort of power?"

"He has that sort of mind. For me, he would be nothing more than a nuisance, but he's enough of one that I keep him close and make him feel safe. It is a sop that costs me very little."

"What sort of man is Elliot in his private life?"

Patrick studied him. "He's the sort of man that if you have a female relation looking his way with anything approaching admiration, you warn her off. Immediately!" He looked away for a moment and then returned to eating his meal. "And if that doesn't work, you spend as much money as necessary to get her out of town and out of his grasp."

He'd certainly not liked Elliot upon witnessing his overt admiration of Anne in Lyme. Seeing him in a position of favour with her and knowing that the family would welcome such advances, he was more than a little disturbed. Now that he had what he considered a true rendering of the man's character, he felt completely justified in interfering.

Wentworth could not help but wonder how aware of Elliot's treacherous nature Anne might be. *Very little of it,* he wagered. However, she had an innate understanding of people, and he hoped that it would warn her when it came to allowing Elliot access into her life.

"You ask about Elliot because of the woman you met in Molland's, am I right?"

"Yes."

"Do you wish to know what the gossips say about her?"

"Not really. The women in your party seemed to think well enough of her."

"Ah, you heard them. They are two of the most rugged scandalmongers in Bath. In their hands, the virtuous are heavily tinged with a whiff of disdain, but I noticed none from them on your lady's account. That bodes well for her. Now, her father is not so fortunate."

Wentworth certainly had his own opinions about the Baronet, some from the past and many from the present. Under any other circumstances, he would decline hearing what others thought, but it was always better to have too much intelligence about an enemy than too little, so he asked, "What about the Baronet?"

"He has come to Bath to retrench. It took him some years, but he managed to run through quite a lot of money in the wilds of Somerset, certainly all his wife brought to the marriage." He paused, and then said, "I hesitate to tell you everything."

"Don't be coy, McGillvary. Spill it all."

"Well, there is a rumour that even if that eldest daughter of his had an acceptable offer, there might be some embarrassment when it came time to pay out the dowry." It was clear that McGillvary had his own opinions with regard to Sir Walter. The smug look on his face at this choice bit of news was usually reserved for tales of his personal triumphs over the French.

Wentworth urged him to continue.

"It is said that the retrenchment would be more efficacious were he to remove himself from the company of people who far outstrip his ability to play the social games. Bath is an old and withering watering hole, but it is still quite expensive. He *will* have to be in all the correct places, wearing all the correct fashions, belittling all the correct people beneath him. His ability to reciprocate entertainments is limited. Camden Place is a good address but not interesting enough to impress the old guard. That means he will have to impress them with what is inside the house. It is amazing how the bills for exotic foods and private soirees can add up."

"How do you know so intimately about the Baronet's money troubles?"

"Our bank bought the paper on a loan of his through a small Somerset bank. He put up part of his estate."

"I thought it was entailed."

"To our friend, William Elliot, yes, but not all of it. There is some first-rate property attached to the estate that, for some reason, Sir Walter has chosen not to put up for sale. His debt would be reduced wonderfully if only he would."

"What do you think are the chances that the retrenchment will succeed?"

He measured Wentworth again. "Not much. My best advice to you is to marry that young woman and give her a roof that won't disappear from over her head."

"Is this what you think concerning her older sister as well?"

Patrick smiled wide. "Perhaps. What would you think of having me for a brother-in-law, Frederick?"

"I think I feel a sudden chill."

McGillvary laughed and pounded on the table. "As you should, my boy! As you should."

Chapter Nine

I am well able to get myself to the concert, Sophia. There is no need to nursemaid me as if I'm a child."

"Certainly not, Frederick, but you are new to Bath. The ferocity with which the First Set attack their entertainments is startling the first few times one engages them." She fussed with his lace and the knot of his neck cloth once more. Leaning close, she whispered, "I still find the uniform of a captain has more attraction than that of an admiral." She half smiled and put her gloved finger to her lips. They both looked at Croft, standing by the fire talking with their two guests.

Frederick lightly touched her hand and whispered back, "I shall not say a word about it, dear." Stepping away, he did the polite and, extricating himself from the little group, made his way to the door and endured another mother-henning from Harkness.

"I am perfect, man; leave it all alone."

"Aye, sir."

Wentworth had noticed when Harkness took offence—which seemed to be more often now that he was a permanent fixture as the Captain's valet—he would fall into using cant naval phrases to express the simplest irritations. As Wentworth put on his great coat, he said, "I will be late and have no need of you."

"Aye aye, sir." It was sharper, more piquant this time.

Wentworth turned to the man as he fitted his gloves and said, "Perhaps, when I get another ship, you should come to sea with me, Harkness. It will give you the opportunity to hone your seamanship and that patois you are developing."

"Thank you, sir. That is a most generous offer. But I think I should stay on land. My skills are of great benefit to the grass combers, sir."

The man is becoming quite a pip, Frederick thought. There was a bit of a shuffle between Wentworth, Harkness, and the footman, but eventually, the Captain was out the door.

For You Alone

~ ~ ~ ~ ~ ~ ~ & ~ ~ ~ ~ ~ ~ ~

The chair let him off a block from the concert hall. He welcomed the walk. As he planned his strategy, he savoured the crisp, late winter air knowing that soon enough he would be stuffed into a large but close room with many of Bath's finest. Through the alchemy of crowds, the heat produced would render the scents, so pleasing at the beginning of the evening, stifling, perhaps even sickening.

He was used to crowds now and walked around the edge of the one gathered at the entrance to the concert hall. There was the usual throng of elderly matrons airing their finery and jewels along with a strong contingent of older gentlemen of dubious strength escorting them. With the peace had come a fair number of men of both the Navy and the Army who now battled for supremacy amongst the more than average number of walking sticks and push chairs. All the jostling around obstacles and for position would call for clever manoeuvring.

He was pleased to find there was plenty of respect for the heavy gold lace of his rank, and he took advantage of the path it blazed straight through to the door where, again, the uniform brought him only a little less deference than he was accustomed to at sea. It was as he divested himself of his hat that he saw Anne.

She wore a flattering soft blue gown with a silk stole. Her hair was simply fashioned with deep blue ribbons. He especially approved of a pendant of deep blue stones and a simple gold chain that she wore around her neck. He put aside thoughts of her on his arm when he saw that her family surrounded her. He cursed his luck. To expect simplicity and ease was foolish when it came to the battle to re-establish a claim on her heart, but he would have welcomed those qualities had they been present. Tonight they were decidedly absent. So be it.

If their one face-to-face meeting was any indication, Anne would graciously acknowledge him without hesitation. If Miss Elliot was any indication, the rest of the family would look the other way. He would acknowledge Anne's efforts with as much delight as a single man was allowed in such a public way and then would stay in the stream of people flowing into the rooms for as long as possible. When he got the lay of the land in the rooms, he would set himself up in a favourable spot from which to listen and plan a further encounter during the intermission.

Suddenly, his plans were thrown completely into confusion when Anne stepped away from her family and placed herself in his path. "How do you do?" She curtsied, and when she raised her face to his, it shone and gave him to hope that his venture out to the concert, perhaps his entire his journey to Bath, would not be wasted. He bowed and then stumbled through his own, similar enquiries. The room was warm, and her unexpected, forthright acknowledgement made the temperature rise even higher.

"I am quite well and looking forward to the music. And you are well? Are the Admiral and your sister well ... as well?" She smiled at the excessive greeting.

"Very...well," he said. Such silliness was a reminder of their past when she was so much younger and he less concerned about whether he'd shipwrecked his life. He was about to elaborate when, to his shock, Sir Walter and then his daughter acknowledged him with just enough genuineness to fool a casual observer into thinking there was true respect between the parties. Wentworth would be an idiot if he thought either heart was in the act, but that was of no consequence. He had no great desire to trade more than insincere gestures with father or daughter. It was only due to an intimate understanding of self-preservation and habit that he was able to return their tokens with one of equal, nay, superior quality.

To see Anne's smile was worth any aggravation the exchange may cost him. Her sister's snub at Molland's had disturbed her. This must seem to her a sort of vindication. *Better and better*, he thought. *She believes I deserve this and wants it for me.*

The rainy weather, the various amusements available to the hardy visitor, and the concert's beguiling promises of musical enchantment were all touched upon in the conversation that followed. There was little left to say that was appropriate for the venue, but he had not come for lively debate or her opinions on the city and its music. He had come to see her and make her understand his presence in Bath was solely for her alone. This being the case, it was time to clear the decks and begin to deal with the most unpleasant topic he could imagine.

"I have hardly seen you since our day at Lyme. I am afraid you must have suffered from the shock, and the more from its not overpowering you at the time." There, he put it out there and was surprised to see her smile rather than turn thoughtful as he expected.

"It was shocking at first, to be sure, but that dissipated as the situation began to right itself. Once we knew she would recover, there was little reason to be always downcast." These were sensible words, words that he had heard repeatedly in the Harville household and repeatedly ignored.

"It was a frightful hour," he said, "a frightful day!" He passed his hand quickly over his brow, hoping to forestall the perspiration he felt now that he was engaged upon discovering Anne's feelings on all that had happened in Lyme. Without naming Louisa Musgrove, he commented on the unanticipated results of sending Benwick for the surgeon.

Anne's face glowed with a smile as she acknowledged her surprise and her hope for their happiness.

He blathered on for a moment about the couple, and then, to his horror, he heard himself saying, "*They* have no difficulties to contend with at home, no opposition, caprice, or delays." And it only got worse from there. "The Musgroves are behaving like themselves, most honourably and kindly, only anxious to promote their daughter's comfort. All this is much, very much in favour of their happiness; more than perhaps—"

He was finally able to control his tongue only after making her blush and look away from him. No doubt, she had taken it as a thinly veiled accusation of her and her family's behaviour in the past. He must do or say whatever necessary to make amends. *The best tack,* he thought, *is to the lee side.*

"I confess that I do think there is a disparity, too great a disparity, and in a point no less essential than of mind. I regard Louisa Musgrove as a very amiable, sweet-tempered girl, and not deficient in understanding, but Benwick is something more. He is a clever man, a reading man; and I confess that I do consider his attachment to her with some surprise. Had it been the effect of gratitude, had he learnt to love her because he believed she preferred him, it would have been another thing. But I have no reason to suppose it so. It seems, on the contrary, to have been a perfectly spontaneous, untaught feeling on his side, and this surprises me. A man like him, in his situation, with a heart pierced, wounded, almost broken! Fanny Harville was a very superior creature, and his attachment to her was indeed devotion. A man does not recover from such a devotion of the heart to such a woman! He ought not; he does not."

The last bit had been delivered too sharply, with too much force. Anne's discontent was obvious. She breathed more quickly and looked about as though she wished to escape. But rather than make excuses and return to her waiting family, she paused and then asked what occupied him while he was in Lyme. He did his best to make what amounted to avoiding his responsibility sound like a holiday by the sea.

"I should very much like to see Lyme again," Anne said. If he was not mistaken, there was wistfulness in her voice that made him believe the feeling was authentic.

He uttered his surprise. "I should have thought your last impressions of Lyme must have been that of strong disgust." There was nothing in her expression to make him think that he was either correct in his estimation or that he had changed her mind in any way.

"The last hours were certainly very painful," she said, "but when pain is over, the remembrance of it often becomes a pleasure. One does not love a place the less for having suffered in it, unless it has been all suffering, nothing but suffering—"

Her words from there faded away. "One does not love a place less for having suffered in it." He knew that to be true. Were it not, no man could endure sailing the seas on ships that encompassed such pain, illness, death, and loss of humanity. But they did. Men did and they thrived because of it. He was the perfect example. Perhaps the principle could be applied to people as well. Perhaps she would agree that a person might not lose all love for another because they had suffered by them. As he had recently come to understand, he had not lost any of his love for her though he had suffered under her withdrawal from him. He could only hope this was her way of telling him that she, too, felt the same even after his former anger and his more recent conduct.

Suddenly, the noise of the crowd rose and drowned out everything she said. Before he looked to see what was causing the clamour, he gazed at her and was heartened to find her smiling and even a bit pink. The crowd separated them, and she moved back to her original place. The hubbub telegraphed the arrival of the patroness for the evening.

She was a middle-aged matron accompanied by a young woman. *A daughter or niece perhaps?* To his dismay, the nefarious Elliot cousin and a ranking lobster he'd seen a time or two around town, accompanied them. There was no place for Wentworth, so he allowed himself to be sluiced into the concert room with the rest of the human tide.

A quick survey of the room led him to a group of men that included McGillvary standing near a door on the far side. The Admiral seemed glad to see him and made introductions all around. The gentlemen were talking business, which held no interest for Wentworth. He positioned himself to view the newcomers to the room as he congratulated himself on the cache of goodwill he had built with Anne. With the elapse of only a few minutes, he saw her enter the concert room with her family and their exalted party.

All the goodwill crumbled away when he saw she was with her god-mother. The sight of Lady Russell always struck him with something akin to fear rather than the mere distaste engendered by Sir Walter and Miss Elliot. Why should he fear the old she-dragon? Aside from her ability to influence Anne, she no longer possessed social weapons powerful enough to ward him away. Her influence with Anne, nonetheless, could be everything. Suddenly, his musings on Lady Russell were cut short by the lobster. He made a show of speaking with the older woman patroness and escorted her to her seat. This left Mr. Elliot—where has he been?— to accost Anne and impose upon her his playing at the attentive gentleman. When the party was finally arranged, he discovered Anne and the cousin were side-by-side on the first of two

117

benches the group occupied, and Lady Russell was relegated to the second. Wentworth was happy to see Anne separated from her, but it came at a demmed high price.

Music filled the air and some of the lamps were dimmed. He noticed the gentlemen surrounding him lowered their voices but did not completely quit their discussion. It seemed that talk during the performance was not limited to unattached men standing on the fringes of the room. Many among those seated were chatting occasionally, flirting outrageously, or earnestly thrashing out matters that may or may not have related to the concert. Anne was not one of these. She sat quietly, smiling in a way that seemed completely unconnected to the room, its activities, or its occupants. Unconnected to him as well, it seemed.

"So, I didn't know you were a music aficionado," Patrick said, nudging him back from his reverie. "Not that this is all that good. This is some protégé of the hideously sparkling creature over there, two seats in on the fifth row." He indicated the older woman seated next to Sir Walter. "A dowager with more pretension than taste, I'd say." Someone drew the Admiral's attention away before Frederick could respond. He cared little what the Dowager had in mind when she arranged the concert; his only concern was how it could be used to further his aims in relation to Anne.

An Italian song began and there was a buzz from the audience and from the gentlemen of the group. McGillvary informed him that the song was scandalous and no Englishman of decent breeding would either sing it or listen to it sung.

"I was not aware that you are fluent," Wentworth said.

"Oh yes, thanks to step-mama. Father got the fool notion that I should speak to her in her native tongue, and so a tutor was pressed into service—swarthy arms and stinking of garlic—and I began my linguistic education. Thank God, Ronan can at least speak good King's English, not that anything he might prate on about is worth its weight in tripe, mind."

Wentworth inwardly laughed at the observations about McGillvary's little seen and little missed half-brother. "I only know enough Italian to bargain for stores or free a crewman from gaol," he said.

"It is amusing to see how many normally upright patrons of the arts find this swill so entertaining. Ignorance of detestable things right under your nose can make life *so* enjoyable. I do crave it occasionally."

As Wentworth pondered this, the cousin began a conversation with Anne that continued for the duration of the song. She turned frequently away from his view and towards Elliot to respond. A program fluttered between them often enough that he could not see much of her expression. He wondered if one or the other of them was fluent in Italian and was mischievously sharing the true meaning of the piece. If McGillvary was correct about the song, a couple even speaking of it might indicate a developed intimacy.

"That looks like one of those domestic discussions that never end well for the man," Patrick said, again inserting himself into Wentworth's private observations. "That is the lady you spoke to in Molland's; is it not?"

"Yes, Miss Anne Elliot."

"Ah, yes, the sister of the inestimable Miss Elizabeth Elliot."

"You are acquainted with older sister?"

"No. I would very much like to be, but so far, she has eluded me." He looked at the group, then added, "Truth be told, we do not swim in the same social waters. By my choice," he added quickly. Wentworth concluded from his tone that McGillvary, for the sake of meeting Miss Elliot, might give the murky waters a try if given the opportunity.

"You would freeze in less than five strokes."

"So I'm told. But think of the fun if I survive."

Patrick was again pulled into another conversation, and Wentworth noticed Anne's expression had grown serious. The conversation's light tone had changed. She looked quite puzzled, and Elliot smiled in a mysterious way. They talked back and forth for a moment or two more; then, she looked over her shoulder to her father.

To Wentworth's dismay, all the gentlemen who had been making up his blind had gradually moved away. He was now exposed to the likes of Sir Walter Elliot, who was speaking and nodding in his direction. Hoping to deprive them of a full view, Wentworth turned towards the front of the room and pretended to listen intently to the salacious song. Energetically ignoring the stares, he recognised a few of the words. He could not help smiling, wondering what the swells might think if they grasped the song's true meaning.

"So, you have gotten the attention of the girl's father. How did you manage that?" McGillvary was at his side a third time. "This is the sort of entertainment the fellow should avoid. The rig he's wearing is the latest cut, and I'm sure that if Daddy has new, so do the daughters. A new obligation or two will be made when they are invited to dine with someone or other afterwards."

"Is there anyone in this room you do not know something … embarrassing about?"

He smiled and looked Wentworth up and down. "You, for the most part. But, I assure you, I only use what I know to protect myself in business. It's good to be certain who to avoid and on whom you can depend in a tight spot."

The sentiment was true enough, and while he was not quite prepared to depend upon McGillvary in any substantial way, he was ready to mine some of his information when it came to the Elliot's cousin.

"It looks like this song is about at an end, sir, shall we step out for some refreshment? I shall buy," he said, indicating McGillvary should lead the way.

Manoeuvring through the crush was difficult but not impossible for two men skilled in such things. Everyone from Anne's party had left the concert room except Anne. For a moment, Wentworth considered leaving McGillvary and going back in to see if he might gain some position, but now that they were out of the room, it was too tempting to stay.

Elliot and the lobster had cooperated wonderfully, placing themselves directly behind Frederick and McGillvary. It may have had something to do with McGillvary waving them over so that he might make introductions. "Know thy enemy, Captain," he had whispered. Acknowledgements were made and now Wentworth knew the lobster to be Colonel Matthew Wallis. He also got a better look at William Walter Elliot.

After a few words regarding business were exhausted, the colonel and Elliot turned away to their own affairs. With this, McGillvary excused himself to get some fresh air, and Wentworth was free to eavesdrop on the others.

"I told you to leave the tactic to me and that I would get you the perfect seat. Make any headway?" It was Wallis speaking.

"A bit. I was hoping she would translate that dreadful song word-for-word, but she is too much a lady and far too clever to bumble into such an awkward situation. She did very well, I must say."

"Was it really so bad?"

"As bad as anything your men might sing in the evening around the fire."

"Bad enough, to be sure, then."

"I complimented her nicely and then begged her to help me to improve my poor Italian. She was quite willing to lend whatever assistance I might require." Both men laughed. Wentworth seethed.

"This is serious! You hate being perceived as ignorant. Having to pretend that you don't know the language…this will be interesting."

"It will only be for a visit or two. The rest of the household will be bored silly by it all and make any number of excuses to escape. That will leave me free to visit with my dear Anne."

"What about the mourning for your *dear wife*, Elliot?"

"Only five more months. Surely you do not think that every wedding that takes place a fortnight after the removal of the crepe is due to a

120

sudden surge of love, do you? She is an intelligent woman and will be more than ready by the time–" They were jostled by a group returning to the concert room, and Wentworth lost his advantageous position.

Wentworth wandered away from the refreshments, the confidence from his encounter with Anne now coming undone. The sight of the whole of her party gathered together was now as good as seeing into Anne's future life. He paced along the back wall of the room, but as he did so, he kept an eye on Anne. She seemed to be moving from place to place on the bench until finally she came to a stop one seat in from the end. As he was about to walk over to her, the Dowager and Sir Walter passed by him to regain their seats. A second acknowledgement from the Baronet did nothing to bolster Wentworth's confidence.

In an interesting turn of events, the colonel seemed to beg off and join another officer in another section of seats. Miss Elliot and the young woman attached to the Dowager snagged Mr. Elliot's attention. Wentworth took pleasure in noting his sour expression when he looked in Anne's direction, but he took a seat with the young ladies. Now that the dust had settled, Anne was free of companions and the complications that they brought. *Patrick is right, go straight at it, man.* He moved the few more steps necessary to put him within reach of her.

"Good evening, again, Miss Anne."

Her smile was worth the exertion. "Good evening again to you, Captain. I know you like music; is the concert performance up to your expectations?"

"Not at all. I am, in fact, quite disappointed in the singing in particular. I shall not be sorry for it to end." As he spoke, little by little her expression dulled. He railed at himself for not thinking up some clever little lies pertaining to the music beforehand.

"I am sorry to hear that, sir. It is disappointing to look forward to an event and have it fall short. But, I think there are many who have enjoyed the surprises that the program has thus far offered."

He understood her meaning immediately and thought she hadn't looked this innocent since the day she was born–clever thing! He was glad to share the joke.

"Yes, my companions said it was rather … suggestive. I smoked out a word or two that were suspicious, but I am not proficient enough to fully understand the complexities of the song."

"It was not, to be honest, very complex at all." Anne smiled and looked away, but not before he saw her cheeks bloom with colour.

He cleared his throat, and she looked up to him again. "I suppose relationships between men and women are not actually that complicated in most cases." He had no idea where the conversation might lead; all he cared to do was engage her in the same light manner that marked their earlier talk.

"Miss, are the seats next to you taken?" a gentleman interrupted, looking from Anne to Wentworth. Before Anne could answer, the woman with him pointed to seats she liked better. The man bowed to them and moved on. *Idiot! Take the seat before it's taken from you and finish the evening in the best of company.*

He was about to join her when a well-groomed hand came to rest on her shoulder.

"Excuse me, dear Cousin," She turned to Mr. Elliot, whose expression, to Wentworth's jaundiced eye, was a cross between a lost little boy and a ravenous wolf. "Miss Carteret is anxious to know what we will hear next." He said some other things, but the blood pounding in the Captain's ears prevented him hearing any more.

The familiarity of the man, the manner in which he touched her and spoke to her, made it obvious their intimacy was established, firmly established. At the cousin's call, Anne had swept Wentworth aside to do as was bid her. There was dutiful compliance on her part and presumption on his. Earlier in the evening, it had been the confidence of an engagement that had enabled her to present herself in public and speak so freely to him. It was that engagement now that drew her so effectively away.

Suddenly, he was exhausted with the charade: hers that had raised his hopes and his own at playing the fool. If only he had discovered his own true feelings sooner or had not allowed pride to blind him in the first place this evening would be very much different. His thoughts and mood were too black for him to remain in her presence or that of the man she had clearly chosen. He would toss off a pleasant farewell and end the comedy.

Just as he was about to bid her good evening, she turned. The musicians were starting and her face became all smiles and pleasantness. Were he not convinced of her feeling towards Elliot, he might think she genuinely wished for his company. "You will excuse me, Miss Anne. I must wish you a good night. I must leave and get home as soon as possible."

She looked disappointed for a moment and as he began to bow, she asked, "Is not this song worth your staying for?"

If he had an inkling that the smile was out of true affection for him, he might stay and take the seat that had held a moment's promise. But he was sure it was habitual politeness that dictated the gentle protest at his departure. "No, there is nothing worth my staying for," he said. As he turned, he saw Elliot giving him a nod and jaunty salute.

To compound the agony, just a few seats over he spied Lady Russell just looking away and beginning to speak to the Baronet. Her expression was light and smiling. He paused for just an instant, briefly toying with a perverse impulse to remain and toss the snake of his presence in the pair's satisfied musical garden, but his weariness overcame his audacity. He left.

Chapter Ten

The tide of music lovers returning to the concert room for the second act was against him. Just as he was about to step into an alcove and allow the current to weaken, McGillvary joined him. "Shall we be gone, Wentworth. The music is tedious and the room is becoming quite oppressive." His expression was like stone, his tone barely civil. He tapped the face of his watch and then let it drop.

The Admiral's obvious intention to flee the hall put him and Frederick in a compact of the minority, bolstering Wentworth's sense of ill use and misconstruction. "Certainly, sir. Lead the way." Again, the colour and rank of the men's gleaming uniforms worked their magic and soon they were collecting their great coats from the attendant in the cloak room—who was much obliged for the very generous tip—and heading to McGillvary's carriage that had evidently been circling the block for some time.

~ ~ ~ ~ ~ ~ ~ & ~ ~ ~ ~ ~ ~ ~

"Thank you for the ride, my friend."

"No thanks necessary. My plans were being thwarted on every side anywise. Offering a service to a friend seemed the least I could do."

"And what, precisely, were your plans."

"They involved meeting Miss Elizabeth Elliot. When I slipped out during the interval, I found her in the hallway. I was pleased to find that she had had a disaster involving the laces of her right shoe. I offered her assistance. She took it but then set out to torment me by refusing to allow me to introduce myself. I decided to play the game only because I'd found a chap who knows the family and was willing to help me manoeuvre her into a position where she could not refuse me." Gesturing with a decanter from which he poured a lovely tawny liquid, he said, "But that weasel, William Elliot, got between us and made himself at home next to her."

124

Wentworth thought it best to keep to himself that Elliot was not the one who had ruined Patrick's plans and was about to reiterate his earlier observations about the woman's coldness; but he thought better of it. McGillvary was a grown man, quite capable of surviving his own tremendous blunders without the aid of a nursemaid.

"I am shocked that you would give up so easily."

"I did not notice you drawing your weapon and putting the little bugger in his place," the Admiral said, handing him a glass of whiskey. He poured just a tot of water in to cause the flavour to bloom.

"You saw that."

"Yes, I did. It seems that both of us have been beaten back by that miserable, under hung, silk-breeched fop. Here's to battling another day." With that, he raised his glass slightly and took the contents in one gulp. "Great stuff," he said, holding the glass to the light and watching the amber rivulets work their way down the glass. "Another?"

"No, this will do for now."

Patrick shrugged and refilled his glass. He took a seat and motioned that Wentworth should do the same.

Frederick had desired to return to Gay Street and lick his wounds, but McGillvary had sensed as much and cajoled him into joining him at Belsom Park for a late dinner. The kitchen at the Park was standing at the ready, for the meal was laid in no time. Wentworth discovered an appetite and enjoyed himself as they talked of younger days and entertaining times when they had the permission of the Crown to chase and break as they saw fit, taking whatever they believed would turn them a profit.

It wasn't until Patrick spilled his wine into his lemon shrub that he noticed how much his friend had drunk with dinner. Frederick was surprised that he had drunk so little, considering his disappointment at the concert. Now that they were in the library, and Patrick had brought out the very good liquor, he was glad of his unintentional moderation. He watched a third glass of the whiskey being prepared and again bit back a warning.

"Your Miss Anne Elliot is a lovely young woman. How did you come to know her?"

He hesitated to confide in McGillvary on this matter. Despite the seeming innocence of the question, the man's bearing was growing more antagonistic with each drink. Wentworth was more than willing to fend off any sort of ridicule or attack directed at him, but he would not allow Patrick to abuse Anne's character to his face. It would be a shame if he were forced to cut out one of his few allies in Bath.

"We met years ago in Somerset. Just after Domingo."

"Ah, so that's where some of that not insignificant prize money went. I always wondered why you crawled back to Portsmouth so broke."

Frederick shook his head. "No, to my shame, none of it was spent on her. I'd already used up most of it by the time I landed on my brother's doorstep. To my surprise, she was willing to take me penniless...for a while at least."

"Marriage?"

He nodded.

Patrick smiled and leaned deeper into his chair. "And here I'd thought you were just a solitary animal. All the while you've carried the torch for a pretty country miss. Why did she go off you?"

"Things just wore out between us."

He shook his head. "Probably for the best. If the feelings can't sustain themselves in the ease of being ashore, they surely won't last through more than a commission or two. Gentle women are susceptible to that more than most, I think. They are like mice, most of them. Just one good-sized cat in opposition and they run squeaking away."

This childish characterisation of Anne angered him until he realised that, childish though it was, it was almost exactly how he'd viewed her all these years. He credited himself with a bit more sympathy in his mental depictions, but Patrick's down-to-earth picture was most apt.

"Little brown mice. Harmless looking until they have nibbled through all your moorings and left you completely undone—"

"Have you figured out another plan to meet Miss Elizabeth Elliot?" He could not hear his friend go on; the accusations were directed at him as much as at Anne. Miss Elliot seemed to be the only topic that might distract him. It was worth a try and, perhaps, worth a listen.

"I suppose I shall meet her eventually. Bath is much like the Navy, small and everyone eventually finds themselves connected to everyone else. Because a woman such as your Annie—"

"Don't call her that. Please." He could not stand the thought of McGillvary, feeling as he did about Anne, calling her the endearment Frederick longed to use.

"Your Miss Anne Elliot," McGillvary said, lifting his glass in a mock toast. "Anywise, they live behind the eyes, dear boy. They live so much in their brains that you can never possibly know all the machinations and thoughts and dreams and desires that go on up there. And you will likely never be enough to satisfy her mind. Or satisfy her in numerous other ways, either."

Frederick had known his friend was not happy in his marriage. When McGillvary's wife, Claire, had died years before, there was little of Patrick's behaviour that had changed. He'd not been faithful to their vows in life; grief held no spell over him, either. If he stayed much longer, he feared he would know more about the failure of the marriage than he cared to know.

"No, they are all smiles when in your presence. Nothing is ever amiss; they endure bravely, never saying a word that might let you know they are unhappy. I should have known, though. After each commission it took longer and longer for us to become...reacquainted. I suspected nothing until after our daughter was born and returned to find that Claire had become a patroness of the arts." McGillvary kicked off his pumps and slouched in an armchair. The wool of his breeches slipped a bit against the glossy red leather. Wentworth held his breath for a moment, concerned that Patrick would fall to the floor, but his friend was still sober enough to right himself and continue philosophising. "The last fellow she was patronising was a poet—a very young poet. The rascal showed up at the funeral. He sat in the backbenches and sobbed into a huge blue handkerchief; I saw it as I was leaving. The sniffing echoed through the church. And there I was, ramrod straight in the front pew, shedding not a tear."

He had been talking in the general direction of his feet but now looked straight at Wentworth. "Whom do you think everyone pitied? Which of us presented the perfect picture of a man mourning the woman he loved?"

"But you were her husband. Surely, no one faulted you, and no one denied you the consolation you deserved."

McGillvary began to laugh. He laughed very hard, at one point slapping the arms of the chair. "You are such an idealist. No, no, you are a Romantic through and through."

There was that damnable notion again. It had come from all directions and from various sorts of men. Wentworth grew warm, not at the suggestion of it but at the idea that one day he might have to come to grips with it being true. To lure Patrick away from his hilarious opinion, Wentworth asked why he thought that Miss Elizabeth Elliot would be much better as a wife.

"It is quite simple. Women like Miss Lizzie Elliot measure everything by its presumed value. The more places to the left of the decimal in the price of any gift, the more heartfelt and meaningful. They are highly practical and never sentimental. The arithmetic is quite simple, my friend. Being given things and being taken places in which to show them off mean happiness. If they are sad, refer to the previous and voila! Everything is all better."

There would be nothing gained trying to refute Patrick's logic, for it was flawless except that it applied only to some women, not all. Knowing Patrick's opinion of the likes of Anne and Claire, Wentworth forgave him his sweeping accusation and felt he understood his friend's amoral behaviour better now.

"They are like a maze, you know. They keep you going round and round, down blind alleyways and retracing your steps endlessly. All for what? To reach the centre and be devoured or to be put aside by spotty-faced poets with big blue hankies."

The Admiral was not passed out, but was not far from it. Wentworth rang for the butler. As he waited for the man, he watched the rain pelt the window glass. In his mind, he resolved to see her again.

"Yes, sir?" the butler asked.

"I am off. Call his man. He's done for the night."

"Yes, sir. The Admiral said to make his carriage available to you. It is waiting out front."

That was Patrick. He always knew himself and always planned accordingly.

~ ~ ~ ~ ~ ~ ~ & ~ ~ ~ ~ ~ ~ ~

Rain was sheeting down causing progress to Gay Street to be protracted. There was more traffic than any sensible person might expect on such a dirty night. *Not only did the denizens of Bath attack their entertainments with ferocity,* he thought, *they are quite willing to risk life and limb as well.* A party letting out from a large, private residence had ground any forward movement to a halt. Wentworth's amusement at watching the hunched figures dodging around the carriages, puddles, and each other wore off quickly.

He wondered how Anne would be getting home. She had arrived apart from Lady Russell but might have plans to leave with her. Worse yet, she might have plans to allow Mr. Elliot to take her to Camden Place in his fine new barouche. This thought was dangerous and caused even more havoc in his tense and disappointed emotions. As the thoughts were his to command, he immediately installed Sir Walter and Miss Elliot into the carriage as well. Unfortunately, both disappeared nearly as quickly as they took their places, leaving Anne and her cousin, sitting side-by-side, enjoying the comfort of the finely appointed seats.

"The bricks feel wonderful, Cousin."

"Yes, I'm sure they do. Ladies slippers are so thin and the sidewalks are freezing cold. Here," Elliot said as he reached across and pulled the curtain closed. "The thick brocade will keep out the chill from the windows. Is that lap robe enough, or do you need another?"

"This is fine, thank you. You certainly spared no expense in outfitting your carriage," she said.

"Why should I? I have the money. And it is my hope one day to have a wife who appreciates the finest things in life." Elliot reached down and pulled a small hamper into his lap. "I took the liberty of seeing to a late dinner. I hope you don't mind, Anne." He opened the lid.

"You must have been confident that I would accept your offer to take me home...and confident that Father would allow it." She took a breath. "Your little repast smells delicious. I must admit that you seem to know me very well."

"Cousin, you are a true gentlewoman of grace and beauty. Only a complete imbecile could misunderstand you." They studied one another for a long moment. Elliot broke the spell by turning his attention to the hamper. "You must taste some of this smoked quail." He held up a tiny leg. She reached to take it, but he moved it out of her grasp. "No, I shall hold it for you."

Anne delicately nibbled at the tiny leg. She smiled in approval. "It is delicious."

When she'd finished, Elliot carefully wiped his hands and said, "I think you will like this as well." He uncovered a small crock of pungent, creamy cheese. "You must never tell."

She sniffed it. Her eyes opened wide. "It is French, surely."

"Surely," he said, taking a knife to spread it. "Tell me about Wentworth. That was the name of the fellow at the concert?"

"Yes, Captain Frederick Wentworth. An old acquaintance."

"You must have known him when he was a more amiable fellow. I found him to be rather disagreeable and not very appreciative when it comes to music."

Anne took a little round of bread with a minute wedge of cheese perched on it. "Let us not speak of him or his ill-mannered ways. I spoke to him only out of politeness. He looked so out of place when he arrived."

"That is another mark of your superior character, my dear Cousin, gracious even to the undeserving." He offered her a slice of an orange. "They are Spanish and bitter, of course, but a real treat this time of year. And then, we have wine." He held up a bottle. "The white is appropriate. Dry and refreshing to the palate." He then lifted another. "But, as we are taking liberties this evening, perhaps we should be wild and try this red." Elliot did not wait for an answer, opening the second bottle immediately.

They each took a drink and discussed its many pleasing qualities. After the bottle was nearly finished, Elliot corked the rest and took Anne's glass. He leaned against the seat, facing as much towards her as possible. She followed suit.

"Anne, I have to tell you something. Though I am still in mourning for my dear, late wife, I already know that her love spoiled me terribly and that when my time is ended, I want to be quickly married again."

She sat up. "This is wrong to speak of, Cousin. Not now. Not yet."

He sat up besides her. "Anne, please hear me." He was silent and merely looked at her. Anne looked away, but he touched her chin and gently pulled her back facing him. *"I desire a woman's touch again. I desire..."* Elliot merely *stared.*

"What is it?" she asked.

"The wine has tinged your beautiful lips the tiniest bit. They are lovelier than ever..." His voice faded and he moved closer.

Thankfully, the carriage jerked. Wentworth's preposterous fantasy ended and he was headed to Gay Street once more.

~ ~ ~ ~ ~ ~ & ~ ~ ~ ~ ~ ~ ~

The night was miserably spent tossing and turning, endeavouring at first to outrun a dream featuring Anne and her cousin. They approached him, smiling, arm-in-arm, and begged him to join them at the church, for it was their wedding day. The pews were far from full and occupied only with her family, but wherever he tried to sit, he was refused and told roughly to "push off." The ceremony was beginning and his dream self was becoming overwrought when an unseen hand gave him a shove. He found himself leaning against a wall to the side and rear of the chapel. From this distant vantage, he was forced to watch as the couple exchanged vows. As a long, postnuptial kiss was blatantly played out before all those in attendance, the scene madly shifted to a hazy, chaotic wedding feast. Again, he was excluded by the guests and forced away from the main body of events, straining to observe from afar. Another abrupt shift brought him into the centre of everything. In this new and unfamiliar situation, contorted and contemptuous faces, some very familiar and others completely unconnected to Anne, surrounded him. An unseen someone roughly put a glass of sparkling champagne into his hand. He was commanded to make a heart-felt toast to the health and prosperity of the bride and groom by a threatening voice in his ear. As he raised the glass, he woke with a start and was relieved to find nothing more menacing nearby than the flowery, lace-trimmed bed curtain he was grasping.

In another fine frenzy of a nightmare, Anne was by his side. They were in the room where the concert had been held. They were alone, but Italian music loudly filled the space. She was dressed as she had been at the concert, and she smiled brightly at him. Her gloved hand touched his arm, and they drew close together. She spoke very softly to him. "I wish to name them all after you, Frederick, even the girls. For, had I not broken our engagement, I would not have been free to be joined to the man who truly loves me." Before he could answer, she handed him a squirming bundle to add to the armful he was now juggling. To his consternation, the swaddled wads were chirping. He soon realised their little voices were calling his name. Anne kept smiling and thanking him; the bundles increased in numbers and began to reduce in size. They continued to multiply and shrink. He was embarrassed to find that he could not hold them all. His efforts to gather them were useless, and eventually, they all fell to the ground and rolled away. Anne was nowhere to be seen, the music was louder than ever and he was left to face his own uselessness.

~ ~ ~ ~ ~ ~ & ~ ~ ~ ~ ~ ~ ~

The clock struck seven. A maid had come at five to build the fire. Harkness had stuck his head in to inquire about the Captain's breakfast preferences and was told to go about his business. By this time, Wentworth had thought through the entire previous evening and the hideously bizarre night several times.

The dreams were particularly rich for consideration. Which of the elements disturbed him most was unclear. Was it Anne's gladness at being permanently and so fruitfully attached to Elliot? Or, perhaps it was her desire to use Wentworth's name. He chose to forego investigating what the meaning might be of shrinking babies, but he owned that watching himself bungle such a responsibility was the cause of a good deal of the agitation he felt. Finally, he became tired of the mental maze and resolved to discount the dreams entirely and began to concentrate on the facts as he knew them.

Anne had, in the past week, taken it upon herself to step forward in two very public places and speak with him. In both cases this was done in the sight of members of her family. In particular, at the concert she had seized the opportunity and engaged him in more than just polite, indifferent conversation. Considering the social climate of Bath and the appetite for gossip of its residents, such actions would be marked in the minds of anyone who had observed them, especially her particular acquaintances.

When she spoke to him in Molland's, it was only the appearance of her cousin Mr. Elliot that cut the exchange short. The arrival of the evening's patroness had done the work at the concert. He could only speculate that, left up to Anne, they would have spent much more time together. Not to be forgotten as well was the grudging acknowledgement of the Baronet and Miss Elliot.

Anne harboured friendly feelings towards him, of that there was no question. But was there more for him? He then considered Lady Russell and what part she might have to play. The woman had certainly made her opinion known. Her intense look on Friday and her stares at the concert were enough to let him know she was not pleased with his presence in Bath. Nevertheless, how much did Lady Russell still influence Anne? The fact that Anne talked to him during the concert's intermission, under the very nose of the woman, suggested some independence.

He believed himself intelligent and intuitive enough to understand the motives of most people. His life and fortune depended upon understanding his enemies. In such a case, he acknowledged, he was analysing a man like himself, bent on winning by the basest and simplest means known—combat. With enough men, enough lead, and enough brains, a victory was almost assured. The only worries were the caprice of the weather and foul luck. When it came to love, there were only two combatants, and the others involved mattered only in their importance to the participants. Weaponry was not a factor, and intelligence seemed to count for little. He must change his strategy.

This was not a battle of armies; it was hand-to-hand combat. It was all about keeping your wits about you as you concentrated on the actions of your opponent or, in this case, the object of your affection. Everything came down to watching and waiting for the proper opportunity and crushing anyone who might try and draw you off. In his case, the distraction was Mr. William Walter Elliot.

In the stillness of the room, as he finished off the knot of his neck cloth, the heir to the Kellynch estate seemed suddenly present. His intimate contact with the family was undeniable. It was senseless to compare the evening's grudging notice of Sir Walter to the place Elliot held. At this thought, a charge went through him as though he'd been struck by lightning. Anne was *not* her family.

She was scrupulous to show proper respect to her father and godmother, even when it worked against her own interests as it had in '06. To her extended family, the Musgroves, she was respectful and kind. She possessed a natural sincerity. For that reason she disliked games, be they for entertainment or advancement.

"I have little natural talent for them," she had told him when he tried to teach her to play a new card game. "If I am to expend this much mental energy, I prefer it to be in a good debate, or at least an interesting conversation, not trying to trick my opponent into believing I hold the highest cards."

"It is not trickery. It's strategy," he had insisted.

"Call it what you like. My winning is still dependent upon hoaxing you into thinking something which may or may not be true." She had soldiered on to the end of the hand, but there was no enjoyment in it for her. It was only her innate kindness that made her agree to play with him at other times that summer.

No, Anne Elliot played no games. What he had perceived at Uppercross as indifference was merely the reflection of the chill of his own cool lack of interest. Her warmth now was as genuine as it ever was and indicative, perhaps, of something more substantial.

With this realization came others, fast upon its heel. The gossips in Bath had William Elliot marrying Anne Elliot as soon as his mourning period was done. The man himself was of that mind from what he had overheard at the concert. Who was there to deny it on Anne's behalf? A loving father would be the most likely person. Unfortunately, for Anne no such person was available. It was in the Baronet's best interest to keep the Elliot name in the social swirl, and he was not likely to contradict news of an engagement even if he knew it to be false. As for Elliot himself, why would he deny such a thing? To be connected with a woman of Anne's rank was to promote his own standing. This assured that he would do nothing to stop the chattering masses.

The only people who knew the truth of the matter were Anne and William Elliot. To this point, Anne's behaviour left enough doubt that she was attached to Elliot in any irrevocable way. Until he heard the words, "Why yes, I am engaged to him," from her lips, he would give no credence to the rumours.

Chapter Eleven

L ife on Gay Street was quiet all Wednesday. Frederick's soul was restive and physical exertion in the form of walks and pacing did little to alleviate the circumstance. On Thursday he did the same, pacing the floor until his sister's complaints drove him into the rain, where he tirelessly watched for anyone from Camden Place that might be out. Having exhausted the fashionable haunts of the city, his feet turned to those less favoured. It was as he traversed Westgate Street that he was more than a little surprised to see Anne's godmother deposit Anne onto the street. He was further astonished to observe her make her way confidently to the door with the horribly peeling paint visited by her cousin the week before. When the door opened, she smiled and spoke to the person admitting her. He watched until it was closed behind her, and then he looked around to see if he'd failed to notice Elliot's carriage. It was nowhere along the street.

That the cousins shared an acquaintance with the same person residing in the Westgate Building was too much of a coincidence to be believed. This fantastical twist of fate could only be surpassed by them each knowing separate individuals and their visits having absolutely nothing in common. To ask either of them about the house and its occupant was impossible. The matter required further intelligence.

There were several people on the street, but the majority were absolutely aghast when approached by a man in a well-cut suit and good shoes. He was informed by one raggedy fellow that, "You may be rigged out more generous than most, but I can tell a man with legal connections lookin' to bring trouble to the undeservin' poor." The man made sure Wentworth knew his opinion of such fellows by spitting on the ground just to one side of Wentworth's left foot and the string of very choice oaths murmured under his breath as he shuffled away.

"Pay him no mind. He's got all sorts of troubles. Can I be of help?" a woman's voice asked. He turned to face an ancient, pleasant-faced woman with an enormous hump and a hat thick with tiny feathers. "I live up there." With some difficulty, she pointed to the building next to the sidewalk on which they stood. "Way up, where them tiny windows is on the second floor. I could see everythin' from there until they put us all out."

"I am wondering about the place with the peeling door." He pointed across the street.

"May Evans" she said, before she even turned back to face him.

"A woman named May Evans lives there?"

"That's right." She looked at Wentworth as though he might be a bit simple. "She takes in boarders. Only ladies."

"I see."

"No men allowed. No exceptions," she said firmly, now looking at him as though he was immoral, "unless you're a relative." The woman's eyes narrowed. "You been there? You look familiar."

"No, I don't know anyone here on Westgate."

"I know I seen you."

He could easily lie and say she was mistaken but to what point? She would in no way harm his enquiry. "I was here last week taking a walk."

She straightened as much as her crooked spine would allow. "Yeah, I remember. You was with that fella measuring."

"Yes." He hoped that identifying himself with McGillvary would not ruin him.

"He's the one wants to toss us out with the trash."

Patrick's cavalier attitude about the occupants of the area was confirmed by the old woman's inelegant suspicions, but Wentworth had no direct knowledge of whether McGillvary intended to buy the building or what he had planned for it. So, he said, "The man did not share with me his intentions. If you remember me from the other day, perhaps you remember a man in a fine carriage that visited at May Evans's that day as well."

"Oh yes! Beautiful work! Honey coloured hair he had...but there was a woman in the coach."

Wentworth smiled. "Yes, that's the one. He was in Mrs. Evan's for about an hour. Do you know the man?"

She shook her head but said nothing.

"Have you seen him go into there before?"

"No, never."

It was Wentworth's turn to be silent.

"Maybe he's just a good son visitin' his old mum." She laughed and leant close to Wentworth. "If he such a good son, what he doin' drivin' a new barouche and makin' the ol' gal live here, I ask you." She winked at the joke.

Indeed, what good son would do such a thing? He thanked the woman and gave her something for her troubles.

Wentworth decided it would not do for him to be seen on the street when Anne departed. He'd done enough obfuscating in the past days to suit him. He headed back to Gay Street. As he made his way through the streets of Bath, he wondered if Anne and Mr. Elliot were merely visiting a poor relation? He'd put off that notion when he'd first seen him enter the building, but now he was not sure that was not a reasonable explanation. He wished he'd asked the woman with the feathers if she knew the identities of any of the boarders at May Evans. All his snooping had accomplished was to give him even more baffling bits and pieces to ponder as the day wore on.

~ ~ ~ ~ ~ ~ ~ & ~ ~ ~ ~ ~ ~ ~

On Friday morning he sent a note to McGillvary, inquiring if he was at leisure for a visit. There was no immediate answer. Wentworth decided to proceed to Belsom Park and, if he found Patrick home, make a nuisance of himself.

With the added hope of engineering a casual meeting with Anne, he made an unhurried stroll down Milsom Street, looking in shop windows and observing the passing human parade. This tactic proved fruitless. Occasionally, as he passed through the lower parts of town, he met with a familiar face. None of those he met seemed interested in stopping, and for this Wentworth was glad. He had no desire to redirect his energies away from thoughts of Anne or his pursuit of her.

"Captain Wentworth!" The voice came from behind him. Turning, he anticipated meeting another acquaintance but was shocked to find Mr. William Elliot addressing him.

"I am told you reside on Gay Street. You must be a great walker to be so far afield." The man's tone was engaging and his look open and amiable. It was no wonder Elliot was able to insinuate himself into good society. Were Frederick not familiar with the damaging information McGillvary had shared, he might be at war with his own interests and be quite disposed to share Anne's good opinion of her cousin.

"It is a trivial distance on such a good day, sir." He offered nothing that could be construed as an invitation to talk. Frankly, the shock of Elliot's speaking to him left him with nothing to say.

Elliot smiled, touched his hat, and bid him good day.

Considers me quite an idiot, I'm sure, Wentworth thought. There was nothing to be gained in examining Elliot's greeting, and he needed to begin moving closer to a place where he might cross the river. He chose his course and was heading to the bridge when he heard his name again called out. He turned and observed a path clearing on the sidewalk. Coming through the opening, Charles Musgrove approached him with his customary straight gait and grinning countenance. Behind Musgrove, Timothy Harville struggled with his walking stick to keep up.

"It is you!" Musgrove called from half way across the street. "I told Harville I thought it was you. He doubted me, but I never forget a man's stance once I've seen him shoot." Musgrove touched his hat and grabbed the Captain's hand, pumping it with an enthusiasm usually frowned upon in the cultured environs of Bath.

"It is indeed me, Musgrove," Wentworth replied. He answered Musgrove's eagerness with an equal measure. There was something about the heartiness of it all that made him want to give in return. A red-faced, heavily-breathing Timothy Harville joined them finally. "I am surprised to see you in this fleshpot, Timothy. I thought you were tucked up all safe and pure in Lyme."

Captain Harville glanced at Musgrove. "Remember my telling you that Elsa and I were to help in seeing Miss Louisa home to Uppercross?"

To Wentworth's embarrassment, he did not. He said nothing.

"I have an errand to carry out for the groom. One thing led to another, and here we all are." Harville glanced again and again towards Musgrove, who showed no sign he even noticed.

"All?"

Musgrove explained that Mrs. Charles, Mrs. Musgrove, and his sister were also in Bath. For a moment Wentworth was concerned, but this was put to rest when Henrietta was mentioned by name and that she was helping to choose wedding clothes for herself and Louisa.

"You must come to the inn and say hello to mother. She's in high gig with the weddings coming up and all the visiting that entails. I've also secured a box for tomorrow night for a new play that's all the rage. If you would visit as well, it would be a splendid touch for the day."

Before Wentworth knew it, he was following in Musgrove's wake and accepting an invitation to join them at the theatre the following evening. The Musgrove party was close by, encamped at the White Hart Inn across from the Pump Room. As they crossed through the common room to the stairs, Charles Musgrove shared a steady flow of humorous, though moderately abusive comments about the inn's patrons. "Mother's most likely holding court in the dining room. With all the friends she's sent notes to, the shopping Mary and Henrietta are planning, and all the sample books for fabric and trimmings that's been delivered already, that place is a shambles," he said, making his way to the second floor. "Harville, if she's here, you should ask Miss Anne if she knows of a reliable framer for Benwick's portrait," Musgrove said over his shoulder as he entered a room.

Wentworth came to a halt and motioned Harville in ahead of him. The possibility that the object of all his desires lay on the opposite side of the door was unnerving. It had not occurred to him in the rush of meeting Musgrove and Harville that their arrival might happily put him in the way of any number of opportunities to be in Anne's presence. He thought it odd that he'd spent hours imagining what he might say and do if they met by chance on the street, but now, with the possibility very real indeed, his mind was completely blank.

The room was as crowded as Musgrove had predicted, but finding Anne in the sea of female faces and frames was not difficult. She was seated at the table at Mrs. Musgrove's elbow. She looked at him with an open expression that he returned with a curt nod. There was no way to draw closer to her without insinuating himself into the ladies circle. He was soon relegated to a chair too far away from her to say anything.

"Anne, there is Mrs. Clay, I am sure, standing under the colonnade, and a gentleman with her" Mrs. Charles said, making sure her voice carried over the commotion of female voices around the table. There was nothing interesting in this until she revealed the gentleman to be their cousin, Mr. Elliot. Wentworth had no idea where Mr. Elliot lived, but perhaps he, too, was rather far afield. Considering that he was again meeting Miss Elliot's companion alone, the Captain wondered how much Anne knew about their association.

Immediately upon hearing the full details, Anne's attention was engaged. It troubled him that Elliot's affairs was of such interest to her. Then he considered that perhaps her interest was roused more by the gentleman's choice of companion. Might this be a confirmation of something she already suspected?

"No, it cannot be Mr. Elliot, I assure you. He was to leave Bath at nine this morning and does not come back till tomorrow." As she spoke, she coloured a bit, and even before finishing the statement, she frowned and glanced in Wentworth's direction. Was her knowledge of Elliot's activities such a secret that she was embarrassed to have let them slip in front of her family? He was again frustrated to think that Anne was privy to her cousin's plans.

"Of course, it is Mr. Elliot. Come and see if I am not right," Mary said, tapping the glass. Anne did not stir from her seat and appeared unconcerned. Then a flurry of clearing throats amongst the visiting ladies drew the attention of them both. Three of the women in particular seemed to express their own private code of lifted brows, tilted heads, and suppressed smiles. When he looked back to Anne, she was redder than before and fumbled as she rewound a small rack of lace.

"Do come, Anne, come and look for yourself." Mary's voice rose as she begged Anne and then reported that the man was departing from view. "Not know Mr. Elliot, indeed. You seem to have forgotten all about Lyme."

Again, Anne glanced Frederick's way, but he could not see her eye. She sighed and joined her sister. Even the most interested of the visiting ladies would not have noticed Anne's posture straighten slightly as she looked out the window. Her fingers lightly touched the sill and slid along the glass pane. Wentworth perceived from her response that she was quite interested in Elliot's meetings with her sister's companion. If that were true, perhaps the nefarious side of the cousin was coming to light. He took satisfaction in hoping that all the speculations of the good ladies of Bath on Anne's behalf were beginning to crumble.

When Anne turned away from the window, she looked surprised, but that quickly changed to an expression of calm disinterest. "Yes, it is Mr. Elliot, certainly. He has changed his hour of going, I suppose, that is all—or I may be mistaken." Her tone was bland as she shrugged her shoulder and returned to her chair. He sensed she was putting on an air of disinterest but was puzzled as to why. Another ripple of penetrating looks worked their way through some of the visitors.

So, the whereabouts of Mr. Elliot was not of supreme importance to her. He would take her actions at face value and give her the benefit of the doubt. If he was right, there might be hope for them.

The visitors stood and gathered their purses, bidding the hostess farewell. Charles was by the open door bowing to each as they departed. "Ladies, it was wonderful to see you. A delight, madam. Come again soon." Musgrove was all smiles until the last one passed by him, at which point he crossed his eyes and pulled imbecilic faces as he closed the door. Without seeing a thing, Mrs. Musgrove understood what her son had been up to and said as much. Quickly, Charles moved to her side, knelt and immediately began to tell her his plans for the following evening. "I have engaged Captain Wentworth," he nodded in Frederick's direction. Looking to his sister-in-law, he added, "Anne will not be sorry to join us, I am sure. We all like a play. Have not I done well?"

She smiled. His rude caper was forgotten. "Charles, a play is just the thing to add to our enjoyment, if your sister and all the others are—"

"Good heavens, Charles! How can you think of such a thing?" Mrs. Charles was adamant in her reminder that they were invited to Camden Place to meet with Lady Dalrymple, the woman's daughter, and Mr. Elliot. The Elliot Pride bloomed full and fragrant in Mary Musgrove. At first, she allowed that her husband might have forgotten the engagement. He did away with that notion post haste. She replied that he had promised her father they would be in attendance. Musgrove countered he had made no such promise, shoring his claim with quibbles about the exact phrases and the particular words he'd used.

Harville had obviously made peace with being caught up in such familial banter. He was occupied with Mrs. and Miss Musgrove as they discussed fabrics and trims. Wentworth looked to Anne for a moment. She was following the exchange between her sister and brother but was noticeably uncomfortable that they had chosen to bicker without the slightest concern for the setting and the company.

"Don't talk to me about heirs and representatives! I am not one of those who neglect the reigning power to bow to the rising sun. If I would not go for the sake of your father, I should think it scandalous to go for the sake of the heir. What is Mr. Elliot to me?" Charles snorted, his tone half-serious. Wentworth doubted that anything, even a summons to meet with the Elliot heir, could dampen his appetite for jesting at the expense of his wife.

The question was a good one. Who *was* Mr. Elliot to Charles or to anyone else? He looked to Anne and was surprised to see her observing him. "*Who is Mr. Elliot to us, Annie?*" he wished to ask her.

The Musgrove's exchange continued in the background, but neither he nor Anne paid it any mind. If her interest in the question was half as strong as his, they could talk until dawn. Each shifted in their seats and then glanced around to make certain no one observed their lack of interest in the main attraction. The impulse to rise seemed to be on both sides, when Anne's name was spoken.

"–if Miss Anne could not be with us."

Anne turned her attention from him to Mrs. Musgrove's statement most reluctantly. This pleased him, and he was more pleased still when Anne made it clear that she would take little pleasure in the party and would be all too happy to change it and attend the play with the rest of her friends. However, she knew what was due her father and sister and would reluctantly forego the temptation of such a kind offer. When she finished her piece, she did not look his way, but he was confident she had spoken so directly so as to make it clear his company was preferred over that of her family and their social concerns.

The energy of his suspicions drove him from his chair to the fireplace. It brought him physically no closer to her but would work to his advantage. He would take his time and listen as Charles began again to hector his wife, for now, even with his mother's pronouncement, Charles was threatening to miss the party and attend the play. All the occupants of the table were busy ignoring them, including Anne. She was paging through a book of fabric scraps. He suspected that she was not very engrossed in them. With everyone thus occupied, he advanced the six short steps from the fireplace to Anne's side. She detected his presence immediately, closed the book, and looked up.

At the concert, he'd been careful to keep a respectable distance. This was the closest he'd been to her since their silent, anguishing ride from Lyme to Uppercross. Fortunately, the silence was over. He could now speak openly—within reason—and hope that they could make a new beginning of things. If he found that her heart was truly engaged elsewhere, he would deal with that later. For now, they were together in this place, amidst an intimate group of friends who were not yet burdened by any expectations or suspicions. Frederick could not help but delight in the great freedom of the circumstance.

Though there was great freedom, there was no knowing what might be overheard. "You have not been long enough in Bath to enjoy the evening parties of the place." Something impersonal and bland was a suitable start.

"Oh no, the usual character of them is nothing for me. I am no card player." The statement was earnestly said. Immediately, her expression softened and her cheeks glowed. Perhaps she, too, was thinking of his misguided attempts years ago to heighten her interest in cards. If given the opportunity, he would assure her that he had found it charming then and would enjoy an opportunity to instruct again.

"You were not then, I know. You did not use to like cards; but time makes many changes." Her smile widened at that, and he realised this was the first explicit mention of their past together since his return to Somerset. He could not help but wonder how their reunion might have been different had he been more frank earlier.

"I am not yet so much changed," she said. She seemed to have more to say but chose not to.

Did she refer to her dislike of games? Or was she signalling that her feelings for him had remained unchanged all these years? His heart began to beat harder, and he needed to breathe deeply. He was about to mention how stuffy the room had grown and suggest they take a walk when Miss Henrietta approached, ruining his plans.

She smiled at the Captain then said in a low tone to Anne, "We must hurry before we are set upon again by another gaggle of Mother's friends." She smiled to each and left them.

Anne watched her move away. Her expression, he thought, mirrored his own of disappointment. She stood. Neither of them realised how close to her chair he'd placed himself. He did not mean to press in on her, but it took a moment for him to step away fully. Her smile was nervous but friendly as she, too, moved.

"I am perfectly ready, Henrietta." She looked to the girl and then to him again. Voices outside the door drew everyone's attention. In an instant, looks passed between those preparing to leave which lamented not doing so soon enough. Charles rubbed his hands at the prospect of new victims to taunt. Mrs. Musgrove adjusted her cap in preparations for meeting another wave of her friends.

The door opened wide, a footman entered and announced, "Sir Walter Elliot and Miss Elizabeth Elliot."

This announcement suspended everything in the room: laughter, time, breath, anticipation of pleasant things, comfort. He was not certain if all those things were pulled out the door past the new arrivals, or if their ruthless sophistication so filled the room everything good was pushed past the panes of glass in the windows. Either way, the pair's arrival demanded everyone's attention.

As they entered, they surveyed the room. Frederick contemplated Dante's reference to surrendering "all hope" when entering certain places. It struck him that the thought applied equally to a place being entered by certain people. Wentworth also observed that a visit to this place, with this assemblage, was everything that Sir Walter and Miss Elliot could possibly want. There was no one of equal status with whom they might be compared. What's more, there was no one of superiority to require their fawning or detract from their excellence. They were far above all and could revel in the absolute pleasure of looking down on everyone else. Wentworth bristled as their unified gaze swept over the room and blatantly settled on him.

Contrived smiles in place, they crossed to Charles. The Elliot connection made acknowledging him a priority. Mrs. Charles's deep curtsey was duly accepted with a mumbled greeting and heart-felt clasp of her finger tips by the Baronet. She beamed as she received a frigid peck on the cheek from her sister. Poor Mrs. Musgrove was out of her element, uncertain of the protocol. She began to stand, but once Sir Walter saw she was willing to stir herself, he felt properly acknowledged and could employ his false modesty to the fullest extent by mouthing phrases like, "family circle" and "no formality needed."

Miss Henrietta and Timothy Harville were in turn forced to greet their betters. Wentworth detested having to watch the annoying social game that must be played out. He knew his time was coming, but the annoyance he felt was stripped away when he looked at Anne. His heart ached for her. She stood motionless, still facing towards him but watching her father and sister. Her purse in hand and partly opened as she was preparing to leave, she stood just a few steps from him. The disappointment was gone, replaced with utter mortification.

"Captain Wentworth." He was finally being summoned to make his obeisance.

"Sir Walter." He made a most proper bow, only stopping himself from tugging his forelock. For an instant he felt a stab of guilt. When such gestures were directed his way, he freely accepted the acknowledgements of authority and greater rank. *Pride is a nasty, insidious thing,* he told himself as he bowed prettily to Miss Elliot. When he rose, there was a subtle smile on Anne's face. He doubted she could read his mind but took it to be satisfaction that he was again, openly, being given his due.

Miss Elliot took from her purse some cards and waved them just a little so all could see them and would know they were important. "I am sure you have heard that we are having a small, intimate gathering. It is to be tomorrow evening. Just a little fête to meet friends, nothing formal." The delivery of the invitation was elegantly and properly done. It was also clear, most unashamedly so, that as little trouble as possible was being taken on the part of the hostess. Miss Elliot laid down the cards on the table in front of Mrs. Musgrove. Frederick was grateful she'd said her piece and that father and daughter would be disappearing soon.

To his dismay, Miss Elliot picked up a card and moved in his direction. As she had spoken, the young woman had glanced about the room a time or two, but he was certain he was the only one with which she had made eye contact. And now, she was boldly approaching him, a card in her smartly gloved hand. "Captain Wentworth," she said, placing herself in the small space between Anne and him. He took the card and thanked her. She gave him a gracious curtsey, rose with a smile on her lips, and turned away. Anne had to step aside to allow her sister to pass, her distress and embarrassment palpable.

His first impulse was to tear up the card, but he would not embarrass Anne, himself, or his friends in such a rude manner. Pondering an alternative was not necessary; Sir Walter and Miss Elliot announced that their social schedule required they immediately take their leave. He observed them just in time to nod.

Life and breath and movement returned to the room. Even his heart knew when it was free of the presence of the Elliots, and it began to beat more normally. Voices began to fill the room again, and the plans that were halted were being renewed. He could not help but stare at the card. He turned it over and over. The printed side, "Miss Elliot at home," alternated with the stark white of the blank side. Wentworth wanted neither the card nor the attention of the Elliots. A card party with his own gentlemen friends would be enjoyable, perhaps profitable. A card party at Camden Place could only be enlivened by the Musgroves.

Charles began prodding Harville to go out again, and Wentworth was naturally included. The ladies were gathering themselves as well. They went as a group down the stairs, Frederick trying all the while to overhear the ladies' plans. No places mentioned were familiar to him.

Short of outright stalking, there would be no opportunity for him to separate from the men and accidentally meet with the ladies.

Once on the sidewalk, Mr. and Mrs. Musgrove bid one another a teasing farewell, and the ladies and gentlemen split apart, heading in opposite directions. He looked over his shoulder for one last look. Anne did as well.

Chapter Twelve

I enjoy the company of the Musgroves, don't misunderstand, but sometimes the bickering becomes like a hurricane: no choice but to batten the hatches and wait it out," Harville said, as they made their way through the crowd near the Abbey. Charles had earlier left them for a shop he'd spied dealing in leather goods. He was keen on having a look at a new saddle scabbard for his prize shotgun and saw this as his chance to investigate the possibilities without his wife present.

"They have been extraordinarily kind to us. I think they feel they owe us for taking care of Louisa."

"They are kind people. Loud, but kind," Wentworth said. He wished to ask about the unexpected attraction between Miss Louisa and James Benwick. He was a bit shamed at having already made his opinion known freely enough to Anne and to his own family, based on little more than supposition. He wanted to know, but then again, he hesitated.

Harville laughed. "They are that. The children, our normally sweet and quiet children, become screeching banshees when they've been with them for a period. It amazes me." They walked on for a moment, and he continued. "There are many things which amaze me these days."

This was an invitation, but an invitation to what? Frederick wondered. Maybe he had some opinion concerning Anne's family, or he had observed his conversation with Anne and wanted some intelligence of his own. Of everyone he could name, Frederick knew that Timothy would understand his feelings if he were to take the man into his confidence.

Harville took something from his pocket and offered it to Wentworth. "This amazes me. He had it done at the Cape. It was to be Fanny's wedding present." Frederick took the miniature painting. It was a good likeness of Benwick.

"The fellow was German," he said. "Those Germans are very good artists, if this is any indication."

"It is very good. Not amazing, in my opinion, but good." The picture was a very true likeness. The cheeks were a bit too round and florid, but it was essentially the enthusiastic Benwick who had looked forward for so long to marrying Fanny Harville. This was surly the perfect picture of a young man determined to make his fortune so that he might finally claim his bride and set up house in comfort. He'd seen this eagerness in Benwick when he'd been taken aboard the *Grappler* in July. This bright young man had died the moment Frederick had informed him of Fanny's death. He was still of the opinion that Louisa Musgrove was not woman enough to revive his friend.

"It's not the picture that amazes me, but that he wishes me to see it framed so that he can give it to her." Harville's voice was raw with emotion.

"I do like her, Frederick—please, don't think otherwise—but how could he claim to love my sister for two years and then, with such ease and speed, give his heart to another woman?" He was about to answer, when Timothy continued. "To ask me, of all people, to do this for him! He can't see anything past his own nose." Harville extended his hand to take back the painting.

Wentworth took his handkerchief, swathed the painting in it and tucked it into his breast pocket.

"I will need that. Miss Henrietta was able to tell me of a place to do the job."

"I shall see to it," Wentworth said, not looking to see Harville's response. Timothy sighed.

"Benwick is happy again. Of course, he can't see past his own nose. And what he *can* see is full of Miss Louisa," Frederick said. He was definitely more in sympathy with Harville than Benwick, but he also knew that time would heal Harville's hurt feelings. There was no sense in dividing loyalties by denigrating their mutual friend.

"I am thoroughly confused how a man so intelligent, a man who was so completely in love with a woman like my sister, his equal in every way, could settle for a giddy, silly—" Harville was suddenly silent.

Wentworth looked back to see if Harville had taken a spill. He hadn't but had fallen behind for reasons of his own. "I'm sorry, Frederick. I shouldn't speak about her so, knowing you once felt for her."

Wentworth laughed. "I never felt nearly as much as you and Elsa presumed. Yes, I suppose I was attracted to her, but it was more because she was an enthusiastic, vibrant young woman, and my life needed some vibrancy at the time. I never loved her, and I should never have acted in a way that could leave anyone in doubt of that."

"Well, that's good to know. No damage there, at least."

"None! Anywise, I can see that Benwick's picture is framed for you."

"Thank you. Considering what you did for me in July, this is over and above anything." They walked on in companionable silence for a quarter of a block or so. Harville stopped before the window of a print shop. "Look at this nonsense," he said, pointing to a print of a small boat with two men aboard. "It is quite obvious that this artist is not sailor."

Wentworth joined him at the window. "There is no danger of mistaking him for one. This must be the place of which my brother-in-law told me. They have more such folly inside if you'd care to look."

"No, I've not the stomach for it," he said, moving on down the sidewalk. Again they were quiet for a time. "I miss the sea."

"You live right on the sea."

He sighed. "You know what I mean. I miss being at sea. When the Musgroves asked that we accompany them back to Somerset, I turned them down. It was Elsa who convinced me that we should take some time in the country. Though Lyme is not much of a seaport, it is hard living by the rhythms of the tides and knowing I shall never again sail."

For some time Wentworth had suspected Timothy was unable to return to duty, but nothing final had ever been said. He did not wish to cause his friend further pain by enquiring. Though he might be able to lend some comfort, the subject was still a reminder that, despite robust health, he, too, might never return to his former life.

"So, I went to the country to get away from the sea and now find myself in this blasted city." He nudged Wentworth's arm. "But I am relieved to find my good friend here and to find others here, as well. Knowing I shall see Miss Anne on occasion is something I look forward to very much." He laughed. "Now that you tell me you never cared deeply for Miss Louisa, I can see that I am no good judge of romantic matters. At one time I had thought James was quite enamoured of Miss Anne. He spoke about her all the time, it seemed. You remember, don't you?"

"Yes, he spoke of her very warmly, very often as I recall." Of all the possibilities concerning him and Anne Elliot, thankfully James Benwick was no longer one of them.

"Now, were he to have come to me and said it was Miss Anne he fancied, I think I would have had no objections to it at all. I wonder why that is."

"In the same way that Fanny was James's equal, Anne is as well." He would have to take greater care in using her Christian name, lest he say anything that might rouse Harville's suspicions.

"True, true. I respect Miss Anne Elliot's mind and her ways. If James were attracted to a woman like her, it would be easier to understand. He seems to have settled—" Harville sighed. "I am too hard on the girl. She is likeable and kind. Louisa Musgrove will make him a good wife." The statement was said with determination and the beginning of conviction.

In the same vein, Wentworth added, "If anyone can enlarge Miss Louisa's intelligence, it would be James. Out of self-defence, she will learn all the major poets he loves, and he will, perhaps, learn to smile more often."

"I suppose you're right. Elsa and I have amended one another. Marriage does that quite naturally."

Wentworth contemplated what changes might come were he to marry Anne. Their tastes in literature were similar in theme, though her knowledge far outstripped his. He enjoyed cards, and this afternoon she made it clear that her preference in that regard would not soon change.

"—I said have you ever considered Miss Anne?"

"Considered Miss Anne how?"

"Romantically, of course." Harville was smiling, but it soon faded. "No, I suppose not."

"Why not, may I ask?"

"Well, as we were talking about, she is quite intelligent and enjoys a good deep conversation. You, on the other hand..." Harville let the sentence dangle and continued walking away.

"I, on the other hand, what?"

Harville turned. "I just don't think the two of you would get on, now that I put my mind to it."

"I see. Benwick would give her the challenge you fancy she desires, but I am a man with a head full of straw." He joined Harville.

"Hardly, Frederick. It's just that your intelligence runs more to the practical...and devious. Hers is more in the line of great thoughts and notions."

"Devious, you say! When have I proven to be devious?"

Harville stopped, and turned to smile at him. "Study your bank accounts, my dear friend. For every pound, there was a wily plot attached. Devious and practical." He continued down the sidewalk.

"I never thought of myself such. Perhaps I should find myself a devious, practical wife and settle down to the perfect marriage."

Harville stopped again. "Now you're angry. I didn't mean it that way. I will admit that, away from the quarterdeck, you are not in the least bit sly. And, if you like, Miss Anne would be a perfect match for you." He pressed on. "With her kindness and intelligence, she might teach you some humility."

Wentworth laughed a little. *Timothy, if you only knew just how much I wish to be taught.*

~ ~ ~ ~ ~ ~ ~ & ~ ~ ~ ~ ~ ~ ~

The following morning, Sophia was sorting through a sizeable pile of mail as the Captain and Admiral sorted through their respective breakfasts. "We are quite popular, my dear," Sophia said, holding up a note. The Admiral inquired who had sent it. Frederick paid it no attention. "This is just one of several invitations. It is for a small party at Camden Place. There are some others, but there is one in particular from Mrs. Musgrove. She invites us for a visit today. Anytime we find convenient."

This was interesting. There was a chance Anne would also be invited to be with the family. It would not look strange if he accompanied his sister and brother, not that he really needed any sort of excuse to visit the Musgroves.

"So, we are invited to Camden Place. That is a little surprising."

"Why surprising, dear?"

"We've been in Bath for a while now. This is the first hint of interest from the Baronet's quarter."

Sophia smiled as she refolded the fine stationary packet. "We should really attend. It is wise to keep the landlord happy."

"I suppose so, my dear; though, I do not look forward to a quiet evening with Sir Walter and his set."

"It shouldn't be such a trial, sir," Frederick said. "The Musgroves were invited, and Mrs. Charles was particularly interested in being introduced to members of Sir Walter's set. Harville and I shall be there."

"You were invited?" Sophia said. She raised a brow.

"Yes, I was with the Musgroves yesterday and was invited by Miss Elliot herself."

Her puzzled look disappeared and Sophia went back to the mail. "Well, yes, Miss Anne is very thoughtful about such things."

"I agree, but it was Miss Elizabeth Elliot who invited me. She saw the card into my hand herself." His sister was again perplexed.

"Do you think the affair and the company too exalted for me, Sister?"

"Of course not, Frederick. I merely wonder at it. Miss Elliot is not the sort to include everyone."

"True. I think the invitation was on a whim. It is born of nothing more than the idea that the blue and gold of a uniform would complement the furnishings of her sitting room nicely. Anyway, I am invited if I am inclined to attend."

"You may not?"

"I haven't really put my mind to it." This was true. His decision to attend the party had been made the day before. "I am not otherwise engaged, but depending upon the day and how it goes, I may stay home, drink some of the Admiral's fine brandy, and read a book."

Later in the morning, Sophia asked that he would escort her to the White Hart so that she might visit for a time with Mrs. Musgrove. He readily agreed, knowing that arriving with his sister would be perfect cover if Anne should be there as well.

The walk was considerably shortened when Sophia remarked on the darkening sky. "We'd best hail a cab now, or we'll be caught in it for sure." A carriage was procured, and they were comfortably settled when the first drops thumped on the roof.

"I am surprised, Frederick, that you failed to notice the quickly shifting conditions. Have you been on land so long you are losing your weather sense?" She looked out to watch the now rain-slicked streets clearing of pedestrians. A woman with good taste in perfume had occupied the carriage previous to them. As he watched the streets begin to shimmer with the downpour, Frederick tried to identify the flowery scent. Sophia touched his arm. "Well?"

"We were saved by your superior abilities, Sister, which is good, as I must be terribly distracted."

"Please tell me your distraction is not because of Miss Elliot."

Frederick examined Sophia's troubled expression and realised she was speaking of Miss Elizabeth Elliot. It was obvious this was a continuance of their discussion at breakfast, and he wondered why she would concern herself with the matter. He crossed his arms and leant back a bit. "And what if it is?"

She sighed and looked out the window. Turning back, she said, "I have no objection to marrying for advancement. I could well see you marrying the daughter of an admiral or a well-placed peer, but the daughter of a baronet with no connections to help you?"

"So, you think I would marry for such a reason?"

"I should be surprised if you wouldn't. But you have a good heart and would only marry someone you could learn to love. I do know that much about you. You could not stand being trapped in a hopeless cause."

"And you think a match between Miss Elliot and me would be hopeless?"

"I think so, yes."

"Then, it cannot be so."

The carriage came to a halt, and Frederick opened the door.

"Does that mean then you are not thinking of her?" she asked.

Offering her his hand, he said, "Come, Sophia, the Musgroves await."

She stepped out and avoided a torrent of water flowing along the curb. "I think you are up to something, Frederick."

He paid off the carriage and offered his arm. "I hope you are right," was all he offered in response.

~ ~ ~ ~ ~ ~ ~ & ~ ~ ~ ~ ~ ~ ~

The room was alive with the usual Musgrove enthusiasm. To his disappointment, Anne was nowhere to be seen, but he was heartened to overhear she was expected momentarily. "She was likely held up by the rain," Harville said, joining Wentworth in the chairs by the window. "It has cleared up, ladies," he called over his shoulder to Miss Henrietta and Mary Musgrove. Both were exceedingly eager to be off.

As they were leaving, Charles entered the room and was told he must turn right around and accompany the ladies on their shopping expedition. He looked longingly towards Harville and Wentworth, both of whom gave him a sympathetic shrug, but he wisely chose to live to fight another day and left with his wife and sister.

"Poor fellow," Harville said, only a little seriously. "He's not got it too bad; though, that may depend on what the ladies are shopping for today."

"Quite true," Wentworth agreed. Having little experience of it, he wondered how dire shopping with ladies might actually be. He reached into his pocket and withdrew Benwick's portrait. Just then, the door opened. Both men turned to see who joined them. It was Anne. Everyone and everything was forgotten as Frederick admired the brilliance of her eyes and her flushed cheeks. Her bonnet strings were carelessly tossed over her shoulders by the breeze. The effect had charmed him in Somerset. The effect now was trebled.

She looked about the room and greeted Harville. For him there was a momentary hesitation, a smile and then a murmured greeting as well. He fancied her gaze lingered a bit on him. His sister smiled and spoke to her warmly, for which he was glad. It occurred to him that their conversation in the carriage might have been enlivened if he had shared with Sophia his hopes concerning the future and the second Elliot daughter.

He could feel Harville shifting by his side, but he could not resist observing Anne. The simplicity of her removing her bonnet and laying it on the table, to be followed by the finger-by-finger removal of her gloves was too tempting to be missed. She took a seat at the table and poured herself some tea at the behest of Mrs. Musgrove. If he reached out, he could touch her bonnet—

"Good, you brought it," Harville said, taking the portrait.

The feel of the portrait sliding through his fingers was enough to remove his attention from Anne and back to Harville. Wentworth asked what particular sort of framing he wished accomplished. Harville was so caught up in examining the painting he had to be asked twice how he wished it framed.

"Nothing special or too expensive. A dark frame to match his hair, I suppose, might be fitting."

Taking a seat at a nearby table where a good supply of letter writing paraphernalia was kept, he could not help feeling that the table was situated close enough to Anne for him to be happy and miserable at the same time. It took a moment to find a pen with a tip to satisfy him. Then, arranging the blotter and ink and paper took a moment or two more. When he was finally able to put his mind to the letter, he was unaccountably drawn into the conversation between his sister and Mrs. Musgrove.

"–at any rate, I said, it will be better than a long engagement."

"This is precisely what I was going to observe," his sister replied. Her voice was adamant on the point. "I would rather have young people settle on a small income at once and have to struggle with a few difficulties together, than to be involved in a long engagement. I always think that no mutual–" Her thought was interrupted with a stronger agreement on the part of Mrs. Musgrove.

Wentworth considered what a passionate ally his sister might have made in '06 had she been in the country. Though, in the long run, passion was of little use. He had been passionate in his objections to Anne's breaking their engagement. In the end, it had been the still, small voice of Lady Russell to which she had listened. But here were good, sensible women agreeing that when two young people chose to throw in together, reduced circumstances and the difficulties borne of them were not to be recoiled from and were even preferable to a situation of uncertainty.

An engagement to him had been uncertain. To marry him at that time in his career was to forge blindly into the future. He had been confident of his own abilities, but she could not see the world from his view. Whether she saw their situation more clearly or she had been guided into only seeing what her godmother wished her to see, he could not tell. As a young man he had pushed and scoffed at all the dangers surrounding his chosen profession, while she rightly perceived them. She had been frightened of the prospects.

The shaft of the pen rolled easily between his fingers as he paused in his writing and considered the harsh things he had said when she said she would not marry him. He was once again ashamed of how brutal he'd been in accusing her of ill-using him. Though he feared what he might see, he looked to see if she, too, was listening. He wondered if she was remembering.

She was, indeed, listening. She was looking directly at him as well. Were her cheeks still coloured by the walk from home? Surely, she'd had time to catch her breath, but that would mean she breathed quickly for some other reason. He looked away, conscious that to continue watching her was to put them both in danger of being noticed. The ladies seemed intent upon their conversation, and a glance towards Harville revealed that he remained by the window, still looking at Benwick's portrait. As he turned back to the table, he could hear Harville rising and moving to the other set of windows. Everyone seemed settled. He continued with the letter.

It was simple enough to list the requirements for the framing. He added that he was to receive the bill, and requested that, when the task was accomplished, the portrait be sent to him in care of the Admiral's Gay Street address. *Simple enough,* he thought. As he folded the letter, it occurred to him that it was an excellent vehicle to convey, without excessive confusion, a person's specific desires. One could tell a craftsman precisely what you desired in the way of a service, or one might tell the woman he loves everything on his mind and heart.

If there was another man in Bath who needed such an advantageous vehicle more than him, Wentworth pitied the fellow greatly. As he considered how he might start such a vital missive, he heard Anne rise from the table and join Harville at the window. He was showing her the picture and recounting where Benwick had it made. Wentworth ached for his friend, for the man's voice, deep with emotion, choked as he revealed to her the object's history. "It was a commission to me! I am not sorry, indeed, to make it over to another. He undertakes it." He indicated Wentworth. "He is writing about it now." His voice dropped. "Poor Fanny! She would not have forgotten him so soon!"

"No," replied Anne, in a low, feeling voice. "That, I can easily believe."

"It was not in her nature. She doted on him."

"It would not be the nature of any woman who truly loved."

Wentworth touched pen to paper and opened his heart:

> I can listen no longer in silence. I must speak to you by such
> means as are within my reach. You pierce my soul. I am half
> agony, half hope. Tell me not that I am too late, that such
> precious feelings are gone forever. I offer myself to you again
> with a heart even more your own than when you almost
> broke it, eight years and a half ago.

The words poured out of him. Honest and true to everything he would now allow himself to feel. As he finished his opening, he could hear her continuing, speaking to a woman's lot of being quiet and confined.

"Our feelings prey upon us," Anne said. For nearly nine years her feelings had preyed upon her to the point that she had refused the proposal of a better man and had become almost a nun. No wonder she could have walked by him unrecognised on any street in the city or country. He, on the other hand, had pretended that no such hold was upon him.

"If the change be not from outward circumstances, it must be from within; it must be nature, man's nature, which has done the business for Captain Benwick," she said. The business of which she spoke must be forgetting.

Wentworth wrote in protest:

Dare not say that man forgets sooner than woman, that his love has an earlier death. I have loved none but you.

"No, no, it is not man's nature. I will not allow it to be more man's nature than woman's to be inconstant and forget those they do love, or have loved," Harville countered.

It is not our nature to forget, Wentworth thought. He continued writing:

Unjust I may have been, weak and resentful I have been, but never inconstant. You alone have brought me to Bath. For you alone, I think and plan. Have you not seen this? Can you fail to have understood my wishes? I had not waited even these ten days, could I have read your feelings, as I think you must have penetrated mine.

Her voice continued. He heard phrases such as, "man is more robust than woman, but he is not longer lived," and, "neither time, nor health, to be called your own." It made little sense to him; he'd missed too much of her reasoning. It mattered not whether his thoughts matched her exactly. It only mattered that she knew how he felt and what he wished.

I can hardly write. I am every instant hearing something which overpowers me.

Again he considered, rolling the pen from side-to-side. His thoughts were disrupted when the pen slipped from his fingers and rolled across the table.

"Have you finished your letter?" said Captain Harville. Both he and Anne were looking Wentworth's way. Both were closer than he had imagined.

"Not quite, a few lines more. I shall have done in five minutes," he said, awkwardly turning the pen nib-side-down. The pen hovered over the paper. Her expression had been one of surprise. She looked happy. Being in conversation with someone who respected her intelligence agreed with her.

You sink your voice, but I can distinguish the tones of that voice when they would be lost on others.

He heard few intelligible words and thoughts, but he knew her well and knew that she spoke only kindness and encouragement, even when she disagreed with his friend. A surge of emotion on Harville's part raised his voice somewhat, allowing Wentworth to be privy to the specifics of the conversation once more. Harville spoke in general terms of a sailor waiting for his family, but the Captain knew he spoke from the experience of the spring. Frederick had watched through his telescope as his friend paced the docks, waiting for the *Laconia* to bring him his wife. When Frederick had offered Elsa the use of his best glass, knowing she would see Timothy on the wharf, her anticipation had been palpable. He had surrendered to her the exclusivity of his sacred quarterdeck so that she might have the best view. The conversation between her and her cousin was excited and punctuated with sighs and profuse expressions of thanks to him and his officers. Harville's voice was nearly as full of emotion as he had been that day. And when Anne spoke, she acknowledged it, not directly, but with her sweet wisdom.

"–if I may be allowed the expression–so long as you have an object. I mean while the woman you love lives, and lives for you. All the privilege I claim for my own sex–it is not a very enviable one; you need not covet it–is that of loving longest, when existence or when hope is gone." He chanced a look their way. Both Harville and Anne were consumed with their conversation.

Too good, too excellent creature! You do us justice, indeed. You do believe that there is true attachment and constancy among men. Believe it to be most fervent, most undeviating, in me, Frederick thought.

"You are a good soul," Harville said, eventually. "There is no quarrelling with you. And when I think of Benwick, my tongue is tied." Before Anne could answer, sounds from the main table announced the rising of its occupants. This would signal to Harville that they could leave for the framers. The time was short for him to finish.

I must go, uncertain of my fate; but I shall return hither, or follow your party, as soon as possible. A word, a look, will be enough to decide whether I enter your father's house this evening or never.

"Here, Frederick, you and I part company, I believe," Sophia said. "I am going home, and you have an engagement with your friend. Tonight we may have the pleasure of all meeting again at your party," she said to Anne. "We had your sister's card yesterday, and I understood Frederick had a card too; though I did not see it. You are disengaged, Frederick, are you not, as well as ourselves?"

The paper was being uncooperative as he tried to fold it. It was crooked, but it would do. Slipping the letter to the framer into his pocket, he said, "Yes, very true; here we separate, but Harville and I shall soon be after you; that is, Harville, if you are ready, I am in half a minute. I know you will not be sorry to be off. I shall be at your service in half a minute." For a moment, he panicked and worried he'd switched the letters. He opened the one and held the stick of wax over the candle. To his relief, it was the letter to Anne. As he'd fiddled with the letter, he'd held the stick of wax over nothing, and now had to wait another moment more for it to soften.

Wentworth replaced the wax, seal, and pen. Harville was bidding Sophia farewell and returned to Anne to take his leave of her as well. Wentworth shoved the ill-folded lump of paper under other scattered sheets on the table and walked to the door. They passed into the hall-way, Harville speaking about his just-finished conversation. Before he pulled the door closed, Wentworth looked through into the room. Anne was moving towards the table while Mrs. Musgrove remained seated.

It was possible she might find the letter on her own. Perhaps she would straighten the sheets he'd left scattered, but an equal possibility was, out of her respect for the privacy of others, she would leave the papers alone. He had scuttled enough chances with her over the past few weeks and knew he must put his hand to the tiller and guide the letter into her hands.

Fortunately, his gloves were on the table. They would be the reason for his return. He stepped through the door, begged Mrs. Musgrove's pardon, explained his return and crossed the room. His appearance startled Anne. She hesitated. He turned his back to the main table and, moving aside several of the sheets, revealed the letter. Her eyes were on him and then on the letter. Assured she understood him, he took his gloves and left.

Chapter Thirteen

A re you certain? I have no plans other than seeing to this." Wentworth was confused by Harville's change of mind concerning the portrait.

"I know. You've more than gone out of your way to help me, and I had every intention of having you do this for me. God knows I've asked you to do worse," he said, referring to the dreadful task in July. "But, I still think of him as a brother, and it is only right I fulfil this one request he has made of me."

"As you wish." Frederick could not help but delight in Harville's sudden determination to take Benwick's portrait to the framer on his own. With the task out of his hands, there might be opportunity to meet Anne and discuss the letter. He had no desire to wait until the evening party to know her feelings.

"Go on. Bath is a big place, and I'm sure there are other, more important things you need to see about." Harville took the packet and the letter.

Wentworth bid his friend farewell in as unrushed a manner as possible. When Harville turned to enter the shop, Frederick dashed away, back in the direction of the White Hart. *She may not need me*, he thought as he wove his way through the sidewalk, *but perhaps she might want me.*

The street was crowded, and no matter how he tried, he seemed at every turn to be thwarted by Bath's human traffic. As he slowly made his way, he became aware of numerous groups of giggling women. Perhaps they laughed since they took up the entire sidewalk leaving the rest of the population to shuffle along behind. There were far too many of the ancient or ill with their canes, chairs, or nurses slowing him down as well.

He scanned the crowd ahead and caught sight of a familiar bonnet. Charles Musgrove and Anne were now within an easy distance. He vowed to join them only if her manner indicated she accepted his letter as sincere. Even if her reaction to him were cool, he would begin a relentless campaign, inventing other chances to make her understand his wishes. He had squandered too many opportunities in the past weeks. He was now determined to press his case.

A women with a dirty, ill behaved little boy clutched to her was the only obstacle between them. The little beggar smashed a toy into his knee as he passed. He glanced back at the smiling little creature but did not stop. Even in the crowd he could hear his own breathing and the rhythmic sound of his leather heels tapping the sidewalk.

He was within steps of them. It would be rude to insinuate himself into their company without invitation—suppose they were taking this opportunity to speak privately? But then, they were all friends, and what would Charles have to say to his sister-in-law which could not be heard by him? He came even with them. Anne gave him a quick look and then another. It was time. He slowed to keep pace with her.

"Captain Wentworth," Charles greeted him. "Which way are you going? Only to Gay Street, or farther up the town?"

"I hardly know," replied Captain Wentworth, surprised. He intended to follow Anne wherever she went, but he could hardly tell Charles such a thing.

Charles then stopped and said, "Are you going as high as Belmont? Are you going near Camden Place? Because, if you are, I shall have no scruple in asking you to take my place and give Anne your arm to her father's door. She is rather done for this morning, and must not go so far without help, and I ought to be at that fellow's in the Market Place. He promised me the sight of a capital gun he is just going to send off—" Wentworth could not care any less about guns and ignored the rest of Musgrove's explanation. All the same, if Musgrove's penchant for guns opened an opportunity for him to escort Anne Elliot to the moon or any star she might fancy, he would be more than happy to give assistance.

"Certainly, Charles, I shall be happy to see Miss Anne home." He ignored the exasperated glances of those passing them whose way their threesome blocked. He ignored Charles and looked only at Anne. Hearing no reply, Wentworth glanced around and saw the retreating figure of Musgrove making haste for a glimpse of the beloved gun.

Anne was smiling as she, too, watched Charles. Wentworth offered his arm. She took it with no pretence of playing the coy miss surprised by the attentions of a new suitor. It was his hope that the deep-rooted familiarity he felt at her touch was equally strong for her as well.

"Bless Charles and his obsession with weapons." Frederick walked in a direction he assumed was towards Camden Place.

Anne laughed. "Yes, bless the dear man."

"I shall always say that his love of guns is one of his finest qualities." She laughed again and leant into him. Memories of their past boiled up with the warmth of her voice and the gesture.

Anne cried out, and his arm jerked. A careless young man walking with his own lady had knocked into the pair. He stammered an apology to Anne. It was uncertain who blushed more, the fellow or his companion.

"Please, don't trouble yourselves," Anne said, smiling at them both. They began to walk again.

"That fellow should be more careful. He'll send someone sprawling."

"I suspect they are young and in love and were paying no attention whatsoever."

"We all have that much in common then." She left his statement unchallenged. He felt hopeful as he steered her to a little path off hectic Union Street. "I intend to be too occupied to be on watch for careless swains." There were others on the path, but most seemed to be refugees from the busyness of other places and were more willing to make way for the lovers and their leisurely pace.

"I read your letter." Anne's tone was direct.

"Good, I intended that you should. And what did you think?"

"I understand you were writing in haste, and so made allowances for the blots and such." Anne's voice made no hint of animation.

Her toying with him was both agonising and enjoyable. "Points off for carelessness. What of the content?" he asked through gritted teeth.

"I thought the composition very fine. You made your points rationally and in good order."

He sighed deeply and loudly. No doubt he more than deserved her good-natured torture, but it was maddening none the less. She stopped and eased them off the path.

"I was very glad to read it, for I have loved none but you." Anne's gaze was steady and expectant.

"My heart is as much yours now as it was that summer. I wish us to be married, Anne. There is no good reason to cover old ground with delaying."

"No, no need for that. It's been a long time, and we should explore new territory." They walked on. Even with such an acceptance to look ahead, the past ten days were examined individually and as links in a chain. Their scrutiny led them inextricably to their present joyous moment.

"I thought you were jealous of my cousin, Mr. Elliot."

"Certainly! Who could blame me? It was his admiration on the beach that roused me to see you more clearly. When I discovered his identity and that he would be staying in Bath, I realised the two of you were bound to meet somehow, though you tried to counter the idea. Almost immediately upon setting foot in this gossip-ridden place, I began to hear rumours and speculations about your future with him. I managed to get hold of myself for a day or so, but the concert was the real blow."

She glanced his way. "I do not think he was purposely driving a wedge between us, but I am certain he was trying to curry my favour. He overstepped himself greatly once or twice."

Elliot's confident boasts to Colonel Wallis, particularly the jolly sa- lute behind her back, reminded him that the man knew precisely what he was about. Frederick chose not to counter Anne's assumptions. He suspected when Elliot learned of their engagement, her cousin's reaction would be dramatic.

"In any case, the following Friday when we met at the White Hart, your determined show of indifference as to his comings and goings gave me some relief."

She squeezed his arm. "I am glad. It was all I could do to keep from shouting that I did not care about his being nearby or a hundred miles away. His manner was never to my liking, and I have recently learnt things about his character that make me glad I did not listen to anyone about his eligibility. My only concern that day was making you know, by any acceptable means, that I cared nothing about him. Had it been in my power, I would have spoken more frankly."

"It began the work. It was your conversation with Harville today that finished off my jealousy. I know eavesdropping is wholly improper, but I couldn't help myself. Just listening to the sweetness of your voice was a pleasure. To hear you state your case so eloquently and even defend us poor men on some scores was all I needed to screw up my courage and tell you what I felt."

"And I am glad you did."

"I meant every word, you know. There's nothing in that letter I wish to amend. My only regret is being too blind to say it all the moment I saw you that first morning." He wondered if such a declaration might have brightened her tired eyes the first morning he'd met her again. His misplaced anger at her decline shamed him now. "Like you, there has never been anyone else. You ruined all women for me. There were few who could come close to your beauty, and it only took a few moments of conversation to make me know they lacked your intelligence and special sort of humour."

Anne laughed, and a pair of passing gentleman looked sharply her way. "I believe you are the only person who thinks of me as a wit."

"That is *my* superior intelligence at work."

She laughed again. "I suppose so."

"Truly, there has never been another. I have been completely constant to you, although, I will confess, it's been unconscious and unintentional. My soul's desire, I thought, was to forget you. That is why I came to Kellynch. I reasoned, as you were nothing to me, I had nothing to fear. So I thought. When I *did* hear of you, I felt immune to you. But when I saw you, I was angry all over again. I felt the pain of the rejection again. I would not see your true, honest nature because I had been made to suffer by your honest consideration of our situation. I deemed you weak even then. But I know now that you are not weak. Your strength and fortitude lie behind your gentle and loving nature."

Anne was quiet as they strolled through a thicket of trees. There were few people nearby and little to distract them. He glanced her way in time to see her touch the corner of her eye. If there were tears, he knew they were tears of relief or happiness. Their walk was a perfect time to speak of all these things, and he continued.

"As I said, your cousin set my mind and heart in motion. Then, Louisa's stubbornness and subsequent fall on the Cobb was the perfect counterpoint to your clear-headed patience and calm. You were even the perfect counterpoint to me! I have never felt so rattled–never by something as innocuous as a fall–but you kept your head and kept us all from losing ours."

"May I tell you something?" She looked up at him with an expression he could not read. "When the surgeon came to tell us he thought there was reason to hope for a good recovery, everyone was elated and rejoicing. I heard you, rightfully, thank God and saw the look on your face. I knew you were truly grateful, and I could not help but fear it was because you *did* love her. Even just a little love under such circumstances might grow to more."

"I was grateful that she would likely recover, but I think it was more relief that my inattention had not outright killed her."

"When you asked me to stay and care for her, I was flattered that you thought me so capable. You asked me so tenderly. I was delighted that you trusted me again."

"I trusted that you were the one person who could pull my completely unworthy fat from a particularly ugly fire." They both laughed.

"I wanted to stay. I would have, gladly."

"I know. But, it was Charles's to decide, and he chose differently. Now I'm very glad for it."

Anne's expression changed from thought provoking to curious. "You were quite angry, as I recall. Why, now, are you glad?"

"Had you been left behind, Benwick's mournful countenance and his sombre poetry might have worked on you in the same way it has obviously worked on Miss Louisa."

She looked surprised at the idea. "Well, then it is a good thing we shall never know." Her smile indicated his jealousy of Benwick and the dangers of rhyme were not much of a risk.

"At any rate, I can say I never loved Louisa Musgrove and could never have done so. I had loved the perfect woman once, and Miss Louisa is not of the same stuff as you. After the fall, I had more than enough time to revisit the past and torture myself with the knowledge of having thrown away so many opportunities to reunite us."

Frederick told her about the Harvilles and their belief that he and Louisa were engaged. "I had behaved inexcusably and must abide the consequences. I had trapped myself through careless and incircumspect behaviour. Fortunately, Edward had been dunning me for a visit, and I reasoned that leaving the scene might be a good way to test the genuineness of her feelings." He leant close. "I think the current state of affairs proves any feelings for me were feeble at best." She laughed quietly, almost to herself. "But, having no idea such a thing was even possible, I left knowing that, if nothing changed, I would return eventually to Kellynch and do what was required."

"You would have married her?" Anne's tone was low and uncertain.

"Yes, I would have, in honour, been bound to marriage. I hope you can understand me; I think we would have found a sort of happiness. Nothing extraordinary, mind you." He stopped and faced her. "Nothing that resembles the feelings I have for you. Do you believe me?" She nodded in the affirmative. He took her arm, and they continued. "The saddest part is that my actions would have deprived her of being loved as well as she ought to be. By marrying her, I would have been denying her the best possible life."

"You would have been denying yourself, as well."

"And you...and Benwick. I would have damaged us all." They continued down the lane, past a bakery. The scent of fresh bread reminded him he'd not eaten since breakfast. "I was six weeks with Edward," said he, "and saw him happy. I could have no other pleasure. I deserved none. He inquired after you very particularly and asked if you were personally altered, little suspecting that, to my eye, you could never alter." He was gratified by her smile. It pleased him to let her know that even when they were far apart, he still spoke glowingly of her.

"What did you do all that time in Shropshire?"

"I languished. You will be glad to know I suffered daily seeing the great happiness between my brother and his new wife."

"You did not begrudge him such happiness, did you?"

"No...well, a little. He deserves it and more. When I told him I was leaving and going to Bath, I hinted that you were the reason. Knowing what a kind heart you possessed, he hoped you would have pity on me."

"I think I am able to muster just a little pity for you, sir."

"Thank you, Miss, you are very kind." He told her of his hopes on his journey and the one encouragement he had possessed. "I could never doubt that you would be loved and sought by others, but I knew to a certainty that you had refused one man, at least, of better pretensions than myself. I could not help wondering."

"I overheard you speaking with Louisa that day."

Now it was his turn to be silent. Her quick recall of the episode made him believe it had carried some weight in her mind. He endeavoured to remember everything he said, but only the pictures and satisfaction of helping her into the Croft's carriage remained sharp in his mind.

"Your speech about the beautiful, glossy hazelnut made me know how you felt about my weaknesses. I suspect you thought me weak again in turning down Charles." She could not look at him.

"I assumed Lady Russell had intervened again, that she once more had persuaded you against a man not to her tastes." It was the first time the spectre of Lady Russell had arisen.

"I never told my godmother about the proposal. She knows it occurred, of course, but even now, we have never discussed why I refused him."

"Was it for me?"

"Yes."

He could not help himself. His heart ached with happiness that she had loved him through so much misery. "I feel sorry for Charles. You would have been a wonderful wife to him and a great influence on his family."

"But again, he would not have been loved in the way he deserves."

They re-visited their meeting on Milsom Street and Molland's that first day. The concert had been an agonising mixture of excitement and dread. They came to understand that each of them was vulnerable to misunderstanding the other, although Wentworth was quick to admit that he was more prone to that danger than she.

"I thought I had lost you, but I realised that if so many could be wrong about Louisa and me, then all of Bath could be wrong about your attachment to your cousin."

"They certainly were! There are still some who have hopes in that direction."

"They shall be greatly disappointed when they learn about us."

"They certainly will." She stopped and he realised they were at the door of Camden Place. "Thank you, Captain. It was a lovely walk." She offered him a courtesy.

He bowed, regretting that she did not live farther away. "Thank you for the pleasure of your company, Miss."

"I look forward to seeing you at the party."

"I look forward to everything concerning you."

His words made her blush, and she stumbled against the door thinking she'd opened it. She was in no real danger of falling, but he took her arm and brought her close to him.

"We shall talk more, later."

"Yes, there is so much to say." The door opened and she left him.

Chapter Fourteen

T hank you, Elise," Anne said, stepping out of her dress. She glanced at the mirror and observed the faint smile which, upon notice, broadened. His influence was in everything about her now. There was no task so mundane that could not be infused with thoughts of him and made enjoyable.

Elise approached and put her nightdress over her head. As she loosened her hair, she said, "I don't care for it braided tonight." In a few weeks time, Frederick would see her just as she was now. Her cheeks coloured scarlet. She turned away from her reflection and went to the bed.

"I am glad to see you enjoyed yourself, Mademoiselle," Elise said, as she lightly brushed Miss Anne's dress. She smiled then went back to her work.

"Thank you, Elise, but how do you know I enjoyed myself?"

The French maid's history was vague, but she had been with their mother first and was now shared between Elizabeth and Anne. She had watched the girls grow into women and was of strong opinions concerning each of them. She smiled over her shoulder to Anne, placed the dress in the closet, and began to gather and fold her undergarments. "Well, Miss, normally, you are unenthusiastic when dressing for such a party as tonight's and are quite glad to be done with it at its end. You come up immediately after the last guest leaves and are ready to retire. But tonight is different."

Anne played with her hair, interested in the maid's observations. "How is that so, Elise?"

"You were dressed before Miss Elizabeth, and you went down early. That is something you very rarely do, Miss."

~ ~ ~ ~ ~ ~ ~ & ~ ~ ~ ~ ~ ~ ~

She *had* gone down early, hoping the Crofts would be precisely on time. They were not, which was a disappointment, but they and Frederick arrived within the hour. By the time they arrived, the Baronet and Elizabeth were down and receiving all the guests.

There was never any reason to blush for her family's manners; though Anne was quite sure their sincerity was not so faultless. Both had made Frederick very welcome. Elizabeth had even taken him by the arm and shown him all the points of interest in the salon. He had found the refreshment table well appointed with many of his favourite foods. Then, when Elizabeth had made the mistake of bringing him to Anne and he remarked how well she looked this evening, Elizabeth made certain he knew that Anne absolutely refused to play cards. She wondered aloud why, considering her distaste for games, her sister bothered to show herself at such affairs.

"I can understand such sentiment, for unless I am playing for money, I find that observing others is, by and large, a more interesting pastime," he said. Elizabeth suddenly thought herself needed elsewhere and left the pair alone. He apologised for any offence if it was given.

"I think she is not offended, merely put out that you would agree with me. I am afraid Elizabeth and I are very mismatched sisters."

He was about to respond when Sophia Croft joined them. Teasing him, she asked, "Are you boring our poor young friend with a continued recital of all the reasons women should not be allowed aboard a King's ship?" The Admiral joined them and she took his arm.

"No, we were talking about how mystifying it is that siblings can be completely opposite and yet come from the same parents," he said. He turned back to Anne.

Sophia smiled and said, "How true. It can be quite heartbreaking in fact. Take the case of the Wentworths of Liverpool. The eldest brother and the only daughter are quite intelligent, independent thinking and liberal in their ideas. And yet, the youngest son—a scapegrace by all accounts—is the most stiff-necked and hidebound man of my acquaintance. Come, Miss Anne; let me rescue you from whatever nonsense he was spouting." She took Anne's arm, gave her surprised brother a wink, and walked away with his prize.

When Anne expressed worry that Captain Wentworth would be angered by the exchange, Sophia laughed and the Admiral said, "They joust like that all the time. He's a good one to liven up a place. Frederick likes a good tease more than most and will be back later in the evening with a good sharp rebuttal." They continued to talk about him and his sense of humour. Anne wondered if she had changed so much over the years that she might be too dour for him or for his humour-loving family.

166

They met repeatedly over the course of the evening. One meeting, under cover of a large flower arrangement in the parlour, was a particular revelation. Frederick confessed that after the *Asp* was sunk, when he was in possession of several thousand pounds and posted into the frigate *Laconia*, he had considered writing to her in hopes that she would renew the engagement. When she told him she would have done so, he admitted that he was as much to blame for their years of separation as anyone else he might hold responsible.

"Like other great men under reverses," he added with a smile, "I must endeavour to subdue my mind to my fortune. I must learn to brook being happier than I deserve." Upon reciting this swath of affected modesty, Wentworth reached out and fingered one of the leaves of the display.

Anne reached out and stroked the same frond. It bobbed silently against the sound of the card party in the other part of the room. "I think you are not the only one who must learn to endure this unearned joy. I, too, gain more than I bargained for."

He glanced her way and said, "How so?"

"All those weeks at Uppercross, I allowed your horrid mood to put me off. Everyone knew we had been acquainted. I would not have been breeching any sort of propriety in presuming upon it. Instead, I wasted my time politely inquiring after your opinion of the weather or the day's shooting. I am a woman after all; I could have done more." She touched the frond again. "I could have used whatever means available to make you understand me, but I chose not to."

"So, you wish to take the blame?"

She smiled and turned to him. "We shall share it equally, but don't think I will be so generous after we are married."

Just as he was about to explore her interesting reference to the state of their future household together, his sister approached and insisted that he join her at one of the tables.

"I have noticed you are not playing very much; so, I will not feel I am imposing upon you, Captain. Colonel Wallis is sorely in need of a hard set down." After slipping her hand through his arm, she said, "And you are just the man to do it."

Frederick was all smiles and feigned eagerness, but Anne could tell he yearned to remain with her in the plant-filled corner. They could not afford to be incautious, and if there was anyone in the room who might guess their secret, it would be Mrs. Croft. He bid Anne to please excuse them as they went to do battle for the honour of the Navy. For a moment, she considered giving him a token, her handkerchief perhaps, but that would rouse suspicion as well. Overt intimacy would conjure up questions in the minds of their friends and family, and those questions would eventually be asked and require answers on their parts.

"Never let it be said that I would stand between you and your duty, sir," was the safest thing for Anne to say. For an instant, their eyes met and she felt something from him, a little disappointment perhaps. She watched and pondered her impression as Frederick and Sophia made their way to the table.

He drew the chair out for his sister and then took his place across from the sharp-featured Colonel Wallis. Anne couldn't decide whether the man's red uniform gave him a florid cast in the candlelight, or he was responding to the warmth of the room and anticipation of the game. Perhaps it was both. *Better and better*, she thought as she watched her cousin approach the table. He asked that Mrs. Wallis surrender her seat to him. She seemed quite happy about the exchange. Mr. Elliot took the chair with a greedy smile.

Whether Frederick won or lost was of little import–though she hoped fervently that he and his sister would thrash their opponents– what mattered to Anne was watching him. She took the greatest pleasure in watching him cut the cards and speak with animation to his sister as the cards were dealt. After the deal was finished, he picked up his cards, fanned them, but did nothing to change their order. They lost the opening trick, but she could tell by their looks that this was a strategy.

No hand of cards ever held such interest for her, but she soon realised she didn't really attend the game. She examined him. His hands were of special awareness to her. He handled the cards with great surety, never dropping or mishandling them. It was regrettable that she must stand so far from the table. With the low light of the candles, closer study was not possible. She would satisfy herself by watching the movements of his whole person. She savoured them all, especially his triumph.

When the game between the services ended, Mr. Elliot withdrew and Frederick was set upon by Elizabeth and Miss Carteret. Anne was amused to see that Miss Carteret seemed terribly smitten with him. She blushed and dropped her cards quite prettily. He endeavoured to show her how to shuffle correctly. This was a complete failure, and when he was on his knees under the table for the second time in as many minutes, he looked to Anne, smiled and made a silly face of frustration that made her laugh. He continued to play with the ladies and the Colonel in a most gracious manner but didn't look Anne's way again.

For once, she wished she did play cards. She could then manoeuvre a place at a table with him. Instead she must continue her charade of disinterest in the games. Walking around the room would have to satisfy for the moment.

The tables changed. Charles Musgrove, who seemed to be eager to have a go against the army, relieved Wentworth. Frederick smiled as he approached her, and her breathing quickened; but just before he reached her, Mr. Elliot stepped up and asked that he might bring her a cup of punch. She refused but could think of no way to deter her cousin from ruining her next furtive meeting with the Captain.

"I hope you are not too bored by the party. I know cards are not your favourite form of entertainment." Elliot ate a cheese straw and took a drink.

"No, they are not," was all she said in response. Wentworth was staying well back, trying to look interested in a conversation between Captain Harville and Henrietta Musgrove.

"I think you prefer guessing games," Elliot said.

It was an odd statement and one that spontaneously drew her attention. "Guessing games? What would make you think I like such things?" He had found a topic that did interest her.

"You seemed very curious the other evening at the concert about how I knew so much about you before your arrival in Bath. You are still as curious, if not more so, I'll wager."

The arrogant presumption of her cousin was laughable. She wondered what might transpire were she to mention Mrs. Smith, late of Westgate Buildings. If she mentioned knowing the wife of his late friend, what sort of guessing game would this become? Were they not surrounded with so many of her father's friends, she might indeed play, but as he had no idea how foolish he looked to her now, she schooled her features and moved around him to walk along the table of refreshments. "I have always thought it unwise to gamble, sir. After giving it a considerable amount of thought, I have come to the conclusion that as intriguing as your mystery might be to me, you are more anxious to tell than I am anxious to know." With that, she walked away.

The path along the table took her precisely where she wished to be: amongst the naval contingency of Captains Harville and Wentworth. As fortune would have it, Miss Carteret and Miss Elliot joined them. Her sister was all smiles, and while Anne could not place herself near Wentworth, she could enjoy a felicitous view of Mr. Elliot glowering at her from across the room.

Anne said little, but she was gratified to watch her sister's perfect manners carry the day in entertaining both Frederick and Captain Harville. Miss Carteret was enthralled by a tale Harville was telling, and her sister dutifully followed her lead. Frederick bowed out, pointing to his cup. She waited for the right moment and left them as well.

"I have never been so frustrated in my life," Frederick said.

"Why is that?" Anne took a drink from the cup he just filled for her.

"We can never be alone here."

"We will not be alone for some weeks or months, perhaps."

"Months! What do you suppose they would do if I were to announce right here that you have accepted my proposal and that we wish to fix a date?"

She gave a bit of thought; though, it did not take long for a smile to come to her. "I think we do not have enough smelling salts to accommodate all the fainting."

He laughed. "Particularly your father, I suspect."

She was about to counter him but then said, "Perhaps, you're right. Though, the cause would be that someone of your prospects would wish to marry me and not my sister."

The secret moments between them were growing in number, and she was flattered how he continued to find ways to come to her. "I have never before set for myself such a difficult mission as I have this night. Had I known when I accepted your sister's invitation I would be exerting myself to such an extent just to be with you, I might have thought better of accepting."

"Really," she had said, her tone feigned indignation. She even took an exaggerated step away to emphasis her jesting.

He frowned and made every effort possible to make amends. "I must not do anything to make us look any more connected than others sharing the warm punch at a friendly party." She let him worry for a moment or two more and then informed him he was the object of her hesitant try to recapture her lost sense of humour. "I was afraid of this," he said. "All that is needed is to be in the company of my sister for a few minutes and I am dished." He took a drink of punch. She noticed a tiny white scar across the knuckles of his left hand.

"What is it?" he asked, when he noticed that she stared.

"Nothing," she said.

Later, in the quiet of her room, she considered how much she did not know about him. They had been engaged so short a time, she'd known little of him even then. She was young and deeply in love with a man who made his way in the world in a most violent manner. The scar was bound to be just the beginning of things.

~ ~ ~ ~ ~ ~ ~ & ~ ~ ~ ~ ~ ~ ~

"–and tonight you stayed downstairs longer than your sister. Miss Elliot is usually the one who remains and sees to the cleaning up."

"Yes, I did. It was only fair. As you say, it usually falls to Elizabeth." The truth was that Anne wanted to stay in the room he'd occupied. She had gathered the decks of cards he'd played with and sorted through them. His nimble fingers had touched them, and she wished to touch them as well. It was all foolishness. She forced herself to pay attention to Elise. It was important that she not allow herself to indulge in silly, girlish antics in her mind.

Elise was finished with her observations. Anne had missed most of them. The maid closed the jewellery casket, curtseyed, and bid Miss Anne a good night. The closed door did more than close out the household, it gave Anne a private place for her to consider a new life.

On other nights, when she looked about her room, it was merely a well-appointed cell. The chamber was neat and tidy, little more than a place in which a prisoner could be comfortable in body but not in heart. Now, in the same way that everything since Frederick's letter was turned on its head, her room, too, was reborn into a warm and inviting spot to contemplate her future. *Love truly changes more than just the lovers,* she thought.

She reached over to a book of poetry and prose by John Gay. She had purchased it in Lyme that morning she and the Musgrove sisters had walked through the town with Frederick. They had been left alone at one point, and she'd made reference to Gay while looking through a bookstall. Frederick had not recognised the name. Before she could explain, he had been called into the store to assist Louisa. She had taken advantage of the solitude, bought the book, and prayed no one would ever know about her sentimental, hopeless purchase. It was not until she met Frederick in Molland's that she had bothered to unpack it from her trunk and read it. Now, it was her most prized possession.

Opening the letter, she relished the thought of his hands touching the pages and that touch turning to action while he wrote of his feelings for her in such intimate terms. Then there came thoughts of his drawing her attention to it as he distracted Mrs. Musgrove with talk of forgetting his gloves. Energy surged through her limbs and inner parts as she remembered his expression when he pulled it from under the other scattered papers on the little writing desk. The flushed, pleading expression, she now understood, was the product of pouring himself out for her. She held the letter to her heart. It was as if he were touching her.

She looked at the letter and smiled. On sudden impulse, she took it and herself to the mirror. Her colour was high and appealing as never before. "I suppose you are no more immune to silliness than the next young woman," she told her image. It had been a long time since she had thought of herself as young, and it was because of him. Frederick made her feel completely different in every way she could imagine.

~ ~ ~ ~ ~ ~ ~ & ~ ~ ~ ~ ~ ~ ~

When Frederick arrived unannounced at the White Hart, all the Musgroves and their guests were present. Along with many of Mrs. Musgrove's Bath friends were his own who were clustered about the dining table, partaking of bits of gossip gathered all over the city and even a few tender bits found in and about Camden Place the night before.

"I scarcely think I attended the same party listening to them," Harville said, nodding towards the crowded table. "It's hard to imagine that so much goes on around a man of which he takes no notice."

"That is always the way of it," Wentworth said, disappointed that Anne was not in attendance. He was invited to join them for dinner and he accepted, hoping all the while she would appear. When she did, he barely had a chance to admire her when it became clear her presence upset the balance of the table. Happily, such turmoil caused them an unexpected benefit.

"Mama is fretting about the table," Henrietta said, gesturing to the large table. "There are so many, and there are still some dishes to be brought up from the kitchen. She wonders if, perhaps, the two of you won't mind sitting over here, at the little table." She looked particularly at Anne. "I assured her that of all the people in the room the Captain would take the least offence in being asked to be separated from the rest."

"Tell your mother I will be very pleased to take a place over here. I would never wish to make her uneasy about treating me like family."

"Certainly, Miss Musgrove, tell your mother I, too, am quite content with the arrangements."

The girl smiled, but as she left them to tell her mother, she glanced back at the pair. "We may have been too enthusiastic," he said. "I think she suspects something. She just doesn't know what."

Anne watched the crowd a moment. "She will be distracted soon enough."

"I was worried at first that you would not come, and here you are. Then I considered it would be the same game of chase as last night when we could barely scrape out a minute alone."

At that moment, Mrs. Musgrove appeared, bringing them each a glass of wine. "I know I should have had you at the other table with us, Anne, and asked Captain Harville to join you, Captain; but his leg is worrying him mightily today. I just didn't have the heart to stand on ceremony."

"You needn't worry Mrs. Musgrove. I have shared tables aplenty with Harville; it is not often I am able to dine with such a lovely young woman." He raised his glass to her and enjoyed the colour flooding her cheeks. Mrs. Musgrove left them and their chairs were brought. Anne and the Captain were seated. Dishes were brought and served in fine style.

After the footmen moved away, Anne said, "Such effusive praise is going to arouse the suspicions of more than just Henrietta." She took a sip of soup.

"I doubt it. These are the Musgroves and their friends," he said, nodding towards the large table loaded with food and guests. "I suppose, just to be on the safe side, we should be silent and severe throughout the meal," Wentworth suggested.

"Shall we, really?" she said.

"No, to be honest, I doubt I could pull it off."

"We were not bothered by anyone in the autumn when we were on our own. How did we act then?"

"I acted like an idiot. You, I am sure, were perfectly wonderful."

"I was disappointed."

Her statement hurt him, but he deserved it. "I'm sorry for that."

"As I said last night, I am sure that I could have made myself known to you. I believe I didn't really know my own mind."

"We know what we want now," he said, raising his glass, "so, here's to the future."

Anne leant forward. "Do you think we should draw attention by toasting?"

He looked to the table and then nodded its way. "Fortunately, the Musgrove's domestic hurricano keeps anyone from noticing us."

They drank, and Anne said, "Around Christmas time, Lady Russell and I visited Uppercross. She called it the same thing. I believe the two of you—"

"Yes, even Harville has admitted that the din can get on his nerves at times. But they mean well." He smiled and busied himself with slicing a boiled potato.

"We will have to go to her soon after you speak with father. It is only fitting."

"I know, Anne. But today, right now, let us enjoy our privacy. Let us enjoy one another's company without the burden of anyone's family." Just then everyone at the large table laughed all together, drowning out every other sound. He leant close, "Except for theirs, of course."

~ ~ ~ ~ ~ ~ ~ & ~ ~ ~ ~ ~ ~ ~

The walk home in the drenching rain was cosy under his umbrella. When they got to the door of Camden Place, they met Miss Elliot, Mrs. Clay, and Mr. Elliot arriving from an outing of their own. Nothing was mentioned about the Captain and Anne walking together, and he was invited in along with the other gentleman.

They took great care to present themselves as unattached and completely disinterested when they joined the Baronet in the sitting room. Refreshments were called for, and everyone settled in for a comfortable evening.

Anne casually explained that she and the Captain had been visitors at the Musgrove's rooms and that he had saved her a soaking by the offer of his umbrella. For good measure, he added, "Unfortunately, salvation came at a price, and Miss Anne has had to endure my nonsense about weather."

"You are a sailor, sir," Mr. Elliot said, "You could leave the place if you find its weather foul."

"I could, sir, but other parts of the world are not as interesting to me just now," Wentworth replied His tone was smooth, but Elliot could not mistake the warning in his eyes. "The presence of my family here suits me very well. The weather is nothing."

Elliot had no opportunity to respond, for Miss Elliot and Mrs. Clay commanded the floor with their opinions on the weather, the elegance of the party the evening before, and the woeful lack of anything in the way of entertainment in the coming week. After those topics were exhausted, Anne spoke nicely of dining with the Musgroves and the crush of their party. She took care not to mention anything about dining with the Captain at a table to themselves.

It was dark when Mr. Elliot said he must be going home. Wentworth wished to stay but knew his remaining might rouse his suspicion. He decided it was best that he take advantage of the cousin's departure. Though Miss Elliot saw them out, Anne stood at the top of the stairs and smiled as he departed.

Chapter Fifteen

The next morning as Frederick worked his neck cloth into an appropriate knot, he reflected on the need for perfection in everything from his appearance to his attitude for the coming interview with Sir Walter. Much of the previous night had been spent dissecting the disastrous first encounter with Anne's father. Ridicule and dismissal had been the Baronet's weapons of choice. There had never been an outright denial of parental permission. It was not necessary to plunge a knife into a dying man when you could simply walk away, assured that he would eventually die of neglect. *I suspect you are little changed over the years, Sir Walter*, he thought, *but I certainly am.* He neatly smoothed the ends of his neck cloth.

"You have finished then, sir." Harkness had quietly joined him and held open the Captain's best waistcoat.

Wentworth shrugged it on and fastened the buttons. "I've finished this. Is my coat ready?" Harkness left him again. He marvelled at the calm of the man reflected back to him in the mirror. But why not? The fit of the clothing was flawless. The colours woven into the waistcoat suited him well. Just then Harkness returned with his blue coat. As expected, it slid easily over his shoulders and fit him in the waist and in length perfectly. He would meet Sir Walter Elliot, if not as a social equal, at least as an equal in the externals the Baronet so highly prized.

Sir Walter had been all smiles and polite grace when Frederick had presented himself at Kellynch in the summer of 1806. "Captain, please, have a seat. How may I help you?" He was the model of a gentleman more than willing to aid a brilliant young officer rising quickly in the King's Navy. Once he was found to be a young man not given to meddling with their daughters, most of the gentry of Somerset had been pleased with Commander Frederick Wentworth, the Baronet among them. But when the commander had asked to marry the Baronet's second daughter, the country gentleman lost his *noblesse oblige* and had regarded the proposal as an insult to him and to his family's honour.

"If it was your hope to collect a tidy settlement, may I remind you that Anne is not of age? She cannot marry without my consent, and there is no dowry even should something be arranged without my consent."

The statement was nearly a lifetime ago; yet, it still had the power to anger him. Today, Wentworth would meet Sir Walter face-to-face, man-to-man, and Wentworth would be the victor. He was no longer a young man cowed by any theoretical superiority; Captain Wentworth was a superior man who would claim his bride.

"Your coat, sir," Harkness said, brushing Wentworth's shoulders. He stood back, taking one last swipe at a speck of lint.

Wentworth carefully judged the effect of the suit. *Not bad for an over-reaching, unconnected stiver with no prospects for the future,* he thought, echoing the words used to reject his suit that dreadful summer. He knew them to be the opinions held by her family and, to his shame, he'd assumed they had convinced Anne of them as well. He had thrown back against her every protest she made. He had twisted her words, making her say things he knew to be the opposite of her true feelings.

Thankfully, all of that was in the past. His dear Anne had forgiven him his foolishness, and he had made great strides in putting aside his own pride and arrogance. He saw her once again as the lovely, intelligent woman he had known her to be.

"I think I'm finished, Harkness."

"One last thing, sir." Harkness took a brush to his hair. "It needs to be cut, sir. If I'd had more notice, I'd have done it today." There would always be something to keep him from perfection. Except for his hair, he deemed himself well-armed and prepared for battle.

Entering the dining room, he found Sophia and the Admiral at breakfast. The Admiral had finished eating, but he lingered over his coffee. Sophia had gone through the mail, and they were now discussing pressing errands.

"Good morning. Sophia. Admiral." The goal was to eat and leave without being questioned about his attire or plans for the day. His hope foundered immediately on the rocks of brotherly curiosity.

"My, my, Frederick. You look to be married...or buried." The Admiral leant back to take in more of the sight of his brother-in-law.

"I've neither of those planned for the day, I assure you, sir. I am meeting a fellow and wish to make a good impression. You know these city types, all rigged out formally just in case they meet someone of importance while walking the dog. I should hate to reflect badly on the House of Croft."

The Admiral laughed heartily and answered, "So, no marriages and no burials."

Frederick hoped to preclude further questions by making a great show of attacking a plate of eggs and beef tongue. He kept a close watch on them and could not help but notice Sophia's pencil hovering over her list. She studied him closely, and he willed himself to look innocent. In general, it took a heroic effort to thwart Sophia's curiosity. To his relief, she suddenly tapped her pencil and turned her attention from him to the Admiral.

"My dear, have you noticed that Frederick seems to be in better spirits since Friday last, but most especially since Saturday?" His relief flagged. It was clear his sister was in the mood to bait and tease. Unluckier still, the Admiral's smirk told Wentworth his brother-in-law was of the same mind.

"Well, when a man quite unexpectedly meets up with an old mate and good friends like the Musgroves, it is more than enough to bring his spirits to the full. Besides," he said pouring another cup of coffee, "Sir Walter's rout the other evening was much more pleasant than I could have ever imagined. Why should he not be in a fine humour?" He looked to his wife. The baton passed, Frederick braced for Sophia's turn at him.

"While these are indeed things which I think may contribute to his...upturn, I thought I noticed a great change on Saturday. He was in an absolute passion to be dressed and ready for the party." She looked directly at Wentworth, who was finishing with his coffee, preparing to make a hasty exit. "Well, Brother, dear. Am I mistaken or has something of consequence happened which is the source of this changed demeanour?"

Sophia had once told him she learned the value of silence and that people would fill the space it created rather than endure it. He, too, had learnt the same lesson and would normally wait her out, but he was in a rush. He must give her something else to occupy her thinking. "Actually, yes, I was able to gain some information on Saturday which will, in fact, change my life markedly. After my meeting today, I am hoping to have very good news for you both." This bit of intelligence, taken simply, should keep his sister busy for a time. Frederick rose from the table, signalling an end to the discussion.

Sophia, however, was not to be daunted by this obvious ploy. "Might this have to do with a certain young woman?"

Frederick had already started out of the room when his sister had aimed this shot directly across his bow. He stopped and turned to address his sister and brother. "There is a good possibility this, indeed, has to do with a certain young woman." He smiled faintly and continued, "But then again, it could have to do with finding a new manager who promises me four and three-quarters per annum." He returned to

Sophia, bussed her on the cheek and said, "I leave you to decide which has raised my spirits, dear." Straightening, he touched his forehead in salute to the Admiral and left them to think over his mixed reply.

~ ~ ~ ~ ~ ~ ~ & ~ ~ ~ ~ ~ ~ ~

Anne rose and sorted through the flowers in one of the side table vases. When she handed the spoiled blooms to the footman, Elizabeth looked up from the book she was attempting to read and glared at her sister for a second time in just a few minutes. Mrs. Clay looked up from her sewing as well and gave Anne one of her more genuine, practised smiles. *With time*, Anne thought, *the woman's show of fake sincerity will be unassailable.*

Since Elizabeth and Mrs. Clay had no trouble seeing she was unsettled, Anne reasoned she must find some occupation before her father took notice. She would normally go to another part of the house, but with Frederick's promise of coming to speak to her father, she abhorred the idea of missing him. The previous day, spent with the Musgroves, was wonderful. Though they were kept apart by propriety and the large number of people visiting their friends, she felt sure no one suspected them. Having such a secret and revelling in it under the noses of people who knew them both so well, was a rare delight in her normally dull world.

The clock, sweetly chiming another quarter hour, interrupted her thoughts. He had said he would call on her father this morning as soon as would be proper. But here it was, nearly eleven o'clock. The morning was racing forward and still no Frederick.

Anne took a seat—even this warranted another glare from her sister—and took up some embroidery. She began to work a simple chain stitch while listening for the door. After another quarter of an hour, her patience was rewarded when she heard the knocker rap three times. Elizabeth and Mrs. Clay exchanged looks and, after a short discussion, guessed that it was Mr. Elliot. Sir Walter was convinced that Colonel Wallis was come to call and that, perhaps, Mr. Elliot was with him. Anne was amused that Mr. Elliot was so much anticipated by her family. When the door opened and Captain Wentworth was announced, the effect was quite fascinating.

Each party seemed convinced that they were to see *their* preferred visitor walk through the door. When that was not the case, each maintained the appropriate, half-surprised smiles and expressions of happy regard. Only her own expression was genuine—my, how good it felt to smile—when she laid eyes on him. Anne was happy to see that either Frederick did not notice the slights of her family or chose to ignore

178

them. He smiled warmly during his reception and looked her way often. While they were settling into their seats, Anne was surprised to see Elizabeth's expression change. In fact, Miss Elliot and her father were suddenly quite solicitous of the Captain, offering him the best seat.

"Captain Wentworth! I am so happy to see you. This is quite an unexpected pleasure. Come, come and have a chair," Sir Walter said, his arms out flung, offering up all the furniture for his comfort. Elizabeth called for refreshments and took pains to make sure the footman repeated special instructions for the kitchen. They strained to make themselves quite at his service. Frederick appeared to take the arch politeness in stride. In fact, he looked as if he was rather enjoying the attention.

After Wentworth had chosen a seat, Elizabeth, of course, took her place next to their father. Anne took her normal place in a side chair just a little to one side of the sphere of conversation. Mrs. Clay was relegated to being a satellite left in a distant orbit. It was amusing to think that, just for this little while, Frederick Wentworth was the centre of the Elliot galaxy.

Anne knew her cheeks were flushed. Her breath was short and the sound of her heart pounded in her ears. The embroidery she'd been working earlier was at hand, and she picked it up. It was a useless gesture. To try and do even the simplest of stitches would be impossible with her hands shaking so violently. She knew it was the fact that he was here to propose that made her so tense. Why this was, she couldn't guess. There was no risk now. He'd made it clear that he intended on making her his wife with or without her father's blessing. The very thought of Frederick's intentions warmed her further, and she could not resist smiling. She looked up and was surprised to find him smiling at her. Anne could hear the Baronet's voice, but it seemed very far off. The whole scene was a dream. He was actually in her home to ask her father for her hand in marriage. A fortnight ago, she could not have dared to hope, but now–

~ ~ ~ ~ ~ ~ ~ & ~ ~ ~ ~ ~ ~ ~

"I believe this will be to your liking," said Miss Elliot, as she offered him a cup of tea. This forced Wentworth to look away from Anne. He accepted the cup, took a drink and, despite its lack of flavour, complimented the hostess. At this juncture, he decided to use the advantage of surprise against the Baronet's advantage of home waters.

"Sir Walter, I wish you to know that I enjoyed myself exceedingly Saturday evening. I thank you again for the invitation." Quickly taking a drink, he continued before the gentleman had an opportunity to reply,

"Such kindness towards me makes me think you the perfect man to render me a particularly great favour, a favour for which I would be most assuredly in your debt." He took another drink and enjoyed watching Anne's sweet expression shift to one of perplexity over the rim. Sir Walter, too, was mystified, but Wentworth could see the wheels turning. The idea of the Captain being indebted to him intrigued Sir Walter exceedingly. This was precisely where Frederick wanted him. Soon, it was suggested that they adjourn to the library.

On entering the room, Wentworth noticed the want of books. There was a single volume on the desk with only other common desk clutter to keep it company. He noticed one of the lower shelves contained several books on sailing that he recognised. He made his way over and read the titles of several other books of poetry and some noted essayists.

"Those are Anne's. She was quite set on bringing them from Kellynch. For what reason, I haven't the slightest idea."

Wentworth wasn't sure the accusatory tone was towards books in general or the content of these in particular. Either way, the Baronet had little regard for the interests of his middle daughter. He touched the spine of *The Seaman's Life*, moved that she'd searched it out on her own.

"Captain Wentworth, whatever aid I might lend you will be a pleasure I assure you." The man examined Wentworth without the smallest amount of tact.

"Thank you, Sir Walter. Thank you very much for such kindness. To be honest, it is not so much a favour I need, as it is your blessing." He observed the Baronet as he absorbed this. The man's expression went from one of puzzlement to deep thought and then to one of elation.

"May I presume you have come to ask for the hand of my daughter?" He beamed and cocked his head. In his pleasure, he let out a little burst of tittering.

Wentworth thought of Anne and persevered. "Yes, sir. You may presume as much."

Sir Walter rose from his chair and came alongside Wentworth. "I must tell you, I did not suspect your interest until just the moment you asked. But now that I understand you and might reflect on it, the evidence has been there all along; although, she has kept exceedingly quiet about it."

Wentworth was surprised that the Baronet would have observed Anne enough over any period of time to notice anything pertaining to her.

"When did you propose?"

"Saturday."

"You see, I do remember having a passing suspicion when I saw you together at the White Hart on Friday." He smiled wider and clapped his hands together. "Love blooming under my very nose, and I failed to notice! The pair of you are too clever by half." Sir Walter's jollity was disturbing, but the man's change in fortune had perhaps done a work that Wentworth had failed to see until now. Though, Patrick didn't seem to think–

"So, Saturday evening the two of you were playing at charades, eh? Letting us all believe you were indifferent to one another. Though, I did notice you taking refreshments together now and then. I thought she presented a beautiful tableau, her dark beauty and your handsome features. Your uniform was particularly striking against her red dress, was it not? You certainly could not have asked Saturday night, and I suppose you didn't think it proper to come to me on the Sabbath. I'm not sure: is a proposal akin to work? Your brother is a clergyman; is he not? Perhaps, he could advise you. But then, you'll not really need to know, as it is Monday; and I am giving my consent."

He nodded to Wentworth and opened his hands. "Well, there it is Captain. You have my consent to marry my daughter."

Wentworth thanked him, even though he was still making his way through Sir Walter's ramble.

The Baronet took his seat again. He pulled the single volume to him and opened it. He looked at Wentworth. "Do you know what this is, Captain Wentworth?"

"I have not a clue, sir."

"This is the Baronetage. Do you know what the Baronetage is?"

"Yes, sir. I have heard of it. In the Navy we have something similar: The Navy List. It discloses each man's rank and where he stands compared with his superiors and inferiors."

"Ah, the Navy is more enlightened than I would have suspected," he murmured as to himself as he perused the pages. For a few minutes, the man seemed to be lost in the pages of the book. Wentworth was about to speak when Sir Walter closed the book, rose and approached him. With hand extended, he said, "I would be most honoured to have our families allied by such a match, Captain." Sir Walter shook his hand and even made an attempt at patting him on the back. Both were rather weak and, strangely brought to mind images of small girls in pretty sprigged frocks.

Frederick allowed him to continue prating on and shaking his hand, but there was something not quite right about it all. Perhaps he was just over prepared, spoiling for a fight when there was none to be had. *This was good*, he thought. There was no sense in starting his relationship with the head of the Elliot family with a scrap. He continued to smile and endeavoured to attend to the Baronet, but in the next moment the man made no sense. He was jabbering on about Mr. Elliot being a part of the family soon. Didn't the silly rooster know that everyone in Bath had paired Anne with Elliot? Was he hoping that Elliot would so easily shift his affections to–

"–her dark beauty and your handsome features. Your uniform was particularly striking against her red dress, was it not?"

Anne's dress had been blue...pale blue at that.

Good God, Wentworth thought, *he thinks I want Miss Elliot!*

"Captain, I must tell you that I know your taking my daughter as a wife will prove to be not only a charming choice but an advantageous one as well. Elizabeth has been mistress of Kellynch all these years, since the passing of her mother and, I dare say, will do you credit as your position and rank require more of you in society. Yes, she will do you quite proud–"

The Baronet clacked on while Frederick thought not how well Miss Elliot could entertain his society, but how she might react when taken into it. The idea of Elizabeth Elliot joining the Harvilles for a homey, family dinner in their crowded little house under the dock in Lyme nearly made him laugh aloud.

"Sir Walter, I am sorry, but I believe that you and I have crossed our signals dreadfully. I have indeed proposed to your daughter, but it is Anne that I have asked to marry me, not Miss Elliot." As the words diffused the Baronet's pleasure, Wentworth was nearly struck with pity for the silly old windbag.

"But surely, Captain, I am surprised that you would endeavour to renew–Anne! You have asked Anne to marry you? I must say, I am amazed." He sounded more angry than amazed as he made his way back to the desk and collapsed into the chair.

"Yes sir, I have asked Anne to be my wife, and, happily, she has accepted. That is why I have come to ask for your blessing over our marriage." Wentworth would take care from here on out to present this as a courtesy to him as Anne's father, not as a desire on their part for his permission.

The man said nothing as he continued to study Wentworth. The tide of the Baronet's mood was definitely turning. The open look was steadily darkening; the eyes were losing their glow. The muscles in Sir Walter's jaw were working at an alarming rate. The overbearing arrogance of years past was steadily reasserting itself as his glee in adding the Captain to the Baronetage completely evaporated.

It didn't matter to Wentworth. The respite from the Baronet's usual vanity and idiocy had been pleasant enough, but the return of the old man was nothing to him. He'd faced worse for mere money and was more than prepared to inform him that this was merely a courtesy call.

182

If it came to it, he would gladly inform Sir Walter that he and Anne had their own plans that did not require her father's approval.

"If you are determined to marry Anne, I suppose we have some business to discuss, Captain."

"Yes, sir. I suppose we do." Captain Wentworth moved to a chair alongside the desk. Unfortunately, he felt the negotiations would have all the charm of bargaining for stores in a foreign port rather than an affectionate father seeing his daughter into the safekeeping of a loving husband.

Sir Walter stood and went to the window. "We must speak of you and my daughter—of Anne. I am surprised that you have renewed the engagement, sir. As I recall, there was a rather unfortunate ending the last time." He kept his back to Wentworth.

Frederick wondered why the subject of the first engagement was being raised. The incident was between Anne and him and was, to his way of thinking, best left unmentioned. "Yes, sir, that was a very unfortunate time for both of us, but we are in agreement about our future together. I hope you will not think me impertinent in saying so, but I fail to see what our past engagement has to do with our present desire to marry."

The Baronet took a seat. "As you'll recall, there was nothing I *could* do for my daughter in the way of her settlement at that time. I always wondered if that was the reason you decided to decamp on such short notice?" He perched a bland look on his face.

Fie! You old bugger! So this is how you will play me. It struck Wentworth how easily and economically Sir Walter could rewrite the past. With the change of just one word—"would" was now changed to "could"—and the entire scene was new. At this, Sir Walter ceased being a cold and indifferent parent and was transformed into nothing worse than an ordinary man, fallen prey to bad monetary circumstance.

Keep your head, boy. It will not do to murder him just yet. Get his blessing first. "No sir. I left because Anne made it clear she would not marry me. I assure you that the lack of settlement money had nothing to do with my quitting the field. May I say that money has nothing to do with my seeking to regain her favour now." He was suddenly curious as to why the Baronet would be taking him down this particular road. There was no reason to think Sir Walter could have any cunning schemes in the offing. This left only an opportunity to cry poor to be the reason the broken engagement was mentioned.

"Ah! A romantic marrying for love! I suppose those who possess an independent fortune are able to indulge such quaint sentiments," Sir Walter said. For once, the accusation of "romantic" did not nettle him as it did when coming from some others. Anything that placed him opposite this man he deemed first-rate. Whatever the Baronet's beliefs were about such "quaint sentiments" was beside the point. The look in his eye was that of a cynic, not one concerned with tender feelings whatever.

"Your situation is much the same as mine when I married my Elizabeth. We married for love, and though I thought them childish, we participated in the traditions that were all the rage at the time. Parties could only be hosted by the families and attended by only the proper people, only certain foods were eaten by the couple. I think I remember–"

Wentworth listened with interest to the litany of marriage customs the Baronet found silly. Most were still in place as far as he knew. What was the fellow up to?

"–and the dowry was expected immediately, within just days of the announcement."

There it was. There was the pearl in the oyster of this convoluted exchange.

"I was fortunate that Miss Stevenson's father was well-able to manage. He lectured me long on this being his daughter's stake in the marriage and that it would provide a stake for daughters to follow. All utter rubbish," he muttered. "People from Gloucester are rarely so scrupulous about their debts. It was of little matter to me, I could well-afford to forego the dowry completely. I only took it to satisfy the man's old fashioned notions of honour and their outmoded country ways." It seemed for all Sir Walter's foolishness that he, too, had learnt the value of silence along the way and sat quietly while the Captain absorbed his little speech.

Ah! An oyster with two pearls! How fortunate for me, thought Wentworth. Of course the man hadn't the money to pay off the settlement. He would do whatever he must to squirm out from under the obligation, even if that included making Wentworth look like a peasant if he made any sort of fuss about the dowry. In the grand scheme, the money meant nothing and the opinion of Sir Walter even less. But the money had come through the mother and was intended for her daughters. Lady Elliot had wished Anne to have a stake in her marriage, and this imbecile–

"So, Captain, shall we, as men of the world, put aside these superstitions and–"

Wentworth decided to extend the silence. The man had the temerity not only to insult the memory of his late wife, but her people, her dearest daughter, and himself. The man would learn a lesson about what it was to truly be a man of the world.

When Sir Walter began to toy with his sleeves, Wentworth deemed it time to speak.

"Sir, as a man of the world, you will agree that gentlemen do not always see eye-to-eye." The older man's expression shifted in a flash from one of hope to one of aversion. No doubt, Wentworth's elevation of himself to the station of a gentleman was repellent. "That being the case, I must say that I have a great fondness for our good, solid English traditions. As a sailor, I know of no other group of men so steeped in superstitions, a few of whom have saved my life." He rose. "So, if you have no objections to Anne and me being married—" He had not long to wait for Sir Walter's affirmative. "And so there is no shadow over the announcement, we shall speak no more of the settlement..."

The Baronet smiled broadly, rose, and extended his hand in agreement.

Wentworth made no move to receive it. "...until the next quarter day when I shall return and expect us to discuss the payment of my wife's dowry."

~ ~ ~ ~ ~ ~ ~ & ~ ~ ~ ~ ~ ~ ~

The cool air was refreshing to the spirits of the lovers as they made their way to Rivers Street. They departed Camden Place quickly, reasoning it was only right that Anne be the one to tell her godmother before word travelled to her by some other means. One would not suspect they had just received the most indifferent of congratulations from Anne's closest family on the announcement of their engagement.

Sir Walter's announcement was followed by a brief and indifferent kiss on his daughter's cheek and a handshake for the groom, which could have been outdone by any of a dozen old ladies of delicate health. Miss Elizabeth's languid, "Best wishes, Sister," was nothing exceptional. To the couple's surprise, it was Mrs. Clay who gave them a warm, "Many happy returns to you both," and whose expression showed any genuine kindness.

Anne suspected Frederick was not bothered by her family's response. The moment they left the house, he had offered his arm, and when she took it, he placed his hand protectively over hers. She was happy to notice when they met anyone with whom he was acquainted, his hand remained and he merely nodded his greeting. He possessed her emotions and, by his actions, made it clear she was his in body as well. Such care was foreign to her, but she was sure she could grow used to it.

"I shall hail us a carriage. The wind is picking up, and those clouds are darkening." He slowed to look up the street.

"It's not all that far now. Besides, it is a pleasure to walk when I have such a delightful companion." She didn't look at him but grasped his arm more tightly and leaned into him.

"As you wish, Anne." There was a smile in his voice. She regretted the chill weather and the gloves they wore.

Making their way steadily through the crowded streets, she wondered if anyone was half as happy as she and Frederick. She tried to imagine how Lady Russell would take the news of their engagement. This led her to think of Mr. Elliot and the news she had to tell concerning him. Why her father was so angry underneath his cold indifference was also a concern. "Frederick, what did Father say when you told him we were getting married?"

It took some time for him to answer. "He wished us well. He was surprised that we had reunited, but raised no objections."

"He seemed displeased about something."

"What makes you say this?"

"I cannot say. There seemed to be an air of tension about him." She laughed and leaned into him again. "I should think that your taking on my expenses would be welcome to a man in financial difficulty."

"Well, to be honest, I may have made him a bit angry. At one point in the conversation I spoke of myself as his equal. I went so far as to refer to myself as a "gentleman" and saw his displeasure at that."

"Oh, yes, that would do it. But he must learn that the word is broadening in scope. Though you own no land, you are in every other way a gentleman."

"I think he cherished hopes for you and your cousin."

"That was never very likely, but recently a friend has informed me of some very deep shades in his character. I hesitate to speak, not that I wish anything kept from you, but because I have yet to tell even my godmother what I have discovered about him."

"While I have no objections to the world knowing what sort of reprobate the man is, I do think it will be quite enough for Lady Russell to contend with us appearing unannounced with the news we are to marry. To cast a shadow upon her favourite may be too much for her."

"You are probably right," she said. "So, I shall tell you of his grave misdeeds another time."

Rivers Street was quite the most crowded street they had walked that morning. It took a little time to work their way to Lady Russell's building. When they finally reached her door, a die came shooting from behind them, clicking as it spun and skittered against the steps to the house. "Hey, toss it up, will ya?"

Frederick picked it up and looked around to the voice. The driver of a fine new carriage held out an expectant hand. "Up here, fella." The toss was perfect and the driver caught it, turned back to his game and his companion without a word of thanks.

Anne knocked on the door while Frederick examined the carriage.

"Miss Anne. Captain Wentworth." Longwell's expression and tone were all politeness for her, but she noted something disdainful when he spoke Frederick's name. "Madam was not expecting so many for tea," he said, careful not to look at Wentworth.

"Are there others, Longwell? My godmother did not mention anyone else being invited."

The butler was at a loss for something to say. Finally, he replied, "Madam had only the family in mind, Miss Anne." Just as he handed their cloaks to the footman, there was a muted crash originating from down the hall. He directed the footman to investigate. "I will show you to the sunroom."

"Is my godmother indisposed, or have I misunderstood and come on the wrong day?"

"Of course not, Miss, but Madam asked that I tell her when you arrived. I shall return directly."

Before she could answer, the footman returned and whispered something to the butler. He grew red in the face. "Please, Miss, allow me to see you comfortable in the Sun Room."

As they passed by a set of closed doors, Anne paused. "Is my cousin, William Elliot, with Lady Russell?" For the second time in several minutes, Longwell went red. Again, he took his time in speaking. He looked from Anne to the Captain and back

"I can hear his voice in the sitting room," Anne prodded.

"Uh, yes, Miss. Mr. Elliot arrived some time ago."

She turned and faced the door. "As you said earlier, Longwell, this tea is for the family. There is no reason for us all not to be together. Please announce us."

Chapter Sixteen

Longwell hesitated for just a moment. He looked at the Captain, who merely shrugged. Frederick knew it to be rottenly perverse on his part, but he took an inordinate amount of pleasure in the man's clear confusion. Wentworth admitted to himself that this was a moral failing with which he might struggle for a moment or two, but considering their history, its existence could not be surprising.

It was clear Anne was not going to give up, and Longwell would either announce them, dealing later with the consequences of the interruption, or the young lady would open the doors herself. This would leave the butler with a double censure to explain to his mistress. As they waited for him to announce them, Wentworth's superior height afforded him a peculiarly interesting view of the room's occupants. Perched on the front edge of his chair, Mr. Elliot was listening intently to his hostess. Lady Russell, too, was leaning forward, speaking with uncharacteristic animation. When they realised the door had opened, the tête-à-tête ceased, and both moved back in their seats.

"Miss Anne and Captain Wentworth." For an instant, all four were silent and did nothing but stare at one another. Mr. Elliot was the first to make a gesture of courtesy. He stood, and in his haste, his cup of tea rattled delicately and fell to the floor. The liquid pooled around his right pump. He looked down and angrily said something under his breath. When he shook his foot, he caught the cup and it rolled beneath his chair.

"Are you early, Cousin, or am I late?" Anne's question broke the silence.

Elliot was rescued from saying anything by Lady Russell. "You are just on time, my dear, although I did not expect that you would bring a guest." The woman's gaze was steadily fixed on Wentworth as she spoke.

"Happily, I found him at Camden Place when I returned from visiting with Mrs. Smith this morning. He came to speak with father—" Wentworth couldn't help himself and looked surreptitiously at Elliot and then Lady Russell. Neither of them looked as if they were pleased to hear this news. "—and he was kind enough to offer to escort me to Rivers Street. I was happy to accept and thought it only just that I should invite him in for tea."

Lady Russell was too well bred to allow more than a momentary lapse in her countenance before she rose and approached them. She kissed Anne's cheek and gave him a nod. "You know that my home is to be treated as your own, my dear. Longwell, fetch two more cups. Come, Anne; sit with me." The woman was sly in greeting her goddaughter with such warmth, enabling her to ignore Frederick and easily draw Anne from his side. That the two of them might, at some future point, learn to love one another was looking more and more like wishful thinking.

"Please, Captain, be seated." Lady Russell indicated a chair that could not be farther away from Anne unless it was in another room. He took it and then looked Anne's way. All her movements as she took a seat on the sofa next to her godmother were studied and exacting. Her eyes sparkled, and the smile on her face was positively puckish. This was a look Wentworth had never seen. He anticipated how this new-found disposition would play itself out.

"I hope we did not interrupt the two of you discussing anything important," Anne said, looking innocently from her cousin to her godmother.

Mr. Elliot was again seated, and Lady Russell's expression was now serenity itself. The cup of tea she stirred was rock steady in her hand. "We were discussing the concert last Tuesday." Just before she turned to Anne, Wentworth saw her raise a brow in Elliot's direction.

"Yes, we were comparing notes on the last selection and how magnificent it was." He drew a bead on Wentworth and said, "I believe you left just as it was beginning. What a pity, sir, but I suppose those whose whole life has been the Navy have little opportunity for cultural improvement. Such sophisticated musical composition may be beyond their … tastes." Elliot accepted a new cup from Lady Russell with a smile.

Wentworth had to admire the man; he'd levelled his shot excellently. Elliot had, with few words, found fault not only with Frederick's musical acumen and intelligence but with his beloved profession as well. The poor sod would get his just deserts soon enough.

"It was not the sophistication of the composition that left the Captain cold, but the atmosphere of the entire concert. You see, cousin, we—the

Captain and I—are entirely agreed that the lack of discipline in most Italian music falls far short of the well-organised and disciplined music so cherished by the fine English mind. Captain Wentworth, being of a profession which prides itself on order and discipline, was understandably dismayed by such an inharmonious and discordant display."

Lady Russell looked about her in confusion as William Elliot's expression changed from smirk to glacial stare. The tension was relieved a little when Longwell appeared with the extra cups and a maid came to finish cleaning up the carpet. When the parade of servants had departed the room, Lady Russell sat forward to pour for the gentlemen. Anne was before her and quickly took hold of the handle of the pot. "Please, allow me, Ma'am."

It could not escape the notice of her godmother or her cousin that she asked for no instructions as she poured the first cup. She laced it liberally with milk and just a little sugar, then rose and presented it to the Captain.

"I think this is just how you take it, sir." Anne tilted her head and smiled. Frederick accepted the cup with a smile of his own and thanks. The flush of her cheeks was delightful. Taking a sip, he said, "It is indeed how I like it, Miss Anne. Thank you very much."

When she turned away, she stopped before her cousin. "And Mr. Elliot, how again do you take your tea?" Frederick nearly dropped his cup. It was worth any of Elliot's pallid insults to watch Anne at work on him. The man's face flushed angrily. His jaws barely moved as he growled, "Lemon and nothing more."

She returned to the tray and began again to pour. The expression on her face was angelic, and she smiled sweetly as Lady Russell spoke to her about the expected rain. To watch her pour and serve the tea was grace itself. It was then that Frederick realised that, when she chose, Anne could be a merciless opponent with the enviable skill of mastering herself under pressure. Such strength and intelligence would be necessary for the life he was asking her to live.

Everyone had their tea and attended to it quietly until Lady Russell said, "Anne, it has been some time since your last visit. I am not used to such neglect, my dear. You have been attending to your father, I expect?"

"I was visiting my dear friend, Mrs. Smith," Anne replied, "the poor widow who lives in Westgate Buildings."

Again, the clatter of a cup came from Elliot's direction. This time he had managed to set it on the table without incident as he stood. "I am sorry, but I have just realised I have another appointment. I hope you can forgive me for rushing off." Wentworth would normally have been glad to see the back of him, but he was more intrigued to see whether Anne was finished with him yet.

She was instantly up from her seat. "Oh, please, Cousin, can you stay but a few minutes more? I have some very good news I wish to share with my godmother. Since you are here and are family, I would like you to know it as well." She would not be satisfied to allow her cousin to learn about their engagement by reading an announcement in the newspaper. She intended on telling them both then and there.

Elliot knew whatever Anne had to say would not be good for him, and as he returned to his seat, said, "I suppose I can stay a moment or two longer."

"And what news would this be, my dear?" Lady Russell asked. She took Anne's hand and brought her back to the sofa.

"Captain Wentworth has asked me to marry him, and I have accepted. He has spoken to father this very morning, and he has given us his blessing. The announcement will be published as soon as possible."

Lady Russell sat a long moment looking at Anne as if she could make no meaning of her words. Finally, she stood and stiffly took Anne in her arms. "I...I wish you well, my dear. I wish you well."

Wentworth thought that she must continue to repeat the phrase if ever she hoped to make the announcement and the sentiment sound genuine. There was little feeling in her voice and almost no expression on her face. Poor Mr. Elliot looked as though something unpleasant had burst in his hands and he was not sure how to rid himself of it. To his credit, the man did master himself enough to come to Wentworth, shake his hand, and congratulate him. "Welcome to the family, sir," was all he managed to say. He then left Wentworth to speak to Anne.

Lady Russell covered her shock by calling for more tea. When Longwell appeared, she ordered that some wine should be brought as well. "We must toast to your happiness, Anne." She still could not bring herself to address the Captain. The woman's cool, perfunctory sanction stung his pride. The least she could do, for Anne's sake, was act the part of a joyful friend.

"I never stopped loving her," he said. "Through all these long years, I never stopped loving her." He did not think he should have to convince her of his sincerity, but if that was what she required of him, he would do it for Anne.

Lady Russell turned. "Never stopped loving her? Never once at Uppercross? Never once at Lyme, perhaps?"

So, this was how it would be with them. "I said I never stopped loving her. I never said I haven't acted stupidly in all this time."

"It is a good sign that you can admit that, sir."

Longwell arrived with the libations. William Elliot repeated his need to be off. Lady Russell went to see to his departure. Anne came to Frederick and slid her hand into his. Her eyes shone and her smile comforted his angry heart.

"Frederick, I look forward to the day when the three of us will sit together perfectly happy in one another's company." Her eager, hopeful expression touched him. He would work as hard as was necessary to care for Lady Russell. He would put aside whatever hostility she might lob his way and dig as deeply into his own soul to find affection for Annie's benefit. There was nothing he could say; so, he raised her hand to his lips and kissed it.

Lady Russell re-entered the room and, taking her seat, poured out the wine. "You said your father has no objections to this marriage going forward?"

He could feel Anne stiffen by his side. Her cheeks were red. He released her hand, and she turned and faced Lady Russell. "Yes, why should he? I am of age, and there are none of the impediments of the past to stop us."

Lady Russell's expression was strained as she passed around the wine. Raising her glass to them, she spoke with a sincerity he could bless. "Then may my goddaughter find the happiness she deserves."

They raised their glasses to complete the toast. Anne turned to him. Her smile made him forget the hostility he had both felt and received. "I think we should be off, Ma'am." Anne bid her godmother farewell.

Lady Russell said, "Yes, Captain, please see my goddaughter home."

"I will see her wherever she wishes, Ma'am."

"Yes, you have that right now, don't you?" She summoned Longwell to escort them to the door.

~ ~ ~ ~ ~ ~ ~ & ~ ~ ~ ~ ~ ~ ~

Again, the cool air was refreshing as they walked. Anne revisited Lady Russell's responses over and over in her mind. Why was she surprised her godmother would not be happy for her? She knew full well Mr. Elliot was her favourite, and to have her plans upset by Anne's acceptance of Frederick's proposal was to invite the dismal response. The saddest thought came when she wondered if her godmother's opinions of Mr. Elliot and Frederick Wentworth would even change if she were told about the former's behaviour concerning her family and Mr. Smith.

"You are very quiet, my dear." Wentworth chaffed the top of her gloved hand on his arm.

She longed for the day that she could remove the layers of leather separating their hands and they could truly touch. "I was just thinking about the morning."

"I think it has all gone rather well."

"You have been in battles in which you have risked life and limb. I suppose anything not putting you directly in physical danger you consider 'going well.'" She glanced at him. His expression was troubled.

"Your father has given his permission, not that I was asking for it, mind you. Lady Russell has been told. Whatever her response, we have cleared the major impediments and, I feel, are free to enjoy ourselves."

It was all so simple to Frederick. He saw none of the true impediments. To be fair, it actually was very simple. It was her desire for something unidentifiable that drove her discontent. He guided her next to a stairway, out of the flow of the others on the sidewalk. "What would make you happy?" His tone and expression were serious.

Just having him ask the question gave a lift to her spirits. "Father is indifferent at best. Elizabeth...well, Elizabeth is going to sulk for a long time, I think. We need not discuss Lady Russell. We have yet for anyone to wish us joy."

He smiled. "It would be a nice touch, but I think I feel joy enough for both of us. It may not be the same, but it is how I feel." He looked about and she thought he might try to kiss her. Instead, he touched her cheek.

"I know. This makes me sound petty and ridiculous. I'm sorry to make you see my sour mood. I should not put you through this."

Frederick smiled, and then laughed. "First of all, I don't see you as petty and ridiculous. Besides, if we compare this sour mood of yours with my pettiness of the past autumn, I think you will be seen as the more adult of us."

"I still don't care to allow myself such a luxury."

He took her arm and they moved back into the stream of the sidewalk. "We shall go to Gay Street and tell my sister and brother-in-law our happy news. I am sure you will get a smile or two from them."

~ ~ ~ ~ ~ ~ ~ & ~ ~ ~ ~ ~ ~ ~

The last of the housemaids dropped a perfect curtsey before Anne and wished the couple joy.

Anne thanked her and turned to him. "You knew."

"Knew what?"

"You knew that your family would welcome our news in this way. That is why you were so offhand about my pettiness." She raised a brow at Frederick, daring him to deny it.

"I hoped there would be smiles and wishes of joy, but I had no idea of them lining up the servants and breaking out good wine and cake." The Admiral had gone above and beyond anything Frederick might have hoped for the announcement. His own thanks would be profuse, but he was sure that Anne's smiling face and unbridled laughter would make them know what a wonderful gift they had given the new couple.

"If only my own people cared so much." Anne glanced away. Frederick was about to speak when Harkness approached.

"Miss Anne, I wish you joy of your coming marriage." He made an excellent leg to her.

Anne looked at the man closely. "Harkness, from Kellynch, isn't it?"

"Yes, Miss."

She smiled in full recognition. "How is your mother?"

"Very well, thank you. I shall write her and let her know things are once more on course. Again, congratulations." He nodded to the Captain and left them.

"What is he doing here?" She accepted a little more wine.

"The poor man is my valet." He smiled; the man had a thankless chore.

"What do you think he meant by 'once more on course?'"

"I'm not certain, but he made a cryptic comment when I was staying at Kellynch. Might the servants have known of about us in '06?"

She thought for a moment. "I would not have thought it lasted long enough to be noticed. But, there is no keeping anything secret from them, no matter how hard one tries."

He led her to the sofa. "True enough. There are no secrets aboard ships either. That being the case, I would say we have had many wishing us well for quite some time."

The servants were dismissed, and Sophia and the Admiral made a show of excusing themselves. He was grateful they understood his desire to be alone with Anne.

She leant back and closed her eyes. "This is so pleasant."

He took her hand. She snatched it back and sat staring at him. "I am so sorry, Frederick. I...I am not accustomed to anyone taking my hand or touching me like that." Her expression was of growing regret.

"Well then," he took her hand again, "I shall have to hold your hand constantly so that you will grow accustomed to it." He leant close. "I intend to touch you as much as possible." He raised her hand to his lips. They sat back, but he did not release her. "I had forgotten how devoted you are. You never were shy about telling me how you felt."

"Shall I tell you how I feel this moment?" He touched her cheek.

"Please do." She pressed against his fingers.

"I want to be married as soon as it can be arranged." He moved closer. "I shall obtain a license so we might do away with the banns. All we need do is find a day when the church is free." He stroked her hair.

She put her hand over his. "But, Frederick, there are preparations. Having a dress made will take time—"

"You can have all the dresses made you wish after we are married. This second time around, I don't want to waste a moment." He pulled her close.

Anne rested against his chest, listening to his heartbeat. "How can I refuse you?"

"You can't." He stroked her hair and occasionally kissed her temple.

"Then I shan't."

A loud click roused them both. They looked towards the door, but it was closed. "I think we've been caught," he said.

Anne began to sit up, but he wouldn't allow it. She said nothing and settled back against him. They sat quietly for quite some time, enjoying the warmth of the fire and one another's arms. Frederick finally said, "When we are married, we'll not have to worry about spies."

"No, we shall be spared that. But, the household will still know how happy we are." This was a comforting thought after such a turbulent day.

~ ~ ~ ~ ~ ~ ~ & ~ ~ ~ ~ ~ ~ ~

The next day, most of the sharper feelings had succumbed to careful thought and a night's rest. Though every couple in Bath considering marriage had gotten to the church first, they were able to arrange a day within a fortnight. It did not completely suit the Captain, but as he was in no position to change things, he, too, succumbed to some careful thought and a good night's rest.

Frederick's second full day as an engaged man was turning out to be quite profitable. A letter from his prize agent arrived in the morning post notifying him that the amount of £500 had been deposited in his account. It seemed that his first capture of the spring season had carried more than just a hold full of rice. When the wrights began their inspection to determine her value, she yielded a box of jewels secreted into the flooring of the Captain's cabin.

No one claimed the jewels, and though somewhere a woman was without her baubles, Captain Wentworth was now a bit richer than expected. As he returned from a short walk, he decided that since jewels had enriched him, jewels Anne must have. What sort of jewellery, he was unsure, but he was confident that, given an opportunity, Admiral McGillvary could advise him on that score. The footman began to speak as he relieved the Captain of his outer garments but was interrupted by his sister.

"There you are, Frederick." Sophia glanced back into the sitting room and then came to him. "Lady Russell arrived about half an hour ago. She was quite agitated, but I gave her some tea and we began to discuss her favourite subject. She is very much better now."

When he had spoken to Anne the previous evening, she mentioned speaking to her godmother and was pleased to say things were much better between them. For himself, he was little concerned, but Anne needed Lady Russell's support. The woman's presence at Gay Street made him wonder if that truce still held or if the woman had come to discuss her favourite subject of the Captain's gross inferiorities. He asked just what *was* Lady Russell's favourite subject?

"Why, Anne, of course." She patted his arm. "I'm sorry I've no Marine to post outside the door, Frederick, but if you have trouble, call for a footman." She left him in the hallway.

He had expected that if he were to face the old dragon alone again, it would be in her own den. Her appearance in his home caught him off guard and was unsettling to a man who liked to have a firm battle plan. Prepared or not, it was time to face her. He entered to find her pouring him tea.

"Your sister has me quite at home, Captain. Milk with a little sugar, I believe."

"Yes, thank you." He took the cup to his favourite chair and marvelled that she had remembered. "And what may I do for you, Lady Russell?"

"I have had two visits this morning which have left me extremely cross, sir."

If the woman was already cross, he calculated what the chance might be that he was the reason. "I am sorry to hear this, Ma'am," was all he could think to say.

"The first visit was from Anne. She *did* tell you we spoke about your last visit and that she and I have set things right?"

"Yes, Ma'am, she did last night."

"Good, perhaps knowing that will help remove the worried, suspicious look from your face."

He smiled at being caught and took a drink.

"Anne came to me this morning and said she and her father had talked about the wedding, that the plans for his part are very easy and simple and that she is happy about them."

"What she and I discussed was very simple. We wish to be married quickly and that precludes anything too lavish."

"I understand that, sir. Military men are generally in a rush. If that is truly what Anne wishes, I shall say no more about the matter, but Anne will deprive herself of anything she considers unimportant. Anything *you* feel is unimportant."

He immediately thought of Anne's declaration that having a dress made would take time. A dress was, evidently, important to her. If Lady Russell was right, that he had put it aside had made it unimportant in her eyes.

She continued. "The second was from Sir Walter. He was quite provoked about the way you went about proposing." The mention of the Baronet and their meeting left him cold. It must have shown on his face for she said, "He feels you have taken advantage of him."

Wentworth nearly came out of the chair. Restraining himself, he merely leant forward, put the cup down and folded his hands. "And did he explain how I have done such a thing, Ma'am?"

"He said you were making demands of him concerning the dowry which he cannot possibly meet."

"Please be assured, Ma'am, my concerns about the settlement are completely just but nothing Sir Walter should feel pressed about." The statement was cryptic, even to his ears. Before she could speak further, he said, "Is there any other way in which I might help you?"

Lady Russell's expression hardened and colour came into her cheeks. "He also has told me about his version of the plans for the wedding."

The plans Wentworth and Anne discussed were quite simple, quite straightforward. There was nothing about them which would justify interference by the Baronet. Wentworth asked her to explain.

"He feels there is no need for an engagement party and that a modest breakfast after the wedding is all he can manage." Her movements and expression indicated the plans were not to her liking at all.

"I am not very familiar with the wedding customs of Bath. Perhaps, you can help me understand why this is not sufficient."

"Weddings are not nearly the generous events they have been in the recent past, Captain, but a young woman of Anne's rank, the daughter of a baronet, even now should have, at the very least, a dress especially made for the occasion. It should be nothing too grand, something that may be worn again at a later time. A young bride should also have some household furnishings to take into her new home—linens and tableware, particularly." She stopped, obviously hesitant to continue.

Wentworth was completely unprepared to speak about dresses or tableware, but he understood being prepared with the materials one needed to make a successful campaign. He was about to make this point when Lady Russell continued. "As a part of her trousseau, she should also have new clothes." Again she hesitated but carried on quickly. "Anne took it upon herself to economise for quite some time. I know she has had no new things for several seasons. In the past, when Elizabeth and Sir Walter returned from town, she was given a small gift." The furrow in her brow deepened. "That was one area of economy they could agree upon and the gift was done away with this year. I fear Anne needs everything new...everything, if you will pardon my frankness, sir."

He did understand her and was appalled that Sir Walter could behave in such a contemptible manner. Wentworth did not care one whit for the mortification the man brought on himself, but to think he could treat his daughter in such a shabby manner angered him. Sadly, thrashing the man was not the answer—

"I told him I had a certain amount of money set aside for each of the girls. I gave Mary hers when she wed Charles Musgrove, and I told him that if he could see his way to match that amount, I would see that Anne had everything she needed. He said he could do nothing more. Then, I said I would see to everything. He left soon after. When I spoke, I now find that I did so in haste. I will not be completely in funds again until after the midsummer."

He was astounded that she was so forthcoming with what passed between her and the Baronet, not to mention what she revealed about her own affairs. Of course, she needed his help. She needed his money to put the situation to rights. Still—

"I was thinking, Captain, that you would not mind using a small part of the settlement money to see that Anne and your own home will be well-furnished."

This presented Frederick with a quandary. To tell her there was no settlement money forthcoming would further sink Anne's father in her eyes. Such was not really much of a consideration to him, but he did not wish to be the cause of more animosity on the lady's part. These sorts of plots always come to light, and if Anne ever got wind that he made trouble for her father, it would be Frederick that was sunk. He could go along with the plan and give the money. All would be well, except that the Baronet would get away with a great injustice. Why should he, the old poseur? As it had been scrupulous honesty that had boosted his own fortunes this very day, he decided to make truth his friend and tell Lady Russell what had upset Sir Walter about his proposal.

"There is no settlement money."

"Not enough, you mean." She sighed deeply. "Please, do not tell me all the talk of your fortune is piffle and that you need the money for the two of you to live on." Lady Russell held her breath.

It was almost a comfort to know he was still in the familiar territory of Lady Russell's suspicions. "No, I mean there is no settlement." He described briefly Sir Walter's ramble belittling old-fashioned practices. Next, he was careful to point up how the man freely admitted his own father-in-law had seen to his duty and promptly paid the dowry. Though he was certain she would miss the irony of it, he told her how the Baronet numbered them both as men of the world. To his surprise she was not completely obtuse and smiled at this. "While Anne is not yet my wife, I see the settlement money as Lady Elliot's last gift to her daughter. It would be morally wrong for the Baronet to betray them both by withholding it."

Lady Russell looked away. The sadness in her eyes was acute. The woman might be a thorn in his side, but she did care for Anne.

"Poor Elizabeth. She would hang her head were she to know this sad business."

"I dare say Miss Elliot was not touched in the least at the news of my engaging her sister. I doubt any worries with the wedding plans will make much difference to her."

She looked at him, smiling faintly. "Not Elizabeth, Anne's sister, but Elizabeth, Lady Elliot, and my dearest friend." She poured more tea. It was clear by her deliberate movements she was ordering her thoughts. He rose to accept his cup.

"I will give you a bit of Elliot history, Captain Wentworth. Lady Elliot was as beautiful as the Baronet was handsome. Some would say more so. Even her daughter, Elizabeth, lacks a certain something my friend possessed. Anne, though, is every bit as intelligent as her mother. They made an exquisite couple. The wedding was lavish by the standards of her people, and then he took her away to be the mistress of his lovely, large estate in Somerset." She told how she came to follow her friend and to be installed in Kellynch Lodge. "My husband was an officer in the Army and was away most of our marriage. He was glad to have me taken care of so that I was not of much concern for him." At this, her expression changed little. Wentworth could not say whether her look betrayed hardness to the relegation or a hidden pain.

"It did not take long for her to realise that her husband, while handsome, had no head for business or understanding of what it took to manage a household or his estate. His father had passed away only a year earlier, and everything was still functioning under the old man's guidance. It was clear that her husband, if not checked, would make a ruin of everything. So, Elizabeth began learning how to economise and to manage her husband."

As she spoke, Wentworth came to admire Lady Elliot by way of Lady Russell's narrative. The picture from the upper sitting room at

Kellynch was very much on his mind. It presented her as a young, fresh, intelligent woman who would soon be shackled to a fool. Like many before her, for the sake of her children, she developed the skills necessary to deal with the folly.

"I don't know if Anne has told you, but there was a son born to them just two years after her. Certainly, they needed the son to mitigate the effects of the entail. But he was stillborn. It broke my friend's heart. She felt like a failure, and I am ashamed to say, he did nothing to lessen those feelings. The pregnancy was difficult as well. So, when Mary was born two years later, Elizabeth's health was irreparably damaged. She worked hard to raise her girls."

Lady Russell stopped and looked off. He could feel the loneliness of the woman, lamenting her friend's circumstances, no doubt missing her friend's company as well. Had anyone told Frederick in the years following his crushed hopes that one day he would be privy to Lady Russell's most heartfelt confession, he would have laughed. Now, sitting in his sister's house, hearing and seeing the effects of this sad tale, he pitied her and pitied Anne for being unavoidably left to the mercy of her stupid father.

"Cozening and coddling the Baronet took a great deal of creativity and energy. I was with her at the end. The only things she regretted leaving were the girls. To be done with the rest was a relief." Again she was silent for a time.

"With all the restraints gone, he did as he pleased. Elizabeth, though far too young and ignorant, became his hostess and housekeeper. Anne was sent to school, which she despised. Mary was left to a parade of nursery maids completely ill-suited to care for her, and it shows to this day."

He had never seen Lady Russell sit in such a way as to touch the back of a chair. That was changed now. It was clear her recollections weighed her down to the point she could barely sit upright. It was time to call an end to the hurtful memoir.

"Ma'am, I must say, Anne is blessed to have you in her life." He was not certain whether he or Lady Russell was more surprised to hear these words.

"I am sure you have never thought that before." She cocked her head and smiled.

"No, you are quite right in that. It is an entirely new thought for me." He cleared his throat and shifted in his seat. "In regard to Anne, the time is short and I, unfortunately, cannot be seen paying for her dresses, but you can. You can use your powers of persuasion to see that she chooses what gives her pleasure, not merely what would be prudent and serviceable."

"Ah, you know my goddaughter well, sir. Anne has very good taste, but indulges it almost not at all. Adhering to your wishes could be very expensive."

"And I should wait to be surprised at how adept she is at spending money until after we marry? Do what you must to see that she is happy. After what you have told me, I think she deserves it."

"I agree, sir." She looked steadily at him for a moment. "Anne was already aware of her father's ways when you came to Somerset and was intelligent enough to know if things did not change, eventually the family would be in the situation they face today. When she came to me and told me you had proposed, I had nightmares of her far away and in need. I made her to understand that a genteel sort of country poverty was to be preferred to raising her children in a boarding house in a grubby port town, waiting for a man who may or may not return, who may or may not have any money in his pockets."

Wentworth was at first shocked she would paint such a dire picture of the future he offered Anne. He was puzzled why she told him about it now. "At least you did not convince her I was stupid."

"No, Anne could never fall in love with a stupid man. I had taken great pains to school her on the dangers of such a thing. Anyway, do you not find it ironic that I used the spectre of poverty to separate the two of you those years ago, and now, you are returned to save her from it?"

"I do, now that you mention it."

"It is like a ridiculous play come to life."

"The Bard said that the world is a stage and we are all merely players on it."

"And I shall do my best to act the part of a solicitous godmother, urging my goddaughter to pamper herself." She rose and gathered her bag and began putting on her gloves.

Wentworth stood to escort her out. "Anne told me at the evening party it is a great wish of hers that you and I should be friends."

"She would be proud of us today, I think."

"I believe she would."

Chapter Seventeen

W hen Frederick arrived at Camden Place the next morning, Anne asked that he escort her to the home of a friend. She hesitated telling him where the friend resided, and it was not until after they made a stop at Molland's that she spoke much about the person at all.

She handed him the box of sweets. "I hope you do not think ill of her. Mrs. Smith's address is not very fashionable." After he handed her out of the carriage, she took his arm without waiting for him to offer it.

He was heartened by Anne's assuming for herself the privileges of a *fiancée*. Slowly, she would come to her place as the wife of a successful man. He tried not to dwell on what that success might become if he were not called back to sea. Besides his delight in Anne's progress, he was extraordinarily interested to finally learn the mysteries of the occupant of the Westgate Buildings.

The peeling door opened almost immediately, and they were admitted to an ill-lit and dingy hallway. The small area trapped the smells of past meals, wood smoke, and strong medicines. It dissipated as they made their way into a dimly lit parlour. Like all the other upright surfaces of the place, the once cheery wallpaper was peeling and the rest of the room was yellow with the cast of cheap candles. An attempt had been made to make things comfortable with covers placed over the few pieces of furniture.

Mrs. Smith was seated near the fireplace where another woman—introduced as a Nurse Rook—was kneeling, stirring the coals. Both ladies greeted Anne warmly. They greeted him in similar fashion, but he could not but be conscious that he was merely a man in the domain of women.

Anne was recruited to help Nurse Rook make tea, leaving Wentworth with Mrs. Smith. They spoke agreeably, back and forth, comparing Anne's many virtues. Though a fascinating subject to him, it was eventually exhausted, and he thought it was the moment to inquire about things he had observed from the street.

"I shall be blunt. I know that you are acquainted with Anne's cousin, William Elliot, and that he has visited you at least once in the last fortnight."

Mrs. Smith grew pale and her expression turned worried. "Yes, I know the man, but I am not quite sure when last I spoke with him."

"It was just a few days ago. I saw him enter this house."

The woman was slender, nay slight, in her build, but she straightened, becoming resolved. "There is a comfort in having a clear conscience, Captain Wentworth. Your coming here today will help me to complete something I began last week."

He was puzzled with her cryptic speech, but listened intently as she began to tell him about her association with William Walter Elliot. Elliot had been, at first, the Smiths's very good friend. At that time, he had had no regard for the Elliot family or the title he would inherit. It was after Elliot had married a rich and silly woman that he came into the means to indulge himself in any number of wicked acts, which her money admirably concealed, and led Mr. Smith into ruin that directly contributed to his death. It was Elliot who was responsible for his friend's estate and Elliot who had neglected such a responsibility. She quickly, with good cheer, laid out the privations of the past three years.

"And so, when he offered to do what was necessary to settle my husband's estate, I was elated. I was not born to an exalted family, but I was also not born to this sort of life either. The hope of improving my circumstances made taking his part much, much easier."

"Did you not think that a man who neglects a vow to a dying friend would most likely neglect the vows to a wife as well?"

"True, he was not good to his first wife, but Anne is not silly and ill-bred. She would not allow him to treat her with anything but respect."

He said nothing about how much disrespect her family was capable if heaping upon her, and how she managed to put such ill treatment aside. "We haven't much time before they come with tea, I fear. Tell me the rest."

"I had no opportunity to begin my campaign until last week on the Wednesday after a concert I knew she was to attend. I had hopes that he might be one of the party. The gossips have him practically living at Camden Place, and I thought he would not miss an opportunity to be seen with her and her family."

He blanched inwardly. Elliot's accommodating behaviour had been based on his desire to gain Anne's trust and hand in marriage, but could he really think himself any better. He'd acted like a fool and treated her badly on top of it. Anne had dismissed it with good-humour, but he was now even more ashamed. All of Elliot's plans might have been upended had he acted in a manner somewhat resembling a gentleman. Had he only taken the seat offered him, Elliot would have been beaten a day or two sooner.

"When she came to me the next day, I began pressing his case. I feel ashamed, now, how hard I pushed. I intimated she had been in the most agreeable of company and that surely there is no one else she could have wished to be with. She agreed, but then made it clear that person was not William Elliot. May I assume it was your company she enjoyed so much?"

He shifted in his chair. The idea that Anne would consider the evening enjoyable after his tantrum was embarrassing. "Yes, I suppose it was. She was very good to conceal my poor manners from you. I was taken in by Elliot's performance and showed myself to be quite a jealous fool who acted like a petulant child."

Mrs. Smith smiled. "We all act like children sometimes. Besides, I think it was his performance, as you say, that made her state so adamantly that she would never accept a proposal from him. Anywise, with that assurance, I knew his plan was ruined and decided to free myself of his shackles, to be a true friend and tell her about the real William Elliot."

She told Wentworth about letting Anne read a letter concerning Elliot's impressions of various members of the family and about his betrayal of her husband. "As I said earlier, there is comfort in a clear conscience, and while mine is almost completely clear, I fear I shall lose my friend when you tell her of my near betrayal."

"There is really nothing to tell. His plans never came to fruition. In fact, you chopped down the tree by telling her about his character. There is nothing he will do now that she does not view with suspicion. I think I owe you my thanks more than anything."

She relaxed for the first time since their arrival. "Thank you, sir. I will forever be grateful for your kindness."

"And what kindness is that?" Anne asked. She placed a tray with tea and the sweets from Molland's on the table. She began to pour and asked again about the kindness of which her friend spoke.

"The Captain has just been telling me he did not care for the concert last week. I did not know he attended as well."

Anne passed the cups around. "Oh yes, the Captain loves music, but I think it was less the music he disliked than some of the company." She smiled and passed him his tea. As the conversation progressed, Wentworth listened and began concocting a plan to repay Mrs. Smith's unintended kindness to him.

~ ~ ~ ~ ~ ~ & ~ ~ ~ ~ ~ ~

The following morning at Camden Place passed quickly for Anne. She, Lady Russell, and Madame Deauville, the dressmaker, were closeted away in the library, which was now littered with racks of lace, bead trims, spangles, precious metal braids, and the most sumptuous fabrics she had ever seen in her life. To her amusement, the two women seemed to be in a competition to establish who was the more persuasive and able to entice Anne into choosing the most beautiful, and therefore most expensive, fabrics and trims for her wedding dress.

Anne sat comfortably out of the tussle, fingering a piece of heavy, intricately woven gold braid she thought would look lovely on Frederick's uniform. It was entertaining to listen to the trifling squabble between her godmother and the heavily accented French seamstress. When the two ended their thrust and parry, Anne would tell them both she had decided on a fabric and two particularly elegant trims, and that she even knew how she wished the dress to be designed. Until such an opportunity arose, she would sit quietly and wait.

"Anne, please come here." Lady Russell was unrolling yet another length of fabric. "I want to show Madame that this colour would be particularly fine on you. This light is perfect to prove my point." Anne rose to join them as Madame began chattering in French as to why the Lady was completely wrong as she hurriedly unrolled a length of her favourite. Just as she was about to be shrouded in lengths of moiré silk, the door opened, and her father entered the room. *Another opinion,* Anne thought. Her mood elevated considerably when she saw Frederick walk in behind him.

The invasion of the gentlemen sent Madame into a steady stream of reprimands—in French, of course—directed at the "oafish intruders." Her father took exception at being called oafish and began a counter argument by calling into question the woman's taste. Lady Russell tried to bring calm to the situation while Anne and Frederick smiled at one another over the wrangling mass.

Eventually, the whole party adjourned to the sitting room. Lady Russell had managed to placate Madame Deauville, and when Sir Walter examined her complexion and was told she was nearly seventy years old, he was suddenly astonished by the seamstress's magnificent spirit and dynamic presence. As he escorted her to the door, Anne heard him say he looked forward to meeting her again very soon, and the woman departed with a promise of returning the following day.

Anne and Frederick were sharing tea with Lady Russell and Miss Elizabeth, newly arrived from a walk, when Sir Walter returned to them. "Captain, have you shared with the ladies all your wonderful news?"

All eyes were on Wentworth. "No, sir, not as yet."

"Well, you must tell them all of it without delay. It is very good news."

Frederick turned to Anne. "I have spoken with my friend McGill-vary—"

"That is Admiral Patrick McGillvary. His family owns Madderly, Kinclaven and Planque, a very fine, old Bath establishment. I do much of my own business with them." He looked as though he had arranged the acquaintance between McGillvary and Wentworth.

"Yes, very old. Anywise, the bank has a house they are managing for another naval friend of his, an Admiral Townsend, and—"

Sir Walter broke in again. "Sir, you must tell them where this house is located." The man literally beamed.

Wentworth glanced at his father-in-law and reached into his breast pocket. "Uh, yes—" He looked at the back of a calling card. "It is on Laura Place." He winked so only Anne could see,. "Your father tells me this is a very good address." She was confident Frederick exaggerated to make himself sound ignorant and uncertain.

Anne smiled and took the card. "Oh yes, it is a very good address. Coincidently, we have family who live on Laura Place. The Viscountess Dalrymple resides there."

"With such exalted personages in residence it must be a good address." He seemed to be having trouble keeping a serious expression firmly in place.

The Baronet sighed. "The Captain wishes you to go with him to approve the house, Anne." It was clear Sir Walter was disappointed that Anne's reaction was not on the level of awe he thought warranted by such news.

Anne motioned to Frederick as she rose. "Certainly, Father. I should have realised." She started to the door.

"But Captain, you've not told them about the party that Admiral McGillvary is giving us at Belsom Park." His voice was getting higher with each word.

Wentworth and Anne stopped at the top of the stairs. "Miss Anne, Miss Elizabeth, Lady Russell, Admiral McGillvary is giving us a party at Belsom Park in a few days. You are all invited." With that, he ushered Anne down the steps.

"We shall be in a great deal of trouble when we return." Anne was smiling as she put on her cloak.

"If we return, you mean." Frederick opened the door and waved her out.

~ ~ ~ ~ ~ ~ ~ & ~ ~ ~ ~ ~ ~ ~

When they arrived at the Townsend house, Wentworth was impressed by the refinement of the neighbourhood. Anne immediately commented how the house was more than adequate in size for a newlywed couple. A man came out of the house and introduced himself as Mr. Lonk, the representative of Madderly, Kinclaven and Planque. He showed them into the house and began immediately to point out the superior features of the place.

Straightaway, Wentworth could see the house was not to his taste. The furnishings, to be exact, were more ostentatious and intimidating than he cared to live amongst, but when one considered the address and the expectations of the neighbourhood, it was as it should be. He examined the first room more closely and was not surprised to find the rumours about Admiral Townsend's fondness for indecent art were true. The sitting room was fitted up with a row of vile stone statues on the carved mantelpiece. A room used as a library featured a large Oriental-style mural depicting a preposterous seduction scene. The painting itself was of finest quality and the skill with which it was executed was breathtaking. As for the impossible acts it portrayed, Wentworth had to move out of the room to keep from remarking to Mr. Lonk on the bad taste of some people.

They toured the rest of the ground floor, the kitchen, and the small garden in the rear of the house. The first floor boasted three bedchambers; the second was for the servants. Lonk and Wentworth discussed some terms of the lease while Anne explored the bedchambers. In just a few minutes, she walked by quickly and clattered down the stairs.

"Anne, dear, what is it?" Wentworth hurried after her. He finally joined her in the garden. "What is it, Anne? Did you see a mouse?"

She whirled to face him; her mouth was a straight line and her eyes on fire. "I have not seen a mouse, and you, evidently, have not noticed the revolting furnishings in this place." Her reticule swung on her outstretched wrist. He reached out, took her gently by the shoulders, and explained what the rumours said about the Admiral's tastes.

"And you must not think ill of his taste as you have said nothing the entire time," she replied in a tight voice.

"Of course not. Especially not in front of Mr. Lonk." He looked and saw the man watching them from a kitchen window. "I suppose there were more in the bedchambers?"

Anne nodded. "There is a wardrobe in the master's chambers with marquetry all over that depicts the most vile things." She looked away, red faced. "Who could ever think of such a thing? Or buy such an article and live with it in their midst?"

"Obviously someone with more libertine tastes than yours," he said. "You needn't worry about anything. Lonk said anything we wish removed may be packed up and stowed away in the attic."

She crossed her arms. "Yes, I'm sure the mural will quite easily be packed up and stowed in the attic." Her brows were furrowed and her mouth was still unyielding.

He was shocked by her harsh rejoinder. "I hadn't given any thought to the mural." Wentworth realised it was an odd compliment that she felt secure enough to allow him to see her genuine anger. Still, her sharp reply stung.

"I don't suppose you had, particularly if you liked it" This was the crux of the matter. "You've not expressed an opinion as of yet."

She had him there. "I think it is salacious, indecent, and nothing anyone of taste and character would have decorating their home." It was the best he could do to sooth her. "Shall I take you home?"

They thanked Mr. Lonk, and Wentworth asked that he convey his thanks to McGillvary and that he would speak to him soon. They were not in the carriage more than a moment or two before Anne said, "I am sorry I was so snappish." She laughed nervously and smoothed her dress. "You might very well change your mind after seeing such an unpleasant side of my character."

Wentworth leant back against the cushions and studied her. When he saw it made her uncomfortable, he took her hand. "I shall never change my mind about you. It is my hope you will become more comfortable with me, and I suppose, showing me a pettish side is part and parcel of that. But please know, Anne, I am nothing like Townsend. There is nothing so reprehensible inside me waiting to spring upon you." She pulled slightly on her hand, but he would not release it.

The carriage moved on, and for a short time, each looked past the other, through the opposite windows. Anne finally said, "After you left that summer, I was very depressed through the fall and winter. Father ignored it, and Elizabeth scolded me for being so poor a companion. Lady Russell was beside herself with worry." She squeezed his hand. "More than once I awoke sorely disappointed that I had awakened at all. I frightened myself as much as I might have frightened her."

Frederick edged close. "I'm sorry, my girl." He put an arm around her.

She pulled back a little so she might see his face. "I don't tell you this to make you feel badly but to explain myself this afternoon." She settled back against him. "One day, she told me I should be quite thankful I had not married a man of the world."

The phrase was common enough, but it was familiar for some other reason that he could not quite put his finger on at that moment.

"She said that they learn many things as they go about conquering and bringing civilization to the world. They develop tastes and expectations that are foreign to us here but which they expect fulfilled. She said that, thankfully, most seek satisfaction outside their marriages, but that some—"

"You needn't say anymore. I understand your meaning." He could not help wondering what sort of man Lady Russell's husband had been. He remembered telling Lady Russell of Sir Walter's equating himself to Wentworth as men of the world and that she had smiled upon hearing it. He wondered if, as he thought then, she was amused by the irony of a country-bound man proclaiming such nonsense or if the irony was that she still thought of him as a man schooled in libertine ways. "So, this parable of men's wickedness was meant to bring you comfort?"

"As I said, she was desperate. I knew she was trying to portray the breaking of our engagement as an escape of sorts, and I knew the idea that you were like that to be ridiculous. Her attempt gave me no comfort at all." She removed her glove and stroked his wrist. "Does that comfort you?"

The touch of her hand or that she knew he was no reprobate? "To know that my leaving hurt you so deeply? No. But I am heartened that you didn't believe me to be a Blue Beard." Her touch on his wrist was driving him mad, and he took both her hands in his. "Has she mentioned this recently?"

"No, most definitely not. I'm sure she doesn't even remember it. She has nothing but praise for you lately. You might be her son for all the glowing comments."

Thank God! Were she still holding such opinions, being in company with her would be impossible.

"Perhaps I can tell you something which will make you feel safer with me."

"If it involves Admiral Townsend and his house, I have no wish to hear it."

Wentworth laughed. "Nothing involving him, I assure you." For an instant, he wished the sweet comfort of riding idly along the streets of Bath could be done without blathering about Townsend and ideas sown in the past.

"You remember that summer, how I was so confident I would have a ship soon? After our break-up, I had every intention of staying in Monkford until I received orders, but I soon found I could not stand being mere miles from you. For days, I tortured myself, remembering your scent and the taste of the few kisses we shared. Though Edward tried to change my mind, I left and went to Plymouth. I borrowed some money and found cheap lodgings. I went back to the life I knew. Within days, a miracle happened and I was holding a packet of orders for a ship called the *Asp*." The feeling was still bright in his memory. "She was a clumsy old tub, but I knew that if I could keep her afloat and keep my crew alive, I would have learnt more from her than a hundred first class ships." He stopped and chastened himself. This conversation was not for him to relive the glories of the past but to put Anne's spoken and unspoken fears about their life together to rest.

"Immediately, I began making the repairs I could to the old dear, pressing men, and looking forward to making my fortune. Finally, all I could do was accomplished. It was the evening before we weighted anchor. I had spent a good part of the night with a particularly lovely woman–" Anne stopped breathing. "–who laughed heartily at all my jokes. She praised my person lavishly, and when I told her a few of my more exciting stories of battles or storms, she responded with the proper amount of terror of the dangers I faced and relief when I was spared. The evening was perfect."

Anne sat straight. "And this is supposed to bring me comfort?"

He was sorry for her troubled face but continued. "You will like the end, I assure you." She did not return to his side, but leant against the cushions and toyed with her reticule.

"I was quite pleased with myself as I walked back to my lodgings. The ship was ready, and I would make my escape the following day. Suddenly, I was faced with a woman of the same sort I had spent the evening with, only she worked on the streets and was not so pretty."

Frederick paused and looked at Anne. She fully understood what he was trying to tell her about the two women, particularly the first. He hurried to bring her some relief. "She told me her price, but it was what she said after that ruined everything." Anne took a new interest in this.

"She said, 'I'll tell you whatever you wish to hear, sir.' I was always repulsed by paying for affection. After a night so pleasing, it was a marked let-down to be reminded that I had paid for the first woman's flattery and laughter." Wentworth took Anne's hand again. "It was particularly irksome because I had met a wonderful young woman who had taught me what it was to look into a woman's eyes and know she genuinely thought me funny and who genuinely complimented me– when I deserved it and not otherwise–and a woman who, when she listened to my stories, was truly happy that I was victorious or just alive. When it's paid for, affection is not much different than a hogshead of beer, or a cask of dried fish, don't you think, Dear?"

Anne gazed at him as he spoke. Again her fingers caressed his bare wrist. She nodded. "So, you were constant to me."

He edged close and took her hands. "Yes, I admit to that, but as I said the other day, it was unintentional and completely unconscious. Do not credit me with a virtue I do not deserve." He hurriedly pulled off his gloves. Her cheek was soft and warm. "I don't wish you to think of me as if I was a knight who chivalrously surrendered the thoughts of all women because I could not have the perfect one." She pressed his hand more tightly to her cheek. "For two years it was anger that kept me at sea, proving myself to the phantoms of your family. It was that anger and accompanying pride which kept me from writing you in '08. After that, it was simply a desire to avoid being fooled by the craftier sex. If there is any constancy that was clear-eyed and sacrificial, my dear, it was yours."

To his horror, she began to cry. Before he could say anything, she rushed him and kissed him hard on the lips. In his mind he saw images of his more gallant self easing her gently away, but those images were not real and her kisses most definitely were. Eventually, when the carriage jerked violently to avoid something in the road, they came to their senses.

Anne looked out the window as she straightened her bonnet. "It was a lovely house. I mean, aside from the despicable furnishings." She didn't turn to look at him.

Wentworth was putting on his gloves. "Yes, it was; but there are other lovely houses in Bath. We shall continue looking." He was exceedingly glad the wedding date was coming upon them so quickly.

She still didn't look at him, but reached out her hand. "You mentioned that Admiral McGillvary is giving us a party?"

He took her hand and edged closer. "Yes, he is inviting every naval officer he can shake out of the trees. He's sure it will drive your father to distraction. He's especially interested in your sister attending."

She turned at this. "Elizabeth! How does he know about her?" Anne edged closer to him.

"Let me tell you about McGillvary and what he knows about your sister."

~ ~ ~ ~ ~ ~ ~ & ~ ~ ~ ~ ~ ~ ~

Sir Walter had been exceedingly disappointed that Wentworth had not seen fit to take the house on Laura Place. But it was explained to him that his future son-in-law felt a mere captain in the neighbourhood might discomfit more than a few of the exalted personages who called the street home. Such deference to rank could not be viewed by the Baronet as anything but a commendable understanding of the natural order of things.

Any disappointment the old boy felt was made up for on the evening of McGillvary's party. The Admiral sent his finest carriage to convey all the Elliots and Captain Wentworth to Belsom Park. Frederick couldn't help thinking the barouche, with its fine cherry wood and oxblood leather interior, was meant to impress Miss Elizabeth Elliot. Anyone else's comfort was merely a pleasant concurrence of events. Unfortunately, his troubles would be for naught and disappointment was definitely on the menu that evening.

Admiral McGillvary himself greeted them at the door. As their coats were being taken, Patrick drew Wentworth aside. "So, where is she?"

"Miss Elliot is sorry she cannot attend, but she has a very bad head cold and needs her rest." His friend's frozen smile made Wentworth pity him. "Anne says she is truly very ill and, if it makes you feel better, ill-tempered as well." He could see the clarification did no good.

"Blast, cajoling women out of their ill-temper is a speciality of mine. No matter! This party is for you and your lovely *fiancé*, whom I have not met." Patrick gestured towards Anne and her father. The introductions were made and Anne and Sir Walter were brought into the main room.

Belsom Park, for being one of the most fashionable addresses in Bath, was also one of its least seen. Upon the death of Patrick's mother years before, the social life of the place had been winnowed down to business dinners hosted by Patrick's father. Now that the son was master of the house, intimate dinners were occasionally mounted, but the most life in the house came when Patrick's daughter Cleora was in residence.

"Sir Walter, I wanted to make sure you had a good evening and so invited a friend of yours." Admiral McGillvary brought the Baronet to Colonel and Mrs. Wallis. He bowed to the ladies. "Now, Ma'am, Miss Anne, I need to steal the Captain away for just a moment."

As they walked off, Patrick said, "Colonel Wallis will need some good company, he's the only Lobster in the place." He laughed out loud, not caring who looked.

McGillvary's quiet, snug office was welcome after the noise and confusion of the public rooms. As he took an offered seat, Wentworth thought that he would much rather be having dinner with Anne in here than out in the circus-like atmosphere of the party. Patrick handed him a black box from Harvey and Gore of London.

"I thought your Mr. Bleeker lived here in Bath."

"He does. When he delivered it, he explained the design was conceived when he worked for them. He'd just never finished the necklace you chose. He remarked that ladies especially are quite impressed when given something from those jewellers. I told him I doubted your intended would be. Listen, Wentworth, I remember how steamed you were that night when I spoke about her. I am sorry; she seems like a lovely young woman." He didn't wait for a reply and went to his desk.

Wentworth opened the box and was speechless with pleasure. The necklace flashed of gold and luminescent white in the firelight. Too long to be considered a choker and too short to be a proper necklace, the thirty pearls were each nestled in a golden setting that together cried out for the warmth of flesh.

"So, will it do?" McGillvary asked.

"It sings of Annie." Frederick didn't look, fearing McGillvary would be put off by his impulsive sentiments.

"Sir." It was Jamison, Belsom Park's butler.

McGillvary joined him at the door. "That being the case, I'll leave you two alone." He stepped aside and Anne stepped in.

~ ~ ~ ~ ~ ~ ~ & ~ ~ ~ ~ ~ ~ ~

Anne quietly thanked McGillvary as she entered the room. "He said you wished to see me." She joined him at the fireplace. There was another chair, but wanting her close, he drew her into his lap. He had one hand on the arm behind her; she could feel him occasionally touch her. "I received an unexpected windfall the other day, after the windfall of your accepting me, and I decided I wanted you to have this." With the other hand, he drew the black jewel case from beside him.

Anne was hesitant at first. It was large enough to be something of value. Gradually, she could feel her own expression let go like that of an excited child. She took the case and opened it. All the breath left her. "Frederick," was all she could say. It was a necklace, and all she could do was caress it in its black velvet-resting place.

"Come; let us see how it looks." She rose unsteadily, and turned away from him. He took her gently by the shoulders and turned her back, facing him. With great pleasure, he watched her expression as the cool gold touched her skin. She reached up and touched it tentatively. "There, that is perfection," he said.

She glanced at the fire, just a little hurt that he seemed to notice the necklace more than her. "I am sure it makes me look very pretty." The pearls in their little golden nests were already beginning to warm and the feel of them was a sort of consolation. "You are terribly clever to fasten it without looking." She smiled and glanced away again.

To her surprise, he stepped closer. "Yes, I am. And I didn't mean the necklace was perfection." He put his hand over hers fingering the necklace. "I meant it is now found the perfect resting place—" His fingers trailed up her neck. Her eyes fluttered and her breathing stopped. "—on the neck of the perfect woman." He tilted her chin up and kissed her gently, but firmly.

The wedding could not come soon enough to relieve Anne's growing passion towards Frederick. She should pull away–

"Captain." The voice was Patrick's. "Captain."

Frederick pulled away first, though it took him some time to respond to the call. She stepped away, not looking to the door where Patrick stood.

"Wha–" Frederick's voice was ragged. He cleared his throat and said, "What is it, Admiral?"

McGillvary stepped into the office. "There is someone to see you." He spoke quietly.

Wentworth left her by the fireplace and joined him. "Send them in." Nodding towards Anne, he said something she could not hear.

Anne looked from the flames towards the two men. They were quietly discussing something of great importance. Finally, Frederick said, "Bring him in here. She will have to know sometime."

The next few moments were a blur. A man in a blood-red uniform entered, bowed to the gentlemen and handed Frederick a thick letter. The butler was ordered to take the man to the kitchen to be fed. Anne knew in the depth of her heart what the letter said. The tips of her fingers hummed with energy. All their plans for a quiet, happy life were ruined.

He broke the seal and read. "I report to Whitehall in ten days."

"That's awfully cryptic, Frederick." McGillvary took the letter and read as well.

"I've never heard of such orders, but that's all it says."

McGillvary looked at Anne, then to Frederick. "I'm sure there's nothing to worry about." Frederick glared at his friend. "I mean, knowing those beef-witted sods, they've not decided what to do with you yet. They just want to keep you in easy reach, that's all." He went to his desk.

"As he said, there's nothing to worry about, Anne. I'll report and be told that it's some boring duty, escorting a ship or some such. Nothing to worry over."

"You said you report in ten days?"

"Aye, ten days." He handed her the letter.

The paper was heavy and the seal black as night. The words were straightforward. Knowing from where the orders derived gave them added weight. She handed the detestable thing back. "We are to be married in seven days."

He took it and only glanced at it as he set it down. "Of course, nothing will change those plans." He took her hand. "Once we are married will we have a few days as man and wife."

214

Seven days to wait. Seven days to dread his leaving, all the while her family buzzing around their heads like bees. It would be the longest week of their lives.

"Might you marry sooner?" McGillvary asked.

"No, we were barely able to schedule the church as it was. It seems there is a great rush to marry in Bath," Frederick said.

"Special License? Nothing like the glow of an expensive piece of paper to make an occasion."

Frederick finally looked from her. "You know that the minute I step inside the city limits of London I am theirs."

"Who would know?" Patrick leant against his desk and crossed his arms.

"I would know."

"Ah, yes, that fine sense of honour you possess. I forgot about it."

"What if we were to go to Gretna Green?" Anne offered. Both the gentlemen turned and stared. The answer seemed simple enough. The source, however, was unexpected.

"Anne, I don't think you know what you're asking. It's three, possibly four days journey. What do we gain?"

"Time together without my family making a nuisance of themselves and three, perhaps four, days more as husband and wife."

"She's got you on that one, Wentworth." To Anne, McGillvary said, "Excellent mathematics, Miss."

"Dear, I just don't think it would be a good idea. It is a rough road. Do you really wish to be wed by a blacksmith on the green?"

"I wish to be wed to you as soon as possible."

"The girl sounds as if she knows what she wants, Frederick, and for some misbegotten reason, it's you."

"Patrick, please! Anne, I just do not wish you to be disappointed. Have you thought about when we return? We might have a few days more married, but I would have to leave nearly immediately upon returning and leave you with ..."

"Gossip? 'Tis no more than the idle prating of people who have nothing better to occupy their time. I've been the object of that when I did nothing more than live my life. I might as well give them something genuine to speculate upon."

"I do not wish to leave you in the midst of a scandal and the cost of all of it—"

She reached up to unfasten the necklace. Her shaking fingers could not find the clasp. "Surely the cost of this will cover a journey to Gretna Green." Even bringing the clasp to the front helped little.

"Stop that, Anne! That is not what I meant."

"I have never asked you for anything! I wish to go to Gretna and that we should be married!" She dropped her hands and fought the overwhelming desire to cry.

"Anne, you are being silly—"

"Don't patronize me, please!"

"Frederick, perhaps you should—"

"Shut up, Patrick—"

"Captain!" The men glared at one another. Anne regretted bringing things to such an antagonistic turn.

The Admiral stepped forward and picked up the orders again. "My, my, Frederick, a beautiful young woman is willing to give you a very lovely piece of jewellery to entice you into whisking her off to Scotland to marry her. And you, you muttonhead, hesitate." He tossed them down. "You had better change your mind, or I may just have to allow myself to be bribed."

Frederick's gaze did not waver from her face. His jaw was rigid, except for the occasional twitch. Anne feared she had pushed him beyond reason.

He came close and reached around to the clasp. The tips of his fingers might have been fire as they touched her neck and upper shoulders. Frederick took the necklace and put it in his pocket. "You've bought and paid for me. I suppose you call the tune." His fingers trailed away from her jaw.

Even Patrick had the good sense to know what he'd witnessed and cleared his throat. "So, now that you have negotiated that deal, it is time to celebrate." To Anne he said, "Despite what I may say about him, you've chosen well, Miss, and so has he." Such sentiment only lasted a moment and the Admiral went to pour them each a drink.

"We will need transportation, and that may take a day or so to arrange." Frederick accepted the drink from Patrick and handed one off to Anne.

"Ahem." McGillvary lifted his glass. "To the soon-to-be Captain and Mrs. Frederick Wentworth." They touched glasses and drank. "Now, as a gift, I wish to offer you the use of my travelling carriage. It is newly sprung, and the upholstery is quite fine. It was my mother's, and she insisted that she would ride in only the finest. I think you will find it to your liking."

Anne was relieved that one problem seemed to be solved so easily. Frederick hesitated to accept. "It is most kind of you, Admiral. I am grateful for the offer and receive it with happiness on behalf of myself and my husband-to-be." She touched Frederick's cheek and nodded.

He smiled in return and shook his head. "It seems I have no say anymore."

"You shall have your say, for we cannot leave the party without announcing our departure."

"Ah, no. I think any announcement is the responsibility of the host." McGillvary joined them, smiling at each of them. "I shall give you a half-hour's head start and then share the news that Captain Frederick Wentworth has been called back to sea and that he and his intended are on their way to Gretna Green."

"You are going to enjoy this far too much, Admiral."

McGillvary smiled wide. "Oh, yes, I am, Captain. I have to thank you two; I was afraid this was going to be a typical, dull party." He laughed loudly. "I am very glad to know I was wrong!"

~ ~ ~ ~ ~ ~ ~ & ~ ~ ~ ~ ~ ~ ~

The travelling carriage was sent to Camden Place to await the arrival of the Captain from Gay Street. While his baggage was shifted from McGillvary's small barouche to the traveller, Anne went inside to pack her things. Wentworth was about to enter the house when she came out with a maid trailing behind her.

"Miss Anne, please be careful." The woman handed the bags she carried to the driver. She kissed Anne on each cheek and then took a handkerchief from her pocket to dab at tears.

"Thank you, Elise. I will not be gone long."

Elise waved and returned to the house. As he handed Anne in, he asked what had taken so long.

"Elizabeth wished to share her opinion on our decision. It took some time."

He took a last look at Camden Place. The curtains were parted in one of the windows, and he recognised Miss Elliot. He gave her a jaunty salute. He could almost hear the window curtains snap shut.

The carriage was just gaining speed after entering the main road when Anne looked out the rear window. "Oh, look, Frederick. Fireworks."

He joined her. "It might be a signal flare from Patrick letting us know he's told the party our news."

"It might be Father having heard the news."

Chapter Eighteen

I now pronounce you man and wife. You can kiss her if you got a mind to." The innkeeper snapped the book closed. He put it away and was tying on his apron while his wife loudly blew her nose into a much-patched handkerchief.

The rapidity of the ceremony and the abruptness of the conclusion caught both Anne and Frederick off guard. A small crowd of the inn's patrons had formed, and with the pronouncement and the mention of the kiss, they were noisy and raucous in their encouragement. Anne glanced about, embarrassed. Frederick leant down and pecked her on the cheek. There was general disapproval and disappointment, but when Wentworth announced he would pay for a round of drinks, all the grumbling ceased.

They followed the innkeeper to the third floor, dodging and stepping over several drunken men who had chosen to quit the miserable weather earlier in the day. Anne held tightly to Frederick with one hand, her other over her nose as the keep drew them on. "Now, like I said, Jane has graciously agreed to give ya her room. You're lucky; it's the last to be had."

They entered the dimly lit room to find it occupied by a frail young woman standing next to the bed. She stood as straight as she could with the steep pitch of the roof. Her expression was taut, and she sniffed as she looked them over. Though the room was sparsely furnished—just the little bed, a table next to it, and a small chest—the four bodies filled the place, giving it the feel of the tight quarters below deck on the *Asp*. To him it was familiar, though, unwelcome in the circumstance. He was sure Anne felt greatly oppressed.

Not waiting for an introduction, the woman pulled a shabby bedcover over a single pillow on the very narrow bed that looked nearly as frail as its owner. She took several swipes at the spread as she muttered, "I dun get clean sheets but once a quarter, but for the swells, nothin' but the finest. And me to sleep on the kitchen floor."

The innkeeper dumped an armload of wood in the general area of the fireplace. "Shut up, Janey. You got no cause for bein' mouthy." Turning to the Wentworths, he said, "Pay 'er no mind. The kitchen's warmer anyways."

At this, Jane lit up. "There, you finally admit it! I been sayin' that since I come. And I pay nearly half me wages for it."

"Shut up, Jane, or you be sleepin' in the barn." The man grabbed her by the arm and pushed her through the door. "Leave these fine people to have at it in peace." Before he went out the door, he turned and assured them he would bring their dinner up directly. Frederick caught him at the door and spoke quietly. The man smiled and tucked something in his pocket. "Yes, sir. Right away. The other will take a little bit." Wentworth closed the door after him, glad to be shutting out the world and, in a small way, shutting out all the noise endeavouring to invade their little bit of it.

Anne stood motionless in about the only spot a person could stand straight. The wind whistled through a tiny window he noticed behind the door. She said nothing and made no attempt to put down her reticule, remove her gloves, or hang her bonnet. Instead, she slowly examined the room.

Wentworth took the few steps to the wood, gathered it, and, stepping over the bed, began laying the fire. He could hear her moving around behind him. He feared she would try to leave and looked over his shoulder to see if she was heading to the door.

She was making no move to leave, She stood at the foot of the small bed, her expression unreadable. She had removed her bonnet and now held it, twisting the strings between her fingers. Glancing towards the fireplace, she caught him studying her. She looked hurriedly away and said, "It is terribly small."

"Yes, but the average seaman has a hammock and a mere fourteen inches at the widest. That bed looks to be almost treble that. We have superior accommodations in comparison."

She smiled. "Yes, well, beggars have no choice when it comes to what they receive."

Turning back to the fire, he viciously jabbed a teetering log. The wood had stood in the weather. Soaking up rain and drying repeatedly had caused it to rot. It split in half, both parts falling to the floor of the firebox. "Yes, beggars are at the mercy of Providence, that is for certain," he said, reaching in to stabilise the woodpile before lighting it.

Anne left the bed, hanging her bonnet and reticule on a rough peg next to the window. The room was too chill to surrender her cloak just yet. A gust of wind knocked on the roof, and she pulled her cloak closer, reminding him he had work to do. To his relief, she was looking out the window. He hoped the fray down in the carriage yard and the chaos just outside down the stairs would make her grateful for their quiet, though tiny space.

He was relieved that the dry kindling caught immediately. Soon, the fire would warm them both, giving at least a glimpse of the bodily comfort that had been missing over the past few days. He worried that the long and uncomfortable journey had worn her beyond her endurance and that, finding the inns stuffed full of travellers halted by the wind and snow, she might lose sight of the joy of their marriage. Considering their journey, he was heartened that aside from her comment about beggars, Anne was accepting the situation with much good grace.

She joined him at the hearth and knelt close. He said nothing but glanced her way now and then as he worked the fire. He saw the weariness in her eyes, though she looked content. The flickering firelight gave her a rosy complexion that suited her very well.

A knock at the door brought them to their feet. Before Frederick could approach or answer, the innkeeper entered with a large covered tray, followed by a boy with two pottery mugs clacking dangerously in one hand and a brown jug in the other.

"Here ya are, sir. Everything hot and as fresh as we can get in this sort of weather," he said, placing it on the chest. "Wine's all gone, though. The beer's good, and this should get you through the evening just fine." He leant close. "Most fine ladies don't care for it much." He eagerly took a coin and departed. Wentworth was glad to close the door on the boy's whining about splitting the bonus.

Anne lifted the lid on the tray. At once, she replaced it and drew her hand back. "Did you order this in particular for me?"

He joined her and looked. "What is it?"

She gestured for him to raise the lid. "I am not certain what it is. The shape is unidentifiable, and the colour ... it may be the lack of light in here, but I suspect it to be deep grey."

"Ah, yes, that would be boiled beef. What part of the animal is always a mystery, but it is edible. And I am sure our host would assure us those little round stones are potatoes." He was surprised when she reached in and removed one of the white rounds. She looked it over and then put it in her mouth.

"It is ... warm," she said. Her expression made it clear she found the potato barely agreeable. She touched his arm as she passed by to the fire. Her weariness was more evident when she leant against the short mantel. He joined her.

"I never expected that bribery would be a part of my honeymoon." She finally looked up. Her smile was wan, her eyes tired and sad. "I know you did not expect this. We are out of our element." The reflection of the flames flickered in her eyes.

"I know this is not what we bargained for, but it is what we have. And, I am afraid to tell you, this is my element, precisely." He took her hand and led her to the bed. She glanced at it and looked greatly relieved when he sat and pulled her into his lap.

Her spine was straight and her hands folded primly in her lap. He placed his hands over hers. "My dear Anne, when I am at sea, the greater portion of my career involves bribery, cajoling the reluctant to do as I wish, and if that fails, frightening them into submission. I am quite at home here, truth be known."

She shook her head a little and then leant into him, resting her head on his shoulder. The small fingers of her left hand caressed his wedding band. To see their rings together was a revelation. His love for her was all consuming.

"You don't frighten me." Her face was mere inches from his. "Not even a little bit."

"Good." He allowed himself to kiss her. During the course of the journey, he'd been scrupulous about touching her only when absolutely necessary. He'd spent more time than he cared doing calculations of the carriage's speed, looking out the window predicting the weather's vagaries, and labouring to ignore her presence when they were not in conversation. The worst were the nights when he would wrap her in his heavy boat cloak, and she would lay with her head on a folded lap robe resting on his legs. Tonight, there was no propriety to keep them apart.

"I feel terribly about putting that poor girl out of her room." She suddenly pulled away, rose, and walked to the fire.

It took a moment for him to order his thoughts. "Even if we felt badly enough to give up the room, it is reasonable to think she'd not be sleeping here."

Anne sighed and glanced his way. "Of course, that black-hearted soul who married us would just sell the room to someone else."

"Very true." This remark heartened him. She was not as naïve as he thought her to be. "So, giving up the room would be fruitless."

"Of course. And if we did that, we would have to find a place to sleep for the night."

"Yes, and though Patrick's carriage is most finely appointed, we've been in it for too many days, and I am heartily sick of it!" She laughed and joined him once again. He took her in his arms. "And, I have no desire to share my wedding night with the driver and the post boy."

Anne buried her face in his coat, laughing.

'I promise tomorrow morning I shall put on my captain's face and go down roaring for Jane—"

"And why should you do that? The poor girl has done nothing to us."

"It is simple, my dear. No matter where the girl is, no matter what her occupation, if I am perceived as angry she will be brought to me post-haste. I then shall take her aside and give her enough to make her sleeping on the kitchen floor very worth her while."

She shook her head. "Another bribe."

"I told you, I am very at home in this sort of place. Most of the world functions by either threats or bribes. Now, I am going bribe you to eat something."

She took his arm and they went to the hearth. "May I ask, sir, with what would you bribe me?"

As they moved the short distance, he said, "I should say jewels or furs perhaps, but I think, at this juncture, I could have my way for a bit of hot water."

She was surprised. "You know me very well." Just then there was a knock at the door. He looked as surprised as she.

"Here's the water, sir," the innkeeper said, holding out a steaming kettle. Wentworth thanked him and closed the door quickly, feeling not in the least guilty that he had not opened his purse yet again. Holding up the kettle, he said, "So, will you dine with me?"

"I shall, sir."

The hot kettle was stowed by the coals, and Wentworth considered where they would eat. No plates had been brought so dining directly from the tray was their only option. Where to eat was a problem as well.

"We can sit on the floor before the fire. We shall pretend we are dining *al fresco*." She went to the hearthrug and settled herself.

"And who is this Fresco chap?" he said, placing the tray before her.

She removed the lid and looked at the beef. "*Al fresco* is Ital—" she stopped. Her eyes narrowed and she examined him. "You are teasing me. You know perfectly well what it means."

"I am, indeed." He took the lid and discovered that not only did they have no plates, but also, other than a carving knife and badly bent meat fork, they had no other utensils. It was only one more instance of folly on a very long list.

As they sat eating and chatting before the fire on a surprisingly new and comfortable rug, he discovered his wife was as adaptable as any man and unquestionably more beautiful to look at. Even under such difficulties, she never ceased to smile. They spoke of things long past and things to hope for in their future. She ate little, preferring to abandon the bent fork and separate stringy bits of tough beef from its fat that she might offer them to him. On occasion, a gobbet would prove difficult and she would insist on feeding it to him. Once, he caught her hand

222

and kissed her fingers. She let them linger and then gently pulled them back. The only disruption to their enjoyment was the sourness of the beer.

Frederick realised this communion was what he'd seen between Edward and Catherine and had been jealous to have. It was now his. And while he felt exhilarated, he also felt the weight of her joy on him. Some might think that the individuals in a marriage easily remained content, but he was coming to understand that he held keys able to unlock their ultimate happiness or lock them into great anguish.

There was little left on the platter save a few misshapen potatoes and chunks of fat in a pool of congealing grease. He slid it under the bed that they might not tread on it in the night. Afterwards, he fuelled the fire while she looked on.

When he was finished, she sat, looking at him for a long time. He told her how beautiful she was in the fire's light. She thanked him and then said, "I love you, Frederick." She kissed him chastely on the cheek and rose. He absently watched the fire.

"Oh, no." There was real anguish in her voice. "The case with my nightclothes is still in the carriage." She looked nearly panicked.

He had not removed his coat as yet and rose. "I shall fetch it."

She stopped him before he got to the door. "No. As you said earlier, we have what we have. I'm surely not the only woman to spend her wedding night in her shift. I am sure to be in quite good company." She touched his chest. "But thank you all the same."

As she hung her cloak, she asked that he would assist her in unbuttoning her dress. "I wish to make use of your bribe now."

Her talk of wedding nights and shifts was irritating an already increasing yearning, so it was only to be expected that after a while Frederick fumed. "Why are there so many of these blasted buttons? And why so small, and so damnably close together?" He slowly opened the back of her dress and endeavoured not to sound as helpless as he felt.

"If you've not noticed, women are smaller than men. Many buttons, close together, make the fabric lie properly. It would leave gaps otherwise." She started to unpin her hair.

"Can't have gaps," he said, under his breath. He'd always thought himself capable in every circumstance. This task proved that theory to be quite wrong. A lock of hair fell on his hand. It sent a tremor up his arm as it tickled the hair on the back of his hand. For a moment he was unable to work his fingers. Just as her hair fell to cover her shoulders, he finished. He wanted in the worst way to gather it all in his hands and smell it, then pull her to him.

"You promise you will not steal a look as I wash." She looked serious.

"What?" The room was suddenly smaller.

"You will not look as I wash and change into my night clothes." Her arms were crossed and she could barely look him in the eye.

His heart raced. He felt as though he had just run miles. He hoped he didn't look as ridiculous as he felt. Normally, he would say something flippant like, of course he would look, that now he was her husband and eventually see everything anyhow. To tease her like that would be cruel, but teasing was a part of his deepest nature.

"Perhaps just below the knees." He tried to look as innocent as possible.

Despite her nerves, she laughed. "You will always have some part of your own way, won't you?"

"As I said, if a bribe will not work, cajoling might do it."

"All right. But no looking above the knees."

"I promise. Besides, I have a fire to tend." He had no intention to look at all when he knelt at the hearth. *Well, this may be a Herculean effort.* He stabbed, carefully poked, levered, and otherwise harassed the logs. As he worked, he could hear the water falling back into the basin. Musing upon what that sight might be, a small chunk of rough soap skittered to a stop at his feet.

"Please, may I have that back?"

The soap was slick, and it took several attempts to pick it up. When he did, his husbandly curiosity won out over his nobler self, and he glanced her way. He saw nothing. In a moment, he looked her way again. She was just beginning to pull her shift over her head. The sight of her was exquisite. He looked back at the flames and marvelled.

Soon, there was a light touch on his shoulder. "I am finished," she said.

He sat back and looked up at her. The light was soft and flattering to her small frame and lovely figure. "You've warmed it up quite nicely in here. I don't even need the robe that was with the gown." She looked at him, looking at her. "You peeked, didn't you?"

Had she seen him? He thought not, but obviously, he was wrong. Before he could respond, she said, "It's all right, it all belongs to you anyway."

Standing, he took her hand. "I do not own you." He did not wish her to think him a brute that thought of his wife as a piece of property, despite what the law might say.

"Yes, you do, in every way that truly matters." She placed his hand over her heart. "I am yours. I only hope you are mine."

For a moment he was disappointed that she harboured doubts. The soft, much-washed cotton under his fingertips cried out to be caressed and explored, but he would take every opportunity to banish her doubts

224

and fears about him. He moved his hand to her shoulder. Gently toying with the strap, he said, "Whatever proof you need, I will give it to you."

She put her hand over his and then kissed it. "You have been most kind to me tonight, the whole way here, in fact. Do not think it has gone unnoticed that you've taken great care to see to my comfort and not press me with what will naturally come. You do have rights as my husband."

"Yes, I have my rights, but I would rather those things come to me freely than take them from you."

"Well, your patience is rewarded. I think it is time."

They were the sweetest words he'd heard in his life. He unbuttoned his jacket and began to ease out of it. "Please, allow me to help you." She took it off his shoulders and to the peg. She brushed it and then, as she fingered the braid, she said, "It is heavier than I thought."

"I imagine there might be as much gold on that coat as you have in your entire jewellery casket. If anything happens to me, sell that coat first when you need money," he said, beginning to unfasten the buttons of his waistcoat.

"No, please let me." In two steps she was before him. Her soft hands took his away and placed them at his side. She then began working him free of the vest. He was enthralled with her actions. "These are not so small as mine," she said, her fingers nimble and deliberate.

"Nor as many. There is an inherent unfairness in this." He could not see her face, but the way the light danced on her hair and her hands undressing him was a fresh agony. The slight pressure of her work on his chest and stomach was maddening. He thanked God his waistcoat was of the newer style and short, for he doubted he could bear such sweet torture much longer.

"There, I am finished." Her eyes were bright with the fire's glow and, he hoped, anticipation. Her hands eased under the vest, brushing his ribs, and pulling it gently off his shoulders. Everywhere she touched him was set on fire; his thin lawn shirt offered no defence. Stepping closer, her hands blazed a trail the length of his arms before she took the vest and placed it with the coat.

His breathing was ragged and his heart racing. He could only imagine how far she intended to take her "help." She returned and began to untie his neck cloth. "For a sailor, this is not a very complicated knot." He stooped slightly as she reached up to unwrap the cloth from around his neck. They were so close that all he need do was move and inch or two closer and he could take her in his arms, kiss her, and begin to find some relief. But as much as he wished relief, he wanted more to see what his dear wife was about. He suspected her subdued nature quailed at this explicit seduction, but she carried it on, and carried it on most lovingly. Watching her fold the cloth and place it with his other clothes, he could see her hands shake. She took a deep breath before returning to him.

Her fingers grazed his neck when she reached up to unfasten the placket button of his shirt. He took her hand and guided it to his lips. She breathed in sharply. "I must finish." Her voice was thick like honey and so low he could barely hear it. He released her hand, but put his hands on her waist. He felt the button release. It had not been tight, but he felt a little relief with air on his neck. The coolness disappeared immediately, replaced by her lips. He groaned as she kissed the exposed skin.

"Annie," was all he could whisper.

He could feel her pulling his shirt from his trousers. There she stopped. He was almost relieved. The pause gave him time to gather his thoughts. There was nothing wrong with what she did, he was in fact delighted, but there was a danger that he might not control himself as strictly as he wished. He knew her worries, and he was determined that he would give her no reason to think him more animal than any other healthy man in the bedchamber. Her fingers moved, then stilled again. He looked down. Her head rested against his chest. She breathed heavily but did not move.

He stroked her back with one hand. "Is something wrong, Annie dear?" The name came so naturally.

She did not look up but said, "I have come to the end of all my bravado." She turned her head and rested her cheek against him now.

He drew her fully into his arms. "You have been playing a part for me?" He could not help but feel honoured that she would so bravely put herself forward for his pleasure.

Her voice quavered. "I wanted you to know you are not married to a timid little mouse."

The words seemed familiar but he couldn't place them and didn't care to dilute the moment.

"You are a passionate man, and I must learn to deal with it." She raised her head. "No, I must learn to revel in it and be a living part of it."

"You are not timid, my dear. Any woman who shamelessly buys a man to take her to Gretna Green cannot be counted as timid." He caught her chin, forcing her to look into his eyes. "As for the seduction," he smiled broadly, "it is greatly appreciated, but to be honest, you began that work many years ago. And it has held fast." He punctuated each word with a kiss.

He picked her up, but she protested, "You needn't carry me; the bed is just a few steps."

He called up a look he thought seductive and said, "I don't want a bit of your energy wasted by walking." Her eyes widened and she laughed quietly.

Frederick Wentworth was indeed a man of the world, but he knew for certain every locale offered its own particular pleasures.

Printed in the United States
215925BV00001B/18/P

9 780972 852951